OUR SHATTERED FATES

OUR SHATTERED FATES

THE COLD AS IRON TRILOGY
BOOK THREE

KAYLA MCGRATH

CONTENT WARNINGS

This book includes content that may be disturbing to some readers, discretion is advised. Content includes graphic violence (blood, gore, body mutilation, decapitation, murder, death, death of family), sexually explicit scenes, vague mentions of sexual assault/sex trafficking, off the page mention of suicide, substance abuse (drugs and alcohol), and alcoholism.

For those who have been here since the beginning.

CHAPTER 1

Intimacy with one's soulmate creates a whole new kind of lovemaking. I've had plenty of sex in my life, both good and bad. But it all pales in comparison to fucking my soulmate. My king. My husband. My mirror. My equal.

Emrys and I crash against my—now our—bed, tearing at each other's clothes with voracious hunger. I can sense the need in both of us through the soulmate bond that connects us, heart to heart, through the red thread Lady Fate linked us with long before we were thoughts in the other's mind. My husband's mouth is hot and greedy on mine, his slightly sharpened teeth grazing my lip and eliciting a starburst of pain. I do not say anything because I like it, and with my own blunt teeth I pull on his lip and draw a drop of blood. I can feel him smile in response as his hands tear open the corset I wear.

"I've missed you," he growls against my throat, pulling away from my lips and seeking my chest.

"You saw me just this morning," I tease, nails finding the golden skin of his back and digging in. "Did I not satisfy you enough then?"

"Too many meetings between this and the last," he grumbles, nipping my collarbone. "I am tired of generals and advisors telling me what to do. I only want *you* ordering me around."

"Well, allow me to oblige then."

I fuse a hand in his deep, garnet locks, feeling the silk of his hair against my rough warrior's calluses. Such calluses on hands are not meant for those to rule, but rule I do. By my marriage, with my husband's birthright as sole heir—and son—of the former Seelie Queen, Aneira Gwyndolyn, and an unfathomable bloodline link to the Unseelie Queen. Somehow, I am destined to inherit both court's crowns.

Emrys's hands busy themselves with pulling the rest of my corset apart and I guide his head downwards. He pauses against my chest and pries the corset from my breast, baring a hardened nipple before sucking it into his mouth. I throw my head back and moan as he swirls his tongue against the peak, grazing with his teeth, sending sparks of arousal straight

2

between my legs. I press my nails deeper into his back, his hair, crushing him to me. Fusing him to me. As if I can pull him into me and I inside of him. Like our minds.

I can feel his satisfaction in my reaction through the bond and he takes those talented fingers and drags them southward, dipping under my dress. I tense in anticipation while lust turns me wet and wanton. I bite the shell of his ever-so pointed ear and his groan ushers his movements onward. Suddenly, his fingers plunge into my core and I can feel how drenched I am with his touch.

"Goddess, wife. Am I the one leaving you unsatisfied and wanting?" Emrys teases. He pulls his fingers out and swirls them against my clit and I mewl and buck against him.

"Never unsatisfied. Always wanting," I pant.

My hands begin scrabbling in earnest at his clothing, yanking the golden silk of his shirt. The tiny clinking of the pearl buttons freeing from their threads gives me a thrill of delight. Soon, his shirt is tatters on the floor and the broad, muscular expanse of his golden flesh is on display. His chest is finely sculpted, every inch of it touched by my fingers. My mouth. I have mapped his flesh a thousand times over.

As always, I trace the scar over his heart; in thanks, in gratitude, in acknowledgement. He died for me. I will never forget it. Not again. Lady Fate may have given him back to me from the veil of death, but she also took him from me in my memories. I'd forgotten our love. Our marriage. Our everything.

"Don't think about that," my husband chastises me, sensing the path my thoughts were taking. To distract me, he pulls the untended to nipple into his mouth, flicking his tongue over it. His fingers between my legs keep circling and dipping, driving clarity from my mind.

In response to his ministrations, I tear his pants down from his hips and free his cock. He groans, as if the restraint was physical pain. My palm grazes him and he twitches in response. I smile and then wrap my hand around his length, pumping him once.

"*Fuck*, Vanna."

Before I can think, much less blink, Emrys has pulled from me and I am being pinned by his tall form. My skirts are about my waist the next instant and then my legs are parted wide with his head is between them. His mouth dips hot against my core, his tongue laving glorious pleasure with a single stroke. I fist my hands in his hair and thrust my hips with his lick, but he grips my hips and holds me still while his tongue wickedly swirls against my clit. His topaz eyes are devious and lust-soaked as he suckles those over sensitized nerves into his mouth. Pleasure arcs through me, a climax building as he works me up, wringing desire and bliss from my electrified body.

"Emrys, please, I'm so close," I nearly whine.

I pull at his hair, fistfuls of dark red between my pale fingers, my wedding band the only spot of gold. The golden ring having only recently been reclaimed by my hand, yet worn by his for nearly seven years. The seven years I lost him for.

"I'll reward you with an orgasm if you stop thinking of before," Emrys tells me against my slicked flesh, privy to my anxiety-fueled thoughts. "Come for me, wife, and forget all that is done."

He returns to his pleasuring of my sex and my head drops into the pillows, my spine arching from the bed. I bite my lip as I feel the climax cresting. So close.

Suddenly, there's a knock at the door and we both freeze, my barreling pleasure evaporating.

"Your Majesties, you are scheduled to be in attendance at the ball as of thirty minutes ago," a voice primly informs with an undertone of amusement. Enydd. Our former mentor from Century Training and our final pawn in Lady Fate's board. A pawn destined to death.

"We're busy," Emrys growls at the mentor that favored him for one hundred years.

"Yes, we can tell. The guards have been getting an earful." There is no undertone now, it is clearly indicated in her speech. I can practically see the smirk on her cocoa brown face, the cinnamon freckles stretching across her cheekbones.

"Just let me finish up," I snap. This is not the kind of edging I'm into.

Emrys cocks an entertained brow.

Chortles from behind the door sound in response. "As much as I wish you could, Your Majesty, we are on a tight schedule."

I sigh and begin to pull away from my husband but he drags me back beneath him. His mouth is returned to my needy pussy and he is *ravenous*. He performs some sort of magic with his tongue and teeth because in seconds that vanishing climax is now tearing through me and has me soaring off the bed. Stars burn beneath my eyelids and ecstasy floods my veins as I arch off the viridian velvet and moan.

Laying there, panting with my husband smirking at me with such a devilish smile of satisfaction, I debate on telling Enydd to formally fuck off. We've been ensconced in meetings all day, most of which have involved political maneuverings, tactics, plans, alliances, and everything between to salvage this crumbling kingdom. The ball tonight is meant to be a balm on the burn that our secret—and now revealed—identities have inflicted. Enydd herself has thrown herself into our advisor's position with the same vigor she trained us with all those years during Century Training—albeit sans whacks upside the head. It's an unspoken thing that her position as both our advisor and among the living is limited and impermanent. Enydd knows as well as we do that her living is only granted by the goddess, and that same goddess will pluck her soul from our realm when the time is right. Enydd, luckily, seems to have come to terms with that fact. I'm not sure Emrys and I have, though.

Regardless, she is a warlord against the tide of our reluctancy to face all those we'd dismissed or destroyed as the Revenant and the Harbinger. We may be the rulers of the Seelie Court, but we are as equally the king and queen of hate and deceit.

Sighing, I drag myself from the intoxicating touch of my husband and adjust my skirts. Silently, Emrys reties my corset strings, hands sure on my ballgown. I smooth wrinkles from our vicious and lust-fueled attack and tuck mussed hair behind my pointed ears.

"Your turn comes later," I warn Emrys with a coy lilt to my voice.

Emrys smiles ever so, a crooked little thing that exposes his slightly pointed incisors. "Of course, My Queen."

The title is said with so much weight. Affection and acknowledgement, teasing and lust, reverence and power. It's near unbelievable how I came to bear it so—two times over. I was raised to be a warrior, not a sovereign.

After I'm properly affixed back into my clothing, I assist Emrys with his, righting a new blouse as I glance down at the silk I tore from him, and buttons I forced. I order his deep red waves back into submission—or what they allow me to do—and press my palm to his sharp jawline.

"I love you," I murmur worshipfully.

"I love you, too."

Happiness gleams in his eyes at the words that I was locked from saying for so long. I may have fallen first, but he lost me, and he labored all these years under my disdain and hate. I've seen to rectifying it every chance I get. Starting with telling him the truth every day.

The two of us move towards the door and there Emrys opens it revealing an impatient Enydd and two flushed guards. As I predicted, below that impatience is that smirk. She was our mentor for a hundred years, of course I came to know her, too.

Unaffectedly, I slip on my knife shoes, painting my face blank and not revealing the shame that should color me from knowing all present here just heard me orgasm.

"If you took the royal chambers—" Enydd begins before I cut her off.

"No, I've already told you I'm not ready to take Aneira's suites. Not yet. Mine will do just fine."

"It is up three flights of stairs," Enydd points out.

"Good observation. All the better to deter those from abducting me from my bed."

"No one would dare abduct you."

"Then this is a non-issue."

Enydd thins her lips and glances at Emrys from the side of her eye. My husband shrugs and Enydd scoffs. She always favored Emrys over me and it seems that affection still stands today. Luckily, she doesn't detest me. Not like some of the other mentors did. Nor how one liked me too much.

Emrys squeezes my hand as thoughts of Osian pervade my mind and leak through the bond. He has as much reason to hate the mentor who tried to force himself on me and blackmail me into faking a relationship. More actually, because once upon a time that mentor killed him, and it was I who took his vengeance.

My teeth grind together until my husband's soothing presence and circling thumb on the back of my hand relax me.

"Your hair is all fucked up," Enydd finally says.

I twist my lips in amusement. "Do you dare to wonder why?"

"Goddess, fucking hell, girl, you try my patience."

"As I always have."

Enydd exhales sharply and steps forward, fixing my hair none too gently, smoothing stray strands and righting braids that had come from their pins. "It's not perfect, but it'll do. Your crown should hide most of this mess." Enydd searches us. "Where *are* the crowns?"

"Oh!" Emrys says startled as he darts back into the room and retrieves our crowns that were tossed onto the chaise lounge that I've still yet to have repaired.

"Those are heirlooms! You can't just toss them about the room when you decide to fornicate."

"Don't worry, Enydd, sometimes we wear them during the act," I tease. If Enydd were wearing pearls, she'd be clutching them. "Besides, we wrested them from the Winter Carnaval. Do you wish to wonder what defilement they endured there?"

Enydd throws her hands up in exasperation. I am quite trying, I know.

Emrys rests my crown atop my head, the thorns and spikes of gold and obsidian sitting atop my silver locks with such rightness that for a nebulous moment all feels fated. But then it shatters and I'm left with a crown, that while designed for me, *shouldn't* be mine. Not really. Not like this.

My husband places his own crown of horns and thorns and roses upon his garnet waves, and then links our hands together. A united force. King and queen. Revenant and Harbinger. Equals. Mirrors. Soulmates. I incline my head and then he nods to our entourage.

"Proceed," the king commands.

CHAPTER 2

All of the previous events of the court have been held in the throne room. As customary, the throne room doubles as a ballroom. A show of power and a flaunting of the massive throne hewn from three ancient tree trunks, veined in Seelie gold magic. The very same magic that undulates above in the false gold ceiling.

The ball tonight, however, is being held in one of the various ballrooms to be at least once removed from the recent tragedy of the Gwyndolyn-Vanora coronation. It was a bloodshed as much as it was a crowning. The Wild Hunt had announced their allegiance to the Dark Court, standing as an omen before the Vampire Court had descended upon the infancy of our reign. The vampires were like a gloom of death, heralding the first marks of battle in the rule. Once the midnight hour had tolled, the Unseelie Court rose up and attacked.

It was only the revelation of my being Caethes's true heir that stalled them into retreat.

Emrys and I are surrounded by guards with Enydd holding the point position of our formation as she guides us through the polished earth walls of the Seelie Court. Gold and emerald and viridian and gilt-edged finery pave our way until we're met with grand double doors of solid oak, arched like a cathedral, and embossed with golden chrysanthemums—the official flower of the Light Court.

Enydd steps aside as the doors groan open, pulled by two fae with gossamer wings of pearly iridescence. Before us, through the grand entrance, is a polished floor of ivory-veined gold marble, the enormous slab made not through nature's means. Trees wrought in auric metal climb the walls and cast down a canopy of alabaster leaves, the foliage which behaves as normally as its verdant green cousin, and similar to the golden ivy that winds its way throughout the court. Even here, some of that famed Seelie ivy is wound up table legs and around door frames.

Courtiers and high-ranking fae mill and pause with our arrival, nearly every variation of Seelie fae present. I sense a handful of Unseelies turned Seelie and it just reminds me even more that I am the same. I was born to the Dark Court, but I made the choice when I was too young to remember to convert or pledge allegiance to the Light. Amongst the fae are notable individuals—ones loyal to us. Namely, Wisteria whose Greyvale magic is enough to mimic and fend off Caethes's chaos magic, and Julia, the human girl and leader of the Crows from Aberth, as well as Violante, the rescued teenage vampire, once one of Aberth's lottery winners—though the prize is nothing to strive for.

Everyone in the room drops to a knee.

"Introducing, King Emrys Gwyndolyn-Vanora and Queen Evelyn Corianne Gwyndolyn-Vanora of the Seelie Court," Enydd booms from beside us.

We tilt our chins in unison, a show of power and solidarity as we take seven deliberate steps into the ballroom. Fractals of light, from the crystalline chandeliers hanging above us amongst the draping white catch on all the gold, sending iridescent shine around us like a corona. Blooming flowers of emerald gems dangle heavily from the artful fixtures, shouting decadence.

"You may rise," Emrys says cooly, voice full of easy, regal grace. I can sense his anxiety through the bond, the feeling of being an imposter bleeding out of him. If not for my proximity to my husband in every fashion, I would not have been able to detect his unease. Where, I would wonder, he pulled that grace from. An outsider wouldn't know. As with I, Emrys was raised to be a warrior. This crown was foisted on him as suddenly as it was with me and we are still learning all there is to holding it.

"Welcome," I call out, my husky voice loud over the soft silence of the crowd, pierced only by small tinkling's of jewelry on wine stems. "It is the pleasure and honor of the crown to have you all present tonight. Please, eat, drink, dance, fuck, be merry!"

A cheer of hurrahs and delight follow my remarks, then music and conversations resume.

A passing tray of sparkling waters stops before us and I quickly pluck one up, exhaling sharply behind the glass. I take a deep swig heedlessly, unworried about the potential for poison due to mine and Emrys's practiced mithridatism from Century Training. Even should someone want to poison us, it would have no effect—not unless it was a several times over a lethal dose, and at that point we'd smell it before we ingested it.

Beside me, Emrys has copied the action, staying in solidarity with me against my internal battle against alcohol. There are moments like these, of high stress, that have me wobbling from my seat on the wagon, but it's my soulmate's firm presence beside me that steadies me.

"Your mind is racing, my love," Emrys chides lowly.

I smile into my glass. "I'm just starting to think about all the naughty things I'm going to do to you when this is over." I emphasize this with a mental image of me naked and on my knees, bending down over him as my mouth opens and takes his—

He groans before I finish putting together the picture. "You are a menace on my composure, wife."

"Is this the part where I say you wouldn't have me any other way and then you tell me there are several ways in which you'll have me?"

Emrys chuckles and wraps me in a tight embrace, pressing his brow to mine. "I was wrong, you are a *villain* on my composure."

"Good," I sass back, then kiss him quickly. But it is not as quick as I intend, because he deepens it with a working of his tongue along my lips. I can taste the sparkling water and the essence of my orgasm on his mouth.

As much as I would love to continue the kissing of my husband—and all the other wicked things he can do with his tongue—we are here for a purpose tonight. An underlying purpose. And that purpose is to assuage the doubt in our rule and the disdain our secret identities has unveiled.

Silently, we come to the same conclusion and separate, taking each other's hands politely. Internally, we share the list of names of individuals whose conversation tonight is essential. We begin with a commander whom Emrys had an altercation with—which ended with my husband slicing off half the fae warrior's horn.

Instead of two curling ram horns, the faerie possesses one fully intact spiral, and the other ending with sudden abruptness. The end line of which matches a silvery scar on his brown cheekbone. Aside from the slight scar, his face is unlined and unmarred, smooth with the fae's graceless age. He could be twenty and he could be two hundred, yet he only appears to be in his third decade. Though, I know his true age is somewhere closer to the latter.

I sigh internally and plaster on a false smile. As we approach, the faerie gives us mixed looks. It is admiration mixed with disregard, and hesitation mixed with ire. I keep my smile steady.

"Commander Baphet, thank you for your presence here tonight," I start. "I cannot thank you enough for your defense of the Seelie Court all these decades. And most importantly, the valiant prowess you displayed in the onslaught of the Wild Hunt and the Dark Court's machinations."

Faeries love flattery. I would know, I am a vain creature.

Commander Baphet's lips twist into a reluctant smile, his chest puffing beneath his blue velvet doublet. "It was my honor, My Queen."

"Even still, your loyalty in the face of such tumultuous times is invaluable. I would like that acknowledged, praised, and most of all rewarded."

Baphet raises a dark brow. My saccharine smile brightens. Faeries love a good deal, and anything surrounding a reward or favor will have them hooked.

"Your Majesty, that is a grand prize and I would be a fool to refuse it." Baphet tries and fails to rein in his excitement. "How may I accept such a bounty from the Light Court's sovereign?" Baphet's eyes flicker to Emrys, a clear memory flashing through his eyes. "I am curious to see how this new reign will repay ages old loyalty in the face of...recent allegiance."

"I assure you; your king has every devotion in mind with this court." I plaster my smile tighter and my façade feels as if it'll crack. "I have every faith in my husband and that he will bring this court to heights that have yet to be established."

Baphet eyes us pointedly. "I have known you, my queen, since you were an infant. I watched you grow, to become the warrior you are, and later the spy balancing the fringes of this court and that. I hope to see the truth of all your identities come to light and remain *within* the Light."

"You shall have no concerns regarding my wife's candor and devotion to her mother's way of ruling," Emrys interjects. "It is this crown's pleasure to personally reassure you of that fact, and to cement our grace with a formal offer. We would like you to become general and to spearhead the battleplans with the aid of Lady Maelona and Commander Tirnoc."

I watch the contempt from Baphet flood and release with Emrys's offer. His earth brown eyes warm, like sunshine on soil, and his chest, which had already previously puffed, puffs again.

After studying ledgers and former archives and journals, it was clearly evident that Baphet strove for the general position without ever having been granted it. From the records the only hesitation on the crown's part had been Baphet's penchant for gambling and the debts he'd accrued some fifty years ago to an Unseelie official. It was discovered later by Maelona, that he'd paid those debts with a command over an unstipulated heart's desire. A liability and something that would impede anyone from ascending rank. But I have a contingency for that one.

"I would be honored to accept, My King." Baphet turns to me. "My Queen. I thank you."

"Then it is settled. We shall send for you tomorrow afternoon for battle strategy," Emrys informs. "In the meantime, enjoy the party."

Baphet nods and wanders off, a considerable pep in his hooved step.

I collect another sparkling water from a passing server and drain it.

"Fuck me," I say breathlessly. "That was just the first one?"

Emrys caresses my back. "Do not worry, wife. You have it all in hand."

"I wish I had it all in the past."

Emrys laughs as he guides us to the next political maneuver.

Over the course of the following two hours, we flatter and reward ten members we'd somehow wronged as the Harbinger and Revenant. Or those whose displeasure over the most recent events of the Seelie Court were most vocal. Other courtiers question us about intentions in our rule and how we mean to reassure the members of their safety when the Unseelie Court has succeeded on so many attacks. Emrys uses his silver tongue to work the worries from them and we continue on with our plans of establishing enemies and allies. He reveals Unseelie secrets that were entrusted to him as one of the highest ranking members of the Dark Court—ones that he'd already revealed to myself and our counsel—which earns much favor. Most react similarly to Baphet, getting offered things having been out of reach during Aneira's rule—though others are like the Admiral.

The Admiral is a Seelie spy, having coined her name from her wings, the namesake in which matches the bright orange, dusky black, and spotted white of the butterfly. She operates within a small network organized by Aneira, a network I had belonged to once as the *Ceidwad Cudd*. We have...*difficult* blood.

She inclines her head at our approach, her ebony lips curving with suspicion. She wears her long half-black and half-white hair split down the middle and styled loose with two space buns decorated with flower petals. Her dress is autumnal in shade which fades out to a shadowy hue at the hem while the sleeves taper to a snowy point over her middle finger. I can see her golden thigh peek out from one of the two thigh slits.

"Evelyn Vanora," she greets cooly.

I bite my tongue at the clear lack of my title. "Aveda Cassel. I'm glad we could take this moment."

"I'm certain we could have had this moment several hours ago, if not for you saving my reward for last, and if you had not been so busy fucking to be an hour late to your own ball."

Fury fires down the bond from both Emrys and I. I try to quell the flaring of the emotion with a firm hand on my husband's arm under the guise of a wife's gentle physical touch. The Admiral doesn't miss it for what it is.

"I don't care about whatever you have here to offer me," Aveda snaps. "What you took from me, you cannot give back. You cannot rectify which you have wronged."

I knew she was going to be the most difficult to appease. In addition to the clear favoritism the former queen bestowed me, Aveda desperately wanted the task of taking down the Sugar Ring—an adjacent group to the Winter Carnaval. So, not only was she passed up once, but twice when Maelona and Corvina assumed the position after my abduction to the Yukon by the halfling, Jacob Dugal. Not to mention, she also wanted the honor of being selected for Century Training, and my recent reveal has soured an already bitter relationship. If it hadn't been for Aneira installing a disguised human by the name of Raina Caldare with a Queen's Glamour—with the same Seelie version of the Unseelie coin that was hidden beneath my skin—she would've never discovered she'd been duped by an imposter in her spy network for a whole year. Alas, she was, and now she is doubly pissed.

"Are you threatening to defect from this court?" I say sharply.

Aveda's lips turn into a snarl. "What, are you going to charge me with treason now?"

"Dependent upon your answer, perhaps."

"You haven't even tried to garner my trust."

"I have known you for many years, Aveda. If you do not want to do something, there is little one can do to convince you to do otherwise."

Aveda purses her lips and I watch as she deliberately shutters her glittery black eyes, contemplating. "What if I request something? And if I am given this boon, I will swear newfound allegiance to the Gwyndolyn-Vanora rule."

I try to hide my surprise. She's desperate.

"Speak of your request," I command softly.

"I want to lead the takedown of the Winter Carnaval."

"There is currently no active move to attack the Carnaval."

"I want there to be one and I want to be the one to do it. I do not want your half-truths of saying you'll do your best. I want confirmation. I want assurances that I will not be deceived."

I blink. She's looking for notoriety and praise and the ever-highly sought after power and reputation that'll be garnered by such a feat. And though it is an admirable quest, I am unsure if I can fulfil it. And I certainly cannot lie.

"I will think on your ultimatum before I supply you with a proper answer."

"I will not swear fealty without this," Aveda warns.

"I know," I reply. I also know that if I do not give her this, she can take all the Seelie secrets she knows and defect to the Unseelie Court. It would be a risky choice on her part, but it is wartime and Caethes would not let the advantage slip her by. Even so, Aveda must know that I would be required to kill her, should she turn on us. So, it begs the question: What sort of leverage, blackmail, or ammunition does she have to prevent this?

I make a mental note to inquire further and speak to Maelona about any unrest in Aneira's former spy network.

"Then we are understood," Aveda concludes.

"We are."

"Have a good evening, Your Majesties."

And with that the Admiral strides away and we are left staring at her retreating back, wondering if the faerie I'd once thought of as an ally will transform into my enemy.

CHAPTER 3

There's little else I imagine less tolerable than an early morning battle brief meeting after an evening of politicking. I sit in my seat to Emrys's left, dressed in fighting leathers of softest black, my husband wearing a similar garb. Across from us, Baphet pushes documents into piles, while a line of chess pieces perch on a glass tablet. Enydd, at the foot of the table, splays her hands on a list of positions that still need to be filled and likely candidates. Beside Baphet is Bleddyn, my mother's lover, who still grieves her loss and the pain of which still shows in his eyes as he pores over ancient battle strategies. Then there's Julia, the leader of the Crows and the person in charge of secret information relay from the Unseelie Court. She is also the only human present, but she does not let her status deter her as she keeps her folded hands over a crisp piece of paper. I notice her golden Seelie tattoo glittering on her neck. At the head of the table is Lady Maelona, leading the meeting.

The hour is obscenely early—or ridiculously late—for the Lady. Maelona is well known for keeping near nocturnal hours, and disrupting her sleeping patterns is tantamount to a threat.

Maelona twists the long fall of her onyx hair over her shoulder as she begins to list newly defected Seelies. We lost four to an undetermined status or to the Unseelie Court. It is bad, but it is less than we had projected, so the ball—which had been suggested by Enydd—has succeeded.

"…and the fourth is Afan Ignis," Maelona reads off as her red painted nail lines the paper.

"I knew that little shit was no good," I mutter, crossing my arms. Ever since he'd questioned me after the Aberth slaughter, he'd left a poor taste in my mouth. Evidently, it was warranted.

Emrys's amusement trickles down the bond, but he says nothing. I send him a droll look and a reminder of how I'd…*serviced* his needs this morning.

I wasn't able to follow through on my promise to Emrys when we retired from the ball. I had immediately crashed upon the bedspread and fallen asleep, one heel off, the other dangling from my foot which hung over the side of the mattress. When I awoke some hours later though, I was sure to rectify my grievous wrong and crawled between his legs. Thankfully, my husband had had the energy to strip from his finery and it took so little for me to pull aside the blankets and take his lovely cock in my mouth. He'd woken with a start and a moan, immediately fisting his hands in my silver locks.

"*Vanna*," he'd murmured sleepily as I'd bobbed my head up and down. Being woken up that way has always been one of his favorites.

I had hummed my appreciation low in my throat as I continued, and his golden eyes opened to slits as he watched me take him deep. He'd finished and had been eager to get me off too, but I'd hushed him and urged him back to sleep, wrapped in each other's arms.

I'm brought back to the present when Maelona begins to speak.

"During the ball last night there was an attempt made on a supply caravan heading to the outpost we've been keeping the human residents of Aberth at," Maelona informs, voice cool and efficient. "It was intercepted and handled swiftly. The two fae responsible for the attempt were solidary fae, banished from the Unseelie Court, hoping to garner some favor with Caethes. They misjudged their skills and have since been dispatched. The humans are safe."

"That marks the third attempt since the coronation," Emrys intones gravely.

"It is wartime," Maelona acknowledges. "But yes, they are testing the boundaries of this court's strength after recent losses."

"Have our retaliations against Caethes paid off?" I ask, crossing my legs in irritation. I hate having to be stuck behind this table and beneath the crown. My very skin itches at the restriction. I am not meant to be this idle.

"Only one," Maelona answers, her dark brown eyes narrowing at a new document. "We successfully infiltrated her kitchens with a volunteer from Aberth. Right now, they are gathering intel from maids and cooks. Anything from unrest, to gossip, to blackmail. Anything we can use to leverage against the Unseelie. Already what our king has provided us is invaluable."

I nod along with this and wonder if Caethes has successfully implemented the same tactic in the Seelie Court. As of our coronation we've slipped a spy in her kitchens and Gideon straight into her bedchambers. Among the other spies we've retained from Aneira's rule.

My eyes flicker to Julia, but the human woman remains quiet, waiting for her turn to speak. Though she and I both know it won't be in the presence of so many.

I tilt my head against the back of my chair, staring at the carved wood ceiling and the golden veins of magic that run through it. I try to count the number of flowers embossed above me, but immediately get a headache at the attempt. Taking a drink of water, I return my attention to the meeting and realize Baphet has begun talking.

"I have some hesitations about the security of the spy network," he says, fiddling with a white pawn piece. "In the absence of the *Ceidwad Cudd* it had begun to fray and now, in light of recent developments it is absolutely crumbling. As it is right now, it is being held together by the Admiral and her loyalty is flimsy at best."

Something I'm unfortunately well aware of. "What do you suggest to fix this, then?" I ask.

"I think we should use it as a façade. Deliberately leave it as it is and let the Unseelie Court think that is where we are weakest. At the same time, we begin to establish a new network with different channels. Beginning with the human you have stashed in their kitchens." Baphet inclines his head. "That way, if or when they attack, they will be attacking little more than ghosts. We will have already moved long before. If Aveda manages to hold the current one together herself, we'll be even stronger without exerting any additional effort."

I think for a moment. "Does this entail leaving the Admiral in the dark?"

Baphet hesitates. "I think that is the best for now. I cannot be certain she will be retained in this court and I don't think it wise to risk this development. Once we are sure of her dedication, we shall move her or inform her as needed."

"See to it that it's done."

"Yes, Your Majesty."

A few more details are read out and then the meeting is adjourned, leaving Emrys, Maelona, Julia, and myself. After being sure the door is shut, Emrys casts a King's Glamour as a shield in the room. Already the room is warded against eavesdroppers, but due to this highly sensitive information, my husband and I trust no one to ensure this security.

"Any news Julia?" I ask, leaning forward eagerly.

Julia inclines her chin and clears her throat. Flattening her hands on the table she begins to speak. "Gideon, thus far, has been successful in earning back some of Caethes's good graces. In his opinion, she still thinks she can use him against you due to being slighted romantically."

"Does he feel like I slighted him?" I question, a pang of guilt reverberating in my chest.

Julia purses her lips. "I don't think so. At least, if he did, he doesn't anymore. To the best of my knowledge, he harbors no more romantic feelings for you."

"That is good."

"Yes. Even so, he hasn't let that on to Caethes, because if she thinks one of her advantages has gone, she's going to lean more heavily on his family."

"Because she has not just his father's life dangling over him."

"Yes, his mother is being closely monitored by both courts. Someone has yet to make a move against her, but it is my opinion that it is only a matter of time. Especially considering that Caethes's anxiety has her moving Gideon's father to a new location soon."

"How soon?"

"Tonight, I have just learned."

"Any other details?"

"I have not been able to ascertain any."

I'm put off by the thought of the father's movement and the mother's monitoring. It was foolish to assume Caethes wouldn't go for Gideon's entire family—which was why Emrys and I instated a rotating watch on her—but knowing that Caethes's illusions on Gideon's feelings for me are the difference...

"It's only been days since the coronation, surely she isn't this impatient," I say, trying to reassure myself.

Emrys sighs. "I've known her for too long, Vanna, and I know that patience is not one of her virtues." He rubs a hand over his mouth. "If Gideon is going to be worrying about his family, he won't be effective for us, and truly will be an unstable weapon."

"What do you suggest?" I ask, eyeing both my husband and Julia. Maelona has kept quiet, letting the information absorb.

"Gideon wants to speak to them."

"No," I say flatly.

Julia's brows narrow over her gold-blue eyes. "Then he wants to speak to you two."

"Ev," Maelona starts, breaking her silence. "Maybe—"

"No," I repeat. "It's too dangerous. It takes one person to spot him near us and it's game over for him and the plight of this court. I will not risk my citizens so he can get familial reassurance. Tell him he can relay his information through you and I will relay whatever we get back from his family via the same channels."

The sudden protectiveness over the Seelies gives me an internal pause and no one but Emrys is aware of it. A flash of pride moves through the bond and the same protective sentiment is reflected in him.

Maelona nods and looks away. I can see her disapproval. "Do you perhaps think that you are punishing him for what has been done in the past?"

I level a firm look at my best friend. "I understand his motivations, I would have done the same. But I have so much more to look out for than a family. I have an entire court depending on me. I cannot be emotional."

"Sometimes that empathy is the difference between the Dark and Light Court."

Hesitating, I stare at Maelona's dark eyes and her even darker hair. Her mood ring hair has belied nothing, she is keeping her own emotions in check. "I can't risk it. Not yet."

Maelona nods, this time softly, as if sensing something in my voice.

"He won't like that answer," Julia warns.

"Respectfully, he doesn't have to," I answer, pivoting to the leader of the Crows. "This was a proverbial olive branch. Us trusting him puts us at just as much risk as him deceiving the Unseelie Queen."

Julia shakes her head and looks aside. Her curtain of dark hair hides half her expression, but I see in her profile that the negotiations on his behalf are not what she hoped, but they are what she expected. "Can you assure him that his family is safe? With proof?"

I weigh the give and take from this arrangement. Gideon is doing us a favor, yes, but it would take so little for him to turn on us. We need to keep him happy. Caethes is offering the same thing we are, but hers is based on a thin lie that walks the truth. Ours is based on an experience lived. If I can call on Lady Fate for him, then Caethes has no chance in securing his loyalty. His family is the difference between it all.

"I will do my best." I move on. "Is there anything else of import?"

Julia's expression transforms, professionalism taking over. "Caethes has been in regular conversation with Joseph Harrow. It seems like an alliance between the Vampire Court and Unseelie Court is growing stronger since the coronation. His theory is that Caethes has something the Vampire King wants."

The meeting continues similarly, the connection between vampires and Unseelies growing tighter. I can only hope the link becomes tight enough to snap. Gideon has begun to feed Caethes false information. Nothing outwardly ludicrous, but enough of misinformation that can be easily spread by other fae. It is effective to have a liar as a spy. After some time, we wrap up and immediately upon our departure we are accosted by Enydd and two guards.

"We must make final arrangements for Drysi's funeral," Enydd announces, not waiting for our excuses. "It's set to take place tomorrow at midday, so—"

"Bleddyn is meant to take care of it," I interrupt, feeling grief begin to swallow me up.

"Yes, but he is busy with—"

"Can it not wait? She's not getting any deader."

Enydd inhales, her plum eyes flaring wide. It's clear in her expression she realizes she struck a nerve. "I will see to it," Enydd says softly. "But these are difficult times and it is an even more difficult time to be queen, girl."

"I'm quite aware."

"Is there anything else you require, Enydd?" Emrys asks the mentor who'd favored him.

She softens towards Emrys. Not in pity like towards me, but in warmth. "No, I think your afternoon is clear. Dinner will be at seven."

"Great, thank you, Enydd," Emrys nods and then the two of us escort ourselves back to our chambers before Enydd can try to convince us to take Aneira's suite again.

CHAPTER 4

I've been to too many funerals of late. There has been so much death in these weeks. Far more than I'd experienced during my two years of exile while being hunted. Now, I am being hunted in a new form and it is wholly undesirable.

Drysi's pyre burns in the stone courtyard, the same one where Aneira's was held. I watch, stone-faced, as her carefully preserved body turns to ash. She's dressed in warrior's leathers, her favorite blade held to her breast, her hands crossed over it. Her long black hair trails over the edge, coiling as it chars. Herbs have been added to the flames so that the scent of burning flesh and hair does not overwhelm the watchers. Near me, and closer to the flames is Bleddyn, tears leaking down his cheeks in silent grief. He keeps his posture rigid, wings seized still, his whole frame tight. I'm sure he's held together by sheer will alone.

Everyone in attendance is in funeral black or Seelie gold, in deference to her and the court she died for. Emrys and I don ebony with gilt edges. Bleddyn wears black only. She meant more to him than his allegiance to court deference.

My heart hurts. I hate this. I'm tired of this. I don't want any more funerals. My entire family is dead. My father, my sister, and now both my mothers. I can't take another loss. I don't know what I'd do if I lost Emrys...

Emrys squeezes my hand, feeling my spiral come on. He reassures me with phantom touches in my mind, intangible fingers stroking through my hair, reining in my despair.

We wait a while longer while a Goldwine witch conducts the ceremony, her magic a distant relation to Seelie power as she settles a warm dome of gold over the crowd, a separate pillar enrobing Drysi and directing the smoke upwards. A hallowed and sacred song that is a chorus of woe flows through the crowd. My throat thickens.

I depart the first moment it is allowed, striding past the throne room and through the halls. I am single-minded as I reach the staircase my chambers reside within. My husband is close at my heels. My teeth grit as I fend off tears, my hands itching for a knife, or booze, or my soulmate.

To my surprise, the moment I enter my rooms, I do not go for any of the things I thought I would. Instead, I am drawn to my desk and the pen that lies there. Immediately, I take it up and begin penning a letter, needing something to do.

Emrys halts in the doorway, surprised by the suddenness of my action and the abrupt departure of my intentions. It's not often I can surprise him now, so that prospect gives me a shallow minute of amusement.

"What are you doing, love?" Emrys queries me as he steps into the room, shutting the door, and doffing his crown. He crosses the space and comes up behind me, wrapping his arms about me.

"I'm writing to Caspian."

Caspian Lockwood is the halfling we'd rescued from the Winter Carnaval when we'd gone after the stolen Seelie Crown. He's also Emrys's cousin on his father's side, sharing the same Lockwood warrior witch heritage. There, we'd discovered his link to Gideon—both of them having been protectors for the Arcana Society—and the untold horrors he underwent in his imprisonment there. Caspian was one of their star showings, used for both the fights and for pleasure, and both were unwilling. My heart pulls at the idea, especially since he's sixteen or perhaps seventeen years old. That kind of torture…

I grip my pen tighter and dig it deeper into the paper to keep from wanting to gouge someone's eyes out of their skull.

"Just to check in with him, or…?" Emrys's lips graze my hair as he peppers the side of my head with gentle kisses. His hands are warm and it's him, his presence, that is enough for me to relax my crushing hold on the pen.

"I want the family records he has on the Lockwoods and Whitecrests. I—" I stop myself, my throat thick. I swallow. "I need to know I'm not alone. That there is more to our family than just you and me."

I stare forlornly at the paper, my eyes prickling painfully with unshed tears.

"Vanna," Emrys whispers. He crouches down and spins my chair—impressive, as it's not one of the seat's functions. "I'm so sorry you're feeling this way. I know it doesn't heal your heart or absolve the loss, but *you* are my family. *You* are my home. And I don't need a bunch of records with strangers' names to be sure of where I'm meant to be in this world." He draws in a deep breath. "But if you need this, I will support you. Just know that I am always here for you. Always."

"But what if you're not?" I breathe, my voice shaky. "I lost you once, Ryss. And we're at war now and I—I just can't handle it if something—"

"Hey, hey," Emrys begins shushing me with his soothing voice and gestures. "Don't think like that. Look at what we've already been through. We fought all of our mentors and won. We killed or banished nearly two dozen members of the Wild Hunt. Against all odds we made it. Yes, there was a moment where it wasn't the truth, but you—*you*—made it so. And I have every faith in you that if it came to it, you wouldn't let the goddess take me again."

Those prickling tears spill over my lashes. "I wouldn't."

My soulmate quirks a crooked smile. "I know."

Emrys resets me in my chair, but does not let me go. He keeps his arms wrapped around me, his hands on my ribs, his face in my hair. I can smell leather and vetiver on him and his scent soothes my every nerve.

Finishing the letter to Caspian, I seal it with viridian wax and dust it with gold. Setting it aside, I begin penning something new. A niggling thought that won't let me go. A plan. The ideas unspool in my mind and I feel Emrys's eyes on my thoughts, watching where it goes, the strategy he follows.

His head lifts from my hair, unseeing past the desk, viewing my thoughts as they formulate.

"The father," Emrys responds, answering my unspoken question. "He's easier to access with this move and he's how we hold the greater leverage."

I stop and look at the paper before me. On it, I've mapped out Gideon's family and where they are. How they're monitored. What risk they pose to the court if we don't have them safe. All the odds lean to Gideon's father being the key.

"I agree." I pull up paperwork I already have on the Zhao patriarch, a list of his medical history, his contributions to the Arcana Society, and connections to the courts. Where Caethes might move him. I narrow it down to three places.

The whole reason we're in this mess is because of Gideon's father to begin with. He was the emissary between the courts. He's how Gideon even knew about the cabin that the courts created. He's why Gideon found me. He's how I rediscovered my Harbinger and *Ceidwad Cudd* identity.

If it weren't for the Zhao men, would Emrys or Corvina have found me first? They were looking through Unseelie Yukon. Emrys was interrogating and torturing Unseelies in an effort to find me. Corvina ventured into enemy territory with the faint hope I might be here.

I shake my head. There's no sense in wondering about the past. It cannot change, and it cannot bring Corvina back.

"Why, though?" Emrys questions.

I shift uncomfortably. "I can't just sit here and do nothing. I'm so tired of the inaction and giving orders. I'm not meant to sit on a throne, idle, while everyone else takes the risks. That's not what I was designed for. You know it, you get it, because you feel it too."

I can feel Emrys's jaw tighten against the side of my face. I can feel him internally fighting the rebuke. The lie. He may be a king but he is still fae. If only by half. And that half keeps us both from telling untruths.

"Would you still be doing this if you weren't constrained by the crown?"

I debate for a moment. "Yes, I think so."

"Without Aneira's knowledge?"

My heart stutters over the name. "Yes. The risk is worth the reward."

Turning again to the paper, I glance at Gideon's mother's details. She's working still, watched by both courts, kept at bay by Dark and Light warriors. She is completely unaware of the position she's in. I can just picture it; her walking into the hospital in her scrubs for a night shift, tote bag over her arm filled with snacks and a book, badge in hand as she scans herself in, unknowing of the enemies that watch from the shadows.

"Who are you sending?" he asks.

I spin around in surprise. "Do you expect me to let someone else do this?"

"This specific mission pertaining to Gideon's father? Where he's in one of three possible locations? Yes. I think it'll tip them off if the Seelie Queen herself goes on a rescue for a supposed enemy's parent." Emrys softens his tone. "He's too exposed, love."

I deflate, but I know he's right. It takes moments for me to decide. "The Admiral. If she's spotted, it gives us leverage on Baphet's suggestion to let the current network operate as a façade and keeps Aveda busy and in the dark. And as much as it pains me to admit it, she has unparalleled instincts when it comes to matters like this. I've seen her narrow down an exact safehouse from a dozen possible havens."

"Okay, make the call."

I do, and then we wait.

The throne room feels cold and imposing despite the golden glow. Emrys and I perch on the arms of the throne, both of us still clothed in our funeral clothes, the king's crown once again on my husband's brow. We sit in silence, but for the two of us, it is anything but quiet. We converse between ourselves through our soulmate bond. Gentle reassurances, whispers, echoes of pride. Around us we keep only those we trust—even then, it is not everyone we'd assign the title.

Maelona stands at Emrys's right, Baphet at my left. Julia is beside Baphet and Bleddyn is next to Maelona. No one speaks, and the only sound is our breathing. The only one that seems to give off a sense of restlessness is Julia; the human not accustomed to standing so still and patient for this period of time. Even so, her will power impresses me.

Eventually, my internal alarm—gifted to me through some inexplicable mix of my natural fae ability and Emrys's innate Lockwood witch magic through our soulmate bond—goes off. Emrys and I both straighten, ready, and our alertness silently signals to the others.

The Admiral steps through the golden ivy archway of the throne room with a middle-aged man in tow. The pride in Aveda's steps is clear, her cockiness rivaling my own. Gideon's father maneuvers his way in via a wheelchair, assisted by the spy, nervousness evident in the strain of his body and his weakened left side. I recognize him from encounters many years ago. The same black hair only stressed with gray and the same creased brown eyes.

I can sense—in a practical way—he is terrified. In addition to being in the space of faerie royalty, he's also a vulnerable human among so many predators.

I have to give it to Aveda, her time management is impeccable.

"Thank you, Aveda," Emrys intones. "Your skill is marvelous and your efficiency unparalleled."

Aveda curtsys, her butterfly wings flaring in an effort to appear more imposing. I prickle at the unintentional barb she throws by reminding me that my own wings are gone. A thin echo of the same pain is felt by Emrys, his wings too, are gone. Both having been taken from us, only he was a child, and I was not.

"It's always a pleasure to be of service to the King and Queen of the Seelie Court. As the Harbinger and Revenant, it's even more of a compliment. I thank you both, Your Majesties."

Gideon's father's head snaps up at the titles, eyes zeroing in on us. His left side droops ever so, but no lack of expression across his features. There is astonishment there, though. Awe and horror, disappointment, and surprise. Each emotion flitters across his face as he realizes he's face to face with the last two Centurions there will ever be. He was an emissary for the Arcana society, he is one to know a little too much about us.

I thin my lips. "That is all, Aveda. Thank you, you may go."

Aveda leaves with a smirk, her heels clicking on the polished floor. Once she is gone, I direct my gaze firmly on Gideon's father. The crown feels heavy on my brow.

"Hello, Mr. Zhao. Welcome to the Seelie Court," Emrys begins, clasping hands with me. "I am sure you have many questions."

"Please, call me Henry," Gideon's father requests. His voice is pleasant and warm and slightly slurred.

"Henry," Emrys corrects himself. "Are you aware of the events of the last few months?"

Henry glances to the side, uncertainty on his face. "I have been in correspondence with Gideon, but it is sparse. The Arcana society has made me aware of the recent change in Seelie rule. I was saddened to hear of Aneira Gwnydolyn's passing. She was a just and fair queen."

My throat thickens. "She was, thank you for saying so."

Henry nods, not quite looking at me.

"So, you are aware that you have become a bargaining chip between the courts, yes?" Emrys continues.

"Yes, Gideon told me that he—I can't believe he did this—sought out the Harbinger to give to the queen for a reward."

"He wanted a cure for you."

"I'm not sick!" Henry spits, anger in his voice before he recollects himself. "I am not sick," he repeats, more gently this time. "There is no bettering this, the Arcana society did their part and already helps where they can. Gideon knows nothing aside from vampirism will change my condition."

"That's not necessarily true." I don't wait for a response before continuing. "Caethes has promised him otherwise. As have we." I raise a hand to halt any questions. "I will not elaborate on how at this time."

"He told me about you," Henry says, surprising me. "Not that you were the Harbinger, but..." his eyes give him away as he looks at me. Twin spots of red burn on my cheeks in response.

"He told you about him and Evelyn," Emrys states flatly.

"Clearly there have been new developments."

36

"It's a very long and complicated story," Emrys says effervescently, unphased by the mention of his wife's former relationship. "Henry, you were a scholar and emissary of the Arcana society—tell me, did you ever encounter mention of soulmates?"

I startle at this line of questioning. This was not previously discussed.

Henry lifts his right brow, peculiar curiosity rising to the surface. He rubs his smooth jaw. It is softer in shape than Gideon's, but that is to be expected—Henry is not Gideon's biological father. He is just the man who stepped up when his vampire father fucked off.

"Soulmates are rare," Henry begins, eyes pointedly flickering to mine and Emrys's hands which are still interlocked. "Typically, the goddess likes to play with specific families. For example, if you have a sister—" I jolt at the mention, while he continues— "she would likely have a soulmate, too. And if your soulmate has, say a brother, they would likely have a soulmate. From there, that brother's soulmate's cousin may have a soulmate. This chain would continue until it comes full circle and somehow an aunt or a son connects back to the original other half's family."

I'm silent and I stare open-mouthed at Henry. "Isn't that a little incestuous?"

Henry shakes his head, the movement jerky. "No, no one sharing a soulmate bond is related. It just happens to be quite a complicated loop. Think of it as a family tree, only in this case it looks more like a wreath." Henry cracks a smile at his own humor.

"If I am understanding this correctly," Emrys probes. "You have two main families with soulmate bonds, and the bonds will be common within those families, but the general populace does not have a soulmate?"

"Correct. Unless Lady Fate gets particularly bored or has struck a deal—that is the case."

Emrys straightens at the word deal, and I immediately intercept. "How much do you know about her bargains?"

Henry shrugs in his chair. "A fair bit, I've translated many texts with their accounts."

"You can read primordial fae?"

Henry's white smile is blinding. "I can, Your Majesty."

For a moment, I've forgotten my title. That I am a queen. For a moment, I am just a girl discovering all that a goddess has manipulated her into. But reality slams back into me.

I had planned to keep Gideon's father in a safehouse, far from the court—it is as Caethes had done, but the Admiral has revealed how flimsy that was. In a split-second, I decide to keep Henry here. In the Seelie Court.

"Henry, while Gideon is otherwise indisposed would you be willing to assist us? It would further help us achieve our goals, not to mention, get Gideon out of the mess he is in."

"How may I be of service?" Henry glances between us. The two monarchs.

"I have some texts I need you to translate. Your knowledge of the society and other court machinations also could be the tide that changes the result of this war."

For all of Enydd's ancient status, it came as a shock recently that she had been illiterate for many centuries until one day, locked in that cathedral, she expressed the desire to learn to read and write. At that point primordial fae and long stopped being used. The amount of people today who can read the runes is concerningly low.

Henry inclines his head with pride. Despite the slight tilt resulting from his stroke, he holds himself with a stalwart soldier's bearing. "I would be honored."

I turn to Maelona. "Lady Maelona, would you organize an aid to assist Henry Zhao with any needs or services he requires?"

Maelona nods. "Of course, Your Majesty." I resist sniping at the title, but we are in the presence of those who expect it. "What suite shall I organize for Mr. Zhao?"

I don't hesitate. "Aneira's former chambers please. They are the most easily fortified and protected."

Any pertinent or sensitive information has already been removed from Aneira's rooms and deposited in mine. I have stacks of ledgers on my desk and piles of tokens and artifacts. Right now, the suites that Aneira called hers are a shell of what they once were. Now they are beautiful and formal, but utterly devoid of personality and characterization. They're just rooms.

Maelona doesn't react but her mood ring hair does earn a few momentary white strands. "Of course."

With that, Emrys and I dismiss Henry for the night and Maelona guides him out the doors. I hear her call for Enydd, and I smile internally because I know she's delegating. Once everyone files out of the space, I wait a breath until the doors squeal shut and deflate.

This rescue did not give me the fulfillment I wanted.

CHAPTER 5

It's beyond the Witching Hour when Enydd barrels into our suite, heedless of the wards we'd placed on the door. Wards that prevent unwanted guests unless it's an emergency. Enydd's presence at the foot of our bed indicates this is exactly that.

Emrys and I shoot up from the covers, instantly alert. My husband's hair is mussed, but his eyes are bright. I'm sure

I appear similarly. It takes a moment to remember to cover myself with the sheet after our former mentor receives an eyeful.

"Caethes is here," Enydd announces without preamble.

I know now is not the time for joking. Enydd and I have always maintained somewhat of an antagonistic relationship, even now that she has warmed to me somewhat. But the flatness in the set of her face is not her normal stoic mask. This mask is crumbling, held together by will. Hiding anxiety.

"Where?" Emrys demands, sheets pooled about his tapered waist.

"The throne room."

"We'll be down in minutes. Please give us a moment to dress."

Enydd nods sharply and turns on her heel. As soon as she's out the door, Emrys and I leap from the bed and dress hastily. My husband finds a pair of leather pants and a gold silk dressing gown. He haphazardly ties it together, shoving his feet into loosely laced combat boots. I pull on my battle leathers from the meeting.

We're rushing down the hall, Enydd leading a fast pace as I tie my hair up in a messy knot. Not much can be done with Emrys's bed-tousled hair, aside from running a hand through it.

I haven't had much of a chance to contemplate why Caethes is here and why now, but Henry Zhao's current location is a probable reason. The question is, how much of our interference has she figured out? Does she know Henry is here? Does she know who took him? Was the Admiral spotted? Did Aveda double-cross us?

The thoughts rampage in my mind but halt when Emrys reaches out and steadies me. "We'll figure it out. In the meantime, we give away nothing." His voice is slightly roughened by sleep and the private thoughts that invade at the sound are most unwelcome at this moment. But it distracts me.

We arrive at the throne room doors and Enydd opens them for us. We stride through, holding regal poise but afford Caethes none of respect of dressing our parts. We'd even forgone our crowns. The Unseelie Queen knows our place, we do not need to prove it to her. And the lack of seeing her as an adequate adversary surely has her blood boiling.

Caethes stands in the center of the throne room, a pillar of silver in a sea of gold. She is garbed in shimmering mercury, the dress clinging to her body like liquid metal. Like a second skin. It sculpts to her hips, abdomen, and breasts, showing every curve and dip and every breath. And her breaths are coming fast and furious. The diamonds at her throat tremble with her rage, her bared teeth blinding against the onyx of her lips.

"You conniving little bitch," Caethes hisses as we enter. Her hands curl at her sides, her hands turning to claws with her fury. Even so, she remains standing at her post in the center of the room. "Meddling in my affairs? Taking my prisoner? A prisoner I made a member of my court?"

I flinch internally. Seems the Unseelie Queen learned from our Gideon machinations.

"I do not believe he was in your court willingly," I quip elegantly.

"It is a war crime!"

"Then how fortunate it is that we are at war."

Caethes seethes. "I could break him."

I don't need to ask which *he* she refers to. It is obvious the only *he* she has in clutches and can hurt is Gideon.

"The love I once held for him has vanished. You cannot use him against me."

"Then I should just kill him then? Is that what you are saying?" Caethes counters.

My heart skips a beat and I feel my anxiety ratchet up a notch. "That seems pointless. Killing him would only serve you as an outlet for your rage. You should really learn to leash it, Your Majesty."

"You should learn to leash your legs—"

"Hypocrisy and sex shaming?" I interrupt, tsking. "Caethes, blood of mine, I'll have you know that double-standards are quite unbecoming in this court. Are you veiling your embarrassment of sharing a lover with one of your family members with wrath?" I giggle to get a rise out of her. "Shame."

Those black lips peel back over white teeth. "You are a child."

I sigh. "Stooping to petty insults will not do."

As Caethes's nostrils flare, surely gearing up for another trade of insults, Emrys interrupts.

"Caethes, why are you here?"

The Unseelie Queen is visibly taken back. She reels on Emrys, focusing those eerie onyx eyes on my husband. "I am here because my prisoner is gone and you have taken him!"

"Do you have any proof?" Emrys queries, lifting a brow.

"Do not play games with me, boy. I do not need proof. Your wife all but admitted it."

"If we did? What purpose does your presence here achieve?"

"It tells me your wife likely still has feelings for the halfling."

Emrys quirks a mocking brow, but I sense a pang of hurt through the bond. "I believe she already discredited that sentiment."

"Why else take the father?" Caethes growls.

"He's leverage," Emrys says simply. "What power do you hold over Gideon now that you cannot manipulate him with his father's fate?"

"You want him dead," Caethes states as a question. Hedging a guess.

"I did not say that. Do not presume to know my motivations." Emrys's voice has taken on a warning note.

Caethes levels a glare at Emrys. "I raised you, boy. I do know you."

"No. You *think* you know me. You know nothing of who I truly am." I feel Emrys's temper flare. "You did not care. I was simply a weapon for you."

"That is not true!" Caethes protests, a hint of true emotion in her voice. I catch it, Emrys doesn't.

I have to blink away the surprise that flitters across my face. Did Caethes truly care for her precious Revenant after all?

I feel Emrys's anger simmer. "What is my favorite color? My hobbies? How do I feel about whiskey and tartlets? Do you even know what color my eyes are?" Emrys casts a King's Glamour before his gaze. "Hmm? Do you have an answer?"

Caethes's mouth opens and closes. She is silent. Rage leaving her body. She ducks her head but I see her jaw working. Emotion boiling. Not rage. Sadness.

"You have your mother's eyes."

Caethes speaks so low I almost don't catch it. She lifts her gaze to Emrys's. He has let the glamour fall.

"Not in the color—though it is quite similar. Yours are brighter. Deeper. But they are like hers in the way they light up when you joke or tease. Or the way they narrow when you smirk. Hers did that."

Caethes looks wretched. Defeated and full of sorrow. I see an internal battle that she is fighting. I see loss. I see far too much of my own reflected in her. She lost her precious Revenant—whom I'm rapidly discovering she probably did care for more than she let on—and more unsettling is her devastation and grief about his mother. Aneira.

The former Seelie Queen, who had raised me, held some sort of power over Caethes. Even still. It's become painfully, and upsettingly apparent that Caethes cared for Aneira. In a way that I am greatly understanding, was not platonic. That some time ago, whether it had been millennia or centuries, *Caethes loved Aneira*. Maybe still, even in her death. But how could she have been part of the orchestration of her demise? Caethes's hand is the one who fed Arawn, and Arawn was the one to finally deal that death blow.

But more over, and devastating to myself, is did Aneira reciprocate these feelings? Did my queen and mother love Caethes as the Dark Queen loved her? Why keep this such a secret if so? Did I really know Aneira as much as I thought?

Heartbreak crests through me and I wonder what else I didn't know.

Aneira kept a whole child from me. And now, I've learned a whole relationship.

The memories cascade over me. Moments of altercation between the two warring queens. The quips. The jabs. The glances I was too blind to see. It all makes sense.

The worlds come crumbling down around me and I feel the stones of my mental fortress rearrange and try to form some mockery of a mirror. The shards like that of Aneira's likeness. What I once thought she was. What she is now. Put together like some jigsaw puzzle, cracks striating her face, webbing her once beautiful features.

I blink away the emotion and refocus on our enemy. I can wallow later.

In the absence of my sudden doubt and grief is anger. I feel it rile up inside me and I feel my husband stiffen beside me.

Vanna, he whispers warningly within my mind. *Do not. She is fragile right now. I've never seen her in such a state. She is more dangerous than ever.*

I want to heed my soulmate's caution, but the fury at Aneira's deception all these years has become a wildfire. The vitriol I wish to spill in her name chokes me, threatening to break my teeth to be let out.

"You do not have the right to speak like this," I hiss, stepping one step out of my husband's reach. Emrys reaches a hand forward but I shake him off before he touches me. "You do not get to reminisce and act as if you have lost. Your flagrant disdain of your denizens has lessened any affection you may have held for anyone."

"I have done what is needed. You do not know of my heart," the Dark Queen returns.

"Oh?" I say mockingly. "Then tell me, Caethes, Queen of the Unseelie Court, what is the desire of your heart?"

Rage. Undiluted rage fills the queen's face.

Requesting a heart's desire is already offensive. Requesting a heart's desire of a monarch is one of the deepest insults one can deliver. If not for the current climate of wartime, this alone could be grounds to call upon battle. It is why I can get away with it now.

"You tarnish the title of queen with your blasphemy," Caethes manages haltingly. Her frame shakes with the power of her wrath.

No. I realize, with the most unfathomable foolishness. She shakes with the power of her chaos. Of the magic she has been harnessing during this exchange.

Caethes is one of the few of the fae who can transform chaotic energy into a tangible force. A force she can—and does—use as a weapon.

"Fuck," I mutter.

In my own emotions, in my own head, I have ignored Emrys's nerves. His agitation and fear as it mounts and builds. It's here, in the bond between us, that his prediction of this altercation does not bode well.

"You are a mockery of all that came before you. You are a worthless scrap of flesh. You are not worth what Aneira believed of you," the queen's words shudder through her, in the same manner her lip quivers. She inhales. "I will seek it as my life's mission to end you."

My cockiness, a significant downfall to my personality, rears its ugly head. "As if that's anything new." My voice is filled with exasperation, but only to hide what turmoil truly writhes beneath.

Caethes bares her teeth. "*I* will be your demise."

I tilt my head to the side and don a small smile. "But dear queen, blood of mine, heir and succession laws prevent that. Don't you recall?"

The Unseelie Queen lets out a sound and it is flooded with chaos. She lifts her hands and pushes them at me. Her wall of chaos strikes me, dead in the center of my chest and I soar backwards. Crashing against the polished earth floor, before the dais steps of the Vanora-Gwyndolyn seat of power, I wheeze. On my side, I grit my teeth, and ready to explode.

Emrys rushes to my side.

Caethes too, has flown backwards. Her silver gown bears marks of her assault and landing. She looks on with a wildness befitting a faerie queen. She, like me, cannot attack. Not outright. And it seems despite her chaos's power, she cannot hurt me unless she is willing to bear half the brunt. And I can tell by the realization dawning on her features, followed by the truth of the matter, that she is not willing.

I get to my feet just as Caethes does, taking Emrys's proffered hand. She inclines her head, the jewels caught between her antlers reflecting the golden light of the Seelie sky. I am reminded, once again, of how I'd once imagined her to be a moon goddess, and here, I am now realizing how accurate that depiction was.

If she were goddess of the moon, Aneira would have been goddess of the sun. The two would forever be star-crossed.

And with that reality I am furious.

I can feel Emrys combing through my thoughts. Trying to weed through the array of conspiracy and discovery. I sense his intention to garden through my mind, find the root of the diseasing sentiments, and pull it out. To dispose of it where its plague can no longer rot within me.

"I think it is time to leave, Your Majesty," Emrys says softly. "You cannot harm her and she cannot harm you. And I do not wish to fight with you this day." His voice takes on a warning note. "Please bear in mind that I hold no succession to your court—not in the fae way—and nothing beyond my will can stop me from harming you."

"You will not kill me," Caethes announces, determination in her voice. "I was all you had for so long. You are not able to forsake me as easily as you defected my court. I was more than just your queen."

"Do not be so sure."

Caethes appears crestfallen. "I know I did not show it, but I I—" Caethes chokes on her words and I wonder if she's trying to force a lie. She swallows. "I loved you. In my own way. I named you. I gave you the last name I made for myself."

Gorlassar.

That's the name Caethes created in secret after she ascended to the throne from slavery. I'd never heard her say it. I've never heard *anyone* say it.

The words strike so deep in Emrys's heart I feel them pierce mine. Loneliness and neglect surge to the surface of his mind. Child-like desire to be wanted and loved invading all the walls that protect his mind. I see a surplus of memories cascade between us, flooding through the bond in his vulnerability. Moments stemming back to infancy of reaching for the moon-haired queen and being denied. Of him at five years old showing a completed carving of a Wild Hunt's horse, his fingers nicked and bloody, that she waved off. The first moment she paid attention to him; when he accidentally severed an instructor's hand when they went to slap him.

That memory is crystallized. The way Caethes suddenly sits up in her seat. More than twenty years before, yet the un-aging queen appears no different. Braids loop about her antlers, a spider web of diamonds strung between them, an obsidian and ruby arachnid perched in the center. She steps down from her throne, descending as the instructor screams, clutching his stump while scarlet floods the marble floor. Emrys shakes with fear but he does not let go of the dripping sword, holding it at his side as he meets his queen's endless black eyes.

She takes a finger to his chin and tilts it up. The action so gentle I have to hold my breath, waiting for the deception of a blow.

"You will be a marvelous warrior," she pronounces upon crimson lips. "Come, boy, you have much to learn."

Caethes takes him by the hand, sword still clutched in the other, as she leads him out of the throne room.

Emrys composes himself enough to shake himself free from the memory and reconstructs his walls. Steadied once again, he meets the queen who'd decided his fate.

"It is too little, too late."

Hurt festers across Caethes's face, like a bloom in decay. The rose of her vulnerability turning to ash, hardening with the permafrost of the earth.

"I suppose it is," Caethes says with finality. Her jaw is tight as she gives one succinct nod. "Good morrow, Your Majesties."

And with that, the Dark Queen, Caethes of the Unseelie Court, departs, a wave of terrible power following in her wake.

CHAPTER 6

I do not go back to sleep. I am far too riled from the encounter with Caethes. From all the revelations she brought. Instead, Emrys and I go to the training room to spar. It has been far too long since I have had a good practice with someone—especially with someone as adept as my husband.

He is my mirror. My other half. Everything in all ways. Even during this tumultuous time, both of us struggling to grasp the realities of a multi-faceted Caethes—albeit in different ways.

We both take up a short sword and a dagger, palming the blades and leaning the familiar comforts. There, on the mat we face off. Emrys has retied his laces and forgone his robe.

"That is an unfair advantage," I whine, gesturing to his wonderfully sculpted abdomen and hard pecs. My eyes devour all the exposed golden flesh and the scar that mars the space over his heart.

Emrys smirks, revealing those slightly pointed teeth. "You could always do the same. I'm sure the equal distraction would be welcome."

"You know as well as I do that the moment my shirt is off; we'll be fucking instead of fighting."

"Would that be so bad?"

My blood heats and wetness pools between my legs. I picture Emrys taking me down to the mat, pinning me down, and fucking me hard. I can almost feel my back arching up from his wondrous thrusts, eager for more friction and touch. I imagine his hands in my hair, pulling roughly to the most exquisite point of pain.

I have to forcibly remove my thoughts from their lewd direction.

"As much as I would love it, it would not be effective for our current needs."

"Fucking is always effective for our needs," Emrys retorts, his eyes dark and his erection pronounced.

"Ryss," I chide, licking my lips. Eyes betraying my want.

"Yes, wife?"

"Fight."

I leap forward, slashing with a high arc of my sword and a quick shot with my dagger. Anyone else, I would've gotten first blood with a kidney strike, but Emrys knows me and is prepared. What I also hadn't realized is that he can anticipate every move because he is in my head. But I am also in his. Emrys battles back, lunging with the dagger and swiping low at my hamstrings with the longer blade. I lean backwards and jump over the slash, sending my body into a backwards roll where I come upon my feet. I use the momentum from my feet and launch from a crouch to an ascending attack.

Emrys, whether by knowing me, or seeing the intention, twirls away and comes up behind me. I whirl, dagger raised to his throat, short sword at his inner thigh. But he has done the same. The flat of his sword presses against my jugular, the blade right at the apex of my thighs.

"Husband," I taunt, "Do you really intend to damage your favorite place?"

"I could ask you the same of your favorite toy, wife."

I arch a brow. "Do you think my favorite toy is that appendage? You know I quite like your tongue, too."

Emrys's lips twist in amusement. "I'm certain there would be some degree of sadness to see my cock go."

"Perhaps," I tease.

We back off slowly and return to beginning positions and this time it is my soulmate who goes on the offense first. Emrys comes at me with a flurry of his blades, his movements lightning quick and I have seconds to react. I drop down and roll between his legs, hastily getting to my feet and lunging on his exposed back.

I drop the sword, but keep the small knife as I tackle his back, climbing up his sweat-slickened skin and arriving upon his shoulders. I then go to twist around, but Emrys throws my weight, using the momentum and sends us both crashing to the mat. We are both without our swords, armed with only daggers as my wrapped legs maintain their hold around my husband's neck. We struggle for a moment, pinning hands that wield blades, and in the process, he breaks my hold. Shimmying up my body, he presses against every plane and curve. I begin to lock my legs around the first available area and find his hips tucked into my pelvis, our heaving chests pressing together. His hard length presses directly into the delicate and aroused center of me, and it takes every ounce of will I possess not to grind up into him. Our hands are clasped, pinned to the dark mat, blades clutched between us.

"Stalemate?" I ask breathlessly.

"Stalemate."

"Good," I announce. And then I pull him in with my hooked feet to press a desperate kiss to his mouth.

He answers in kind, the force of his mouth punishingly divine as he forces our lips apart, his tongue diving between. Simultaneously, we let go of the daggers and our hands find every bare expanse of skin, finding sweat and desire slickening us. Emrys grinds his pelvis into mine, his hard cock delivering blissful friction to my needy clit. I feel my pussy pulse with want, the yearning making me moan into his mouth. His hands find the laces on my leathers, diving beneath them and palming my breasts.

"Please," I whine. "Touch me more."

His thumb finds my nipple and flicks against the hardened peak. Arousal surges, sending a bolt directly between my legs. I arch. I want his mouth there. I want his teeth against my breast, his tongue swirling my nipple. I need his face between my legs, teeth grazing my clit. I want. I need.

In our frantic clawing and pulling of each other, we both neglect to notice approaching presences until the very last moment.

"Oh," a softly slurred voice squeaks, while a second voice joins in an amused chuckle.

Emrys and I break apart, eyes rounding on the intruders.

"The king and queen are quite...active in their affections," Enydd declares in her low brogue.

I glare, getting to my feet. "A knock could have been beneficial."

"Yes, but you proclaimed you were not to be disturbed after your late-night visitor."

"Is this not disturbing us?"

"Unintentionally." My former mentor smirks.

I blush furiously, trying to penetrate Enydd with any sort of damage through my eyes. The former mentor simply flutters her lashes innocently.

"Good morning, Henry," Emrys greets cordially, clearly more put together. He has reassumed his role as a respectable king, though the golden robe does hinder the professional elegance by a touch.

Henry Zhao tries to hide a blush, smiling softly. "Good morning, Your Majesty. I hope the day is treating you well?"

Emrys cocks a brow, entertained. "It is early yet."

"Yes. Yes, of course."

Shirtless, Emrys's scar is prominent on his chest and Henry's studious mind does not miss it. His eyes zero in on the mark that gave him his Revenant identity, mouth dropping open ever so slightly, and it's clear that questions are brewing in that brain of his. Emrys notes this too—as I see through the bond.

"I was just showing Mr. Zhao around," Enydd announces. "He has only seen formal areas of the court as an emissary and I thought it would be prudent to show him around."

"Certainly," Emrys responds. "But also..." he turns his attention to Henry, "when you have a spare moment, I'd like to ask you some questions."

"Me?"

"Yes, mostly pertaining to any and what information the Arcana Society maintains surrounding the Harbinger and Revenant. For educational purposes."

Henry blinks. "Yes, certainly. Of course, I...I would also be honored if—"

"If you could also ask questions about our identities?"

Henry nods fastidiously.

"We'll make the arrangements. Are you free this afternoon?"

The plans are made and then Henry and Enydd leave us be, our former mentor gracing us with a wave and a quip:

"A royal heir will not be made while you two still take your tonics!"

With their absence, Emrys and I look at each other in shock and amazement.

Children.

We'd never really discussed if we'd wanted them. It is not required of monarchs in the fae courts; however, it is unusual if sovereigns do not procreate. Both Caethes and—falsely—Aneira are two such examples. Emrys and I were raised and conditioned to be warriors, both of us not expected to have babies. Children born to warriors is as rare of an occurrence as rulers not having them.

We were together for decades during Century Training, but even then, our worlds and thoughts were absorbed by not getting caught and surviving the training. Most days we were so exhausted. Most days that sort of future felt much too far away to consider.

"I hadn't thought—"

"Neither had I," Emrys answers softly.

"I'm not in the right headspace to be thinking of babies, I just..."

"I know, me neither. But we have plenty of time to figure it out."

"Right, right," I agree. But some niggling thought has planted a seed of doubt and I feel more now than ever that time is running out.

I am riled and antsy when we return to our suite. Even when we undress to finally go back to sleep, I am anxious. I lay next to Emrys and stare into his golden eyes. The fight helped but not by much and even if he couldn't read it through my thoughts, he can see it in my face.

"I still need to do something," I murmur into the darkened area of our bed. The heavy velvet curtains are drawn around us, but some of the daylight filters in. "I need to be out there. I am not meant to be idle."

"You want to try another rescue."

"Yes, but this time, *I* want to do it. I want to be the one directly responsible for taking one of Caethes's advantages."

Emrys's lips thin. "You're going to go for his mother."

I wonder how much of this is preordained by Lady Fate. How many of my choices are truly mine. How many have been influenced by her. How many have been predetermined by her. Is Gideon's mother a pawn in the goddess's game? Is she meant to be a piece for Caethes's side of the board? Was anyone changed when the lullaby was written for Corvina and I? How did this all shape up so messily?

Regardless, I am choosing this, whether it be my own, or a goddess's will.

I don't answer but it is written across every line of my face and revealed in my thoughts. I've been over the papers, I know her routine, I know the rotating watch. I can do it, I'm certain of it. But I am queen and there are invisible strings holding me back. I am more a padded monarch than I am the fearsome warrior, and I despise it.

Emrys reads all of this. "Tomorrow then. Together."

Something brightens within me. "You're with me?"

"I'm always with you, Vanna."

Emrys wraps me tightly in his arms, pressing his warm body against mine, tucking my head beneath his chin. I breathe in the scent of leather and vetiver, the slight lemon and musk becoming my world.

I smile softly. "I love you."

"I love you, too," he returns.

Somehow, after that, I fall to slumber.

CHAPTER 7

Emrys gets up without disturbing me. I discover this when I wake sometime later to cool sheets next to me when I stretch out. I check the timepiece at my night stand and see the late afternoon hour. Surely, Emrys is already with Gideon's father, pressing him for information on our Centurion identities.

Tentatively, I reach out mentally and discover my husband is in fact with Henry, the two of them ensconced in the library. Hesitantly, I make my mental presence known, like a knock on his open mental door, and sit just inside the fringes of it.

The two of them converse cordially, my soulmate seated on the edge of a plush cushion, while Henry sits in a high back chair with a footstool. His wheelchair is tucked into a corner. If electricity were reliable in the court, he would have been able to bring his electric wheelchair, but as the Seelie Court does not possess any outlets, he could not. Typically, electronics of any kind are unreliable due to the dense Seelie magic that curtains so much of the court.

Henry sips on tea and ponders a question I clearly missed.

"I don't think it was known to anyone that your wife's identity as the Harbinger was hers, nor the fact that she is evidently female," Henry says. "Yours however, had been narrowed down, though not wholly determined. The seven of you who were always within Caethes's entourage made it obvious."

Emrys nods, sipping his own tea—some kind of black blend with a hint of cinnamon. "What I'm surprised by is how no one figured out who she was by the fact of her being one of the winged fae." Emrys mentally strokes down my nerves, apologizing.

"I think too many were preoccupied thinking the Harbinger was male to consider anything else."

"Perhaps." Emrys takes more tea. "Did you have dossiers on either of us regarding speculations?"

"Of course," Henry says flippantly, evidently eager to sell Arcana secrets. "Your whereabouts were tracked as much as could be. Hers were less so, though in recent years more theories started leading to her about the *Ceidwad Cudd*."

"Ah."

"Ah is correct. May I ask a few questions now?"

Emrys waves his arm in welcome. "I welcome it."

"The rumors and evidence have pointed to you and your wife being enemies, but that does not seem the case anymore. Particularly considering this morning, which I deeply apologize for."

"It is not needed," Emrys offers.

"Thank you, Your Majesty. So, what I am curious about is—what merit does the assumptions of the Revenant and Harbinger being enemies hold? Did you ever hate each other? Try to kill one another? Is she the one who killed you to earn your name?"

Emrys chuckles. "That is more than one question, but I am fine to answer them all. Firstly, as you can tell, the Revenant and the Harbinger are not enemies, and up until recently and for most of Century Training, we were not. Second, there was a time in training when I thought I hated her. When I was deceived." Memories of Osian surge up between us in the bond, our matched fury smoldering beneath the past. "There was a time, also, until recently that I believed she hated me. Or at least it was something close to it."

I never hated you, I whisper through the bond, an intangible touch like fingers running through his hair accompanying it. *Even when I didn't remember, a part of me loved you. The goddess couldn't take that from me.*

Emrys smiles on the outside. *That is nice to hear, wife. Thank you.*

"As for did we try to kill one another?" Emrys continues. "Somewhat. But was she the one who killed me at the end of Century Training? No. That was the mentor who'd tricked me and coerced her." A wicked smile twists his mouth. "She took care of him in the end, and I sincerely hope he suffered when she did." He pauses and then says almost

61

conspiratorially, "I was otherwise indisposed—being dead and all."

"So, the accounts of that battle...?" Henry starts.

"Are half-truths. We did fight the mentors and the Wild Hunt. It truly was thirty against two. She really did command the goddess."

A lightbulb goes off over Henry's head. "That's how you hope to persuade Gideon against Caethes. You plan to use the goddess."

"I've planned nothing of the sort," Emrys deflects. "My wife has a plan; I do not question it."

Henry's gaze narrows, clearly reading the lines of the faerie trickery and mistruths without falsehoods. Emrys smiles behind his cup.

"Any other questions?"

"Actually..." Henry begins, lapsing into a query about a squabble some years ago that both Emrys and I had been inadvertently involved in.

I slip away from Emrys's thoughts and back into my bed. I lay there for a moment in the silk and velvet sheets, staring up at the canopy of the bed. Tonight, I get to do something. Tonight, Emrys and I don't have to be the protected sovereigns. Tonight, we get to be the warriors we were always meant to be.

Calling for a meal to be brought to my room, I wrap myself in a sage silk robe and pull my hair up in a jeweled claw clip. Barefoot, I wander over to my desk and ponder some documents, some made by my hand, many not. Pushing most of them away, I reach for the messy scrawl of the plan to retrieve Gideon's mother.

Gideon's mother, Natalia Zhao, is a licensed practical nurse, currently working a rotation of four-on-four-off twelve-hour shifts, switching from night to day every two weeks. She is currently on the third of those four nights on a surgical unit. I look over a few documents detailing the hospital's security systems including the location of cameras and what security guard's routes look like. Previous monitoring from fae guards disclose guard schedules and habits, where certain guards slack, how other guards pause for an unauthorized cigarette or cellphone break. I memorize all of it.

Once the food is delivered, I sit at my desk with the golden platter of fruit and meat and cheese, picking at it as I pore over more information. My eyes are glued to the pages so intently that I don't realize I've consumed the entirety of my meal until my fingers meet the empty plate.

I sigh and rub my forehead with the heel of my hand. Getting up, I stretch my legs, pacing my floor and extending my arms above my head. It's at this very moment that my husband decides to return to the room and finds my robe scandalously high on my thighs, just barely covering the most intimate parts of me. I retain this pose as I hold his eyes, giving him a sultry look and pivot just so, so he can see the curve of my naked ass and the parting of my robe to his favorite place between my legs.

Emrys's eyes heat, the topaz burning with desire. "Wife, you are utterly irresistible."

"How so?" I ask innocently, batting my lashes.

Emrys strides across the room, determination and arousal clear in every line of his body. He gathers me up in his arms and his hands instantly go beneath the robe, cupping my ass and kneading. I giggle as he growls against my throat, his fingers digging in like a deep tissue massage, rubbing down the backs of my thighs.

"Do we have time?" he asks, yearning in his voice, aching in his cock.

"I think so," I say coyly.

Just then a knock sounds at our door.

"Oh, for fuck's sake!" I groan. "Tell them to go away."

Rotting anger begins replacing my horniness. My temper is wound so tight that I dream of nothing more than slapping whoever is interrupting this time. This is the third fucking time.

"Goddess fucking tits and damn it all," Emrys grumbles as he releases me and turns to the door. I straighten myself out as he swings open the door. "Can I help you?" Impatience clear in his tone.

"Oh, so sorry," Maelona replies, striding in past him. "Was I interrupting a fuck session?"

"Does it look like we'd gotten there yet?" Emrys growls, slamming the door with a flick of his wrist.

Maelona peruses him pointedly, her chocolate eyes falling on Emrys's straining pants. "I think not."

"Mae," I start. "I love you, but why the hell are you here?"

Maelona takes a seat on a green velvet pouf and tilts her head at me, her long black hair falling like a cascade of ink. "I think we're losing Gideon."

I deflate. "Why do you think that?"

"Something Julia said in training today. She mentioned Gideon withdrew from her. I suppose he is anxious about his family and wants assurances that they are okay. Apparently, Caethes had quite the meltdown last night. Broke many things. Perhaps she took out some sexual frustrations on him. I am not sure."

I narrow my brows. "Julia wasn't set to meet with Gideon last night."

Maelona shrugs, the shoulder of her champagne gown slipping. "Perhaps she wanted to check on his status after

Tirnoc made comments about the events involving Henry and the Admiral."

I blink, but Emrys beats me to it. "Tirnoc wasn't supposed to know about Henry's rescue."

Lady Maelona's hair flashes an indecisive color. "The Admiral may have been boasting to a few secure people."

"*Secure people?*" Emrys echoes, anger lining his words. "What does that mean?"

"Tirnoc, Bleddyn, Wisteria, and Julia that I am aware of. She may have also been in the presence of Violante, as well."

I pinch the bridge of my nose. "Perhaps Baphet was right about Aveda."

Maelona casts an arm over my empty drink cart. "Perhaps he was. So, what are you going to do, Your Majesties?"

"Stop calling us that," I snap, inhaling sharply.

"You're always so prickly if you haven't orgasmed in a while. Right, pretty boy?"

"Thank you, Mae," I mutter irritated. "You can go now."

"But I just got here." She fake pouts.

"Out, Mae."

"Fine, fine. I hope you get fucked soon, maybe you'll have a sense of humor again."

Maelona leaves with a little twinkling wave, shutting the door behind her.

"Goddess help me," I mutter below my breath.

"We should send Julia to officially meet with Gideon tonight," Emrys says, clearly thinking aloud. "To ensure he *is* okay still after Caethes's visit and threats. If she thinks Gideon is worthless to her, we have only a thin chance of securing his safety."

"That's probably a good idea."

"If he isn't though, we need to organize a rescue of Gideon."

I look at Emrys in surprise. "As well as his mother?"

"If Caethes has no use for him, there's nothing stopping her from retaliating against his family. You and I both know she will kill on a whim."

I'm instantly reminded of Tadgh, a surprisingly docile Unseelie whom Gideon and I had caught and interrogated. He'd found his demise at Caethes's hand simply for her to prove a point. I remember how she'd swiped her claws against his throat, how his severed head had rolled and the geyser of blood that had been a fount from his neck. The arc of crimson that had splashed the queen's gown. I remember dual-pupiled Prussian blue eyes, still open in shock.

He'd died for his loyalty, his payment forgotten by his queen.

Pulling myself from the memory, I rub my eyes. "You're right. We'll tell Julia."

It becomes painfully clear that I will not be engaging in any lovemaking with my husband right now and that just sours my mood further. Maelona's comment flashes through my mind and I snort. My former casual lover would know that detail about me, even so, I need not be reminded of it.

Emrys pens a letter for Julia, sealing it with viridian wax, and calling for a messenger. The note is instantly swept away and we await answers. We wait, and for what feels like eternity our plans are on hold. We continue the rest of the afternoon and evening by going through the motions. But then at seven we receive an answer.

Gideon is fine and still in Caethes's good graces. He still wants to continue. He adds additional reassurances in case we aren't convinced. I can't help but appreciate the words.

The rescue plan is resumed.

CHAPTER 8

Emrys and I step onto the streets of Vancouver, inhaling the night scent of city life. We'd deceived our guards and entourage, feigning an early night, only to retire to our chambers, dress for the mission and slip through the Faerie Roads. A King's Glamour took care of the ripple in the wards and our absence in the bedchamber. The room meanwhile, was charmed by my husband to falsify subtle sounds of lovemaking. I just pray that no more unexpected guests arrive before we can return.

We glance around and extend our shared ability outwards, picking up a few signatures of supernaturals— mostly witches and halflings, a vampire or two. Typically, in a city setting such as this, the fae are practically unheard of, the surplus of iron a caustic agent on their lungs. Long exposure without effective mithridatism will sicken and weaken the fae. It is why most fae—Seelie and Unseelie alike—remain in their courts or in their respective territories of wilderness. Wilderness like the Yukon or the old forests of Europe.

The hospital which Gideon's mother works at is several blocks away, as we couldn't risk stepping out of the Faerie Roads so near her monitoring grounds. For all we know we could trigger some wards that Caethes has placed or we'd walk directly into a patrol. No, it's better to approach from afar and assess from a distance.

Stepping from the alley, Emrys and I keep to the shadows, darting under blown streetlights, and away from unaware pedestrians. The air for June is warm, fluctuating between heatwaves and late spring showers. The scent of petrichor is heady in the air, indicating that there was a recent rainfall, despite the fact I do not see, nor skirt any puddles. Side by side, we continue our route, our black booted feet eating up the distance and growing my anxiety. There is a slight thrill in my blood at being on this mission. Of being queen and having such a foolish task ahead of me. The freedom is like a drug, unhindered by the jewels and gowns and crown of the throne. For a while it is just Emrys and I, the Revenant and the Harbinger. Like old times. It gives me a rush and the smile that spreads across my face is dark and wicked.

"What is that smile for?" Emrys inquires, a quirk to his lips.

I glance at him from the side of my eye. "This is what I needed. Can we make this a habit? Perhaps a monthly secret mission? Just to keep the crown from chafing."

My husband cocks a brow. "Like a date night?"

I grin. "Exactly like a date night."

"Only you would get excited at the prospect of a forbidden mission date."

"It's one way to keep the romance alive."

"Love, there are so many ways I can keep this romance alive. Say the word and I'll do my worst."

"Oh, will you now?" I tease.

Emrys makes a flirting sound of affirmation before turning us past an alley and through some construction.

Heavy metal bins hold garbage bags, old insulation, and drywall. Plastic sheets flap in the wind from a series of scaffolding, paint buckets left for the night, tools haphazardly strewn about. Large orange construction cones are stacked with some pallets as a basic display of laziness from the previous day's workers. Anyone could—and would—steal those cones, just for the hell of it.

"Well, next month we should—" I immediately stop as a too close fae presence pings on my internal radar. And then more.

I whirl, pulling out a golden dagger and getting into position beside Emrys. He too, has reacted, his sword, Heart's-Desire drawn.

From the waving plastic, a seedy-looking faerie steps out. He brushes aside the opaque sheet, murky with a film of construction dust and graffiti. The faerie is distinctly Unseelie, his signal flaring his allegiance to us. His face is gray and wan, cheeks sunken and marked with black scratches. Beneath his two sets of noxious green eyes are hollows, the rings beneath his eyes the deepest violet of bruises. Greasy black hair hangs limply over his brow, partly pushed back and slicked down.

"Emrys Gorlassar," the faerie says between blackened teeth. Stepping further into the light I notice a pair of silver antlers sticking out from his hair, moss draping from the tines. "Your favor is being called in."

Emrys's heart sinks, I can feel it through the bond. In response, without knowing exactly why, mine does the same. I sift through his thoughts, trying to figure out what favor could possibly be getting called in. And then I find it.

The club in Prague. What he had to do to get us into the Winter Carnaval.

I remember the conversation.

"How exclusive is this event really?" I'd asked.

"Very," Emrys had responded.

And then I had begun to ask what he did to get us the in. And then his response.

"Later. I told you I'd do anything for you."

I hadn't questioned him further. I hadn't even thought about his words after that, too consumed and distracted by the rekindling of our relationship. Of our marriage.

"Ryss," I whisper, devastation hinting my tone.

Emrys beseeches me, apology and grief written in his burning gold eyes. "I'm sorry, Vanna. I made an empty debt. The favor is binding or forfeit."

If I thought my heart sunk before, it's nothing compared to the lead that drops into my belly now.

Favors with a forfeit clause lock the promiser into a debt or vow under the consequence of death. If the faerie who promises goes back on their word, they forfeit their life. Immediately. Just like a heart's desire command gives the user rule over the giver, the promiser of a favor is indebted for eternity or until the favor is fulfilled. If Emrys offered an empty debt, he has to do whatever this faerie wants of him. Or he'll die.

Anger lashes through me, propelled by fear. The absolute terror that rises with the tide of wrath chokes and consumes me. I feel it crawl up my throat, flood my mind, and spray all rational thought wide. Everything is panic, everything is chaos, everything is desperation. I cannot lose Emrys. I cannot survive if I lose him again.

Regret fills Emrys, leaking into the bond and crashing against my fury and fright like the tide meeting the surf. They sizzle against each other, breaking and combining, turning the bond into an absolute state of disaster. But no one is the wiser to our inner turmoil. The fae before us cannot see the horror rampaging between us. On the outside we are cool, standing with our blades and taking in this seedy faerie.

"It is no longer Gorlassar," Emrys corrects after a time, his voice full of power its clear he doesn't feel. It's also clear he wants to shed Caethes's name. "It's Gwyndolyn-Vanora."

"Of course," the faerie responds, voice practically sticking to us like slime. "How marvelous it is to have an open debt to a faerie king."

"It wasn't completely open," Emrys rebukes. "Only whatever is within my power and does not cause me to forsake my chosen court or harm select people."

The faerie's four eyes narrow. "Yes, convenient now that you have defected from the Dark Court."

Emrys remains silent. I do too, but I'm almost certain everyone present can hear my racing heart.

"I would like to speak of the favor in private," the faerie continues when Emrys doesn't speak.

"You may say whatever you need in front of my queen, she can be sworn to secrecy."

The four toxic eyes narrow on me. "Can you swear this meeting to secrecy, king's wife?"

The title he gives me rubs me the wrong way, but I bare my white teeth in a vicious smile. "Sure."

Despite knowing I am fae, he does not trust my truth.

"I swear the occurrence of this meeting and the contents of his favor will not be revealed by the hands nor lips of mine."

The faerie inclines his head in acknowledgement and turns back to Emrys. "You are being tasked with framing a vampire of Joseph Harrow's court for the murder of Annabelle Laroche."

I instantly feel the favor lock onto Emrys, binding him. But at the same time, my eyes widen in shock.

Annabelle Laroche was an unidentified supernatural who'd gone on auction at the Winter Carnaval. She'd sold for a record sum to the King of the Vampire Court, Joseph Harrow. Emrys, Maelona, and I had seen her in Joseph's clutches, not having the power to do anything against him in our quest for the Seelie Crown. Guilt pangs in my chest at the memory of those wide blue eyes and soft blonde curls. She'd been so small. So young. And now she's gone.

"Who am I to frame?" Emrys asks. "Any vampire of my choosing? Or is it a specific vampire in mind?"

"Christian Duchannes, is the name of the vampire who will be taking responsibility."

"Is there any further information?"

"I have a folder of documents for you to read over." The faerie's four eyes flicker to us. "I will give it to you after you say your goodbyes to your wife. You must do this alone and she may not follow. You have fifteen minutes."

The faerie slips away, back through the construction and I wheel on my husband. Shock and fear, sadness and anger, all tumble within me, each one rearing their ugly heads for dominance, urging me to lash out at Emrys. Emrys draws me into the alley we'd passed, facing me. I sag against the brick wall, needing it for all the emotional support.

"How could you?" I whisper, tears burning in my eyes.

"I didn't think it would come to this."

"This what? That an empty debt could lead to you committing a crime?"

"That we would be together. That it would be like this when the debt was called." Emrys glances away. "I thought there was a chance I would be dead before it was called."

Those tears spill down my cheeks. I see his thoughts clearly.

"I knew I was running out of time to fulfill Lady Fate's bargain. That Lady Chaos's intervention gave me only months more to live if you didn't love and lose. And you were gone for so long and when you came back you still didn't remember everything you needed to. And you were so lost in yourself..." Emrys's gold eyes go hazy. "I figured I wouldn't have to answer for this. But I still made sure that I had some stipulations in case, including not telling Caethes about the favor."

Now it is anger's turn at the forefront and I push off of the wall.

"So, you were just going to throw it all away? You weren't going to fight for me? You were going to give up just like that?" I shout, tears streaming freely down my face. "You were going to let it all go like we meant nothing? I fucking love you, Emrys! I still loved you even when I didn't remember it. I began falling in love with you again, even despite the goddess's block on my mind. Why did you put us in this situation?" My words come out stumbling, my breathing ragged. My anxiety is replacing that wrath that had just erupted and now I feel empty and too full.

"I was fighting for you for so long, Vanna. For years. You didn't want to see me, or hear me. You forced me to swear against things I didn't want to. I was losing hope. I've had the torture and the pleasure of loving you and it was so painful to see you in Aberth with Gideon, having no idea who I was. What I meant to you. What you meant to *me*."

The memory flashes through his mind and I see what he took in. Gideon and I in room number seven. Gideon shirtless, scratches down his back from the sex we'd had the night before. My hair mussed. Hickeys on our skin. The scent of another male all over me. The emotions surge forward, too. The murderous rage. The heart-wrenching devastation.

"I was at the end of my rope, Vanna. This was a last-ditch effort. I wasn't expecting to get you back."

My lip quivers, the insecurity at his wavering faith in me festering between us.

"Vanna," he whispers, stepping forward. "No. I wasn't losing faith in you, or in us. I was losing faith in the goddess. In myself. I feared she had played an impossible trick on us. That there was no way you could love me without Century Training. It took years back then for us. I didn't think seven was enough. I didn't think I was enough."

"No." I push him away. "You cannot soften this with lovely words."

"I'm trying—"

"You're not trying anything," I bite out. "You were going to martyr yourself and leave me a grieving widow when you were gone. You were going to put me through hell—again. All my memories would have come back and I would know, but you'd be fucking *dead*." I grab him by his leathers, fisting my hands in the material and shove him against the opposite wall. "You were going to take half my soul from me."

"I'm sorry—"

"Sorry isn't enough!"

A flicker of rage and something else darkens Emrys's golden gaze. Suddenly, he takes my hands and tears them from his leathers. Gripping my wrists, he whirls us around so now I am back against the wall.

"I would like to speak now," Emrys says lowly, bringing his lips to my jaw. "You keep interrupting me, wife." He nips the lobe of my ear and my knees go watery, heat flooding between my legs. "You kept my heart locked away inside you, fucking other men and women—"

"I—"

"I am not finished yet," he interrupts, pressing his front to mine and moving to capture both wrists in one hand, his other going to my thigh. He hitches it over his hip and grinds his pelvis into my core. "I do not hold that against you. You were free to fuck as you wanted because you had no memory of us. I did not carry that curse. I carried another, that I could not fuck anyone else because I was destined for you. No one held a spark of attraction. No one could match up to you. I didn't want anyone else. I was tormented by the memory of you. Of your scent, your taste, the way you moan when I eat that pretty little pussy."

I whimper, said bit of anatomy in question clenching. Desire mounts, flooding my blood with its heady drug. I don't care that we're in the middle of the city, ensconced in an alley. I want him. I want to fuck him right now, even through the rage and fear.

"Sorry is the smallest thing I can offer, but it is what I am starting with," Emrys continues. "I will continue being sorry for this deal for the rest of my life. But for now, you can be angry, just take that anger out on me in a different way."

Emrys's cock throbs against me, and suddenly I'm grinding my hips into him, begging for friction.

"I want you to fuck me," I command, heated. "I want you to take me in this alley now and fuck me. Punish me for tormenting you all those years."

Darkness eats up all the gold in Emrys's eyes and a sudden hunger floods through him. His mouth is on mine, devouring and battling. Our tongues and teeth clash, our lips are pulled and bitten, love and anger burning through us. Emrys's hands are on my ass, hot over the leather. They're in my hair, pulling, yanking my head back.

He exposes my throat and strikes out at it, delving down with kisses, between my breasts. He pulls apart the laces on my leathers, expert fingers working the knots and ties with such precision my head spins.

Between one moment and the next, Emrys has untied my leathers and exposed my breasts to the night air. My nipples are instantly peaked with arousal and chill. I feel them pinch with want as Emrys's mouth comes down to one and pulls the hardened bud into his mouth. He flicks his tongue over the peak, swirling and flicking in a way he knows I love. I drop my head back on a moan, and fist one hand into his garnet locks, the other going for the stays of his pants. His cock is already painfully hard, straining against the crotch of his pants.

He continues pleasuring my nipples, switching between them as his hand works to free me from the rest of my leathers. My top is completely open, hanging off me and baring my midriff. His fingers now find the laces of my pants, working them free as I struggle to do his. He has mine open before I have his—impressive considering I'd had a head start.

Pushing my pants down my hips, Emrys exposes all of me to the night city air, all my white flesh on display. My skin heats.

"King's Glamour?" I ask breathlessly, my mouth buried at his neck. I deliver love bites upon his golden skin. "Unless the risk of being seen is part of my punishment?"

The prospect makes me wetter and Emrys senses it through the bond.

"No glamour," he growls, plunging his fingers into my core.

I cry out as bliss begins winding through me, of Emrys's fingers dipping into my dripping center and then coming out to swirl my clit. I whine and buck my hips for more.

"I am going to do things to you that will make you scream, but you have to be quiet unless you want to get caught," Emrys warns. "It's your punishment. Do you understand?"

"Yes, my king," I say hoarsely.

"Good girl," he responds, rubbing heavenly circles on my clit.

My breasts heave with excitement and arousal. I catch glimpses of my husband in the moonlight, his eyes, feral for me, his lips, constantly touching me, his hands, slick with my lust.

He pushes my pants down the rest of the way until they're at my ankles. Kneeling down, he works one leg free from the leather constraints and the boot. Then, from his kneeling position, he feasts on me.

His mouth between my legs is ecstasy. His tongue curls around my clit and flicks it. He swirls and suckles, tasting me, enjoying me. His hands are on my ass, his fingers kneading into me.

"Oh, fuck. *Yes*. Don't stop."

Suddenly, I'm hoisted up the wall as Emrys stands, still eating me out. My legs wrap around his shoulders, my hands dig into his hair. I try to thrust against his divine worship on my clit, but he pins me harder into the wall, one hand stealing between us. A finger enters my center and I feel my pussy clench around it as he continues licking.

I moan, throaty and desperate, feeling my climax build and rapidly approach. Emrys keeps thrusting that finger inside me, curling in a come-hither motion, rubbing that ultra-sensitive spot inside. I feel my orgasm begin to swallow me up—to crest.

"Ryss, I'm going to come. I'm so close," I pant.

But before the orgasm can take me, Emrys stops and slides me down the wall. I cry out in frustration and shock.

Meeting my soulmate's eyes, I see the devious look in them. He kisses me and I taste my arousal on his mouth. When he pulls back, he fists his hands in my hair and gently urges me to my knees. I drop.

I know what he wants, and I grow wetter again, even though I just nearly came. We've never played like this, but this is something I certainly could get used to.

Emrys frees his cock from his pants, and his proud length is excruciatingly hard. A pearl of arousal beads at the tip of him and I instantly lick it away, tasting the salty flavor on my tongue. I stare up at my soulmate as I take his cock in my mouth, bobbing up and down his length. Emrys groans, his fingers tightening in my hair, his hips slowly thrusting against my face. I begin to take him deeper, carefully pushing my subpar gag reflex. I adjust. My hands cup him, one to help pump his cock with the motions of my mouth, the other on his firm backside.

Fuck my mouth, I tell him through the bond. *Fuck it like you hate me.*

"Vanna," he moans as I swirl my tongue against the underside of his dick.

But he does as I ask.

The hands in my hair become more forceful, moving my head in motion with his pelvis as he fucks my face. His cock bumps against the back of my throat and I feel tears well up in my eyes. Still, he continues thrusting, and I continue taking.

After a short time, he begins to lose his rhythm and I know he's close.

Are you going to come for me, husband? Do you want to come in my mouth? I taunt through the bond.

He thrusts once more before withdrawing and suddenly he pulls me to standing and shoves me against the wall. The brick scratches against my sensitive breasts, but the feeling of being handled like this turns me on beyond belief.

Emrys wraps an arm around my hips, his fingers delving between my legs. He brushes his thumb against my clit before he plunges two fingers into my core.

"No, wife," he whispers at my ear, his tongue tracing the shell and nipping at the lobe. "I'm going to come in here after I've well and truly fucked you."

He dips his fingers in and out, his thumb playing an exquisite melody on my clit. Pulling my ass against his hips, he grinds his cock against me.

"Put your hands on the wall," he commands me. I do, and suddenly his fingers are gone and he's sheathing his cock inside my pussy with one rough thrust.

My mouth opens in a silent scream from the pleasure-rippling invasion. His fingers work on my clit while his cock pumps in and out of me, his other hand is on my breast, rubbing and pinching my nipple between his forefinger and thumb. As he takes me from the back, I push against his harsh thrusts, feeling him hit the deepest places within me. I begin to see stars as the pleasure mounts.

"Is this perfect little pussy mine?" Emrys asks, still fucking me.

"Yes!" I cry out.

"For how long, my love?"

"Forever. Always. Eternity. I'm yours."

"Good girl."

I feel my drenched core clench at his words, squeezing his cock as he fucks. He groans and I feel my cresting orgasm begin to take me.

"I'm going to come, Ryss. Please let me come."

"Come for me, My Queen."

My climax hits me like lightning. I moan and gasp, feeling the waves of the orgasm pummel through me as Emrys's cock pulses within me as his own climax takes him. He groans and I feel his heat fill me, his thrusts slower and harder as he comes down from his orgasmic high.

My husband kisses down my spine, gracing each vertebrae, and withdraws from me. I feel empty without him inside me.

Wordlessly, Emrys tucks himself away and drops down to his knees, helping me back into my leather pants. I still do not wear undergarments, so it is just leather against my over sensitized flesh. He helps lace them while I work on the top, fixing what little of this disheveled mess I can.

I am breathless as Emrys wraps me in his arms. All I smell is the aftereffects of sex and leather and vetiver. He presses his forehead to mine and looks down into my eyes, gold meeting silver.

"I *am* sorry," he repeats from earlier. "I cannot be without you. You are my reason for living."

"As you are mine," I breathe. "I have loved you from the moment you held my hand during our first dose of ricin. I just didn't know it yet. I have loved you since the beginning."

Emrys cups my cheek. "I love you."

I clutch his chest. "I love you too, but I am still very angry at you. You cannot ever doubt me again."

"I won't."

"Good."

We seal our promises with a kiss that tastes of the other.

CHAPTER 9

When we step out of the alley, I'm sure our fifteen minutes of farewell has more than passed. The Unseelie leans against the orange construction cones, arms crossed over his chest. A displeased look is on his face, judgement in each of his four eyes.

"Took you two long enough," he quips.

I shrug, knowing I look amess. Emrys looks only a fraction better. "We made the minutes count."

"You certainly did," the faerie retorts dryly, looking at a non-existent watch. "It's time to go."

Emrys squeezes my fingers and turns to me. "Do not continue what we were going to do tonight, please?"

The pleading tone gets me. I nod. "I won't."

He places a desperately tender kiss on my lips—he still tastes like my essence.

"Come back to me."

"I will," he swears.

I watch Emrys's retreating back, fending off tears. I'm standing in the shadows just beyond the alley, mist rising around me. Every step takes my heart a little further from my body and I feel the stretch, the bond grow taut. It's as if I can feel physical heartstrings wrenching. It's still there but the separating of our physical selves has the bond resisting.

My soulmate turns to look at me over his shoulder, my feelings mirrored back at me in Seelie gold eyes. I bite my lip and wave. He waves back and suddenly my husband and his blackmailer slip into an inbetween and onto the Faerie Roads.

I don't know how this faerie found Emrys. I don't know if they were expecting us to make an attempt to free Natalia or if somehow they tracked us. All I know is that they have him and I am alone.

Drawing in a shaking breath, I step into the alley and through my own inbetween.

Even though we've both stepped onto the Roads at virtually the same time, we've arrived at different points. The Roads do no lie parallel to whatever world is above and beyond. The Roads cater to their own way of being and this dimension cares not for the reality that the laws of men abide. It is why it is always necessary to have a fae escort in the Roads.

The trek on the Faerie Roads is long, drawn out by my own sadness and mourning. Bioluminescent mushrooms guide me back to the Seelie Court as I wallow in my failed endeavor. I try to turn off my thoughts as I stare at the ground ahead of me, polished by thousands of footsteps, the walls rawer without the touch of hands. The ceilings drip dirt every so often, the growth of the dangling roots disrupting the cavernous space's roof.

As one of the fae, I have an inherent sense of navigation, and as one of the Seelie Court, I have an intrinsic bond to sense the presence of the court. This ability has only become more heightened with my newfound royal status. I idly wonder if this also extends to the Unseelie Court as my "destiny" to become the next Dark Court heir.

When I arrive home, I ignore the guards and their surprised expressions. They look at each other, slight panic ringing their eyes. I wave them off. As I arrive at my doors, I notice the guards who'd been posted there hours ago have dispersed, likely scared off by the King's Glamour Emrys had laid that mimicked our fucking. I am not certain for how long it was timed, but it has long since stopped. There is only silence at my door.

And the presence of a halfling inside.

I withdraw a blade and approach cautiously, unlocking the suite and swinging open the door. It hits the wall and I find Gideon standing at the steps. He jumps at my arrival and flushes scarlet.

"What the fuck are you doing here?" I demand, surprise written all over my face. "How did you get here?"

Did the wards fail?

Gideon lifts empty hands in supplication as I enter my chamber. He steps back until he's at the edge of the descending stairs.

"I can explain."

"Get talking then."

"I brought a peace offering. A symbol of our former friendship and a display of my use." Gideon turns to my empty drink cart where he suddenly produces a hunk of metal, beside it is a rare and powerful witch amulet meant for cutting through wards.

I lift a brow in confusion. "What is this supposed to be?"

"It's your glove. From when we hunted and interrogated the Unseelies together."

At a closer inspection I realize it is my garbage gauntlet, indeed. Back at the cabin, back when I thought I was still human, I had fashioned a basic mechanic's glove with bits of iron stolen from about our sanctuary. It had served me well when we'd needed to use physical force to get our captives to speak.

"I can't deny the nostalgia associated with it, but why is it any use to me?"

"Caethes had it locked in her trophy room. I took it. Don't worry, she won't notice it's gone."

Caethes has a trophy room?

"And I'm supposed take your word for that?" I ask archly. "Gideon, you're not well known for telling the truth at the best of times. Why should I believe you now?"

Gideon deflates a little, the gauntlet lowering. "I deserve that. I just...I need you to believe me."

"Why?"

"I need you to know I'm truly on your side. I never gave away your identity. That has to count for something."

I incline my head in acknowledgment. "It does."

His spine goes a little straighter. "I can get into places I shouldn't be able to. Places you can't. Maybe if Emrys was still part of the Unseelie Court he could, but he's not and can't. *I can.*"

The mention of my husband has a pang going through my heart. I can feel the bond still between us, but the distance has strained it, placed a fog on it. It's like squinting across the sea during a storm and trying to see the neighboring island. You know it's there, but it's vague. Hazy.

"Please, I need to prove myself." Gideon swallows and looks away. "I need you to tell me my dad is okay."

I flinch. That's what this is about. "Your father is fine. He is safe."

"Where is he? Can you give me the safehouse coordinates?"

"Absolutely not," I snap. Gideon flinches and I soften. "It's too risky." Gideon doesn't need to know that his father is literally only a few wings away, safely tucked into the bed that belonged to the last reigning monarch.

"Can you at least tell me how he seemed?"

I debate for a moment, hesitating in my feelings of trying to save Gideon's feelings, and my oath to this court—to protect it. I weigh the pros and cons and sigh.

"I will allow you one hour to talk. But not here," I tell him, glancing around my room. My husband's room.

The chambers are no longer the chaos they were weeks ago, but it is not tidy and shows signs of living with piles of clothes—both mine and Emrys's—as well empty platters and glasses. I internally thank myself for locking away all my documents before leaving, that's one thing I'd begun drilling into myself upon my return.

"Where?" Gideon asks.

"The library," I say, casting a Queen's Glamour over Gideon so he appears just like a regular fae guard.

One perk of becoming Queen of the Seelie Court is the ability to cast powerful glamours, strong enough to rival both Emrys's and Caethes's.

We traverse the halls in silence and I internally extend my perception outward, ensuring we don't run into anyone who will catch us out. At the library doors I pause, ensuring there is no distinct human presence hiding in the stacks. There isn't. I push open the doors and direct Gideon in. Filing in after him, I lock the door behind us. I still hold my blade in my grip.

Pointing to the armchairs by the fireplace, Gideon takes a seat and sits at the edge. The firelight and faelight play across his sharp features and strong, squared jaw. Against the crackling flames his eyes seem even more amber than usual.

Gideon laces his fingers together in front of him, resting his forearms on his knees. He's dressed in jeans and a white Henley, the sleeves of which are rolled up above his elbows. I, in contrast, remain in my sex-ruffled black leathers.

The halfling lets out a sound half between a scoff and a laugh. "This has nothing to do with my dad, but it just got me thinking." He meets my eyes, holding the amber to my silver. "This is in no way to offend you—"

"I'm already starting to feel offended."

He repeats that half-and-half sound. "I just don't know why I was so drawn to you. Like, I understand some of the basics—you're beautiful, of course—"

"Thank you."

"But, beyond being forced into survival together, I felt there was...more." He shakes his head. "How wrong I was. As soon as Emrys came around—the bloody *Revenant*—it was clear that I really did mean nothing. I don't know. I just don't get it, I guess."

My heart clenches in guilt. I remember his fears from only months ago—was it so recent? —when he worried about me being fae. About being discarded and suddenly meaning nothing. I look away, that guilt climbing a little higher, digging a little deeper. I twirl the blade in my hands before tucking it into my thigh sheath.

I know why. I could assuage his feelings, ease my doubt. But at what cost? I'm revealing information gifted to me from the goddess—via second-hand through Enydd, mind you, but still. I internally debate back and forth. His father already knows so much about soulmates, how Lady Fate operates within families and pulls those bonds. I decide he has a right to know. Corvina would have wanted him to know.

Still looking away, I whisper. "I do."

Slowly, I turn my head back, meeting his gaze. Gideon's eyes are narrowed, he's leaning forward, listening.

"You do what?"

"I know why you were drawn to me. Why we were drawn to each other." I pause, inhaling and rolling my lips together, fighting this internal battle still despite my decision. "You were drawn to me because Lady Fate decided to give us soulmates."

Gideon's brows shoot into his hairline. "Soulmates are rare—beyond rare. Are you saying...?"

"No," I rush, running a hand through my silvery locks. "Emrys is my soulmate. But Corvina was yours."

Gideon blinks once. Twice.

I watch the gears turn in his head, the computing going on within his mind.

"Corvina," he deadpans. "Your twin sister."

I nod. I swallow. "Yes."

"The faerie who found us at the cabin."

Corvina had come upon us at the cabin when we'd been drinking whiskey on the patio. Right before we'd nearly kissed. She'd stumbled across the anti-Unseelie wards, dying. We'd rushed to her as she fell and then she'd died in our arms. In the arms of her twin sister and her soulmate. Her sister who didn't recognize her, and her soulmate who didn't know her. Possibly the two most important people in her life had buried her in a shallow, unmarked grave like she was *nothing*. The tragedy strikes me like a physical blow, bringing back all the ache of her loss.

I set my jaw and nod once.

"Oh."

Gideon falls back into his chair and casts his eyes to the fire. I watch his jaw work, emotions flooding through him as clear as if they were spelled out across his face. I watch regret, grief, loss, hope, frustration, sadness, and despair swirl over him like a kaleidoscope. But instead of vibrant colors it's every emotion I'd never want to feel after learning about my soulmate.

It feels like a cruel trick. To tell him that he has a soulmate, only to instantly realize she is dead and he has no chance to fulfil the bond.

"I thought I felt—" he shakes his head, "I thought I felt something towards her when I saw her, but I dismissed it as an adrenaline rush or something. Never did I think she was—" he breaks himself off. "This...this kinda fucking sucks."

"I know," I whisper. "I'm sorry."

Gideon is silent for a beat before he brings his destroyed expression to mine. "So, we were never supposed to be."

It isn't a question, but I answer it anyway. "No, we weren't."

Even though Gideon and I were never meant to happen, even though he was always meant for my sister, I have to thank him for having temporarily been mine once. Without him, I may never have gotten Emrys back.

I draw in a breath, trying to soften another blow. "I know what you're feeling—to a degree."

"How?" Gideon's voice is hollowed. He may not have known Corvina, but he lost her all the same. He lost his future with her. His love with her.

"Emrys died once," I whisper.

I remember Gideon's journals, his aspirations of becoming a writer, his fascination with the Harbinger. And then I tell him the true story of the Harbinger and the Revenant, once never truly known, now finally revealed.

Gideon listens as I tell him about Century Training. About Osian's deception, about falling in love with Emrys and having to hide it to save his life, about the truth of the blackmail and then our marriage, about the battle once we'd completed our training, of killing our mentors and the Wild Hunt. Of Emrys's death by Osian's hand after we thought we'd won. My grief, so powerful it has summoned a goddess. The bargain I'd struck. The memories I'd lost. The torment Emrys endured. All the while, the halfling is silent, taking it all in and letting me speak.

When I finish, Gideon's eyes are trained on my left hand. On the gold and emerald ring there.

"And through all that, you two found your way back to each other," Gideon murmurs.

"We did," I say softly, twisting my hands together. "I truly am sorry, Gideon—for what I put you through. And what you lost. Corvina was…" I draw in a shuddering breath, full of pain and love. "She was lovely. She was everything I'm not. She was kind and sweet, she loved jewels and finery for the sake of them being pretty. She was intelligent and clever. And warm, and funny, and optimistic." Emotion thickens my throat. "She was the very best of us—of the fae. She was *truly* good."

Gideon nods, sadness in his too-orange eyes. "I wish I could have properly met her."

"You would have loved her," I manage thickly. "What I wouldn't give to have another moment with her."

And then I realize I'm being unnecessarily cruel. There is so much I would give up for more time with Corvina, to bring her back just for a while. I miss her desperately, but there's nothing I can do because she is dead. But Gideon's father is not. He is very much alive and it is well within my power to grant Gideon moments with him. I could do a small good deed, something Corvina wouldn't have even needed to hesitate on.

"Give me one moment," I tell Gideon and slip to a bell pull.

Tugging the golden rope elicits a tinkling bell and summons a servant. Immediately, a faerie with gauzy white wings enters the library after I unlock it. She curtsys quickly and it causes her short periwinkle curls to tremble.

"Your Majesty, what can I do for you tonight?"

"Please tell Enydd to wake our guest and bring them to the library. She will know who I mean. And please ask someone to bring tea for three."

"Of course, Your Majesty. Right away."

The small faerie skitters away, racing for Enydd's chambers on the second floor, one wing away from this very library.

I return to my seat and Gideon assesses me critically.

"What are you doing?" he questions.

"Trust me," I tell him simply.

The tea service arrives before his father does, but the moment Henry Zhao enters the library in his chair, I hear a small gasp and tears stream down Gideon's face.

"He's here?" he asks, his voice catching on tears.

"He is here," I confirm. "You have the rest of the hour to spend with him. Enydd will take him back when it is time." Enydd walks behind Henry, pushing his chair as fast as it'll reasonably go. Relief and happiness and every possible emotion associated with reunion crests across his face. When the two Zhao men meet, both are crying, crushing each other to their chests, squeezing like they'll never let go.

I get up and pause, setting my hand first on Henry's shoulder, then Gideon's. "I will take my leave now, make the most of your time together tonight."

Gideon looks at me over his father's shoulder, both of them quaking with emotion. Tears fill Gideon's amber depths. "Thank you," he whispers.

I wave it off but something in my chest warms. "It is the least I can do."

"It means the most."

I nod and depart from the library, ascending the steps toward my chamber. When I enter my room, it is cold and empty without my soulmate's presence. I inhale, still scenting some of his leather and vetiver and lemon in the air. Standing there, I take it in for a moment, feeling everything I do, and sigh.

Gideon has left my makeshift gauntlet on the drink cart and I walk over to it, fingers tracing the bits of iron. It does not burn. It does not sting. I pick it up and see hints of blood still marring the surface. Sticking my hand inside, I feel it out and flex my fingers. It doesn't fit. Not in the physical sense, because it never did, but in the spiritual sense. It made sense for Human Evelyn, but it doesn't make sense for Harbinger Evelyn, or Queen Evelyn. It feels like a false face, like a mask or like a dress several sizes too large. It is not me, but it was a part of me in some intrinsic fucked up way. It was a key to my survival, and for that I cherish it in the same weird, fucked up way.

I put it down and go to my washroom.

Alone, I go to the bath and fill it with all the scented oils that remind me of Emrys. Stripping off my leathers, I slip into the tub and soak, luxuriating in the smell of home and the memory of my soulmate's touch. From far away, I hear Emrys whisper in my mind.

I miss you already.

Tears fall down my cheeks.

I miss you more, I return.

CHAPTER 10

The day after Emrys is blackmailed to repay his favor I oversee the training of Wisteria, Julia, and Violante, with Maelona. Maelona had invited me to watch after witnessing a stellar breakthrough with Wisteria's magic.

Evidently, if a witch—or magic user—dies while Wisteria is copying their ability, she keeps it.

So, when the Fairwalker witch was murdered during the same attack that took Aneira from this realm, Wisteria retained the replicated ability. Now, the Greyvale witch, with her inherent ability to mimic and share magic, can also heal.

It begins to beg the question though. Is this a regular Greyvale ability? Or is this something special unto Wisteria herself? How many other Greyvales like this exist? If the incident were to repeat, would she have two additional abilities to keep? Or would she lose one for the other? Are these anomalous Greyvales out there hunting down magic-users and killing them to steal their ability? Surely not. Surely, we would have heard about such a problem by now, whether it had been in the texts, through the spy network, or either of my hidden identities.

Wisteria shows the ability in question off to me when Maelona slices Julia's forearm with her blade. The human girl hisses in pain and at the same moment, Violante's eyes grow dark, carmine veins standing out on her cheekbones. Her fangs are exposed as Maelona gets between the hungry vampire and the bleeding human. This training is not just for the self-defense purposes of Julia, nor the magic honing for Wisteria, it is also the reining and taming of the Violante's bloodlust.

The entire event takes seconds, and in those seconds, Wisteria's eyes eerily change color—lightening to the deceased Fairwalker's eyes—and Julia's cut heals instantly. It leaves not even a white mark against her toned, russet skin.

Maelona applauds everyone for their success during my witness and a flash of pride goes through me at my best friend's prowess. Maelona was built for this. She is a natural born leader.

I still wonder why the warrior princess did not inherit more of a title. The warrior princess moniker was informally bestowed years ago, her parents having been important people in fae politics, but truly no royal blood runs through Maelona's veins. And there is a wrongness about that. She is meant for this. I know it.

An idea unfurls in my mind, but I discard it. I cannot think of things like that right now, because those things begin to make me think of things that hurt. Of Emrys's mission. Of being apart from me. Of Aneira's death. Of the crown she left us.

"You're incredible at this," I tell Maelona, dragging myself out of my despairing. "Truly, I could never have the patience."

Maelona takes me in and looks me up and down. She reads me like a book. "You're in a mopey mood, but you're not as prickly. Glad to see the king tended to your needs."

I tilt my head. "You seem quite focused on this issue. Is there someone not attending to *your* needs?"

"Oh, I know you're not offering, so I do not see why it is relevant."

She's deflecting. I smirk.

"Oh Mae, shall I arrange for some fair maidens to descend upon the realm? Do you have a preference? Redheads perhaps?"

Maelona fights a smile and loses the battle, laughing. She lifts her index finger and points it at me. "Do not. I have no trouble seeking bedmates."

"Mmhmm," I murmur teasingly.

"I don't!"

"I could say I'm just teasing, but I could also be serious. I know what you're like."

A devious smile creeps across the Lady's face. "I could say something to knock your ego down."

"My curiosity has been piqued."

Maelona visibly fights not to laugh. "It has not been difficult to find a better lay than you."

Gasps and giggles erupt from the girls around us.

I gape in dismay. "Are you saying I'm a lousy lover?"

"You said it, not me."

"Mae!"

Maelona cackles. "Well, if you mind your own business, maybe your feelings won't get hurt."

"You remember that the next time you tease me about my sex life."

"Oh, I have no illusions about my prowess compared to your husband's. I have fingers and a tongue, too, but I know I cannot compete with your preference for a cock." She pauses but then mutters under her breath. "Though the ones I've tried have been less than subpar."

"Mae!" I chastise again, blushing furiously.

Wisteria raises a hand, a somewhat sheepish look on her face. "I have to agree with Maelona on this one. I've had a lot of bad dick, but the women seem to know how to get the job done."

Julia seems to contemplate this. "I've never been with a woman."

Maelona flicks a look over her shoulder, flirtatious and coy. "Want to try one?"

"Maelona Eidolon!" I splutter.

Julia flushes bright scarlet, from her hairline to neck, her golden tattoo glimmering against the blush. Wisteria elbows her playfully, laughing and jostling. Violante is noticeably silent. The young vampire was changed at sixteen years old and I'm uncertain if she ever had the opportunity to lie with a man, a woman, or even someone inbetween.

Maelona arches a brow. "I'm just asking. I am a realist, Ev."

98

"Evidently."

Maelona twists her red lips in a smile. "Speaking of the male species...where is Emrys?"

My stomach drops. "He has some private business he's attending to."

"Oh?" Maelona quirks a brow, waiting for me to elaborate further.

I do not.

There is silence.

"Well, thank you for the instruction today, it was most revelational," I say, stilted. "But I have matters I must attend to."

I begin walking away before my emotions can be read by everyone in the room, but Mae's voice halts me.

"Ev, is everything okay?" There is a soft edge to her words. "I understand we are at wartime, but something else seems off. Has something happened recently? Is there a new development?"

Holding still. I breathe deeply and plaster a false smile on my face. The fae may not be able to lie with our words, but we can lie with our faces. "New things are constantly happening, Mae."

"That is a very non-answer, answer."

I shrug. "I'm dealing with it. Don't worry, it's nothing to concern yourself with."

"Ev," Maelona chastises and strides over to me. She looks over her shoulder at the other girls when she reaches my side. "If there is anything you need, you know I am here to help. Don't you?"

I smile, and it's the first real one I've felt today. Clapping one hand on Maelona's shoulder and the other on her forearm, I look at her deeply. "I do, and I appreciate you more than you know. But trust me, it's nothing you need to worry about."

The unspoken "yet" hangs in the air and Maelona picks up on it.

Rearing her head back in surprise, white strands of shock weave through the chameleon-girl's hair. "You'll let me know if that changes?"

"I promise."

We separate with nods of understanding and false smiles. Maelona returns to training, I wave to the girls, and then I leave.

In my chambers I am installed behind my desk, poring over letters and pleas from all over the Court and Seelie territory. Rubbing a small ache that begins at my temple, I try to decide how to best manage a scrimmage on the border of Dark and Light.

Prior to my announcement of war, the Unseelies had broached a northern town encompassed by the Seelie territory. At the time it was an attack that allowed retaliation, but after my declaration, they were held in a stalemate. While the Unseelie usurped what is rightfully ours, the Seelie cannot take it back during our parlays—which we have not been advertising—so all attempts to retake have failed. Light Court soldiers are wondering where our support lies and if our reign is failing them already.

Inhaling deeply, I scribe a letter and inform of the meetings and the impact they hold for all of the court. Penning less sensitive court details feels dangerous, though I rationalize to myself that for all intents and purposes these are public knowledge already.

Once finished, I set it aside and add a second letter to that tangent, asking General Baphet to visit outposts and Seelie fae who are not currently residing in the bubble realm of the court. Part of the Seelie territory is British Columbia, and most of it allows the fae to roam freely, but I begin to wonder what that freedom has garnered.

Are they becoming antsy? Eager for change? Do they still hold faith in this court? How many have defected to the Dark Court in our changeover? Do we need to worry about the rare fae beasts becoming wild under our rule?

The Seelie Court may be known as the Light Court, but we are by no means *good*. We partake in trickery and battle, lust and deceit, too. Though in a much milder manner. As a whole, the Seelie Court does not ascribe to the tastes and flavors of the Unseelie—of lotteries and slaughters, cannibalism and slavery. We are both debauched, yes, but what the Seelie do, the Unseelie take tenfold.

Suddenly, I decide to deliver the letter by hand. I push away from my desk and cross the threshold, striding purposefully through the court. As I walk with my mission, I run into Commander Tirnoc.

"Is General Baphet in the council room?" I ask without stopping.

Tirnoc reels and rushes to catch up to me. "He is, Your Majesty. Is there something else I can help you with?"

"Good. And yes, follow me."

He does without question, his long legs matching my pace. His leathers squeak ever so slightly in the din. We keep our silence as I clutch the letter in my fist and push open the council doors.

Baphet looks up in surprise, his polished ram's horns catching the golden light. Surprise lights his eyes before he stands to attention and fists a hand over his heart and bows lightly.

"Your Majesty. To what do I owe this honor?"

"Take me to one of the outposts."

He blinks. "I beg your pardon?"

"I want to see the skirmishes up close. Bring me to one."

"Your Majesty, I don't think—"

"If you tell me that you do not think it is wise, I shall tell you that I don't think it wise to question a furious queen, no? I am a warrior, too. Please remember that, General."

Baphet snaps his mouth closed, recalling he is not just speaking to the Seelie Monarch, but the Seelie represented warrior.

"When do we leave?" I press.

"In a half hour," he says on a suppressed sigh.

A half hour later, Baphet, Tirnoc and I have journeyed through the Faerie Roads and to a decimated faerie revel. Tents and campfires smolder beneath the destruction, food and drink is smashed beneath muddy boot prints, fabric is shredded amongst the ruin. Fae bodies have been carried aside and covered near the more densely wooded area, while Seelie forces speak amongst each other—preparing.

"This revel of undeclared fae was attacked by Caethes's forces," Baphet tells me as he spreads a war map upon a broken table. "Our ally in her ki-court…" Baphet cuts himself off, glancing around at his near slip up around the others of sharing our kitchen spy. His eyes are panicked, but I nod to continue. He clears his throat. "They said that once we come to assess the damage as she expects, there will be a second wave—we are now prepared for it."

"How long ago was this siege?"

"About three hours ago. When they return, they intend to raze it."

"Well," I start, grinning ferally. A shiver runs down the bond. "Let us raze them, then."

We meet with the rest of our soldiers and warriors, planning strategy. Most of them are shocked to see their queen on the battle lines, but it's clear they remember who I am first—the Harbinger. Once all in formation, we wait.

I twirl Oath-Sworn while I stretch out my sensing ability to the fringes of the ruined party, feeling along the edges of the inbetweens, touching ever so slightly on the Faerie Roads. I can feel them intrinsically now. With the power of the Light Court soaring through me, my ability is heightened and I can sense every entry to the Roads in the general vicinity.

Suddenly, like a plucked guitar string, a vibration rises through my gift and I zero in on an inbetween.

"There," I say—moments before Unseelie pour forth from the Roads.

We meet the flood with blades shrieking, the piercing shing of metal on metal renting the air. Battle cries and groans fill the forest as I become my blade.

I cut through enemies—through their armor and glamour—and one by one dwindle down Caethes's numbers. Oath-Sworn strikes true through a heart while my dagger drinks its fill on the lifeblood from a jugular. I whirl, sliding Oath-Sworn out and arcing it through the air as it connects with a neck and passes it. My golden blade drips gore as my feet dance across the bloodshed, dipping and lunging, stabbing and swiping.

Tirnoc fights with lethal grace, two short swords gliding in his double-jointed hands as he takes on two opponents, earthen eyes turned to hard stone. Beside him, Baphet has a large battle axe that he hefts high and deals obliterating blows with. A nameless warrior nearby delivers fast strikes to cover Baphet while he hauls the dangerous and heavy weapon. They're a concerted effort—haul, heft, parry, swing, dodge, decimate, reengage, repeat.

In nearly every set of eyes I douse the light from, I see surprise that the Harbinger is their demise—that the Seelie Queen is fighting a battle as small as this one. But I am hounding it into each and every person that I am claiming my title as queen, but I am not forsaking the one I trained a century for.

Faster than we expect, the fight ends until every Unseelie is dead or has fled. The death count is disproportionate on a one-to-seven level despite having had near equal numbers to begin with.

As I end my final opponent I stand there; Oath-Sworn dangling, blood running down my face, rain beginning to fall from the heavens, painting all the lines of battle all the more dramatically.

Despite it all—I smile.

CHAPTER 11

Once again in my room after being hurried from the battle and urged to bathe, I sit, clean and redressed before my desk. Gritting my teeth at the never-ending stack, I select a weighty envelope and absently pick up my Unseelie blade that connects to Emrys's. When I read the sender, though, I pause.

Caspian Lockwood, of the Arcana Society.

I slice through the red wax seal and eagerly tear into the contents of the envelope. It is large and puffy, stuffed with so much more than I expected Caspian to glean. All of it is nicely tied together and a second sealed letter, this one similar in size to a postcard. I read it first.

Evelyn & Emrys,

Here are copies of all the official records I could find about the Whitecrest and Lockwood lines, plus some family documentation from my side. I did some reading myself and honestly, it's a little concerning how intertwined the families are—not to worry, you two are not related.

Let me know if I can help with anything else.

Yours in Debt,

Caspian

Setting aside the letter, I unwind the cord around the thick file and let it fall open before me. Papers flutter up, held together in organized sections with paperclips and other bindings. This, I realize, is going to take far longer than the two hours I'd allocated to this ordeal.

Checking the timepiece on my wall I mentally shift around some duties and manage to squeeze another hour to dedicate to this. It won't be enough, but it'll have to do. Had I not absconded to fight Unseelies I could, but I did and now I must deal with the restrictions as they are. I immediately dive in.

The contents of the documents and records absorb into my brain like a sponge. Anything pertaining to Emrys and I is like glue to the place I hold my memories. Some of the accounts are even written by Gideon's father when they've skewed towards the fae, and of course, because they are connected to two half-witch faeries, it is frequent enough.

I discover that Emrys's father, Ansel, was the brother of Caspian's mother, Vanessa. They are first cousins. A half-witch faerie and a half-witch vampire.

106

Suddenly, a name—that previously would have sparked no familiarity in me before—jumps out.

Christian Duchannes.

The vampire whom Emrys has been sent to frame for Annabelle Laroche's murder.

Diving into the documentation, horror begins to unfurl within me.

Joseph Harrow had been experimenting on supernaturals back in the 1940s and discovered how to splice and combine our DNA. This recount details how Aneira, who'd once held a tentative alliance with the Vampire King, declared him an enemy of the Light Court after discovering he was kidnapping and experimenting on her faerie citizens. After that truce was shattered, he had to pivot to more Unseelie guinea pigs and the few he could still steal from my former queen. Much of it led to monstrous and catastrophic creations, but at some point in the late 20th Century, he hit a goldmine. He was successfully able to create hybrids—vampire parents mixed with other supernatural types.

I reel from the information. Vampires have historically only been able to birth halflings when a male vampire and a female human procreate. The offspring is always male. Due to the vampire DNA being so aggressive, it attacks anything perceived as a threat. So, if a male vampire and a female Seelie were to attempt to reproduce, the vampire genes would destroy the faerie portion, and ultimately itself in the process. Even witches, with their magic, are too strong of a threat oftentimes—it is notably rare for those like Caspian to exist. The only thing subservient enough to vampires are humans. Therefore, it leaves halflings technically sterile since no female halflings exist and female vampires cannot carry a fetus.

But it seems Joseph has found a way around that and has created hybrids.

Annabelle Laroche was one of these hybrids.

And Christian Duchannes is the father of another hybrid.

He is also Rhodes's half-brother.

My uncle.

And whoever this other hybrid is, is my cousin.

Throwing myself back in my chair, I stare at the ceiling in shock and terror. What kind of abominations has Joseph Harrow worked in the process of trying to make a new creature? What lies beneath the labs of his experimentation? What other unholy fucking things has he done?

At the bottom of the documentation is a signature, signing off on the funding and support of all discoveries.

Caethes.

Now all I see is red. Rage transforms my vision to scarlet, tilting my world on its axis. The Unseelie Queen is truly a monstrous creature in all aspects. I cannot see a single redeeming quality in the Dark Court monarch. She has no empathy, even for those who have suffered so similarly to her. She cares not for those who were enslaved and does so the same herself, just using a different word. She punishes because she hurts and because misery loves company.

How am I possibly related to such a beast?

All the injustice strikes me and suddenly I explode.

I manage to cast a Queen's Glamour to soundproof the room before I let loose a feral scream.

Standing from my chair, I pace the room and pull my hair at the roots. My teeth are gritted, grinding together with punishing pressure. I feel a crack threaten, but I do not stop. I can feel the rage flowing through me, injected like venom through my bloodstream.

Casting my gaze at the stained glass ceiling, I force myself to look past the panes. "Lady Fate! I command you to speak to me!" My breaths heave through me. "Lady Fate, as Queen of the Seelie Court, I command you to answer me!"

My hands are outstretched at my sides, my fingers curling and unfurling, as if turning to claws. My feet are planted, grounding myself in the realm of the Seelie while I furiously condemn the goddess.

"You spoke to me once!" I call out. "I am asking you again."

I wait, anger boiling in the quietude. Seething against the injustice of it all, I internally curse the goddess. From a distance I can sense Emrys's concern, but with all the space between us the communication is vague and it is easier to block him out. I feel tentative phantom fingers reach for me, wanting to help, but I shut down.

"Lady Fate!"

Again, silence. I stay like that for a few more moments before deflating.

"Coward," I scoff, and pull down my Queen's Glamour.

Instead, I seek someone else that can help. Maybe visiting the Prophet Witches will be enough to draw the goddess's attention.

The Prophet Witches live in the Stone Vale beneath the Seelie Court. As in the Seelie, Prophet Witches also reside in a separate Stone Vale beneath the Unseelie Court. These witches are dedicated to the goddess, forsaking their mortal sight for premonition. Unlike Whitecrest witches who naturally possess precognition, Prophet Witches can hail from any line of witches as long as they make the same dedication.

Once, I'd visited the Prophet Witches, seeking a prophecy after Gideon was taken. It was made abundantly clear that Lady Fate did not wish for me to receive a prophecy at that time and refused me. When one of her acolytes, Bambalina, tried to defy her, the goddess punished her in return. Another, Sybella, gifted me a lullaby, a half defiance to Lady Fate—which now I see as very brave or very stupid.

I have not visited since and am unknowing of what happened to the small, dark-haired witch, nor the beautiful redhead.

When I depart from my room, guards silently flank me, drawing paces behind me like magnets. I ignore them and descend low, into the bowels of the court. The stone stairs turn from dry rock to damp and glistening as I enter the witches' territory. My guards stay back, not stepping one foot into the vale.

The burbling of a stream and the steady thrum of a waterfall meet me. I walk into a glade, lush greenery capping rocks, abundant flowers filling the air with the scent of freesia, jasmine, hyacinth, and the slight cinnamon tinge of carnations. Blooms erupt all about the walls and dangle their roots like fingers through the tranquil waters. Above, the sky is gold, capped by the Seelie magic that pervades all of the court.

As I walk further into the Stone Vale, Sybella steps out from behind a rock.

She is wet, her white shift sticking to her like a second skin, her autumnal red hair sleek down her back. Over her eyes, and obscuring the stones that press into the sockets is a white silk band.

Sybella smiles without seeing me, yet knowing my presence anyway.

"Queen Evelyn," Sybella intones. "It honors a girl to be met with Your Majesty's presence." Daintily, she dips into a curtsy. "May a girl guess why a queen would deign to visit her?"

"Guess away."

"The queen is here to demand direction from the goddess, but that is not today's fate."

"Then what is?"

"A girl once came for a prophecy and left with a lullaby. Today that girl comes as a queen to seek direction and shall leave with prophecy."

"Oh, will she?"

Sybella smiles softly, pressing her hands to her abdomen. "She will."

Hope blooms within me, crushing it beneath its devastating weight. I hadn't anticipated how much I'd truly expected to be denied again. Some of the rage falls from my sails and I'm left slightly off balance.

"Before we start, I need to know. What happened to Bambalina?"

Sybella twists her lips. "A daughter does not speak out against the wishes of the mother, therefore she is no longer among the Prophet Witches."

"She's dead?"

"No. A fate worse than that, the girl known as Bambalina has been banished to live a human existence, sightless and faithless."

"That is cruel."

"It is just."

I bite my tongue and change conversation. I'll seek out Bambalina another time. "What prophecy does the goddess hold for me?"

I've communed with the goddess far more than the average fae, already. Already once, I'd summoned her and demanded a favor out of her. I am not so disillusioned to believe she did it out of the goodness of her heart. She did it because it was *fun*. Because it afforded her the ability to rig a game and play with the pieces. So, while I don't intend to take her name in vain—again—I do not devote myself to her with flowery words or the value of my sight. I am far too selfish and pessimistic for such designs.

Briefly, I wonder how old Sybella truly is and how long she has been speaking prophecy. How did she get into such an ordeal? Was she forced or sold? I realize these are questions I've never asked, and yet she is a denizen of my court. Do I have power as the queen here? Or does the goddess's reach far surpass mine?

"Please put out your hands," Sybella commands.

I do, and the Prophet Witch takes them in hers. Her skin is warm and dewy, her hands soft in mine. I look at her, staring at the white band across her face. She hums low and I feel magic thread through us. When I look down, I realize I am not just feeling the magic, I'm seeing it, too.

Gold winds around us in ribbons of iridescence, slipping beneath our flesh and wrapping around our hands.

"There are two outcomes," Sybella begins.

"What are they?"

"A girl cannot say."

"But it's Fate, your goddess."

"And Lady Chaos counters her, and Lady Karma counters her."

Fury boils my blood. "This isn't fucking Rock, Paper, Scissors."

"It is more like it than you know."

"This isn't chance."

"Isn't it? Chance—Fate. They're quite similar."

"Is this what my prophecy is to be?"

"No." Sybella shakes her head with a small smile. "This is—"

The golden magic fusing between us warms, permeating us with a glow.

Suddenly, the voice that was Sybella's is no longer wholly hers and it is not spoken by her mouth. It is whispered in my mind.

All those you have ever loved will die
Once their hearts collide,
The future carves to vie
With crowns divide,
A choice to combine
Or a decision to rend,
Stars must align,
Where this will end.

I stagger back from Sybella, horrified and tingling. "What the fuck kind of prophecy is that?"

Sybella stares with her sightless eyes and gives a dainty shrug. "A girl did not make it, she just delivered it."

"Does this apply to both outcomes? You said there were two. Am I to lose everyone either way?" Anxiety sets my heart hammering.

Sybella pauses, contemplating. She is silent, as if mentally communing with the goddess. An odd look crosses over her face, something I cannot decipher. Her lips twist.

"Yes and no."

"That can't be true."

"A will assure a queen, it is."

Sudden hatred for Lady Fate burbles in my chest. I can feel my nostrils flare and I bite down. "This is bullshit," I spit.

This is my one and only prophecy and all it spells is death, and more death. I feel like I've wasted it. I feel like all this prophecy is going to do is send me into a spiral. Why did I even seek it out?

Everyone I love will die. Emrys, Maelona...

What of former lovers?

"This was a mistake."

And then I turn on my heel and leave, not letting Sybella get another word in as anxiety consumes me.

CHAPTER 12

Promptly after my borderline meltdown in the Stone Vale I realize I'm late for a meeting with Julia. I race through the halls until I find myself in the designated council room we'd chosen for receiving Julia's intel. I'm cursing my time management every step of the way.

When I arrive, Julia is pacing at the head of the live-edge table, a small stack of papers in front of my chair. The human girl looks up and as usual I'm taken aback by her startling gold-blue eyes. She rushes to her seat and tucks her long dark hair behind her ears, waiting for me. Nervously.

The room is typical Seelie décor—gold and viridian, heavy woods and verdant ivy. Fae magic weaves in the room, veining the walls and striating the ceiling. White chrysanthemums are painted on the paneled walls, ascending and transforming into constellations. There is no stained glass here, as this chamber is underground.

I take my own seat and glance over the papers, imagining something terrible set to befall the Seelie Court, but there's nothing immediately of note.

"What do you have to report?"

Julia nods her head at the papers. "All the necessary details are documented there, but to be blunt, Caethes is planning an assassination attempt on you—"

"What's new?"

"And apparently she has something that will provoke you into a rage."

I cock a brow. "Do you know what this thing is?"

"No. All I know is that it does not involve Gideon, whatsoever."

"You're certain of this?"

"I am."

"How?"

Something flashes across her face, a look gone too quickly to decipher before she trains her eyes on me. But she is not meeting me, not really, she's looking through me. Odd. I file away this peculiarity for later.

"Caethes was gloating. She said it was a prize. Whatever it was had her too delighted and distracted to have Gideon in the bedroom."

"I see." I pause. Those words once would have my stomach churning and coiling, but now they echo through me and dissipate. Now, I worry about the prophecy. I loved Gideon once, does that mean he is still destined to die?

"Anything else?"

There's red on Julia's cheeks. "No, that's all."

I eye her with concern. "Are you sure you are up to continue this?"

Julia's gold-blue eyes flash with fear and surprise. "No! I mean—yes! I want to keep doing this. Please. After everything Caethes has pulled in Aberth...I want to see her *burn*."

I'd hardly considered Julia's motives in agreeing so readily, but I suppose it makes sense. She was the leader of the Crows—a human organization bent on taking down Aberth's annual human sacrificial lottery—and has continued training. Their mission in Aberth was only usurped by my interference and I feel a small pang of guilt for it. How different would the lottery have turned out if Wisteria and I hadn't plotted? Would Elliot have still died? Would Caethes have reacted so savagely?

I'll never know and it does not do to dwell of what-ifs.

"Who originally contacted you and conscripted you for the Seelie Court?" I ask. I point to her golden Seelie tattoo. "I know Ghislain did that, but who did he owe a favor to in order to have it done unsanctioned?" I'd looked at the records, and there was nothing of the sort, despite the tattoo being real.

Julia's nostrils flare as she breathes in. "The Admiral—Aveda—did. She was my contact after she discovered the town last year. I met her at the Anemone nightclub one night. It was after the lottery before last had taken—taken someone from me. She sensed my anger and asked if I wanted to get my revenge even if it would take some time. I agreed immediately."

Of course, it was Aveda with her spy network. It shouldn't have been surprising that she'd taken it upon herself beneath Aneira's nose in my absence. She would've had no one thwarting nor investigating her.

I internally curse. It matters not that it worked out eventually in our favor, it was risky. For all she knew, Julia could've turned on her and imparted this knowledge to Caethes. Luckily, this wasn't the case.

I shake my head from my mental argument.

"Three days hence will be the next meeting. Please be safe when in contact with Gideon."

Julia nods, a blush of pride on her face after not having this responsibility taken away. "I will."

"Good."

Julia fidgets with her hands and while I do not show it, I sense something off. I watch her for a moment before exiting the chamber.

Is Gideon withholding information from Julia? Is he telling her not to inform me of everything? Is Caethes planning something bigger than my assassination?

Discomfiture is not new to me, not with this heavy crown, and not when I've slipped into new identities as often as others change their clothes. Queen, wife, warrior, spy, girl. They're all me. I have grown from the inception of the prophecy—I am more than three. I keep earning titles, new facets to my name, outgrowing whatever was first designed.

Has Julia outgrown her name too?

Unease curdles in my stomach. How I wish my husband were here. What I wouldn't give for Emrys's comforting presence now. But he is away, and I am stuck in the deception of his wake.

"Your Majesty," General Baphet suddenly says from an adjacent hallway. "I'm surprised to find you here. Are you not scheduled for a meeting with Lady Maelona?"

I mentally check through my responsibilities for the day and mutter a curse.

"Thank you for the reminder General Baphet, I'll be on my way now."

And again, I race through the halls for another late meeting.

Maelona is in the training room, having finished up a training session in lieu of Julia due to her Gideon duties. The Crows have since dispersed, but evidence of their presence is still clear—sweat marks, human scents, and a basket of rags. The Lady is brushing off her hands after shutting a cabinet door housing staves. She turns to me, dressed in black leathers, her long black hair braided back.

My heart pangs at the sight of her. She is my best friend. I have loved her for years. Is she doomed to die as well?

"I'd make a comment about your lateness having to do with your husband, but seeing as he seems not to be at court, it's just you."

I give a start, but my words hurry on. "I'm sorry, Mae. I was late to another meeting as well. I got side-tracked by personal issues."

Maelona sighs and looks at me drolly. "Were these fun issues or problems?"

"Problems. Definitely problems."

"Anything I can help with?"

I debate for a second, assessing my best friend and her warm, open brown eyes. I won't tell her about the prophecy, but I decide to divulge a small concern. "Have you noticed anything peculiar about Julia's behavior of late?"

Maelona raises a brow. "Not particularly. What are you seeing?"

"It's not so much I'm seeing anything, but more wondering."

"About?"

I bite my lip. "I think she's hiding something."

"Something bad?"

"No…but, I'm sensing she thinks I'd disapprove of it, and I am not sure if I truly would."

"Do you know what you are sensing or speaking in riddles?"

"Oh hush," I say, lightly smacking her shoulder. "I don't know. I just feel it."

"Trust your instincts, Ev. Have they ever led you wrong?"

I ponder. "I have made many poor decisions."

"And rectified many of them. Including what was between us. It was fun—the romance—but it did not fit."

Guilt flashes through me. I never thought romance was a problem for us. For me it was as easy as switching the needs on and off, but now I wonder if that was only my perception of it. What if for Maelona it was more painful than that? Of having emotional whiplash from our different encounters, never sure if she was going to get Lover-Evelyn or Friend-Evelyn.

"I'm sorry," I say.

Maelona shrugs. "We tried, that's all that matters."

"I just never realized how different we experienced the years with each other and I need to apologize for my selfishness. I didn't realize how much the sexual part effected our friendship until now."

"I appreciate that, but truly the feelings are not hard and the pains do not exist." Maelona shakes her head. "But back to your original concern. I have not noticed anything off with Julia, but I will be sure to keep attentive of it from here on out."

"Thank you." I exhale. "Now, onto our boring meeting."

"Ah, yes that. Well, the mission to rectify Baphet's heart desire is underway and the Crows are improving with their two-handed weaponry."

On my recently repaired chaise lounge is a box wrapped in parchment and twine. I approach it carefully, concerned about who was in my chambers in my absence. A thin tag reads my name in Caethes's handwriting. I finger it gently and slowly, without bumping the box—or its contents—I lower my ear to the box. I hear no ticking and no growling. There is no sound emitting from it.

Erring on the side of caution, I cast a Queen's Glamour about the room, both soundproofing the space and obscuring me from view in case whatever is inside the box is indeed alive and bloodthirsty. It won't stop it, but it will be enough for me to gain the advantage.

I am not worried about poison. I've practiced enough mithridatism for it to be virtually a non-issue, but if it's a booby-trap set to drive a knife through my face…well, no amount of practicing will make me immune to *that*.

Cutting the twine with a knife, I tear the paper and break the seal on the box. With the knife-tip, I flick it open and wait. When nothing jumps out, I peer in cautiously.

Inside I find bits of ash and leather. Atop it sits a piece of paper, penned in more of Caethes's scrawl. I dip my hand inside, pluck up the paper, and shake it off.

Jacob hid them well, but I found them. I didn't anticipate this delight when I hired him.

Confusion crosses my face before I notice what the paper obscured.

Beneath the sheet is a horn, as long as my hand from wrist to fingertip. There's a slight curve before it arches to a sharp point. Ebony and glossy, even beneath the layer of ash.

Instantly, I realize.

Jacob hid them well.

My heart hammers.

But I found them.

And then it shatters.

The ash, the leather, the horn.

These are my wings.

I drop everything and step back, hyperventilating. Pressing a hand to my chest, I try to calm my thundering heart and gasping breaths. My vision swims. I go down on a knee and try to gather myself through the haze.

Distantly, I sense Emrys peering into me, my horror deep enough to reach him as far as he is. I can't determine anything he's saying or wants to say aside from a thin sense of fear, comfort, and concern. It's enough to bring me from the waters that are threatening to drown me.

And then I scream.

I don't care who sees me now. I don't care what they think. I slam open my doors with a satisfying and furious crash, storming my way to the Unseelie Court.

Courtiers and guards leap out of my way, stumbling back from the waves of fury that leech off me. I make my way to the Seelie throne room, and rip the curtain of ivy that contains the Faerie Roads. Every step through the tunnels dabbled with bioluminescent mushrooms and dangling roots brings me closer to the object of my fury. It dances at the edges of my sight, egging me onward, burning the fuel in my steps.

Innately, I find the correct turns, and when I see the flanked statues of Emrys and I, my wrath is renewed by the wings my stone likeness possesses and what I only have as ash in a box. Ascending the gabbro staircase, I let the passion of my anger lead me. I do not formulate coherent thought. I am guided by the worst of my emotions.

Vanna, no, Emrys whispers in my mind. The power behind it is enough to transcend the distance.

At the top of the stairs, I find myself in the mountainous, night sky and glass view of the Unseelie Court throne room. Unseelies gather in an informal party, dressed in gauzy layers of chiffon and sheath, most garments baring legs and cleavage, arms and backs on display. Most are bedecked with some amount of silver glitter, dancing against the moonlight like stardust.

A blue haired faerie-woman with her feet in the lap of a black-haired male, pauses as a white-haired male feeds her light green grapes.

"Your Majesty," she calls out, directing her head towards the diamond Unseelie throne. "You have a guest."

Caethes rises from her diamond throne, wearing a dress of luminous white and silvery ropes, metallic tattoos of her court's signature color twining her arms and legs with flora and fauna that reflects those wrought on her throne. Her hair is straight and sleek down her back, her diadem perched primly between her antlers.

The diadem that burned me and named me her heir.

"Hello, Evelyn Vanora."

I step into the throne room, seething with rage. Dozens of eyes watch me. I have willingly walked into the lion's den, and yet I am not afraid.

"Hello, Caethes," I return through my teeth.

"Did you receive my gift?"

"I did." My words are flat.

"What did you think?"

"Your gift-giving services could use some work."

"Is that so?"

"Indeed. But I came here to tell you something."

Caethes's lips twist. "Certainly. Do you care for an audience?"

Said audience is rapt, greedy. The chaos between Caethes and I surging and feeding their insatiable appetite. I wonder if these whet urges will send them into a frenzy as a battle may. I realize my fury blinded me and there is more than just fae presence here, there is a halfling.

My gaze zeroes in on the left of the room, and there, Gideon sits in a chair, a glass clutched in his grip, panic on his face. He hides it as soon as I make eye contact. I blink, and return to Caethes.

"I do not care. Let them hear what spells the descent of your rule."

Caethes cackles a laugh. "Dear girl, I will not forsake my crown."

"You do not have to. We are at war, and I assure you, you do not want this battle."

"It is exactly what I want."

"No, you wanted war with Aneira, not me." Her name is like acid on my tongue. "I will ruin you. Your legacy will be less than ashes. I will obliterate you from history. It'll be as if you never existed."

Caethes hisses and inclines her chin. "I'd like to see you try."

"This court is slated to be mine and it's too late to choose another. The crown has recognized me. I am your heir apparent and nothing will change that."

"You *stupid* little girl."

"Perhaps if you had not been so selfish with your own court and had named a successor, you wouldn't have gotten yourself in this mess. But you have, you short-sighted dolt, and now you reap what you sow." I pull back my lips over my teeth. "This will be mine, and I will take everything you care about with it."

In a flair of dramatics, I take the stairs and disappear into the Roads once again.

CHAPTER 13

Maelona is in the throne room when I return and her hair is burgundy with wrath. Her dark eyes are midnight pools and her hands are held in furious fists. When she catches sight of me, her lip curls back over her teeth.

"Do you have any idea how many people told me you were on a rampage and had no idea where you were going?" Maelona starts furiously. "The guards were too afraid to confront you, but I do not hold the same sentiment. So, I ask now: Where were you?"

I cross my arms over my chest, still feeling waves of anger radiate off me. The air between us is filled with danger. "The Unseelie Court."

Maelona is taken aback. "Why the fuck were you there?"

"Caethes left me a gift."

"A gift," Maelona deadpans.

"And a note."

"And that was worth running into Caethes's clutches?"

"My wings were."

Mae freezes, her hair flickering black—white. "What?"

"She had my wings and she mutilated them." I grind my teeth together. "She burned them and left enough pieces so I knew."

"Ev."

"That's why I vowed to take everything from her."

"Did you not once consider that you were violating the rules of war?"

My heart stutters at my folly. "I did not."

Maelona's hair is once again wholly merlot. She steps up to me—slowly. "I empathize with you. You lost your wings, and were devasted at seeing them so brutalized. But you do *not* get to allow your emotions to let you make foolish decisions." She's even closer now. "You risked the entire court—selfishly—because Caethes slighted and tormented you. You put countless lives at risk without a second's consideration."

"She humiliated me."

"Then humiliate her back!" Maelona's voice is bright with anger. "You are our queen now! All your decisions reflect on us! All your choices determine our lives! You have to think above your own interests. You have to give a fuck about others—especially since Emrys is nowhere to be found and you're our only option. As a queen you don't *get* to act independently!"

"Then I shouldn't have been queen! *You* should have!"

"But I'm not! You are, and you have to deal with it."

"I don't know what I'm doing! Neither does Emrys!" I break. "We're trying to figure this out, but he's caught up doing something he never should have had to, and I'm here hoping it all doesn't fall apart."

Maelona softens. "What is he doing?"

I try to answer but nothing comes out. My throat works. "I can't say. Fucking oaths."

"Fucking oaths," Maelona echoes.

We're silent a moment, the anger dissipates and Maelona's hair is once again ebony. I pinch the bridge of my nose.

"I'm not cut out for this," I whisper.

"Well apparently you're wrong, considering you have a claim on both crowns."

"I never should have."

"Aneira and Corvina never should have died, but it happened anyway."

My heart clenches, thinking of the loss of two women I loved. Of how Maelona—according to the prophecy—is destined to die, too.

"I miss them."

"So do I."

On the peripherals of my internal alarm, I sense a new presence and immediately my hackles go up. I pull a knife out of my thigh sheath and without having had to communicate, Maelona has produced a blade of her own. We stand back-to-back, weapons ready.

From the ivy, leading to the Faerie Roads, a familiar figure steps out. Her body is covered in iridescent scales and her hair is slick as oil with the rainbow hue of gasoline. Too green eyes contrast against onyx lips and a forked tongue is caught between sharp teeth.

Tegwyn.

She bares a blade, aloft in one hand, so like the one I'd once stolen from her. Once, when I thought I was human. Once, when I thought it was simple monsters hunting me in the Yukon.

"What are you doing here Tegwyn?" I ask, a note of warning in my tone.

Tegwyn hisses softly, fear written across her frame. "I have been commanded to kill you."

I lift a brow. "An assassination attempt?"

"*Yes*," she hisses harshly.

"That's probably a very bad idea."

"You are right."

"Then why try?"

"I told you; I have been commanded."

A heart's desire.

If a person has been divulged a heart's desire by one of the fae, that person holds a command over them. One heart's desire equals one command. Gideon held one over me when I foolishly told him mine when I thought I was human. He possibly holds two more. I can only think of one person who may have had Tegwyn swear a desire.

"You gave Caethes a heart's desire?" I inquire.

Tegwyn scoffs, slowly advancing. "Us Unseelie must. It is a stipulation to be invited to join her court, another to be closer to her confidences."

White hot horror races through me. Does Caethes possess a heart's desire over Emrys? Surely not. Surely, she would have tried to use it by now. Surely, my husband would have told me. Right?

"And this was what she requires of you?" I pause. "Tegwyn, she must know you are no match for me."

"She does." And I detect a hint of sadness in her voice, repentance, or desolation. "But I cannot stop until I complete the task or you kill me first. I have disappointed my queen and this is my punishment."

I feel a pang of remorse. Tegwyn may have tried to kill me once, but her own queen sending her to her death is a whole other sort of killing. The *betrayal* she must feel.

"It doesn't have to be this way," I reason softly. "We can put you in the dungeons, hold you until Caethes passes and the command evaporates. You don't have to die."

"Holding on that long might just kill me anyway."

It's true. The longer someone fights or does not complete an active command, the more painful existing becomes. After long enough, the agony can kill the fae. Something like this could take weeks, perhaps months, but even then, I'm unsure how long it will take to eliminate the Unseelie Queen.

"What if—"

But I'm not able to continue because Tegwyn launches herself at me in a messy attack. She doesn't even get close before Maelona steps around me and strikes out, slamming her dagger into Tegwyn's chest. The blade punctures straight through her heart.

Anxiety spikes in me, but it is not my own. It is my husband's. Even from so far, he can sense the goings on. I can only imagine his fear, knowing his soulmate is experiencing some sort of danger, yet there is nothing he can do. I don't want to contemplate when the roles are reversed.

Tegwyn looks down slowly in shock, blood dribbling from the corner of her black lips. She lifts her poison-green eyes at us, sadness and acceptance coalescing in them.

"So, this is it?" Tegwyn whispers, before dropping to the ground and loosing her last breath. The light fades from her once bright eyes and now the color that was too-green now dulls with the cast of death.

I stare down at Tegwyn's lifeless form, a mass of emotion I cannot decipher stirring through me. I am not sad exactly, but I feel an odd mix of relief and disappointment.

This war has so much needless death. Why must Caethes be so cruel? Why must she care so little for the life of another? She did it with Tadgh when she beheaded him before our very eyes. When she tore out Elliot's heart because the lottery went awry. Or murdering the servant after a meeting, just to prove a point. Now, she sent Tegwyn to die, mostly because she could.

Still conflicted, I still stare down at the corpse at our feet. Not saying a word.

Maelona runs a hand through her hair, exhaling sharply. "I'll summon someone to deal with this. You must call a meeting to discuss an assassination attempt." I don't answer and Maelona snaps her fingers in front of my face. "You might be the Harbinger, but you are also the Seelie Queen and you need to start letting your guard follow you. This certainly won't be the last attempt on your life and you are growing distracted." She softens. "For Emrys's sake at least, don't die for nothing."

I nod, but what I don't say is that the attempt on my life gave me a sick rush. That somehow it brought back feelings from my days as the *Ceidwad Cudd* and the Harbinger. Of missions and dispatches. Of things I'm used to. What I know how to do.

131

But I did learn how to become a warrior and a spy. Perhaps I can learn how to be a queen, too. I *want* to learn how to be a queen.

Maelona leaves to delegate the task of body disposal while I enter an adjoining council room, finding sheaths of paper and ink. Penning letters to General Baphet, the Admiral, Bleddyn, and Enydd, I find a servant and command them to be delivered promptly. They are and within a half hour all those I called for are in the council room.

"There was an assassination attempt tonight," I begin. "It failed, but you all must be notified. Caethes is starting the end to this war in earnest and we must act accordingly."

"What do you have in mind?" Aveda—the Admiral—asks.

I meet her gaze. "I have a question for you, and the spy network as you know it."

Aveda lifts a dark brow. "You have my interest. What is the question?"

"We must send an assassin in accordance to Caethes's move. What I wonder now, is should we send someone adept enough to complete the job? Or send someone who is planning to defect to the Unseelie Court and save us the task of losing them by their own choice?"

Aveda blinks, startled by my blunt cruelty and strategizing. "You leave this decision to me?"

"If you would like to make the choice, yes."

"May I think it over?"

"Certainly. Just decide and report back to me once it is done."

The Admiral ducks her head, her butterfly's wings flaring with pride. "Of course."

Aveda is one of the few fae I know who possesses the gift of karma. It is essentially the antithesis of Unseelie chaos, wherein the faerie can sense or manipulate the source of power into their own gain. Unseelies have an internal chaos meter that sends them into a frenzy during battle, this is akin to a berserker in Viking lore. Seelies meanwhile, have something significantly rarer—that being the ability to sense patterns made by choices and therein the outcomes. It is somewhat like a Hazelhurst witch's ability, but it is a finicky gift and the slightest change in decision makes ripples in the end result. Resembling the butterfly effect.

I have seen the Admiral firsthand using this knowledge to her advantage on a mission.

"Do you have anyone in mind?" I question.

"I have three. Two suit the former request, one the latter."

"Excellent." I dismiss Aveda thereafter and she nods before striding from the room. I turn to Bleddyn. "Can we solidify a new joint Kingsguard and Queensguard?"

"Absolutely," Bleddyn says, bobbing his head. "Any specific requests?"

"I will outline specific qualifications, but in the meantime, I default to your expertise."

"I will be on it immediately."

Bleddyn leaves after his task has been assumed and I turn to Baphet, his ram horns recently polished and picking up the shine from the golden ceiling light.

"Have you strayed to the gambling halls recently, General Baphet?"

The general startles and his dark eyes widen. "No, Your Majesty. I have sworn off the dens and halls since you appointed me this position. I will not be risking it by tempting my addiction."

"Good, I am glad to hear it." I switch topics. "My sources tell me you once frequented a hall operated by a vampire by the name of Draven, is this correct?"

"It is."

"Can you get me in contact with him?"

Baphet's eyes turn suspicious, and I can see he wants to ask me why, but wisely doesn't. "Certainly."

"Lovely. In the meantime, could you inquire about the loyalty we previously spoke of?"

"I can."

With that, Baphet is dismissed, the sound of his cloven feet before the whine of door hinges announces his departure.

"What are you planning, girl?" Enydd asks when it is just her and I left.

"Many things."

CHAPTER 14

After the meeting commences, I follow Aveda to her chambers. The spy is not stupid, she hears me—or at the very least, senses me. At her door, she whirls, her split black and white hair flaring.

"Can I help you, *My Queen*?" she says my title as if the words are venomous, burning like bile on her tongue. Her dark eyes narrow and I see the agitation in her wings—I notice it, because I recognize the tells from my own lost ones.

"I want to enlist your help."

Aveda cocks a single dark brow. "Oh?"

"The plans to take care of Baphet's heart's desire command are underway. I want to usurp them."

Aveda laughs—not kindly. "Are those royal bonds chafing?"

I grind my teeth. "I cannot lie, and even if I could I would not do you the disservice of doing so. Yes, title is...constricting. I do not think I was the ideal choice to rule, but I *want* to rule. But I do not want to do it pillowed and pampered. I want to fight. I want to do more than talk and decree."

"You know...I always thought you'd just been handed everything you'd been given. It all seemed so effortless. How easy everything came to you."

"If that is a compliment, it is a poor one."

The Admiral chuckles. "I meant, that I think I misunderstood you. You are closed off. I did not recognize all that you'd suffered beneath your arrogance. That, or perhaps I noticed we were far too alike."

"That could be true."

"It's why," Aveda continues, nearly lost in her own thoughts. "I think, that I understand you. That I would resent the title as you do—to a degree." She smiles. "It's why I will help you. When do we start?"

I heave a breath. "Now."

The Admiral gives me an amused smirk. "All right then, shall I change?"

"Your leathers are fine."

"Then allow me to get my weapons."

Aveda slips into her room and I notice the heavy dark woods and the rust orange drapes, the browns and oranges and blacks on the brocade patterns, the low ambient light of amber in ebony glass. Her suite is much smaller than mine, but still grand, nonetheless. She leaves the door ajar, and I watch her stride purposefully to an armoire, producing a damask blade and a bow. She slings a quiver over her shoulder, buckling it to accommodate for her wings.

Through the bond, I can sense Emrys's anxieties. I do the best to calm him, but the distance muddies our communication unless absolute focus is implemented.

Aveda steps out and shuts the door behind her. She looks me up and down, critically. "Shall we?"

Aveda and I leave the court behind, striding for the Roads. Beneath the light of the mushrooms my hair and the half of Aveda's glow blue and eerie. We walk together in silence, not having explained the plan as we have both been kept abreast of it during meetings.

Draven is a vampire who'd lured Baphet into dreams of fortunes, but in doing so, deceived him out of money and reputation. To rectify it, Draven directed him to a rogue fae formerly of the Unseelie Court who promised restoration of his former status for an open-ended bargain. He'd agreed, and while his renown was reinstated, there was a black cloud over him and his dreams of receiving general status were ruined.

Until my rule.

It was a common ruse, we discovered. Draven and this rogue developed a co-dependent relationship where each one got the power of different forms they wanted. We could kill Draven, but that would do nothing for the command. The rogue is the target.

"I heard a rumor that you fucked Gideon in these Roads and left him here, is that true?"

I sigh heavily. Will I never live this down? "I did."

Aveda makes a sound, almost of amusement. I glance over and see a smirk on her lips, and something like respect in her eyes. "Did he deserve it?"

"At the time? Yes. But looking back now on what it caused...what it made me do? Probably not."

"Hmm."

Neither of us speak again as we traverse the Faerie Roads, but soon enough we find our turn. When we take it together, we ascend to a gambling den.

In a juxtapose in direction, we find ourselves in burrow filled with heady smoke and incense. There, we stand at the top entrance with a railing of raw wood, patrolled by four guards, and look down over tables and booths filled with faeries. This is a neutral territory and anyone present has been sworn to put down arms and stave off killing. Aveda and I, however, have made no such deal, but in order to be allowed to pass the guards and wards, we must.

But I have a solution for that.

In my pocket is a charm created by Caspian to disable wards. It will suspend them while I—or anyone I touch—passes through them. But the charm will not nullify the guards. That falls to us.

Without a second's hesitation, I take Aveda's hand and drag her through the wards. I feel the prickle of electricity as we pass through them and that moment is enough to stun the guards into inaction. We move swiftly, separating and moving to our targets.

We dispatch the guards. The Admiral fires off an arrow and loads a second one as I take out another guard with a blade. As her first arrow kills a horned fae, her second lodges in the shoulder of a winged one. My sword arcs out and my second opponent meets my strike. He falls beneath the second one.

Meanwhile, Aveda and her winged enemy rise in the air and battle it out with daggers in close combat, wings thundering as they crash together, throttling and coming to blows. After a few seconds Aveda gets the upper hand and drives her blade through the chin of the guard. He falls from their aerial battle and falls to the packed dirt floor with a meaty thump.

Aveda lands beside him, dropping to a knee, and looks up at me with a feral grin.

"Just like old times."

I grin back.

We slip down the stairs, glamoured, the patrons below none the wiser to the entrance guards' assassination. Weaving through the tables and booths, we work our way past serving girls and dealers, shouts going up with wins and losses. The Queen's Glamour covers the two of us and without any notice we find ourselves at the back, towards the offices where Draven resides.

It may be a fae frequented establishment, but a vampire runs it.

I slam open the door to Draven's office, sensing the one singular vampire presence behind it, and he jumps with our entrance. The two of us pour in and Aveda loads her bow and aims it before the vampire has a moment to draw breath. I cross to the desk with my blade held out, dropping the Queen's Glamour to his eyes only.

Draven leans back, greasy black hair slicked against his skull. His red eyes widen as he lifts his hands into submission, but I continue forward.

The scent of incense is lesser here, but present is the pungent aroma of marijuana and other fae intoxicants. Slumping bookcases lean against the walls of carved rock, a desk heavy with papers and scales and white powders stands between us and him. The only light offered is from a lamp dangling from a chain, the illumination yellow and watery. A purple tapestry hangs on the wall, dingy with a torn hem, an emblem of a broken crown emblazoned on it.

"Where is the rogue?" I demand, forcing the full air of queenly authority into the words.

Draven hisses, displaying his fangs. I push my blade closer in an advance.

"Where. Is. The. Rogue?" I bite out.

"I wouldn't goad her," Aveda says flatly. Warningly. "She's in quite the mood and she'll kill you with a single flick of that blade."

Draven's eyes flicker between the two of us. "A spy-queen and a bastard-spy."

Aveda looks over at me with irritation. "I just might kill him instead. Maybe drag him into the sunlight first, though?"

"I won't argue with that once he gives us the information we need."

A quick flash of panic lights his eyes. "W-wait a second, we can work something out."

I roll my eyes. The amount of times I've heard that before.

"Just tell us and I'll ask her not to end you," I say.

"She's here. Tonight," he babbles. "Two floors down in the fighting pits. She's watching there. I have a few desperate—"

"That's enough. Do you happen to hold any heart's desire commands over anyone?"

"N-no. No, I left those to Ysandre. Our deal depends on her not taking money and myself not taking commands."

"That's quite insightful." I turn to Aveda. "What shall we do? Tie him up and knock him out?"

Aveda strokes her arrow taut in the bow string. "That's an option. Not the one I'd prefer, though."

140

"Then we—"

A distinct whine sounds and seconds later an arrow lodges in Draven's heart and the vampire's eyes go wide before he slumps over the desk lifelessly.

I sigh with the full breath of my chest. "For fuck's sake, Aveda."

"My finger slipped."

"Accidentally?"

Aveda simply smirks.

I groan and sheath my blade. "Let's go find the pits."

It takes mere moments for Aveda and I to slip unnoticed from Draven's office and down to the fighting pits. We wind down the staircase and to the sounds of hollering. I follow the tide of presences on my internal alarm, sensing only fae presences still. The further down we descend, the louder the calls become. The cacophony becomes clearer, distinct boos and cheers going up.

Skirting the wall, we keep our eyes trained on the occupants of the mezzanine, seeing who appears to be of import. There are several who have attachments to the Winter Carnaval and its adjacent rings, and additional fae who's allegiances do not follow either the Dark or Light Court. But there is one who specifically stands out as all.

She is a fae woman with long golden waves cascading down her back, statuesque in height, with flawless tanned skin, and leonine eyes of amber and moss. Her long, toned legs end in the hooves of a goat, her fingers ending in the claws of a beast, and small horns sprout from her brow.

There is no question that this faerie is Ysandre. The gut instinct is too strong, the energy virtually palpable.

Ysandre smirks, her lips painted blood red as she drops a stack of gold coins into one hand and then the other. Her eyes are trained on the fight below where two faeries of dubious loyalty spar with bloody knuckles.

Still glamoured, Aveda and I weave until we come up directly behind her. Fortuitously, there is a wide berth around her, so when I sneak up behind her and wrap a hand around her mouth and place a dagger below her ear, everyone remains blissfully ignorant.

"Ysandre?" I whisper.

I can feel her heartbeat quicken. She nods rapidly.

"It's nothing personal."

And then I sink the blade into her brain and she collapses against me as blood runs down my fingers. A pang of guilt strikes me, but I squash it down. I am not a stranger to killing, but that does not mean that I enjoy it.

A fault and a bright side to killing someone Courtless is that while they do not have protections, they also don't have repercussions for killing them. Even if it wasn't wartime, no punishment would be dealt for killing the rogue. But that doesn't mean she doesn't have guards and allies that will seek vengeance for her.

Together, Aveda and I shove Ysandre over the rail and into the pit causing a distraction that allows us to slip by the first of her guards. The rest, however, are not stupid, and though they can't see us through my glamour, they know we're here.

Panic spikes through the bond and I sense Emrys's sole attention pinned on me, piercing into my mind. I block him out so as to not distract myself and to keep him safe from whatever it is he's doing. It's clear he's been blocking me nearly this entire time as little to nothing has been revealed on his side of our connection.

Blindly, Ysandre's bodyguards slash at us and Aveda and I dart beneath their swipes, sliding from their attack and dashing up the stairs. We race together and I can see the smile on Aveda's face and I know it matches mine—a product of the thrill and rush of a mission. While I don't find pleasure in all part of being the Harbinger and *Ceidwad Cudd*, I take the parts of necessary evils and accept them to have the rest.

We ascend the staircase to the exit, we weave around tables and booths once again, bodyguards following in our wake, still unaware of our identity. As we ascend the final steps, we pass by the first guards we'd dispatched—still dead and yet to be discovered. In our duration here, it's apparent that no one new has arrived to gamble or fight. It is luck for us, because no alarm has been sounded. Until now.

It blares overhead and patrons startle drunkenly, looking to the commotion and seeing a ghost chase. I spare no more looks as I drag Aveda through the wards once again and into the Faerie Roads. We do not stop, we keep running, our booted feet hitting the packed earth like thunder. Time passes so quickly, and in a matter of minutes we're turning back into the Seelie Court, no one the wiser to our disappearance and unsanctioned mission.

Aveda and I stand in the throne room, breaths heaving, grinning ear to ear. But realization seems to strike her and that smile falls. Reservation entering her eyes. She's remembering her dislike for me, but I see in her dark gaze it is not nearly as potent as it once was. She's warming to me. Not enough to change her mind. But enough to make her hesitate.

"Thank you, Aveda."

"You're welcome, Harbinger."

It's a step in the right direction.

Back in my rooms, I sit quiet and still on the floor. With my legs crossed, I shut my eyes and place my palms on my knees, searching within my mind—within the bond. I follow the trail of that red soulmate thread, pushing past space and time, urging on a headache from the distance.

I'm burrowing deep into my psyche, following the tug and sensation of my husband. Flickers of his awareness touch me and I latch onto it. Pulled along, I find myself deep in my mind's eye and seeing out from Emrys's golden gaze.

The scent of leather and vetiver suffuse me before the further hints of blood and booze assault me. Emrys starts at the intrusion of his mind, but settles once he realizes who the presence belongs to.

Hello wife, he whispers silently. *What are you doing here?*

Worrying about you.

Worry less. I am well.

This is your definition of well?

The black marble expanse of the Vampire Court is grand and a disgusting display of wealth and brutality. Scarlet runs rivers across the floor, bodies leaking from arteries and veins while vampires feast. Emrys is surrounded by the bloody vampires as he parades as a courtier, donning an elaborate King's Glamour. He takes on the illusion of one of Caethes's six, pretending at a fae by the name of Rowan. With brown hair, blue eyes, and moon pale flesh, he does not resemble my husband in the least, especially with the magically altered features.

He chuckles softly. *I am fulfilling the command—and as soon as I do, I will be home with you.*

"Rowan!" a bawdry voice calls out, black hair mussed, red coating his jaw. His eyes, like every vampire's are red, but I gasp when I notice the shape. And then the other features that register.

Is that—?

"Seth Winters," Emrys, disguised as Rowan, greets. "How fares the Carnaval?"

The creator of the Winter Carnaval.

And evidently Emrys's uncle.

Caspian's father.

I feel sick to my stomach.

The family resemblance is undeniable. Seth, as a vampire is eternally frozen around his early thirties, therefore, his features are perfectly preserved and a horrible match to his son's.

The son whom was taken by his own organization and abused.

"Delightfully busy," Seth finally responds, wiping his lip with his thumb. "We're in the process of moving settings due to a...*hiccup*."

"Oh?"

"It will be a much more delectable experience than last time for you. Which was the last one you attended? The city?"

A thin line of panic slips through Emrys, but he quells it. His features are perfectly schooled, and if I were not in his head, I'd be none the wiser to his unease.

"I do recall the city."

Because he did—if only to pass through.

"Ah!" Seth says, eyes gleaming—is he high? It takes much for a vampire to feel the effects of substances, but enough can do the job—as can drugged human blood. "Well, the next one shall be better—especially once we find more of those little hybrids."

Emrys gives a wicked smile, one that usually has me crossing my legs for friction, but in this case sends a shiver down my spine.

"I can't imagine it being better than the last time I was in attendance."

"It will be made of your wildest dreams," Seth promises, leaning in. He quickly pecks Emrys on the cheek. "Come! Take part in the drink! There's some wonderfully aged wine that is simply divine. Unless you happen to take part in the Unseelie inclination of flesh and blood?"

"That delicacy is not for my palate."

"Well, in that case—wine!"

Seth drags Emrys towards two serving girls who quiver in thin white shifts, one holding a decanter of wine and the other kneeling with a tray of goblets upon her head. They tremble as the males approach.

Vanna, you should leave, Emrys prods, insecurity coloring him. *I don't want you to see me drinking.*

My chest squeezes but I nod before I murmur through the bond.

Please take care of my heart. I've left it with you.

As you have mine.

I slip from his mind like a hand outstretched in farewell, his soothing presence evaporating like smoke. His fingers within our souls are outstretched to meet mine. But we do not touch. Already the scent of leather and vetiver has faded, the warmth of his skin, the comfort of his soul.

When I return to my body, I return to the cold stone and stiff leathers, dirt and blood crusting my form.

I look down at my hands as a tear slips down my cheek.

CHAPTER 15

Days pass after dealing with Baphet's heart's desire, and I grow antsy as war approaches. Every day I'm informed of more battles and hijinks, assassination attempts—on both sides—and information exchanges. All while Emrys is still gone. Meanwhile, I attempt to make excuses for why the queen is the only monarch present—I cannot say much of anything while bound to the oath.

Even so, it doesn't stop those from pushing and prying into the king's whereabouts.

The first meeting after Ysandre's death brings many curiosities. Reports reach our ears about the convenience of her death, bringing with it the nullification of Baphet's heart's desire command. Aveda and I glance at each other knowingly, but do not reveal our participation. Maelona, however, sees through it and gives me a silent scolding through her dark eyes. She flashes the same look at the Admiral, but she simply flips the white half of her hair over her shoulder and shrugs.

"No witnesses can recall who the attackers were, but it's clear they wanted the Courtless to lose their trap," Baphet says, clearing his throat and puffing his chest to hide the vulnerable relief he feels. No longer does the heavy burden of an open command lay on him. "With both Draven Morraine and Ysandre Invicta dead, their ploy of deceit and coercion is over. The working theory is that they—or someone close to them—was a victim of one of these tricks and did not want to surrender the heart's desire command."

"It's a fine theory," I comment simply.

"Do we have to worry about an information leak? Did someone know we were plotting to take her out ourselves?" Tirnoc asks, fresh from a battlefront.

"Not at this point. Our plans differ from the one executed," I answer.

Aveda covers her chuckle with a sip of her water.

The meeting pivots to our spy in Caethes's kitchens, and Baphet looks down glumly.

"We discovered through the girl, Farah, that Caethes is planning a political marriage. One could assume to Joseph Harrow, but she could not determine who exactly. Unfortunately, she was found out and executed. The rest of our spies have decided to lie low, so information will be halted."

My heart aches from the death that is my fault, but as shitty as I feel, nothing will absolve me of it. I must bear the blame and continue. And continue our meeting I do. And I repeat. And repeat. Every day.

Days move, on and on.

I find myself lashing out at everyone and most servants and courtiers avoid me unless necessary. Aveda has let up on some of her hostility, likely placated somewhat by duties I've assigned to her and our joint mission, but more likely because I'm clearly in a foul mood and she pities me. I hate that. General Baphet gives reports succinctly and I appreciate his to-the-point nature. Enydd doesn't give a fuck about my attitude and tells me point blank that I'm being insufferable. She's not wrong.

Bleddyn mostly works through one of the others while assigning new guards for me and Emrys, and I try to soften towards him. He is still grieving Drysi, and aside from Maelona, he is the only surviving member of the former Queensguard.

Maelona is the best person to put me in my place though. Emboldened by our friendship, she has no qualms yelling at me when she feels I need it. And evidently, she thinks I need it a lot.

It's been nearly a week since Julia's last Gideon report—longer since I've seen my husband. We've managed to share brushes of feeling, echoes of words, snippets through the bond, but nothing as clear as when we're in each other's presence. And nothing today. Probably being in completely different realms doesn't help.

I've been blocking any sensations from him today, sensing anxiety and I'm unsure if it's his or mine, or if one is influencing the other. All I know is that I'm in a terrible mood and I need to focus.

I'm meeting with Julia in the same chamber as last time, only this time I am first to arrive. I'm seated at the grand table, previous notes before me, hands folded atop them. My nails have been painted gold and the only adornment on my fingers is my wedding ring. A teardrop emerald, framed by diamonds, set in gold. I stare down at it and miss the male who placed it there.

Huffing, I look away and scan the walls. No longer are there tapestries with Aneira's likeness spaced upon the walls—Enydd took them down when I kept getting distracted by my deceased mother's face—but now there are viridian fabrics done up in gold thread, depicting moments of the Gwyndolyn-Vanora rule. Of Century Training. Of the battle where we'd earned our names. Of our marriage. All courtesy of Enydd.

I shift in discomfort as the images look down upon me. I rearrange the black skirts I wear just as the door opens and Julia arrives.

She is tall—I note absently—almost my height, but that is where our similarities end. She is dark of hair with warm, russet skin, while I am pale and colorless. Julia strides into the room with an uncertain gait, almost wobbling—though she does not wear heels, just leather boots. She's dressed in black pants and a brown, padded, jacket, with a white tee shirt peeking beneath.

As she crosses the space to me, she adjusts her collar before sitting down. I stare her down, taking in the non-verbal cues that all indicate she is uncomfortable and trying to hedge my suspicions.

I decide not to engage in her odd behavior. For now.

"Does Gideon bear news?"

Julia nods and swallows. "Yes. Caethes is growing more enraged each day and tears the heart out of a servant each time she receives intel an assassination attempt is thwarted."

I quickly calculate in my mind. "That's four servants."

"So far, yes."

I receive this information and process it. Should we stop sending assassins after Caethes? None of our attempts have gotten far, and neither have hers either. Tegwyn knew her attempt was futile, but due to the command, could do nothing against it. I pity her for that, and all the following ill-fated souls.

Julia isn't meeting my eyes; she's looking everywhere but at me.

"Anything else?" I press.

"He says he misses his father."

"His father is kept safely ensconced with heavy security. No one sees him—it's for his own protection. But he is well and resting and wants for nothing." I haven't seen the man in days, but he is kept happy with books.

"And he worries for his mother."

"She is being monitored."

I'm not sure how much Gideon's mother knows of the situation, but considering that her and Henry Zhao are married—and he'd given Gideon his last name—I assume she knows a lot and is simply keeping up appearances.

"Can you bring her here? To stay with his dad? It would give Gideon more peace of mind while he risks himself for you."

The request is bold and so is the end claim. But she says it with conviction, despite not meeting my gaze. I let the silence stretch between us, Julia still fiddling with her collar, myself holding still.

"It is being considered."

"Okay."

The silence is met again. I purse my lips.

"Why are you acting so strangely?"

"I'm not," Julia says quickly. Too quickly.

"Don't play dumb with me," I command with the authority of my crown. "Is there something Gideon doesn't want you telling me? Are you worried he's working against us? Is he blackmailing you?"

"No! No, it's none of that. It's—" Color blooms high on her cheeks and she thins her lips, taking in a deep breath. "I have feelings for Gideon."

I blink.

Oh.

Oh, I wasn't expecting *that*.

I blink again.

"And he has feelings for me too. I think just attraction— at least for now—but I was just worried you'd be upset because he's your ex, and he sort of kind of betrayed us once, and I'm also doing this job for you, and maybe you'd think it was a conflict of interest, and I—" she cuts off her babble and bites her tongue.

I hold up a hand while I process this new information. "It does not matter that Gideon and I were once together. That relationship is very much over, and I hold no claim over him. Entanglements can create a conflict of interest; however, if you can keep doing your job proficiently, then I have no need to remove you from the post. He has once betrayed us, yes, but he is working on proving his loyalty. So, for now that is a non-issue. I do not care what you do in your free time as long as it does not make the court vulnerable." I do not mention how hypocritical such statements are. "If you are happy with him, then I am happy for you. Just look out for yourself."

Color is bright on Julia's face and her skin positively burns with mortification. She nods. "Thank you for understanding. I really appreciate it."

"If that is all, you may go now."

Julia takes the dismissal with grace and leaves the room.

I sit in the chair staring at the empty sheet of paper before me, realizing I hadn't jotted down the meeting's notes. I blink down at it, staring somewhat robotically. I did not—and could not—lie when I told Julia I was happy for her. But what I didn't say is that I still hold some kind of mixed emotions from the entire ordeal. Not because I want Gideon—far from it—but because I hesitate to trust him. I do not want to see her hurt over him.

I'm not sure how long I stay in that council room, but it's long enough that a significant passage of time eclipses me.

I just want my husband.

I want to be held and reassured, comforted, told I'm doing a good job. I need validation that I'm not a complete fuck-up. But overall, *I just want him back.*

Closing my eyes, I lift the block and try to focus on Emrys, reaching for that red thread inside me that links to him. I follow it through space and time and realm and fate, tracing my hand over the tether to him. Suddenly, I find him.

And my heart freezes.

He is hurt.

And weak.

In pain.

And the Winter Carnaval has him.

CHAPTER 16

I plan everything horribly and impulsively. I don't tell my Queensguard, the Kingsguard, Bleddyn, Baphet, Aveda, or Enydd. And certainly not Maelona—all I'd get is a tongue-lashing and I'd rather not waste time.

It's the dead of night and about time Lady Maelona will begin to wind down. I leave a note in my chamber with the official Seelie Court seal, proclaiming that I am taking on a solo mission, and in my absence, Lady Maelona is in charge. I also flag down a servant with a second letter and leave him with firm instructions to deliver a second letter to Maelona once she's asleep. She won't be able to read it until she wakes well in the afternoon and by that time it'll be too late for her to stop me from my foolish rescue mission. The letter details my apologies and my faith in her ability to lead the Seelie Court in my stead while I attempt to return the king. I tell her that the Winter Carnaval has him and that I will be doing everything in my power to bring him back—even if it costs me my life.

All those you have ever loved will die.

I ignore the prophecy and make my move.

The Winter Carnaval once had Gideon. It once had our crown. Now it has my husband and I want to see it burned to the fucking ground. I don't know what it'll take to bring down the supernatural black market, but I intend to see it done in my lifetime. It had been my mission once to bring down a faction of it, but I'd failed, and Maelona and Corvina were the ones to successfully dismantle it in the end.

I dress in black leathers, skin tight and padded in vulnerable areas. Knives adorn my person in sheaths along my entire body, and upon my back is my golden sword. My hair is braided in two, pulling tight against my scalp. I leave my crown on a decorative pillow.

Trying something I've never attempted; I merge my latent ability and my soulmate bond. Working them in tandem, I try to fuse my sensing ability with that of the tethering of my husband so that it works as a beacon. It takes some trial and error, and the first pulse of a migraine before I get a ping, but then I do, and my eyes fly open.

"I'm coming for you, Emrys," I whisper to the darkened room.

I depart for the Faerie Roads, casting a Queen's Glamour on myself so that I operate virtually unseen. I skirt patrolling guards and late-night courtiers, making my way to the throne room and therein the access to the Roads. There, I traverse the familiar tunnels and begin a journey I've only navigated once before.

So much easier to access now that I know where to go and how to get there.

The Winter Carnaval is still operating within forgotten realms and the chain of will linking them. Only this time, the destination has changed. When I find the first turn to the first stepping stone, I discover myself looking at the last Winter Carnaval destination. The tunnel down to the caves that looks like it was dug by a giant's fist. The pulleys and elevators, the torches, the raw reddish earth. But this time, there are no screams of terror of pleasure, and the scents that once pervaded this space are muted. Old.

There is no one here.

If this chain follows the previous loop, then I know exactly where Emrys is.

I curse as I begin crossing the forgotten realms and follow the copper light to the next.

Mountain.

Wasteland.

Island.

Manor.

City.

Century Training.

I pause at the edge of the field overlooking the crumbling cathedral and check a hidden timepiece. Fifteen to the hour. It's dusk here, fine shafts of sunlight disappearing with nightfall. The gray stone is in worse disrepair than before, crumbling and another wing has succumbed to the elements.

157

More moss and lichen have overtaken the ruins, crawling over it like an infestation.

There are several vampires here, a handful of fae, a witch, and one soulmate.

I cross the grass, the overgrown length up to my thighs. I take steady steps, anxiously aware of my surroundings and mental alarm. There is no one new. I approach the entrance of Century Training, the grand oak doors painted with rust from the now orange, iron bars. Placing a hand on a latch, I unhook it and open the doors. They swing inward and the ominous creak announces my arrival.

For a moment, it is just dust settling. And then there are footsteps. The signal of the witch draws closer and I renew my Queen's Glamour, tightening it like a cloak. I stand in the entryway as she arrives in front of me. Immediately, I peg her as a Frostsinger.

Her hair is platinum blonde, wavy and long. She stares at me with eyes made of ice, so glacier blue, coldness strikes my soul as she takes me in. The witch is just as pale as I am, but she retains a rosy hue to her cheeks and nose, as if slightly bitten by an unseen chill.

"Who are you?" she demands.

I give her a vicious smile. "The Seelie Queen. Now, I think you have someone who belongs to me."

She opens her mouth to begin her siren's song, but I draw a blade and throw it straight and true at her. It lodges high on her side and she stops, cupping the wound. Blood seeps out from between her fingers. The knife is between her ribs, restricting her lung capabilities, and therefore one of her powers.

I advance on her. "Would you like to take me to him, or would you like me to find him myself?" I draw another blade and brandish it. "Your call, but only one of them requires you living."

Her lips curl back over her teeth. "You could have just asked first."

"I'm asking now. And besides, you were about to sing me into a trance so don't even try that shit again. If I get the slightest inkling that you're going to pipe up, I'll sever your vocal cords before you have the thought."

I stare her down and let the fact seep in that I cannot lie.

She huffs in annoyance and pain, still applying pressure to her bleeding wound. She hasn't taken the knife out yet, which leads me to believe she has some brains.

I place the point of my blade against her spine and fist my hand in her long hair. "Walk."

She does, and as she does, she leads me through the familiar corridors that once housed me for a hundred years. We don't say anything, but I can hear the slight wheeze in her breathing. When we arrive at our destination, a sick splash of irony rushes through me—we're in our old bedchambers.

I roll my eyes.

As the witch opens the doors, she reveals tacked up curtains, blocking the last remnants of sunlight from the space. The vampires in the room turn in unison and I quickly count, finding all accounted for. Four males, two females.

And Emrys.

I feel my heart explode in my chest as I see my soulmate. He's nodding out of consciousness, locked to an iron chair, beaten and bloody, one golden eye swollen, his plush lips split and scabbed. My husband is pale beneath the blood, different shades of it from brightest scarlet to near black showing the degrees of healing. They tormented him a long while.

Fury ignites in me and I want to kill them all.

Time works differently in Century Training—one year everywhere else is a hundred here—which means even though they have just taken him, they have also had plenty of time before I got here to do this damage to my husband.

"What is she doing here?" one of the male vampires asks.

"She's the Seelie Queen," the witch says frostily.

"Yeah, no shit, Phoebe. She's also the Harbinger. Haven't you heard?"

Phoebe sighs. "That would explain her spectacular aim."

"Have you been living under a fucking rock?"

"I've been busy!"

I slightly poke Phoebe's back and she squeals.

"I'd like to take my husband and leave. If you hand him over, I'll let you live. Fight me on it, and die."

The vampires all exchange worried glances. Fucking around with the Harbinger is not something they want to learn about. Even so, I see a spirit in them. They're measuring their odds. Seven against one. Normally unbeatable odds, but they've never challenged me before.

"Think we can ransom her to Caethes?" the first vampire proposes.

One of the two female vampires scoffs. "The Harbinger and the Revenant? We could put them at auction, imagine the price they'd fetch."

"Are you two fucking stupid?" a third vampire chimes in. His hair is dark and his features Grecian. "This prick was given to us because they stole our merchandise. We can't just pawn him as we like, he's retribution for—"

"Shut the fuck up, Aleks!" the first vampire shouts.

The only "merchandise" we stole was Caspian Lockwood.

"Look, I have no patience for this," I cut in, readjusting my grip on Phoebe's hair. "Give me my husband and let us walk, or I'll kill you all. Starting with her," I say, indicating Phoebe.

"Can't do that," Aleks replies. "We don't have that authority."

"Well make it, otherwise you won't be doing another thing ever again."

"Marco—" Aleks starts, looking at the first vampire, but he shushes him.

"We don't have that authority," Marco says with finality, stepping forward. His eyes, like all the others are blood red.

"Then I authorize you to speak on behalf of the Winter Carnaval, as Queen of the Seelie Court, I decree it."

I'm not sure if I actually have that power, but bluffing with official sounding words works just fine for me.

Emrys is still out of it, hardly lucid, but I think he senses my presence. Through the bond I feel him stir groggily, trying to sound out my name. My heart clenches and anxiety rises within me.

Who did this to you? I demand, fire in my blood. I will destroy whoever did this.

He shakes his head.

Who. Did. This. To. You?

Marco. But you cannot kill him.

I watch the memories play out of Marco's sick delight in torturing my husband. The blows that fall on him over and over as he's bound. Marco laughing. My husband in agony.

My wrath is incandescent.

I will kill him.

Trick them, Emrys whispers in my mind. I see the path his thoughts are taking, the plot he's unravelling.

But Aveda—I begin to argue, my fury still bright.

Trust me.

Marco straightens. "If we give him back, do you swear that you will let us live?"

The desire to slice Marco's throat is potent, but I shove it down. For Emrys's sake, adding to his plan. Discreetly I check the time—it'll cut it close. "I'll do you one better. I promise I will let you live today and the Seelie Court may not attack the Winter Carnaval for a period of ten years. This will be sworn in blood and validated with your same oath, in return, reversed. Do you agree to the terms?"

Marco eyes me warily, a dark brow lowered. "That's it?"

"That's all," I say calmly.

"We are not fae."

I shrug. "Humor me."

"Okay, we agree."

I indicate Phoebe as I speak. "May we use her blood to bind the oath? With your authorization."

Marco hesitates. "Yes."

"I, Evelyn Vanora, Queen of the Seelie Court, hereby enter into a sworn blood oath with Phoebe Frostsinger and Marco on behalf of the Winter Carnaval to bind in agreement the former verbalized contract as sworn by both parties without amendment. These words are true, this oath is binding." I prick my finger with the tip of my blade and mix it the bead of blood with Phoebe's. "As I speak, no attack may occur between the participants for a period of a decade, after the minute of the first hour of the next day, to the day, this is sworn."

Instantly, a rush of power goes through the room and I grin.

In addition to my Queen's Glamour I'd inherited with the crown, I also possess the ability to blood bind oaths with those not fae with the same results as if both parties were fae. They are sworn to their word, and because Marco accepted the authorization, he truly spoke for the Winter Carnaval. The Winter Carnaval cannot retaliate, and cannot participate in the war between the Unseelie and Seelie Courts unless they choose our side.

"What did you do?" Marco demands.

That wicked smile is still on my face. "The oath is binding, you're welcome. Careful who you attempt to harm, you cannot inflict injury on a member of the Seelie Court during this time."

What I don't tell him is that there is a minute of limbo, and it is my loophole to get Emrys's revenge. Midnight strikes and I toss Phoebe away into Aleks. I stare for a moment and countdown. I weigh the time, and after a few breaths, I attack. I rush Marco with a dagger held and leap onto his front, my knee driving into his sternum. My blade falls and plunges into his throat, over and over, nearly decapitating him. The swath I open up has blood flooding onto the floor and out of his mouth. Shock flaring his carmine eyes.

"This end has come to you because you dared to touch my husband." I lean in closer, blood spackling his face. "My *king*. My *soulmate*."

Marco coughs and it is only blood.

Behind me, Aleks jumps to aid, but when he attempts to strike me, he cannot. The intended blow bounces off me, unaffected. One of the female vampires attempts the same, with the same result. The minute long window has closed and no harm can come between us during this oath.

Aleks stares at me in horror, and I laugh. I stand in one smooth motion and taunt. "Didn't you hear? As I said, '*for a period of a decade, after the minute of the first hour of the next day, to the day.'* There was one single minute unaccounted for, and it is gone now."

I'd said I'd let Marco live *today*; the day passed. I did not speak the oath into effect until a minute after the hour. I worked to my advantage.

"You tricky bitch," Aleks hisses.

"I prefer clever." I wipe my bloody hands on my leathers. "Now, which one of you has the keys to my husband's shackles?"

I hold my hand out and only have to wait a few seconds before Aleks approaches, delicately placing the keys in my palm.

"Thank you for your cooperation."

I stride over to Emrys unworried but furious, and kneel beside him. I cup my hands on his jaw, lifting his gaze to mine.

"Hello, my love," I whisper, brushing his bruised cheekbone. "I'm here to take you home."

"*Vanna,*" he rasps.

"Yes, husband."

I then set to work, unhooking the cold iron from his wrists and ankles, unbothered by the touch of the normally corrosive metal. The vampires behind me mutter in surprise and dismay over my killing of their comrade, and our joined ability to withstand the touch of iron—cold forged, too. I release my soulmate and then help him to his feet, leaning in to his ear.

"Did you fulfil the command?" I hardly breathe the words.

He nods. "Yes."

"Good."

"I did this on purpose," he continues.

"You what?"

"Later."

I send the vampires and witch a vicious glare and help my stumbling king from our once bedroom. He manages the uneven pavers with muscle memory, his warmth heavily leaning on me and leeching his vetiver scent into me—even through the stench of blood.

"Where is everyone?" I whisper as we exit the front entrance.

"Gone from here. They're securing another realm right now, and as there isn't an event currently ongoing, everyone is attending to their other duties."

"I see."

We traverse the field, now full dark. I keep mental tabs on my alarm system, ensuring no one is hiding in the tall grass. If there are any other vampires here not formally attached to the Winter Carnaval, we are vulnerable to them. Thus far though, it is only those we have already encountered.

Emrys is wheezing in pain as we cross the first threshold, and I distantly wonder if Phoebe will receive any sort of medical attention, or if they'll just dose her with some vampire blood. Vampire blood is an excellent healing agent, but it comes with addictive qualities and a drugging effect—it shouldn't be used regularly.

We make our way in reverse through the stepping stones, faltering slightly as the ground becomes less steady beneath our feet. When we return to the Roads once again, we both heave a sigh of relief.

It's minutes more and we enter the throne room. Maelona is there—pissed.

Fuck.

It seems like the messenger did not wait until Mae had gone to bed.

"What in the goddess's name were you thinking?" Maelona hisses, stomping over to us.

I inhale deeply. "I was thinking we needed our king back."

"Without any fucking backup? Evelyn, what the fuck?"

"It worked out, didn't it?"

"And I'd like to hear how. What did you *do*?"

I cringe a little. "I made a deal."

And then I tell her about the blood oath.

CHAPTER 17

Maelona is, rightly so, enraged. Taking down the Winter Carnaval has always been a plight of the Seelie Court and now I've set us back any attempt by a *decade*. Task forces and spy networks will need to be paused and reined in. It seems the Lady wants to scream at me some more, but when Emrys coughs up blood she bites her tongue.

"We'll continue this later."

I don't bother to comment on her commanding tone, and the fact that Emrys and I are the monarchs, not her, but she isn't wrong.

Maelona silently seethes, hair wine-red in fury, as she silently helps me haul my husband to our chambers. Emrys is lolling between us, and between the two of us, we're half dragging, half carrying him. I unlock the door and my best friend practically pushes us inside.

"Tomorrow afternoon we are talking. No rescheduling," Mae determines firmly.

"Tomorrow," I confirm.

The door closes and I'm left with my husband, wounded and tortured. He's groggy, but I can sense him through the bond. I know he's not on death's door, just very, very exhausted.

I drag him to the bathroom and set him down gently, sliding him down a wall. I turn the golden faucets on full blast, keeping the water hot and adding in oils—lemongrass and ginseng. Then I set to work, cutting away his ruined clothes, and depositing them in a bin. I manage his boots off and once he's unclothed, I strip down myself and help him into the bath.

He groans as the warm water touches his beaten flesh and he leans into me, inhaling against my neck, hands seeking my bare flesh.

"Mm, Vanna."

"Shh, just let me help you."

I take a seat next to him in the enormous sunken bath, feeling the hot water caress my skin and soothe my anxious nerves. Coils of steam rise from the surface and pinken our complexions. Adjusting Emrys against the edge of the tub so that he doesn't slide in, I grab a cloth and some soap, and set to work cleaning away the blood.

Gently, I stroke his face with the white cloth and it comes away filthy. Emrys winces as I graze a bruise on his cheekbone just below his swollen shut eye. My chest aches for him as I continue cleaning, my husband still mumbling and hazy. Concern grows for him and I move closer, our bodies more flush. This wakes him.

One eye opens wide and immediately takes in my features. A small smile graces his mouth. "My Vanna." And then he cups my cheek with a cut-up hand.

I lean into his touch as I wipe the last traces of blood from his face. I'm uncertain if there's any in his hair because of the coloring, but I'm thinking it's more than likely.

"Yes. I'm all yours."

His hand stays on my cheek while the other coasts down my body, tracing my slight curves and slender frame, lightly scratching at my taut muscles. His fingers find my abdomen and it flexes in response. He opens his palm to my belly and covers it, slowly sliding to my side, down to my hip. Butterflies dance in my core, dipping low and spiraling deep.

He's lucid now, but luxuriating in my touch.

Reaching past him, I grab the glass pitcher and fill it with water. Carefully, I tilt his head back and pour it over his garnet waves. The water comes out pink. I repeat this process, running my hands through his hair and nails along his scalp, freeing debris and searching for any lumps or cuts. I find none.

I keep dousing him with water until it runs clear. When it does, I lather his locks with lemon-scented soap and he groans in pleasure. I smile, I don't think I've ever had the opportunity to provide him this slight pampering. It's nice, I like it. I just don't particularly care for the circumstances.

Once the shampoo is rinsed, I use the matching conditioner and massage it in.

"I meant to get caught," he whispers.

169

"What?"

He wriggles. "Don't stop." He clears his throat. "I meant to get caught by the Carnaval."

"Why?"

"For intel. Joseph Harrow is directly working with the Unseelie Court. There were talks of a marriage alliance."

I cock a brow in surprise. "That is confirmation we were looking for. Do you know when?"

"The solstice."

"Oh, symbolic." Particularly since that is the very same day Caethes plans to kill Gideon.

He hums an agreement. "By doing this, we've put a stop to the Winter Carnaval's connection in this war. They cannot participate unless it's for us. And we know they won't."

"But Aveda will turn on us now."

"Not necessarily. We can promise her the mission once the time is up."

"She won't be pleased by that."

"No. But now we can also involve the Arcana Society."

I scrutinize him. "No, they're not allowed to interfere with the courts."

"Unless the society head or a House Council representative is selling secrets to the Vampire Court."

The Vampire Court operates outside of the parameters of the Arcana Society and its governing body, therefore any association with them is treason. They abide by their own rules, but at the same time, they are not protected by the society's laws. They are even further removed than the Seelie and Unseelie Courts.

"And someone is?"

"Yes. Both the Seelie and Unseelie delegates are working with Joseph and Caethes."

My eyes widen at this.

Fae delegates from the House Council must be apart from the situation and unbiased towards the courts. They cannot choose sides in fae court politics either. The only bearing their titles have on the Seelie and Unseelie is that each of the representatives must hail from opposite courts. The two fae govern the House Council with a member of each supernatural species—halfling, vampire, witch, and werewolf. The only reason why two fae exist with seats is because once the court designation did play a role, but now such ideals are nixed, though the seats were not removed.

If the representatives compromise themselves with fae politics without the House Council's first involvement, the House Council and Arcana Society are obligated to intervene on the opposing side and minimalize casualties.

"How did you find this out?"

"I started to hear snippets at the Vampire Court so I followed them. When I got myself taken to the Winter Carnaval, I learned my captors liked to talk—and to brag. I listened when they thought I was unconscious, and I got them to spill secrets with taunts as they beat me. It was worth the pain."

The memory of it flickers through the bond. I see him interrogated, tortured. He's tied to that damn iron chair, vampires circling him. Taunting, threatening, throwing digs about me. Teeth-cracking blows rain down on his jaw, rib bruising punches taking the wind from his lungs. I see the memory of blood dripping from his mouth, his head cloudy with pain. But what keeps him lucid and present is me. Thoughts of me, of us, our marriage, our rule, our future.

Anger burns in my chest. "And what was your plan to get out of this mess?"

Emrys hesitates. "I'm not sure. But I knew it would involve you. Eventually, I was going to reach out to you through the bond."

I look away, furious. Emrys cups my cheek and turns me to face him.

"Don't be angry at me, Vanna. I was doing this for us."

"You could have gotten yourself killed," I say thickly.

Emrys wipes a stray tear from my cheek. "I'm sorry, my love. I didn't want to worry you."

"But you did."

"How can I make it up to you?"

I hesitate, eyes blurry.

"Does this help?" he asks as he presses a chaste kiss to the corner of my jaw.

"A little."

"And this?" He kisses the edge of my mouth.

"A little more."

He chuckles as his lips meet mine. "This?"

"More."

"In what way?" he teases.

I make a displeased sound against his lips as he continues kissing me. His lips move sensually, slowly, taking my lower lip and drawing it out, catching it with his teeth. Emrys's tongue glides against the seam of my mouth and I open for him, relishing in the familiar taste of him.

Something ignites low in my belly and I squirm from it. Carefully, I drape myself over my husband and straddle him. I can feel his cock, proud and hard beneath me.

"Fucking you would make it even better," I tell him as I slide my slick core against his length. The warm water doing delicious things to the friction between us.

Emrys wraps his arms around my waist. "Then ride me wife, I'm yours for the taking."

Slowly, I sink down onto him, impaling myself on his length. The stretch of his member inside my tight channel is divine, and I throw my head back in ecstasy at being so filled. Emrys leans forward and peppers my chest with kisses, sliding his mouth down my breast before dipping low to take a nipple in his mouth. He flicks his tongue against one, sending zings of electricity through my core.

The soulmate bond between us positively glows, as if by joining again we've set a match to paper, and the ember that was the bond all these days is renewed. It blazes between us as I bounce on him, grinding my clit down onto his pelvis, seeking that decadent friction. He presses me down onto him harder, his hands clamped to my hips. Urging me.

I moan as he tends to my opposite nipple, delivering the same ministrations to that one. His slightly sharpened canines scrape against that tightened peak and my pussy clenches around him. He growls and suddenly he's pushing me off of him and turning us around, bending me over the edge of the tub. Fisting a hand in my silver locks, he arches my back and then slams into me in one swift move. I shriek at the new delightful pressure as Emrys takes me from behind, pumping into me with slow, forceful strokes. I push back into him and he lets out a choking sound, his rhythm faltering. I giggle as I continue pushing my ass against him as he pounds into me, our flesh smacking together with loud sounds—made louder by the bath water.

"You're fucking incredible, Vanna. I've missed this, I've missed you."

Emrys leans down, turning my head and nips my throat, drawing harsher love bites down the back of my neck, to the juncture of my shoulder. I can feel the marks purpling as he continues claiming me.

"I've missed you too," I moan. "So much."

"Show me. Show me how much this pussy needs me. Come for me."

Feeling playful, I return his move on him and twist us around so that I am once again on top. I slam him into the edge of the tub and he grunts. I give him a devilish smirk before I'm riding him again, fucking him into oblivion. So much power rushes between us, the bond like lightning. I increase my tempo, feeling my climax build low in my belly, slowly spiraling outward. Emrys plays with my nipples, driving me wild. I keep taking him, loving him, pumping him.

"Come for me, wife. Come on my cock, I want to feel you squeeze me."

My breathing becomes hitched, and I cry out. My orgasm blasts through me, careening through my entire body, zinging from my clit to my toes. I ride Emrys through the waves of my crescendo and moments later he follows me over the edge, pulsing inside me. He clutches me desperately as the last throes take him. I continue grinding on him until he's finished, maximizing both our pleasures.

I lean against him, soaked and sated, my core clenching with aftershocks. Emrys runs his hand down the back of my head and along my spine, trailing over me possessively.

"Next time," I whisper raggedly, "I'm punishing you for this like you punished me."

He chuckles and I feel it vibrate in my own chest. "Is that a threat or a promise?"

"Very much a promise."

"I'll hold you to it."

"See that you do."

I sigh and then it's Emrys's turn to pamper me. He goes through the same motions for me as I did for him, though I try to dissuade him.

"I'm not the one that was just kidnapped and beaten."

"Let me do this for you. It will help me. Make it feel like everything is going back to normal."

I let him. Though, I don't know what normal is to us anymore. Normal is so far outside the range of a recent timeline that it is a completely foreign space to me. I have been a queen for so little, and before that I was recently reclaiming my Harbinger identity after being stuck as a human for two years. It's been painfully long since things were normal, and my old normal was Emrys's hell. When I had forgotten our marriage and our love. When I'd seen him as my rival and enemy— someone I'd sometimes fucked in Century Training, but with no feelings. How wrong I was.

I'm not sure what it is, but I'm eager to find it with him.

All those you have ever loved will die.

The intrusive thought strikes me and Emrys freezes. My husband sifts through my recent memories and reads the prophecy.

"Evelyn," he says sternly, using my full name— startling me. "I have already died once; I am not going anywhere again."

I hitch a staggered breath, relief mixed with anxiety. He's right. He did die once. Does that make him immune to the prophecy? The prophecy never foretold anything of resurrection, so it's entirely possible my husband can subvert this prophecy. Hope floods through me and I cling to it like a shipwrecked survivor seeks a surface at sea. This prophecy is my wreck and he is my buoy.

Emrys kisses my brow. "I am here. I am yours. And I am not leaving you. No goddess will take you from me. Am I understood?"

I nod against his mouth. "Yes."

"Good."

He lathers the lemon soap into my hair and I tilt back as he works it through my tresses.

"So, tell me everything about what I've missed."

I sigh. "I was worried about when you were going to ask."

And so, I enjoy Emrys's touch as I fill him in on our court and the political advances we've made, the assassinations we've thwarted, and all battle and strategy updates. The unsanctioned mission for Baphet's command. I also tell him about my wings and Caethes's delivery of them and when my voice shakes Emrys just holds me. I close my eyes as I let the emotions run their course, and then I continue.

CHAPTER 18

Caspian,

It has come to our attention that a member of the House Council has been working with both the Unseelie Court and the Vampire Court. We are set to produce an official summons to the Society Head, but in the meantime, I would greatly appreciate if you could give us any insight or gossip *surrounding the matter. In addition, we will keep you posted about any results surrounding a hearing.*

Please do not inform anyone of this correspondence and I wish you well. Send word if you require anything— anything at all—and we will be happy to assist you.

Warmly,

Evelyn

I just finish penning the letter to the young halfling protector when Emrys finishes the official documents to send to the House Council and Arcana Society respectively to inform them of a representative's duplicity and now their ensuing obligation. Together, we seal both with emerald wax, the official correspondence with the monarch's seal, the friendly one with my personal one prior to my queen days. By hand, we deliver them to a courier and then we depart the chambers to head to our meeting with Maelona.

We'd spent the night wrapped in each other's arms after bathing together. Hands on chests over hearts, staring into silver and gold eyes. Due to Emrys's fae healing his swollen eye is just a blemished purple and green now, and his split lip is only a pinkened line. Before slumber took us, our breaths were laced with *I missed you* and *I love you*, the sentiment echoed through the soulmate bond.

We arrive in the official council chamber and Maelona is already there, dressed in fighting leathers. Emrys and I are decidedly not clad as such, instead, we don blouses and loosely fitting pants with slippers on over our feet. Of course, we have a few hidden blades—old habits are not shed so easily.

Mae crosses her arms over her chest and stares us down, her sharp cat-eye makeup a long, bold slash across her lids, adding to the severe look. Her claret-painted lips are pursed, and her fingers tap on her forearms.

"Well? Who is going to start explaining both your recent idiocies?"

Despite our royal titles we cringe and launch into our stories, chagrined. Maelona listens but stays silent, her varying facial expressions—brow raises, smirks, thinned lips—and changing hair the only thing belying her reactions. We tell her more about my rescue at the Winter Carnaval and the blood oath, going into detail, and then we try to explain to the best of our abilities how Emrys came to be in their clutches. We try to skirt the oaths, but we can only do so much. Luckily, Maelona is clever and well versed in oaths and is quickly able to put the pieces together.

"So, this mission you completed; it was the payment for gaining entry to that sex club?" Maelona clarifies.

Emrys nods.

Maelona paces, sucking in her cheeks. "Do either of you have any heart's desire commands left hanging over your heads that I need to know about?"

I flush furiously. "Aside from the ones Gideon may possess, no."

"And you?"

"No. Caethes tried once—to force and ensure my loyalty—but I refused. She kept trying for a while but eventually she relented. I'm sure she figured if she kept pressing, she'd lose the Revenant."

I deflate in relief. Caethes possibly holding a command over Emrys was playing on my anxieties more than I realized.

"Okay, and aside from Evelyn's current blood oath, do either of you have any active blood oaths?"

"No," we say in unison.

"Good." Mae shakes her head. "I feel like I'm parenting children."

"We're both older than you," I defend.

"You, no—I am by six months—him, by a couple years."

"Does Century Training count for nothing?"

"No."

I sigh and roll my eyes. "Let me know how it differs if you decide to have children."

Maelona gives me a maniac smile. "Will do. You two will be godparents, of course."

I cock a brow. "Such an honor."

"It's not every day a child's Aunt Ev and Uncle Em are royalty; I must seek the rewards and benefits as they come. I hope for the same honor, should you two decide to reproduce."

Emrys and I share a quick look, our thoughts exchanging rapidly through the bond. Children have been something we've put off discussing, both during Century Training and now with our recent reunion. Truthfully, I never expected to have them because of my status as a warrior and what my duties to Aneira entailed—a child just didn't fit into that role. But now, with my new place, it is something I *can* consider. Beside me, I feel my husband going through the same motions, cataloguing our pasts and meshing it with the future.

Almost like a vision, I picture our children—a little girl with her father's garnet locks and her mother's silvery eyes. My soulmate holding a babe, wrapped in Seelie emerald with my light hair and Emrys's golden gaze. Another who looks exactly like Corvina. All of them have wings, like those Emrys and I both lost.

My heart locks up at the prospect of those babies—our babies. It is suddenly a future I want more than anything and Emrys's answering longing is a match to mine. Without words we have decided on this future, whether it be now or years—even decades—away, we want these babies. Together.

We lock eyes and the adoration shared makes my chest tight. Never have I felt so loved or seen. Never have I been so fulfilled by a prospect. I want to kiss my husband, to wrap him up, and hold him tight. I want to never let him go. I want the peace of a life together.

I am determined to make it.

Finally, I turn to Maelona.

"We'll let you know."

"You better," she teases, "otherwise I will torment you for eternity."

We wrap the meeting up and return to our royal duties. Emrys and I deflect questions about Emrys's recent whereabouts and the presence of his lingering injuries. We notify Aveda about the partial shutdown of the spy network, any current spies or assassins on assignment related to the Winter Carnaval must be pulled back. The Admiral is not thrilled but does as she's told when I inform her it's related to a blood oath. She has yet to learn the full story—that will come later. We also inform Baphet about the blood oath and he remarks about how it gives us an advantage in the war, how the Unseelie Court cannot utilize the Winter Carnaval agents against us—he is clearly thrilled and I wonder if he has new debts, and if they are owed to the Carnaval. I make a note to investigate. Bleddyn is near the end of finalizing our new guards and I check in with him emotionally. The inquiry seems to surprise him, and it's enough for his emotional veneer to crack, but he answers honestly.

"I am solemn, but serving this court is the best way for me to heal."

I nod and continue on. I'm not sure to what degree he was involved with Drysi, but he lost so many people recently, too. The Queensguard he considered his brothers and sisters in arms, the woman he loved, and his queen. It's a difficult burden for anyone to bear.

Days pass and Emrys heals. There is little to no evidence of the brutality he endured at the hands of the Winter Carnaval. It only takes two nights before the Arcana Society and House Council receive and answer our summons, organizing a joint assembly dated for three days hence.

The date arrives and we ascend on the House Council with an entourage. Emrys and myself, Maelona, Bleddyn, Enydd, Wisteria, Julia, Violante, Baphet, and Aveda, as well as our nameless and faceless King and Queensguards.

Exiting from the Faerie Roads and emerging from a three foot wide crack in a monolithic rock wall, we find ourselves taking in the pristine scenery of a barren, glacial mountainside under a violet sky. A pure and untouched stream burbles before us and across it is an ultra-modern structure that blends in with the white and slate gray of the mountains. The building seamlessly merges with the rock—as if it were born from it. The upward slant of the roof diverts the snow into a funnel where it ends in a trickling waterfall that divides the building down the center.

Maelona steps in front of us and pricks her finger on a blade, whispering the word for opening. With the drop of blood on the knife, she slashes the air and parts the wards that conceal the House Council from human eyes and supernatural intruders. The wards part with a soft susurrus in the wind and we continue.

The House Council's headquarters are located in a remote region of Greenland, virtually untravellable without the Faerie Road—unless one wishes to hike for days through desolate terrain.

Several of the walls are made completely up of windows, and the glass brings in the starlight that is beginning to ascend. Guards dressed in white uniforms flank all the entrances and exits, and I can only imagine more hiding where the eye cannot see. When the doors open by an unseen hand, we are greeted by a perfectly temperature regulated space.

The room is modern and sophisticated, enhanced by the crystalline chandelier that cascades into an icicle point. The floor is a single slab, the same shade as the snow outside, and the desk is translucent glass. Behind the desk hangs a sigil for the House Council, wrought in platinum. It's simple and to the point—a six-ringed gordian knot framed by an "H" and a "C" respectively.

A witch with dark hair greets us with a warm smile. "Welcome. Your meeting will be commencing shortly. You are encouraged to wait in the antechamber through those doors and the Council will receive you soon." She indicates a tall pair of silver doors with a slight tremor to her hand. Fear. It is understandable, she's in the presence of the Seelie Court.

Maelona says nothing and simply strides past the witch, pushing both doors open for our group to enter.

We find ourselves in a large waiting room with firm leather couches and chairs encased in geometric steel frames. The tables retain the same modern twist as the sofas, yet are illuminated from within by a pale, cyber-blue light. A miniature version of the lobby's chandelier hangs above, and shards of the crystalline glass make up sconces and lamps.

We are silent and hold a resolute calm, knowing we are compelling their hand. That their duplicity within ranks forces their aid. Emrys and I keep up a steady stream of consciousness and strategy between us through the bond—with no one the wiser.

We do not have to wait long before the dark-haired witch arrives to escort us to the council chamber.

The council chamber retains the same qualities already displayed throughout the rest of the building. The room is encased in glass and I can only imagine the windows are UV treated—it would be impossible for the vampire delegate to sit on the Council otherwise. Rows of shiny metal benches—nonferrous for the fae—take up a substantial portion of the room, and each are limned in that faint cyber-blue light. An identical copy of the House Council's favored chandelier hangs from above a glass-topped platinum table that stretches the length of one wall. Each of the six council members, cloaked in white holds a seat.

To the side is a smaller table with three empty chairs and name plaques—Sonya Deveraux, Everett Kwon, and Liam Holden.

I zero in on the fae delegates first. The Unseelie representative has pastel pink hair in cherubic curls about her porcelain face with large doll eyes of pewter blue. Her mouth however, is a Cheshire slash, sharp teeth behind painted rose lips. A whip-like tail dances behind her. The Seelie representative has a lizard's slitted pupils surrounded by moss green eyes, and long wavy hair several shades of green darker. His skin is slightly bronzed, though in patches it fades into scales, ending in slightly sharpened claws.

Our entourage takes seats on the metal benches while Emrys and I remain standing before the House Council. We incline our heads, demanding reverence. The representatives all duck their heads in submission.

"We thank you for meeting with us so promptly," Emrys begins.

"It is not often we are summoned together by fae, let alone by the king and queen," the vampire delegate—Damian Harper-Contas—responds. "I hear congratulations are in order—both for coronation and matrimony."

"Thank you, there have been some big changes as of late."

"Indeed. Do any of those changes bring you here today?"

The halfling delegate lifts a hand. "Perhaps we should wait until the Arcana Society takes their seats before commencing. I believe I hear them coming now."

As the halfling delegate—Blaine—speaks, the doors are opened by two halflings flanking a vampire. The vampire is a thirty-something statuesque woman with fair skin and strawberry blonde hair tied in an elaborate chignon. Her eyes, as every vampires are, are crimson. She strides in, dressed in a powder-blue pantsuit with wide legs and a tapered waist. Her heels click determinedly as the two slight halflings hurry behind her.

Sonya Deveraux takes her seat at the smaller table, while Everett Kwon—dark of hair and eye—takes on her right and Liam Holden—sandy waves and seafoam gaze—sits on her left.

"Apologies for the delay," Sonya says in a disciplined voice. "Travel was difficult. Please, begin with the meeting."

Sonya crosses her hands over her desk and sits primly. Her attention focused on us.

Damian side-eyes her but trains his gaze on Emrys. "Your Majesty, please inform us of why you called upon us."

Emrys places a hand on his mid-section over his black and gold blouse. "It has recently come to my attention that some of your delegates have been working with the Winter Carnaval and selling secrets to the Unseelie Court."

Damian raises a brow. "That is a severe accusation."

"And yet it is the truth."

Damian cannot challenge this as the fae cannot lie.

"Do you have the names of these delegates?" Blaine inquires.

"I do," Emrys stares into the eyes of the other fae. "Representatives Philomena Trinity and Theine Volo."

All heads swing to the faeries in question. Both of them have burning rage, mortification, and terror written across their faces.

"How do you answer for these accusations?" Blaine interrogates. "Have either of you been working with the Winter Carnaval or selling the Unseelie Court information?"

They do not speak.

Blaine hisses. "It is a simple yes or no question."

Both faeries remain silent. Seething in their pure white garb.

"I demand your answer."

Philomena bites her lip with those sharp teeth, drawing blood. "Yes. I did. I sold information to my founding court."

"That is grounds for termination and banishment, you understand this?" Blaine asks.

Philomena lifts her chin. "I do. But I did not act alone. And neither did Theine." Philomena's eerie doll eyes swivel to Damian. "Our vampire representative has been working with Joseph Harrow and their connection to the Carnaval."

Blaine's jaw drops and several gasps go up about the room. "Joseph Harrow is a sworn enemy of both the House Council and Arcana Society."

Damian's lip curls and his fingertips dig into the desktop. "He shouldn't be. He's a genius."

"He's a self-righteous ego maniac, not to mention inhumane, immoral, and overall, a disease to all!" Carmella Goldwine, the witch representative fires back. Her golden eyes are blazing with her ire. "You are a traitor to the haven, society, and world as we know it. I call for immediate dismissal and banishment of Damian Harper-Contas, Philomena Trinity, and Theine Volo."

Arguments break out. Shouts rise in the room, defenses and accusations flying like knives and shields. Bitter words spit poisonously, threats of blackmail thrown out like darts. It rises to a cacophony and I simply watch and wait, Emrys and I seeing and assessing through each other's eyes.

I take in Carmella Goldwine, easily the youngest representative on the Council. She's perhaps twenty with flawless golden-brown skin and gorgeously sloping features that indicate a Middle Eastern or Indian background.

The young witch stands and plants her hands on the table top. Her thick fall of ebony hair cascading down her back is a stark contrast to the blinding white robes she wears.

"I vote to remove the corruption from this government."

"That is half our number!" Theine argues.

"Then it is clear that half of this government must be dealt with." Carmella snaps her fingers. "Guards! Escort the three traitors out and place them in holding cells."

I balk at the commanding air this young witch displays and am equally more impressed when the guards follow her orders. White garbed figures peel themselves off the walls and then come to the two faeries and vampire, staring meaningfully. There's a hush as I see the three mentally debate the odds, but then acquiesce to the commands.

187

They leave without much ceremony, their empty seats made painfully clear. The doors shut softly behind them, leaving the rest of us in the wake of their duplicity.

The halfling representative rubs his temples. He appears young as all halflings do, but his eyes are tired, belying his age is many times what his youth implies.

"We cannot function with half a governing body."

Carmella has since taken her seat again, but now she is leaning back—casual and nonchalant. "Then admit interim delegates." Carmella eyes our party. "I see many Seelies, a vampire, and a human amongst those gathered. Perhaps we can temporarily instate some of their party."

"They are not removed from the subject at hand," the werewolf representative—Jonathan Clay—inserts.

"Yes, well neither were fifty percent of your former Council," Emrys interjects. "And after you hear the rest of our petition it will not matter because you will be obligated to offer us aid—as will the Arcana Society."

Carmella points to Violante, Julia, and Bleddyn. "You three will take temporary seats. Come. Be sworn in."

CHAPTER 19

The three are sworn in, Julia—the singular human—stepping in for the Unseelie representative role. Their dominant hands are held aloft as they swear a temporary binding, one threaded with fae magic, declaring their current positions are to be held only until a replacement can be found and until such time their assistance is no longer needed. There is also an addendum for our party, considering they're fighting for the Light Court and it is taken into account.

Afterward, Emrys and I fill in the House Council and Arcana Society to the Winter Carnaval and Vampire Court's machinations—how they've been aiding the Unseelie Court and how there is to be a marriage alliance in direct opposition to promises from the Dark. The Winter Carnaval is a sworn enemy of the supernatural governing world, as is the Vampire Court, so any sort of promises to them are held as treason. It takes little evidence at this time to prove our side and the Unseelie Court's disloyalty. In the end, the House Council and Arcana Society are both obligated to fight for us.

"The House Council formally accepts the obligation to assist the Seelie Court in the current political climate," the halfling delegate declares.

"The Arcana Society formally accepts their responsibility and oath to the Light Court," Sonya Deveraux announces. "We are now in alliance."

We all sign on a contract produced by the dark-haired receptionist in black ink. It is bound in blood and sworn with magic. Just as all the signatures are laid to rest, Emrys and I look at each other in alarm at new presences as an explosion blows out the windows.

Vampires and Unseelies descend upon the meeting and within seconds the white clothed guards are splattered with blood. Many of them are taken out before we have a chance to react. Crimson paints the sleek surfaces and starched clothing like a macabre scene, slashes of scarlet and spatters of ruby erupting from throats and chests.

Everyone in our party attacks with vigor, fighting back the attacking forces. We hadn't brought a large arsenal, but we did bring basic weaponry. I take Oath-Sworn and Emrys takes Heart's-Desire and together we cut a swath through the invaders. We work in tandem, natural in our grace and power. Emrys and I know how the other fights, we know how to move together in every way. He is my equal, my mirror, and we eliminate all that come our way.

Aveda and Maelona work back-to-back, both wielding moon scythes, Baphet powers through with all the rage of a bull, Bleddyn is a honed blade against the tide, Enydd is ruthless with her urumi. At the back, Violante, Julia, and Wisteria fend off the stragglers that make it past us, taking on fewer targets but still holding their own. Wisteria's eyes have changed to that of the Fairwalker healer.

We are not fast enough when a faerie with goat horns tears out the jugular of the halfling representative. He immediately exsanguinates and dies at his post.

The werewolf representative has transformed into a large, hulking black wolf with the same green eyes he possessed in his human form. He tears through vampires—his natural sworn enemy—with a ruthlessness that describes pent up frustrations and bottled rage. Limbs fly and dark blood spurts, mixing with the lively crimson of the rest.

Carmella is casting offensive spells while holding up a shield of golden light, a bubble keeping her safe and untouchable as she fends off her attackers. Sonya and her two halflings hide behind her. A group of vampires swarms her and Carmella arcs out with a knife-like spell that severs three throats with the cut of her arm. She continues these Latin incantations, killing and maiming with her magic.

The battle continues, fallen guards and bodies littering the ground. Our party sustains few losses, those of the nameless guard, but with a heart-wrenching yelp, we lose Jonathan to the remaining horde of vampires. We finish off the last of the Unseelies and vampires, the last body falling to Aveda and

Maelona. The two of them lock eyes, breaths heaving as the corpse is cast aside.

Emrys and I look at each other in abject horror, crimson masking our features.

The representatives sold us out.

The thick, coppery tang of blood scents the air, the fog of death hanging over it all like a black shroud. Night air tinged by glaciers and snow whispers through the ruined windows, the breeze doing so little to penetrate the dense atmosphere. Everything that was once pristine white is now desolate and destroyed.

I turn to stare at Carmella, the last remaining member of the House Council. She meets my eyes and her golden gaze is grave as I see her come to the same conclusion. That she is the last and the others completely betrayed her. She seems to process it quickly and then gathers herself.

"The House Council will still honor the promise we gave and we will seek vengeance for this attack this day," Carmella declares with a ferocious tone. "I will ensure Damian's, Theine's, and Philomena's executions are prompt."

"We thank you," Emrys says softly. "Please let us know if you need anything from the Seelie Court."

"I will."

We linger awhile before leave—taking Violante, Julia, and Bleddyn with us—in silence and covered in blood. There is little we can do, but we do call for additional resources, and once they're secure and on the way, we depart.

At the court, I command Baphet to send a formal war notice to Caethes, informing her of the consequences of her alliances and that the House Council and Arcana Society are now officially fighting against them. I do not inform her of the Winter Carnaval's inability to attack the Light Court. I'd rather keep that advantage close for now, and if she learns the hand by verbal channels, so be it, but I will not be the one to bestow the knowledge upon her.

The vampires tonight were not those affiliated with the Winter Carnaval, if they were, they would not have been able to touch or attack any of the Seelie Court.

My nerves are becoming unnumbed after the attack and with every passing second, anxiety rises. Before we do anything else, Emrys and I bathe, washing off the battle and blood, scrubbing beneath our fingernails and through our hair. Once we're clean, we head for a council room and summon a small meal. We eat and then Emrys and I summon Aveda for a meeting.

We've been putting off this discussion for as long as possible, but the time has come. We hold it in our regular council chamber with tea. I run a hand over my forehead as we wait for her, staring at the curling steam rising from the teacups set before my husband and I. Emrys covers my free hand with his, massaging small circles there.

Aveda arrives, dressed in clean black leathers, her wings folded against her back, black and white hair tied in two braids. She does not sit, but she does pour herself a cup of the tea and adds two sugars and some milk.

"Evelyn, Emrys, lovely to see you again."

The Admiral still withholds our honorifics, and despite the fact that I don't enjoy being called by the royal terms, I bite my tongue at her lack thereof simply because of disdain.

Aveda sips her tea and stares at us over the lip of the cup.

"We called you here to discuss the stipulations of your loyalty to us," Emrys begins.

Aveda raises a brow but doesn't rebuke him.

"There have been some changes regarding our stance with the Winter Carnaval."

193

"You're drawing this out."

Emrys sighs. "There are no current plans to attack the Winter Carnaval, however, we would like you to head any such plans."

"What changed? The attack?"

"The timeline."

"In what manner? You are still hesitating."

"We cannot touch the Winter Carnaval for ten years," I cut in.

Aveda freezes. "Ten years?"

"Yes."

"Ten fucking years?"

"That is correct."

"Why?"

I look over at Emrys nervously. "It was the blood oath. To get him out of their clutches as he gained intel. It's how we were able to gain allies of the House Council and Arcana Society."

Aveda's cup clatters against the table. "You knew this was the one thing!"

"I know," I say shamefully. "But we are promising it to you now, with all the resources and backing of the Seelie Court."

"A pathetic promise," Aveda spits.

"I understand the implications of this now. I hope you do, too."

Aveda narrows her eyes and her wings flare—a stab of jealousy and loss goes through me. "Is that a threat?"

"No, it's a natural recourse to the situation at hand."

There is silence between the three of us.

"You two have been fucking up every battle and political maneuver in your already very short rule. You have lost so many denizens to Caethes, whether that be defecting or dying. Your failure is only going to encourage more."

"The courts have never been at war like this in our lifetime," I argue back. "The Unseelie have been our enemies for millennia, but it has been centuries since we've been in a conflict like this."

"That does not excuse poor rulership."

"We came into these crowns when the courts were already at war. Do not blame us for a war the Aneira allowed."

"And who announced that war?"

Guilt strikes me like a bright red arrow. "I may have declared it, but I was not the—" I stop, suddenly unable to speak.

"The catalyst? Is that what you were going to say? But you can't, because you are. You are the one who tricked Caethes with that halfling. And even so, your return as the Harbinger would have done it. You are the one who let it happen. This is *your* fault."

Anger and shame flood me in a noxious combination. My supper sits in my belly like a lead block. I swallow.

"The war is a necessary evil."

"Is it?" Aveda challenges. "Or was it your hurt ego?"

I don't tell her that it was the former love I held for Gideon that ushered in my hasty decision, but Emrys knows, he reads it through the bond. Even if it wasn't Gideon, Aveda is right. Aneira would have sought revenge for my abduction. Caethes hired Jacob to take the Harbinger. We'd be in the exact same place, only with shifted blame.

"These decisions are not made easily," Emrys says softly. "Aveda, we are trying. We want your help. We want to give you the Winter Carnaval mission."

Aveda's nostrils flare. "Your trying is not enough."

195

"I know," Emrys allows. "So, what do you suggest we do?"

The Admiral is thrown for a loop but composes herself quickly. "Ask Maelona, she'd be the better ruler."

And with that Aveda leaves us with her clicking heels and slamming door.

CHAPTER 20

"No."

"What do you mean '*no*'?" I demand.

Maelona crosses her arms over her chest and stares us down. We'd summoned her to the council room after Aveda's departing, informing her of the Admiral's barb. The warrior princess's eyes are hard, her hair flickering indistinctly.

"I mean no. I don't care what Aveda says, you may not be asking me now, but I am telling you that I am not taking your crown. You can make me heir apparent, but you are not stepping down."

"Why not?" I counter hotly. "We clearly don't know how to rule. We've been fucking everything up."

"You don't think anyone else would do the same? Caethes has been ruling for hundreds of years, she knows the ins and outs. You do not yet, but you'll learn."

"I could make it an official royal decree."

"But you won't."

I bite my tongue because she isn't wrong.

"We need to do something else," she says, changing topics. "We need to make a point. An attack."

"On the Unseelie Court?"

"No, that's too obvious, Caethes will expect it." She tips her head to Emrys. "How much intel did you learn at the Vampire Court?"

"Plenty," he answers.

"Use it to attack Joseph then. Hurt Caethes's allies."

An idea strikes me. To hit Caethes where it hurts. Emrys follows this train of thought and I feel his dubious reaction, but then he follows the path to the end destination and realizes. Promptly, he agrees.

"Mae, can you organize an attack with Baphet and Enydd to minimize the vampire forces? Plan an attack in broad daylight for our advantage." I drum my fingers on the table. "We need to speak to Julia next."

Maelona rushes off to commandeer Baphet's and Enydd's attention, the lady eager and resourceful. We flag down a servant and ask him to find and deliver Julia to us. He takes off and we wait.

"Are you sure pulling Gideon out now is the best course of action?" Emrys asks.

"I think he's done as much as we can ask of him right now. Things are escalating and the solstice is drawing near. What if Caethes decides to still go through with killing him? Especially since she plans to get married that same day?"

Caethes had sworn to end Gideon's life by the summer solstice—which is rapidly approaching. Once upon a time the concept of Gideon's death was unfathomable, like it was the end of the world. Now...I don't particularly want to see him dead, but my heart doesn't cry out like it once did. I would feel immeasurable guilt, especially knowing I could have prevented it. Keeping him in the Unseelie Court at this point is a punishment and Caethes's rage knows no bounds. I don't want her taking her wrath out on Gideon. Particularly since she'll just use him and his heart—literally—as a pawn once she has Joseph Harrow in her bed.

"She could," Emrys admits reluctantly.

"He's also one of our pieces."

The King piece of Lady Fate's board. How it's possible, I do not know. It makes little sense to me.

All those you have ever loved will die.

I shove that cynical and cryptic voice from my mind.

I may have loved Gideon once, but I refuse to allow that prophecy to sink its talons into him. He should be safe, untouchable by the disdain of my heart.

Julia arrives and I shake myself free of the mental fugue. There is concern and pleading on her face. I don't even get a chance to begin before Julia is rushing out with a torrent of words.

"Please, you have to save him. You have to get him out of there." There's a thin cry to her voice and I raise my brow. She continues passionately. "Gideon can't stay at the Unseelie

Court anymore, Caethes is pissed you guys survived the House Council attack. She killed three of her courtiers and two human servants in response. It's only a matter of time before she turns on Gideon."

Emrys and I lock eyes and understanding cements between us. We truly do need to pull Gideon now, there's no question about it. If Caethes is willing to decimate her own forces, ending the lives of her closest denizens, then the slight protective factors that I imagined Gideon had are as corporeal as smoke.

There must be strict rules in place, Emrys murmurs in my mind. *He must essentially be under lock and key until decisions are properly made.*

We can bind him.

I feel his nod internally. *I will forge a blood oath.*

We will house him with his father, there is plenty of room in that suite. It will also serve as a reminder to keep him in line.

Agreed.

Emrys and I turn to Julia, poised formally. I clear my throat before speaking. "We will remove Gideon from the Unseelie Court."

Julia is stunned, her blue-gold eyes blinking fast. "Really?"

"Yes. We will send a rescue effort during an underlying mission. It will be a distraction and an opportunity. Please let Gideon know as discreetly and quickly as possible. Tell him not to act any different, but be ready soon."

The human girl nods quickly. "Yes, of course. Thank you, Evelyn. Truly, thank you so much."

Her thanks strikes a nervous cord in me but I dip my head in acknowledgement. "You're welcome."

"That's not all," I continue.

"Oh?" she asks, confused.

"Do you trust your Crows enough to lead a classified mission?"

She hesitates only a breath. "Only the ones I've had since last year."

"Rachel and Lorelai?" She nods, and I continue. "Tell them to gather up a team of five and then I want them to rescue Natalia Zhao. I will supply two Seelies who are familiar with the patrol. She will be kept in a safehouse far from here. I don't want Caethes discovering we had any hand in her disappearance, but we can't risk her near the Dark Court any longer. She's going to lash out, and Natalia does not deserve it."

"Of course. Thank you, Evelyn. Seriously—thank you."

I wave her off with a tinge of discomfort as we wrap up the meeting, and then Emrys and I return to our chambers. I'm sitting at the vanity, brushing out my long silvery locks, and he's tidying my mess of a desk.

"I'm pretty sure Julia and Gideon are together."

Emrys stops at my comment, pausing and looking up. "Oh?"

"Mmhmm," I say distractedly. "She already told me she has feelings for him, but I sense those feelings go both ways."

Emrys slowly sidles up to me, and I see his reflection draw near in the mirror. "And how does that make you feel?"

I shrug as my husband's hand comes to glide around my throat, tipping my head back. His lips graze the sensitive spot below my ear. I bite my lip and my eyes roll back. He draws a hot kiss there and then suckles gently.

"Do you miss him?" He punctuates this with a nip.

Fiery pleasure bolts through me. "No."

"Not even a little?"

"Not even the slightest," I rasp as his teeth draw a love bite on my throat.

"Good. I don't wish to speak of him anymore. I don't want you to think his name. I want you to forget every name but *mine*."

Suddenly, Emrys is hauling me off the stool and setting my ass on the edge of the vanity. His mouth captures mine with such decadent heat that I moan against his lips. He plunders with his tongue, tracing the shape, while his hands go to the hem of my shirt, tearing it from me. He pauses only to pull the shirt over my head and then continues his divine torment. My hands scramble against his pants as his own find my waistband. We're eagerly shucking off each other's bottoms, and as he steps out of his, he lifts me so he can yank them down my legs. My core is flush with him, my wetness painting against his skin. I manage his shirt off just as he finishes divesting me of my leggings.

"I need you," he rasps against me.

"I need you, too."

His hands go to my hips and I feel the head of his cock against my slicked entrance as he tilts me just so. I shift my hips closer as he slowly inches into me. I throw my head back as I feel his length enter me—filling me, stretching me so perfectly. He thrusts shallowly, letting my pussy take him—soaking him, sucking him. He groans low in his throat as I roll my hips with his movement, hooking my heels into his backside.

Emrys sinks fully into me, grinding his hips into my pelvis, my clit receiving glorious friction as I crest my hips to the wave of our tempo. We find a devastating rhythm, working with each other, seeking the sensation and touch and desire of the other.

All I smell is sex and vetiver, yearning and ginseng, leather, lemon, love, and honey. I am drowning in it and I wish to never resurface.

His hands hold my ass and I use him as leverage, planting my hands as far back on the vanity as I can, baring all to him. My soulmate dips down to my chest, and laves his tongue between my breasts, dragging his nose against my sensitized flesh and then over the curve of my breast. He nips the soft underside before moving to a nipple and capturing it with his mouth. He pulls it into the warm, wet heat of his mouth, flicking his tongue against it.

I moan, my filled pussy clenching around him as the first sparks of my orgasm begin to erupt. I feel him flex inside me as his own climax threatens on the edge. Our movements become frantic as he keeps mouthing my nipple, playing with it while fucking me. I fuck him back, my breaths rasping, mewls of pleasure slipping from my throat.

"My fucking queen," Emrys whispers against a hardened peak. "My insatiable little vixen. Come for me."

"*Emrys.*"

"Come, Vanna. Can you do that for me, love?"

It takes two more thrusts and stars explode behind my eyes. I choke on a cry of "fuck yes," and shatter on his cock, shuddering around him as my inner muscles pump him for his own orgasm. His climax meets mine a second later and we ride through it together, my delicate channel squeezing his dick as he fills me with his release. A groan of purely satisfied male meets my ears, his mouth pressed and muffled against my collarbone.

I run a hand through his silky garnet locks, fisting a hand at the nape of his neck.

"I never want you to forget that I love you," I tell him firmly.

"I won't," he promises.

I pray I never put him through that once lived nightmare again.

CHAPTER 21

"Are you ready for this?" Aveda asks, still slightly bitter from the Winter Carnaval faux pas. I just hope she remembers I allowed her to kill Draven.

"Absolutely," I return.

The Admiral and I stand with Emrys, Baphet, Enydd, Bleddyn, and other fae, preparing to descend on the Vampire Court. Maelona is notably absent, currently deployed on the mission to recover Gideon from Caethes's clutches with Julia. Wisteria was forced to stay back with Violante, as the young vampire wanted to help, but none of the missions were safe for her. In the end, her ego was assuaged when the witch suggested she stay with her. I'd met Wisteria's eye and mouthed a thank you, she'd mouthed back that I owed her. I smiled. I did.

We had fought with Enydd and Bleddyn when they proposed Emrys and I remain behind, not risking the crown for this mission. We'd argued against them, stating we needed to be active royals. That we couldn't be pampered and soft. We were trained and raised to be warriors; we couldn't be expected to set our blades down in favor of sitting on thrones. So, after much back and forth—and on the condition of keeping a large guard—they acquiesced to our demands and Emrys and I were involved in the mission.

I'd claimed that Maelona would hold the court in our stead—and she did, if only for a couple minutes—but in actuality, we'd left Wisteria in charge of the Seelie Court.

It's broad daylight, a little after noon, and we stand at the gates of Joseph Harrow's estate—a massive gothic monstrosity in the middle of some North American woods. The gates are black wrought iron, topped with sharp spindles and designed with roses. Briars snarl just inside the fence-line, choked with fat, red roses and scythe-like thorns. The manor house is separated from the gate by a dark gravel drive, the structure of the building stoic gray stone. The windows are all tinted and UV treated, trapped by decorative—and functional—bars to prevent breakage and sunlight attacks. The Vampire Court has wings and courtyards, gardens and fountains, ascending four floors and widely imposing, it is ironically, positively vampiric.

Halflings patrol the grounds, dressed in slate gray, and carrying sleek black guns. It's a jolt to see supernaturals using firearms. Typically, we adhere to blades and bows and the like, as wards and other magic interfere with the firing mechanisms of guns. I suppose Joseph is taking his chances.

Courtesy of a King and Queen's Glamour, we are hidden from sight. I ensure we are all covered and then I nod to Bleddyn who begins to dismantle the wards. We breach the wards with witch-made amulets and fae blood, the action alerting the vampires, but damaging the magic anyway. We cross the lawn, racing on sure feet to the many entrances of Joseph Harrow's home.

The halflings turn to us and open fire despite not being able to see us. We fan out, making ourselves a more sporadic target, only two bullets finding any of our party—neither fatal. We collide with the halfling guards and dispatch them in seconds—surely, they activated some sort of silent alarm—and bust in the doors. A hail of bullets rings out with sharp cracks, the scent of gunpowder thick in the air.

Our forces erupt into the gray stone and crimson carpeted foyer, sliding across black marble floors as we disarm more halflings and terminate them with their own weapons. We steal their guns and fire around corners, taking out waking vampires.

Crimson puddles shine against the lacquered floor, reflecting our carnage back at us.

A rush goes through me, a thrill at the fight. My blood burns with the adrenaline rush, the urge and thrill of fulfilling a power I've always claimed. I feel an echo of the same feeling in Emrys, my husband taking up an abandoned handgun, a blade in his other hand. This is what we were designed for, not sitting on an overgrown magical tree chair and letting someone else do this work for us.

We can rule and fight. We can be warrior sovereigns. There is no rule that states we cannot wield blades and wear crowns.

Suddenly, the idea of our future unfurls within me. A king and queen who fights for their people, side by side, crowns on brows and swords held aloft. In this fantasy, the three children I'd imagined are there—the most important things we fight for.

I blink. Is this truly our destiny? My heart squeezes at the want.

Emrys is too busy fighting to linger on my thoughts and I throw myself back into the attack.

We cut our way through the manor until we find ourselves in a veritable throne room. It is done up in a mockery of an ancient Greek style. Columns and pillars are bastardized in shades of onyx and ebony, dark marble spanning the space, statues of vampires feeding on and fucking humans carved like Michelangelo's. Red mars the space like the splashes of blood we bring, a ruby encrusted throne sits on a dais, deep crimson carpet heralding it like a flood of arterial spray.

Joseph Harrow is certainly one for theatrics.

The king himself is nowhere to be seen, the throne room empty of all save our attacking forces and the halfling guards pouring in through all the entrances. A few vampires have woken from slumber, groggy, yet feral with their red eyes and violent in their attack. We renew our attempts and decimate Joseph Harrow's court.

The time passes in blurs and lulls, cutting and firing, stabbing and shooting. We take on the flood of Joseph's vampiric followers until the flow stops and their blood runs cold on the floor. In the end we stop and take in our surroundings. The devastation. I see a final vampire, terrified and meek peering out from behind a column.

"Where is the king?" I demand.

"With the Unseelie Queen."

Of course.

I shake my head free of the thought and change direction.

"Tell Joseph we've repaid his kindness at our coronation," I call out. "Tell him the Seelie Court sends their regards."

The vampire nods hastily and then takes off through an open corridor.

I look at my husband and I see a light in his eyes, like a frenzy, a high from bloodlust. It is reminiscent of the look the Unseelies get when they receive a taste of chaos. I grin because I know I have it too.

Emrys turns away and addresses the rest of our group. "I want them to know it was us. Ensure there is no question that the Seelie Court does not take an affront lightly. The Gwyndolyn-Vanora rule will not be underestimated."

CHAPTER 22

Our group disperses and we leave the Vampire Court in all its death and desolation, returning to our own court. The Faerie Roads are a welcome reprieve from the bright and the blood of the vampires, the cool and cocooned atmosphere of the false earthen tunnels like a balm against our battle-roughened skin. The Seelie Court is home.

Once we wash and redress for the evening, a meal is prepared for all those who'd followed us to the Vampire Court, those that traveled to rescue Gideon, those that saved Natalia, and those who held down the Court in our absence.

Dinner is roasted chicken with honey and fig, rosemary potatoes, a salad topped with roasted pine nuts, goat cheese, and a blackberry dressing, carrots glazed with brown sugar, and fresh rolls. It is devoured, however, in a primly fashion. Gold wine is served and a flash of longing goes through me. Emrys cups my hand and soothes me through the itch, pouring us both non-alcoholic, sparkling pear juice. I drink it down gratefully, thanking my husband internally. He kisses my wrist and holds me with his topaz eyes.

I am with you every step of the way. I swore it in our marriage vows; I am with you through every struggle, Emrys murmurs through the bond.

And I, with you, I declare.

Halfway through the meal Maelona and Julia arrive with Gideon in tow. All three of them are completely unscathed. They pause in the doorway of the dining hall, taking in the scene. We urge them to take seats.

Emrys stands. "Come, sit, eat!"

I watch Gideon step inside the space hesitantly, and it occurs to me that the last time he was in this room having a meal was when we'd just arrived in the Seelie Court. When we discovered my true identity as the Harbinger. When I'd revealed Corvina as the Seelie who'd died in our arms. I see him realize this, too. His amber eyes darken with memory and flicker to me, a wordless conversation spoken between us. I give him a non-committal response and allow my husband to be privy to all.

Gideon takes a seat near the end beside Julia, and across from Aveda. Beside the Admiral is Lady Maelona.

Immediately, the two faeries are ensconced in conversation, relaying their opposing missions to the other, regaling with the tale. I watch, surprised and curious as Maelona's hair shimmers ever so slightly pink.

The warrior princess is interested in the spy.

Aveda seems just as charmed, captivated by Maelona's melodic voice, her dark eyes trained on her. Like tracking prey. Like watching a shooting star. Like infatuation. It's intensity.

I cock a brow and turn to Emrys. My husband does not miss Mae's rosy hue and Aveda's focus, and hides his smile behind his glass.

I wonder how the two have known each other so long— that I've known them so long—and a romance has never bloomed between them. Was I ever in the way of that? Aveda is notoriously monogamous. Did she not want to compete against the casual relationship I held with the Lady? Or have they been involved and I have just never noticed?

The dinner is met with companionable silence, the slight scrape of cutlery against porcelain, the slight tings of glassware moved, murmurs of conversation. The scent of all the delicious food fills the space with a drool-inducing aroma, and from the distance I detect a chocolate smell for dessert.

"Have you given much thought to the Solstice Celebration?" Enydd suddenly asks from two seats down from me.

I turn toward her, surprise written across my face, fork paused in hand. "Not really, no."

"The first solstice during a Seelie's rule is the most powerful. Solstices are the highest magic point for Seelies while equinoxes are the Unseelie's equivalent. This solstice is your first as king and queen, it should be a large event."

"If you haven't noticed, Enydd, we're at war."

"And?" the former mentor asks with a cocked brow.

"Ask for a ceasefire."

"For a party?" I reply dubiously.

"For a solstice. For one night. Unseelies already receive great power during the seasonal transference, the Dark Queen would be foolish to pass it up herself. She'll want the charge, too. Especially since she plans to wed that day."

"Why is our first so special?"

"Because right now you have all the power of the Seelie Court, but have never been charged by a solstice. As the season wanes to an equinox, you begin to lose that extra bolster, but the court retains the overflow. What remains infuses with you until the next. Until you encounter a solstice, you are not operating with the full potential of this court."

Emrys is frozen, taking in Enydd. "Are you saying that once the solstice occurs, we'll be even more powerful?" The emotion that is running through Emrys right now is not greed, it is awe and a little fear.

"That is exactly what I'm saying."

"What sort of celebration do you recommend?" I query, popping a goat cheese and pine nut bit of salad into my mouth.

"A revel would encourage the rawest amount of power."

My brows rise. I cannot recall the last time the Seelie Court held a revel. Revels are full of decadence and debauchery. Music and dancing, drinking and feasting, playing and fucking. It is all the mythos of fae celebration with all the splendor and none of the horror. Seelie revels do not encourage torment of humans the way Unseelie ones do. Though trickery is encouraged and even prized.

"I can't see Caethes agreeing to that," Emrys says.

"I can," Gideon interjects quietly. "She can touch Arawn then." Gideon pauses, a blush coloring his face when he realizes everyone is staring at him. He clears his throat. "She ignores everyone on full moons when she can physically be with him. Solstices and equinoxes afford the same ability. That, mixed with the power will be something she can't resist."

Will Caethes take both Arawn and Joseph on her wedding night?

I instantly push every thought of that idea from my mind.

Emrys is more startled, but I watch his thoughts play out, theories and intrusive thoughts filtering through. I stare hard and flat at Gideon, pushing through my husband's mental deluge, and then gather myself. I nod. "We shall make the request then."

It's odd to see my former lover and eternal love communicate like this. Rather, it's odd to see them converse at all. There's something distinctly different about Maelona and Emrys talking. Perhaps it's the lack of bitterness and betrayal, or maybe it's because I never loved Maeloa romantically—not truly—and our friendship was always first. That was not the case with Gideon, and everything revolving around Emrys is so much more complex.

Gideon thins his lips in acknowledgement and then returns to his meal.

Shortly after, dessert is served, a moist chocolate cake, fruit tartlets, and caramelized apple blossoms. I have no reservations and I take a portion of each. Emrys smiles at me delighted and through the bond I sense his pleasure over my appetite. It hasn't been something I've acknowledged, but my lack of hunger has been on his mind, and it's been worry enough, but not enough to tip the scales on the war front worries.

Everyone finishes the food and servants clear the plates. After dinner, drinks are served and I refuse all offered liquor, opting for water. Emrys does the same. I try not to react to the surge of pain and nostalgia when I see Gideon accept a tumbler of whiskey.

We'd shared an amber bottle the night Corvina died.

The thought sours in my gut and I have to bite down on my pain, grinding my teeth, as Emrys's hand comes to grip mine. Always. His presence is a constant. The brief distance between us when he fulfilled the heart's desire command is still an ache, dull, but there nonetheless.

Conversation flows naturally among our dinner guests but Emrys and I keep ourselves apart, somewhat reserved and separated. Eventually, the talk dies down and our allies disperse. Emrys and I take our leave, and in our chambers, I respond to Carmella Goldwine's confirmation that the executions have taken place, query into Bambalina's current whereabouts, and pen a letter to Caethes.

Taking heed of Enydd's advice, I write to the Unseelie Queen requesting a temporary ceasefire for the duration of the solstice for both of our court's benefits. I try to remove the antagonistic air I typically summon in ink for her, and instead try for a pragmatic angle. I pray it's enough as I sign it with the Seelie Court's official sigil and my own personal one.

I send it away and then prepare for bed, dressing in silk loungewear of Seelie emerald and a robe. My hair is carefully brushed out and free flowing around my shoulders and down my back. My husband's eyes track the cascade of silver as he reclines on the bed, shirtless and clad in black pajama pants. His dark red hair is tousled and careless, begging for my hands to run through it. Every taut line of his body looks delicious and all I want to do is take my tongue to every crease and ridge, to bite the sharp jut of his hipbone, to trace the cut of his abdominals with my lips. His golden eyes heat with desire as my silver ones darken with lust.

As I advance purposefully toward him, a knock sounds at the door.

The presence behind it is distinctly fae and I handle a dagger just as I open the door, prepared to use it. It's a servant, clearly anxious, and bearing a note.

I take the paper and read it.

I accept a meeting of negotiations. Meet me now, dressed as you are, I am waiting in your library.

Caethes.

CHAPTER 23

The library is warm with the pre-summer heat. The courts may reside in bubble realms, but to a degree they are still vulnerable to the whims of the seasons. It's dark outside through the stained glass windows, yet the golden light from the candelabras offer plenty to see by. In one of the armchairs by the empty fireplace is the Unseelie Queen.

Caethes sits primly, hands folded in her lap, dressed in Unseelie violet. She wears a satin slip beneath a crushed velvet robe. Her feet are clad in dainty slippers, and her head is uncrowned. Her antlers are free of the adornment that usually bejewel them, and their pale, hoary glory is revealed—with the still broken tine from the lottery massacre.

I approach slowly on my own slipper-clad feet, taking the seat directly across from her. As Caethes formally accepted my request, no harm can befall either of us for the duration of this meeting from the other. Though our locked heir and ascension laws prohibit that anyway.

Leaving the bond completely open, I allow Emrys to see all. His anxieties bleed into me and I erect a thin shield between us, blocking his emotions from me during this meeting. If he really needed, he could break down the barrier, but as it sits currently, it serves our interests.

"I called for tea," Caethes begins plainly, a slight note of distaste in her voice. It's softer than her usual, but nothing that'll put someone at ease. "Your servants are absolutely skittish."

"Did you threaten them?"

Caethes waves off my question. "Servants are meant to be subservient. You should be able to say what you please to them."

"And evidently kill them when the mood arises?"

"If that is what a queen commands, then yes."

"How have you managed to run a court this long when that is your attitude?"

Caethes leans forward, a feral gleam in her ultra-black eyes as she grins wickedly. "Through fear."

"That doesn't seem conducive to loyalty."

"I have bought loyalty through terror and force of will."

Right, because she has demanded heart's desire commands from all her subjects. Power. Control. Blackmail. Extortion. All of it effective. All of it heinous.

"How did you turn out so wrong?"

Just then a servant bearing a tea service arrives, hands trembling causing the saucers to clatter in their plates. The sound is sharp in our tense space, and we both stop as the servant deposits the tray on the low table between us.

"We can handle the rest from here, Mathilde," I tell the servant delicately. "Thank you."

She dips quickly and meekly, then disappears through the doors.

"That would never suit," Caethes says to herself as she gazes at the disappearing servant.

I roll my eyes and pour myself a cup of steaming tea.

"I was a slave," Caethes admits.

The revelation startles me and I spill a few drops of tea. I meet Caethes's black eyes and watch her for any cracks in her façade. She stares intently at me, not through me as if reliving her trauma, but at me, as if she wants me to feel her pain.

Emrys's surprise penetrates through the barrier, and I patch up the mental wall before shifting my attention solely on the Dark Queen.

"I was sold to men who used me as their plaything. I was forced into acts I never wanted—that I would never do. Eventually, I managed to find my way to men of greater power, and one by one I took them out, clawing my way out of that horror. I dragged myself from the pits of hell, and found myself in a king's bed. I realized how easy it would be to trick him into giving me his crown. And so, I did. And then I had him killed.

"I was once nothing, and then I became something fearsome. Something to be loathed. I gained a taste for blood and a knack for chaos. I was molded into what I am by the depravity of those who scorned and disdained me.

"*That* is where I turned out so wrong, Evelyn."

I can see the rage burning off her like a visceral thing, turning her silver bright. Her face is hard, cool marble, but her incandescent wrath is white-hot fire. It has been lifetimes since she was used so, but that sort of scar does not fade so easily.

"Are you not doing the same to your denizens?" I accuse.

"No," Caethes snaps firmly. "I do not take sexual encounters from those who are unwilling. All my lovers since have wanted what they received."

I remember once being told that Caethes was sensitive about the word slave and she had a specificity about sexual consent that did not match her penchant for murder.

"That is not what I meant, and you know it."

"Do I?" Caethes cocks a brow and sips her tea.

"You kill. You control. You take."

"And you do not?"

I'm taken aback by this accusation. "No."

"You did not kill Arawn? You did not control your people in attacks? You did not take Gideon or Henry Zhao?"

"You are manipulating the narrative."

"That is politics."

"We are not the same."

"We are more alike than you would ever dare to admit. We are related, after all."

I can't help myself. "Do you know how?"

Caethes inclines her head, flaring her nostrils as she inhales sharply. "I looked into it when it became clear you are my closest blood relation." She looks away. "Your mother—Drysi—was my much younger half-sister. Spawn from the same father."

My aunt.

I am Caethes's niece. She is my aunt. *That* is our blood connection.

I realize now Caethes had some sort of connection with both of my mothers.

"How long were you and Aneira romantically involved?"

Caethes's head swivels to me comically fast. Her large eyes widen. "We kept our past secret. Did she tell you?"

"No, I just guessed."

The Unseelie Queen looks down into her tea, getting her bearings. She is the only thing of purple decadence and cool silver in this Seelie space. Here, it is all warm golds and browns, rich viridians and hunter greens, stained glass, polished earth, hardwood. Motifs of chrysanthemums and crescent moons bedeck the space. Raw edge tables, shelves, and railings surround us. Gilded Seelie magic weaves within the room, the atmosphere suffused with its glow. There is no questioning that this is a Light Court structure. It does not hold the wild cliffside nights of the Unseelie Court—it is embracing earth and cozy burrows.

Caethes finally speaks.

"It was three centuries ago, and it was for several decades." *Decades.* "I was new to my reign and by that time Aneira had already solidified herself as a paragon of a queen. This horned and golden deity-like creature was the longest reigning monarch to ever grace either court. I was enamored by her. Utterly enraptured and captivated.

"I had so much hope for change back then. Aneira saw something in me, I suppose, a spark of goodness that was quickly crushed beneath the whims of the Dark Court. But she was so hopeful, and she saw potential in me.

Kayla McGrath

"We thought we would unite the courts—a feat never accomplished by any monarchs before us. We thought we were different." Caethes scoffs. "We weren't. We were the same as all the rest before us.

"Our advisors whispered in our ears. Sowed doubt. We were played against each other. Eventually we committed unforgivable sins against each other and no amount of pleading or explanations about extortion were enough to repair it. We were sullied, broken, ruined. Our hopes and fates were torn asunder, and we further poisoned ourselves to each other to the point that nothing remained of the people we once were. The people we loved. We were strangers to ourselves and each other. And yet, we looked exactly like we once did. For all eternity."

I don't know what to say to Caethes's declaration.

"I've never told anyone that," Caethes murmurs from behind her teacup. "It is nice for someone to know, even if that person is my enemy."

"So, you loved her?"

"Deeply," Caethes confirms. "And I've never loved anyone again."

I gaze into the unlit fireplace, tracing the gray stone with my eyes. "One of the mentors during Century Training desired me," I begin, opening up as Caethes did to me. "He tried to take by force what I would not give him, and made me to play along with a ruse—to pretend we maintained an intimate relationship. If I did not, he would kill Emrys because he knew I loved him. He thought if he couldn't have me, no one could. So, he orchestrated a plot for me to make an attempt of Emrys's life."

Caethes raises her brows.

222

"I loved Emrys for decades while he hated me. He truly thought I tried to kill him to prove my alleged attraction to Osian." The words taste bitter on my tongue.

"Did you ever want your mentor?"

"Never. I hated him."

"Did you kill him?"

"Yes."

"Good."

I almost want to laugh that we're not at each other's throats.

She eyes me. "Was he the one who killed Emrys?"

"He was."

Caethes twists her lips. "Then I am also glad you got vengeance." She pauses. "I should have known Emrys was Aneira's child. He looks like her—goddess, even when he had his wings, they looked like hers. But wings are not uncommon for the fae and I dismissed my theories and made him keep his peculiar abilities to himself. Anything that made him stand out in the wrong way I wanted gone. I wasn't going to risk him." She scoffs. "But I lost him anyway."

"I didn't know he was Aneira's either," I whisper betrayal from my chosen mother bleeding into my voice. "Not until the crown was thrown at him."

Caethes cocks a brow. "That is surprising."

There is silence between us and then Caethes speaks again.

"Do you still think we are truly so different?"

It occurs to me in a wild thought that we aren't, and that unsettles me deeply, In some twisted way, I can see her justification. Her vision of what is right and just and deserved. And that terrifies me.

It's also abundantly clear that to a degree we resemble one another. Pale hair, pale skin, the same slender build, the same height—minus the antlers—and something I'd never noticed before, we have the same mouth. The same full pout, the plush shape.

"It doesn't change anything."

"No," Caethes responds after a brief pause. "It does not. But I will accept a ceasefire for the solstice. For Aneira and what we once were. For my own selfish reasons."

"It's reason enough for me."

"Are you hosting a revel for the solstice?" Caethes asks, seemingly off tangent.

"We are."

"And it is your first since becoming monarchs?"

"It is."

Caethes lets out a harsh, barking cackle. "Oh, have fun with that one, Little Queen."

"What does that mean?"

"You'll find out." The Unseelie Queen finishes her tea, deposits the empty cup on the saucer, and stands, looking down at me. "It is settled. I still hate you, but I see you differently."

I stand and meet her abyssal eyes. "The feeling is mutual."

Once upon a time the might of Caethes's power terrified me, that the Dark Court Queen could weave her chaotic magic, and wield her horrible influence in a massive web, netting us all in her path. I feared to be taken down, drawn, wrapped up in it. To be wound into her spider's nest and feasted on when the mood struck her.

But I know differently now. And I know that I hold much of the same power as she does. She has the Unseelie Court's backing, but I have the Seelie Court and the Revenant. And that is more than the power we've crippled her of.

It has to be.

We trade brittle smiles, and then the Unseelie Queen leaves the Light Court. I stare after her as she vanishes, and breathe a sigh of relief. I let Emrys in and all of his anxieties flood through me and out of me, washing like the crash of waves on the surf. And then I'm left with his love and adoration, his belief and hope in me. His effervescent will and untamable determination.

He is something she will never have.

I soak in the feeling for a moment and then I return to my king, eager to perform wifely duties that I was so robbed of.

CHAPTER 24

Over the next few days we prep for the solstice. As it seems, Caethes has also let up on the attacks preceding the celebration. I'm mistrustful of her game, but I do not tempt fate or her ire by attacking first during this time.

Food is curated carefully, and drinks are selected to honor the solstice theme. Everything is golden and gilded, honoring dawn and dusk, a twilight transition to represent the exchange of power from the equinox to the solstice. From Unseelie to Seelie. Invitations are sent out and RSVP'd, tailors are hastily employed, jewels and cosmetics are obtained. Musicians audition, everything from cello to viola, harp and flute, keys and strings and horns. Most are fae but there are a few talented humans—who are paid handsomely and fairly, unlike the experience in the Unseelie Court.

Enydd finds Emrys and I in a council chamber after meeting with Commander Tirnoc who has been on battle lines thus far. Him and Baphet are now learning how to spearhead this war together. Enydd however, cares little for their bitter squabbles and easily puts them in place. Perhaps they listen because of her ancient age—it is a number I haven't dared calculate, nor ask, but I know it is great, and she is the oldest living fae I know. But is she truly living? From my understanding she is standing on borrowed time gifted by Lady Fate.

The eldest faerie crosses her arms in her olive gown, the draping sleeves hanging past her waist. She leans against the wall, assessing us with her censorious plum eyes.

"Have you two prepared for the Rite, yet?"

Emrys and I glance at each other in confusion. He speaks first. "What is that?"

Enydd cocks a dark brow. "You have not heard of it?"

"Should we have?"

"Oh, goddess." Enydd sighs. "The Rite is a performance displayed by rulers of a court with consorts or spouses to start off the festivities. After the ceremony, you two are to participate in a public coupling before the rest of the couples are encouraged to take to copulating in secret and then return to dancing. These unions will take place at various points throughout the night."

I blink rapidly. "When you say 'coupling' do you mean fucking?"

"Yes."

My husband and I stare at each other in shock. How have we never heard of this Rite before? It does occur to me that neither queen has had an official consort, nor spouse of any sort during their reign in our lifetime. But surely it would have been mentioned in passing at some point? How long had it been since Aneira had had a lover? Emrys's father? Even then, that pairing was a brief, secret thing, and so was her subsequent pregnancy.

"Is it too late to cancel the revel?" I ask, already knowing the answer.

Enydd looks at me drolly. "Do you know the amount of times I caught you two during Century Training and never said anything? Or how you seem to have no qualms about finishing before attending balls?"

My face colors. I don't even have to look at my soulmate to see him having a similar reaction. The same mortification bleeds through the bond.

"I assure you, you two will be fine. Most couples pair off before the climax. And after having heard of your performance to gain entry to the Winter Carnaval, I think you will be just fine."

The memory of the Prague club draws heat into my face for altogether a different reason. Maelona, Emrys, and I entered a private sex club under the guise of participation to receive an invitation to the Winter Carnaval. There, the three of us pretended to lapse into intimate touches, and it became clear very quickly that Emrys and I were not pretending and he took me to completion right there in the scarlet booth in front of everyone.

The thought of the lewd act of voyeuristic pursuits sends a thrill through my body and slickens my core. Emrys immediately reacts to the new wetness between my legs, sensing it through the bond and by scent, and his eyes darken in response.

"Stop that," Enydd says, slapping Emrys upside the head like she did all those years ago during Century Training. "I know you are thinking it, but I do not wish to see it play out."

"You're the one who suggested the solstice celebration," Emrys accuses.

"For the power transference, not for the free pornography."

"Seems like a two-for-one special."

Enydd smacks him again.

"So, we're leading our first orgy," I ponder aloud. "This should be fun."

"It is not an orgy," Enydd argues.

"For all intents and purposes, it certainly seems so."

Enydd sighs in vexation, utterly fed up with our bullshit. She murmurs to herself—or maybe to the goddess. "Why did I agree to come back?"

"Because you adore us and find our company absolutely spectacular."

She gives me an exasperated look but does not rebuke my statement.

"So aside from the orgy, is there anything else you need to speak to us about?" Emrys inquires.

"No," Enydd says after another sigh. "You're free for the rest of the evening."

"Lovely, maybe we'll practice our orgy-making skills."

This time Enydd lets out a groan, throws her head back, her arms up, and exits the room without a further word.

The solstice dawns bright and eager. There's a tangible energy to the court, a palpable power shift growing and swelling within the atmosphere of the day. It is not a sensation I am familiar with, but I am certain it is due to my connection to the court via the crown. Did Aneira always feel this power shift each solstice? Is this a taste of the power to come tonight? Through the bond I can sense Emrys experiencing the same thing.

Emrys and I are dressed for the revel in scraps of gold. The materials leave so little to the imagination.

My husband wears a gauzy shirt, so sheer the gold fabric just looks like glittering skin, and the chains that hold it together are fine and silken. His loose-fitting pants have a bit more substance and opacity, but they are slung low on his hips, cutting the sharp V of his jutting hipbones to desirous degrees. He wears sandals of gilded chains and butter soft leather, and more chains bejewel his person, hanging from around his neck and in hoops along his ears. Slight cosmetics line his eyes and brush his cheekbones, gilding him like some glowing god. Upon his head is his horned and floral crown, the crescent moon curved at its center.

My dress—if it can even be called that—is of similar fashion. Fine chains lace around my arms, swooping in arcs to my elbows and wrapping my nearly bare waist. The sheer and shimmering panels of my golden gown cut down my body, hardly hiding my nipples and baring all of my midriff down past my navel. The skirt has two wide slits reaching above my hip bones, covering so little. My heels are made of chains and silken ribbon, wrapping along my calves in tandem, while more decorative chains wrap my thighs like garters. I, too, wear gilded cosmetics, and my golden crown. My silvery hair—like Emrys's wavy locks—is left free and unbound.

"How did you know Aneira was your mother?" I blurt, nerves coloring my voice.

Emrys quirks a brow and eyes me. "She told me. When I was barely old enough to remember. She told me that I was her son and that she had to give me up, even though she regretted it, but now she was asking forgiveness. I asked her if she'd take me back and she said she would not, that she had daughters to care for now. So, I told her I do not forgive her and never will."

"Ryss…" My heart breaks for him. Aneira gladly abandoned Emrys—and continued to do so—because of me.

"It is in the past Vanna, do not fret. I do not blame you."

He kisses my hand and some of my heartbreak diminishes.

We stand behind the doors before our entrance to the throne room, the room used many times over for events. I can hear the sound of the orchestra playing, voices talking, the clink of glassware. I inhale slowly and twine my fingers with my husband's. We meet each other's eyes, and then nod for the doors to open. When they do, we grace through them, leaving no signs of our anxiety.

The room seems to hold a breath as we enter. The throne room has been transformed into a golden forest. A false carpet of gold grass has been laid out, and sprouting from it is a forest of gleaming auric trees, the branches reaching high into the depths of the rippling magic ceiling. Some to the trees have twined together to create burrows and private alcoves. Courtiers and patrons are dressed in little more and even less than us, some in nothing but body paint. Everyone pauses and turns as we enter, flutes of champagne stopped between fingers, bites of fruit hanging in stasis.

Emrys and I walk through the gilded woods, hands held and upraised as we walk towards the Seelie Court throne. The tri-trunked and magic veined seat holding so much of the court's power. We pass by everyone as we ascend the dais. When we take a seat, it's with Emrys first and then me upon his lap—evidently, he has not torn the throne asunder as he had the crown.

I curl my hands over the arm rests of the throne to hide my shaking nerves. My anxiety is leeching off me in waves— waves which Emrys would be able to feel, even without the bond. My husband winds an arm around my waist, and dances his fingers on the bare skin there, gracing my ribs and trying to calm my racing thoughts.

Ghislain, a faerie with a goddess-blessed ability of Seelie magic imbued in his blood, steps from the rear of the room. His very veins glow with the pulse of power, turning his ochre skin even richer. His bright green eyes and vibrant red hair are a striking contrast against everything else. He is dressed in a loose tunic and pants of such light, oaken green that the shimmer appears threaded with even more gold.

Stepping before the Seelie throne, Ghislain extends his hands in welcome. The guests remain silent and focus their attention on the faerie. His face is placid as he begins the revel with ceremonious words.

"We cherish this time and season of change, seeking the blessings of transference and light. Here, we celebrate our new reign, that of the Gwyndolyn-Vanora rule, and with it, the new surge of power they shall inherit."

His voice is power and it fills the court, winding through every person present. The scent of decadent food and fruity wines are immersed with that of fresh rain—of magic. It's sharp and heady, like petrichor.

"We acknowledge the goddess for this transition of power. Thank her for the fading equinox to have this solstice bless our king and queen, and imbue them with the rightful power of their court."

Thunderous applause meets the conclusion of Ghislain's speech, and then my anxiety ratchets up to nauseating degrees.

Enydd steps up to the dais, her shimmering emerald wings fanned open, her gown spun-gold and liquid. She opens her arms, as if cupping the magic of the court.

"We thank the goddesses for the blessing of this solstice, and in the honor of their names, our king and queen will begin the revel with The Rite." My terror crawls up my throat with Enydd's brogue, her every word a barb. "As a gracious offer to the three goddesses of Fate, Karma, and Chaos, the Seelie Monarchs offer their bodies in a coupling to accept the power of their reign."

Enydd steps into the crowd and then we are left on display.

For some reason I didn't think we'd be paraded on the throne. For some reason, I'd figured we'd start in a quiet corner somewhere, or perhaps somewhere where no eyes can see us. Perhaps dim lighting. I realize now how foolish that thought process was.

My fingers itch for a bottle.

Though my soulmate has some anxiety himself, it is nothing compared to mine. I can sense his resolve build, and as he does, he slowly glides his fingers across my skin again. Relaxing me.

He guides my face to his and bestows me a tender, yet passionate kiss. His tongue playing with mine, his hand cupping my throat. My eyes flutter closed as I respond, moving my lips against his. He breaks the kiss and then slides out from beneath me, seating me firmly on the throne. In front of everyone, he kneels at my feet and looks up at me with heavy, lust-addled, topaz eyes.

"Eyes on me," he whispers. "It's just you and me. No one else matters."

I nod and swallow, tasting lemon and vetiver.

How I wish I could've imbibed in just a little alcohol. But I know that's a slippery slope.

Emrys parts my legs, his fingers grazing up my calves and swirling behind my knees. Carefully, he spreads me wide and shifts the thin panel of fabric that covers my pussy. The sight of him yearning for me has me wet. My core clenches as he presses his face between my legs and laves up the center of me.

I gasp at the stroke of his tongue, feeling that talented mouth of his work against me. My eyes roll back in my head as I fist my hands in his ruby locks, grinding my clit to his face. He focuses his attention on that bundle of nerves, and I feel my body grow loose, my nerves softening. Suddenly, I don't care about all the eyes on us, all I care about is the pleasure that my soulmate is wringing from me.

Biting my lip, I chase an orgasm that builds through me. My hips undulate with the rhythm that Emrys drums into me, his tongue flicking, and tasting me, his hands gripping my thighs, keeping me wide open for him.

My nipples are painfully hard and tight and I know they're showing through the thin fabric. But I don't care. I don't care about anyone but him and I.

"*Emrys*," I moan, breathy, thready.

I close my eyes as he purrs his approval on my clit. I nearly cry out from the sensation. My climax is on the very

234

edge, the precipice rushing up to me. Emrys feels it and increases his efforts. I'm flung from the cliffside as I come, bliss a crescendo through my being, unfurling from my center to my toes. Exploding out of me. I let out a cry of ecstasy as my husband takes me through the waves.

I'm limp, panting, and utterly sated.

Suddenly, my husband helps me off the throne and on shaking feet, I stand. I turn to look over the crowd but Emrys cups my face and forces me to look at him.

"Don't look at them. Look at me."

He pushes me up against the side of the throne and wraps my legs around his waist. My soaked pussy is pressed against the fine silk of his pants and I can feel his throbbing cock through it. He kisses me desperately and my arms wind around his neck, fusing in his hair. He reaches down between us and shifts his pants, freeing his hard length. With a few ministrations, he guides his cock to my entrance, and I readily take him.

My husband enters me, slamming to the hilt. I whimper into his mouth and he takes that sound, smiling against my mouth while I taste him and my climax. He's so thick and fills me so well, stretching me to the perfect point. He begins pumping into me, his hands gripping my thighs where I feel every touch and bite of his many rings.

"It's just us," he says into me, his breath raspy.

My hips roll against him as he thrusts, our skin slickened and slapping together. I bite his neck, nails digging into his back. His mouth is on my collarbone, nipping the hollows there.

Suddenly, a rush of power, unlike an orgasm rushes through me. I gasp and so does Emrys, golden light filling us. I look at my husband, positively glowing, his topaz eyes burning with divine power. I can see through the bond that my silvery eyes are incandescent too. Gold Seelie magic pours into us and spills out of our very pores. I feel it fill me, comfortably warm and right. The remaining power of the Seelie Court, preserved and withheld by the solstice enters us and through the goddesses will, accepts us.

The solstice transference is a sign and around us, the sounds of the orgy take off. Couples take off together to the burrows and alcoves, to the walls and even to the floor. I hear moans start up, rending fabric, slapping flesh.

Emrys and I stare at each other, love and power flowing through us.

"Do you want to finish this somewhere more private?" I ask, breathy.

"I would love that."

Emrys pulls out of me and tucks his cock into his pants. He rearranges my skirts before setting me down and then takes my hand. The two of us descend the dais, the sounds of fucking paving the way, and take off down a corridor.

I chance a look behind me and see mostly gold and flesh, long hair wrapped in fists, breasts bared, and legs parted. Hands are on multiple partners and many body parts, fingertips and nails digging, touches grasping and scrabbling.

Down the corridor, a couple has already claimed the wall. The female's front is pressed flush against the wall, her cheek turned from us. Her ass pushes outward as the male takes her from behind with slow strokes, his one hand between her legs, the other pulling her hair. She moans and he groans, and I startle when I recognize the voices.

Gideon and Julia.

I blush as we quickly dip into a room before they notice us, and I realize it's the council chamber that we always seem to find ourselves in. Emrys slams the door behind us and locks it. Before I can think, much less act, he pushes me against the table and splays me upon it.

Without hesitation, my husband tears the tissue paper dress from my body and bares me completely naked. My hardened nipples tighten against the cooler air and I lift myself up on my elbows to watch my husband visibly devour me with his eyes. He comes between my legs and drags me to the edge of the table, his mouth going to my breasts. Biting a nipple and rolling it in his mouth, he pinches the other with his hand, driving exquisite pleasure through my body. His free hand goes between my legs and immediately he hooks two fingers inside me and pumps them in and out. He rubs a glorious spot inside me and I gasp and thrust my hips. The heel of his hand grinds against my clit, and I realize I'm about to come again.

My hands tear the fine chains on his shirt as I search for purchase as I chase my orgasm. Emrys feasts on my breasts and plunges his fingers inside me while I keen and moan, shredding what remains of his clothing. Somehow, I manage to loosen the waistband of his pants and they fall.

My orgasm climbs through me and up my throat and I explode, screaming. As I come, Emrys removes his fingers from my drenched pussy and drives his cock into me. I screech at the filling as he slams into me, punishingly full. He ramps up my orgasm with his pulsing cock, and I'm utterly at the mercy of the waves of bliss.

"You're fucking perfect, Vanna. Fucking perfect, and all mine."

"I'm yours," I cry out. "I'm fucking yours."

"That's right. And you're going to come for me again like a good girl, aren't you?"

I gasp, but he's not wrong. I feel another orgasm spiraling within me from the fae magic. From the fucking solstice. Wetness rushes out of me, soaking him and gushing around his cock.

"Fuck Vanna, did you just—?"

"Yes!" I interrupt, pleasure flooding me.

The prospect is too much for my soulmate because suddenly he's coming, his climax releasing into me, hot and throbbing. He groans as my delicate inner muscles clench with my own orgasm, squeezing every moment of pleasure from both of us.

Emrys finishes and pulls from me, collapsing on the wood next to me. I'm panting and sweat-slickened, splayed on the table. Both of us are spent and sated, limbs languorous and hazy. This is bliss.

I don't know whether to call this lovemaking or fucking, but it's incredible.

We lay there a while, getting our bearings and then eventually we dress in what remains of our ruined clothes. When we exit the hall, Gideon and Julia are nowhere to be seen, thankfully. We weave through the orgy, more flesh than fabric now as the orchestra plays around them, and servants mill with trays, attempting to remain oblivious to the fucking all around.

As we pass an alcove I catch sight of a flicker of color, black and red and pink. I look over and I find Maelona in an intimate entanglement with Aveda. They're wrapped in each other, hands between each other's legs, fingers working as their mouths meet in a passionate battle. Their eyes are closed, so they don't see us and we hurry past.

Weaving down the halls towards our chambers, I'm surprised to find Wisteria sitting on a bench and looking out a window, a glass of champagne dangling from her fingers. She looks forlorn and contemplative.

Sensing our presence, she half turns, reassures herself, and then goes back to her stargazing.

"I couldn't bring myself to participate."

"You don't have to," I say softly.

"It's not that I didn't want to—I'm aro, not ace—but it just felt like too soon. After Elliot."

"I understand."

She turns to me and her teak eyes are hard. "I want to be the one to kill her, Faerie."

I don't even have to ask who she means. I know she means Caethes. The Dark Queen who murdered her boyfriend, publicly, and horribly, by tearing out and eating his heart at the annual equinox lottery in Aberth. The memory replays in my mind like a gruesome film reel.

"I want to see her suffer while she dies by my hand."

"I know."

"Can you make that happen?"

"I can try."

Wisteria drains her champagne, tilting back her head of coppery curls, and then plucks up a second glass I hadn't seen before. "That's good enough for me."

CHAPTER 25

Despite the bloated feeling of being swollen with so much power, it feels like there's a lull. Like a calm before the storm, something wicked brews. The next day I can sense more in the reaches of the court. The intricacies, the nuance, the very fiber of it. I can feel the threads that hold this pocket realm together and how to manipulate them to ever so slowly speed up or slow down time—as Caethes had done to us during the equinox lottery in Aberth.

Thoughts of Aberth have me drawn to the Yukon. As if I need to be there. There is a pull on my soul—a tether—yanking me to the wasteland that was the basis of my survival for two years. It's restless. *I* am restless.

Even though my husband can sense this tireless energy through the bond, I tell him.

"There's something telling me that we need to go to Unseelie territory," I begin, feeling the weight already lifting off my shoulders. It feels good to speak my worries into existence, to share them verbally—not just mentally. "I think it might be Aberth."

Emrys, just finishing up his breakfast pastry, lifts a brow. "Then let's investigate. We should never ignore our gut instincts."

"My first gut instinct had me calling you, my enemy."

"We should sometimes ignore our gut instincts."

I smile as my husband brushes off his hands and stands, buttoning up his maroon lace blouse—though keeping it open enough that I can still see the decadent cut of his collarbones.

Before we leave, I notify Maelona of our temporary departure, even though the sleep-addled Lady immediately retires back to bed. A bed where a spray of white and black hair lays across silk pillowcases. I give her a look of teasing and impression but my best friend simply rolls her eyes.

"Do not start," she warns, as she closes the door and returns to her bedmate.

Emrys and I travel to the Faerie Roads, and wander the tunnels, marveling at the ethereal blue of the bioluminescent mushrooms, the near pulse of life we can now feel through the earthen paths. Intrinsically, the Roads are part of both the

Unseelie and Seelie Courts and through our solstice celebration it reacts and feels different. Living. Beating. Tangible.

I follow the draw through the Roads and step out at a turn, Emrys content to follow. We immediately arrive on the fringes of the field entreating Aberth. The copse of trees we exit from hold no trace of the inbetween that belies the Faerie Roads, and the empty field betrays no wards to prevent access from them either. Nonetheless, they are all there.

Crossing the field, I pick up on the eeriness of the place. The grass shushes against our boots, but unsettlingly, no sounds prevail from the ghost town. At the first edge of Aberth, we find empty houses with lights off and no signs of living. Closer to the center of town we begin to see more destruction. Ash and char mark the roads where carts tipped from the lottery had wreaked fiery destruction. Banners and lights hang ominously, tattered and shattered across the streets, broken bulbs littering the ground and violet fabric peppering the ground like ruined confetti. Rotten food blackens on the pavers, blood streaks the stones in rusty lines, still yet to be washed by the rain or picked at by scavengers.

Aberth was an odd town, but it had been lively. This…this desolation is wrong. It speaks of apocalyptic endings, wakes of natural disasters. But nothing about this is natural. This was a slaughter and a theatre, all held by the Queen of the fucking Unseelie.

In the town center, the stage is still erected, having been abandoned by all—citizens and Unseelie alike. Bodies have been cleared away, but not their evidence. On the forefront of the stage, I can see a large bloodstain and drag marks. The place where Elliot died. Where Caethes tore out and devoured the heart of Wisteria's gentle-mannered boyfriend.

A rage rises in me at the devastation that the queen has so callously entertained. Wrought. Condoned. Encouraged. She

242

is monstrous. She is the product of worse beasts. I want to kill everyone who made her so terrible, so that I can eliminate everything her murderous touch has corrupted and taken.

It occurs to me that this rage is probably what drives Wisteria every day now. That thoughts of Caethes dying beneath her hand give her the strength to continue. To avenge Elliot. I suddenly want it for her more than anything.

In the distance I can see the inn and the nightclub—the Anemone—both of which give me sick twists of nostalgia. Of when I believed in Gideon. Before he betrayed me. Of when we were together and new and full of hope and fear and desire. Before I remembered my husband. The thought sickens in my gut, turning my breakfast over in my stomach like lead.

Emrys simply wraps an arm around my waist,

Standing just before the stage, I look at the discord and realize that even though I was drawn to the Yukon, I was not drawn to Aberth. My own mindless wanderings brought me to the sacrificial town, not the pull in my being.

"This isn't where we need to be," I say to Emrys into the open air. To the silence around us. "I don't feel the draw here."

"Then show me where it is."

We turn on our heels and exit the town once again, walking through the field. At the edge, I step into an inbetween and take Emrys with me. We take a few steps through the Faerie Roads before the tug becomes painfully insistent and we take a right. When we come from the inbetween, I freeze at the scene before us.

Tall evergreens, alpine trees, rocky earth, and loamy soil. Patchy grass and spots of mud, puddles and roots. Foliage that holds berries and verdant leaves, ferns and windfalls. The scent of pine and fresh air, an undertone of burning. A dilapidated structure and magic.

The cabin.

Still a charred mess. Still a ruin. Still a broken memory.

There are scorch marks on the earth where Corvina's corpse was desecrated and cremated. A lump forms in my throat and burns my eyes. I swallow and look away. My soulmate draws me close.

Together, the two of us head towards the cabin and I follow that tether. It leads us directly before the anti-Unseelie wards gating the premises. I whirl and take in my surroundings. At my feet is a puddle. I look down and gaze in.

Suddenly, I feel enthralled, magically compelled to keep staring.

Before my eyes—or maybe in my mind—I see a battle play out in the reflection of the pool of water. Weapons of blended metal. Swords clash and metal rings out, armor flashes silver and gold beneath a ruby sun. Flickers of night and vampires, glimpses of dawn and fae. The smoky apparitions of the Wild Hunt. The cycle of nightfall and sunrise. Midnight sun.

I see the advantages we get. How we can use the natural disadvantage of sunlight against the vampires with the increasing daylight hours in the north. What we can do with our weapons.

I take in the scene.

"This is where the war will be."

Emrys nods, seeing all that I do through the soulmate connection.

"I think you're right."

I draw in a breath and hold it. This place that was my sanctuary for years is now the tipping point—the pivotal place—that will decide the continuation or commencement of my life. Of my reign. Of my future and family with my husband. Everything leads back to the beginning.

The question now is; how is this decided?

The answer becomes clear back at the court when Henry Zhao reveals a book on faerie wars and the laws surrounding them. The inciting court chooses the grounds, but said grounds must be on enemy territory to give them a "fair" advantage, since they're technically "unwilling" participants in the battle. Fucking semantics.

Henry also has translated the primordial fae that I'd struggled with. One of the terms that neither I, nor the previous translator could figure out was soulmates.

Lady Fate favors soulmates—or twin flames—and is oft more known to answer their calls. Even then, to do so is not recommended. Evidently, I've elected to ignore that particular warning. Which is why we specifically are playing her game while everyone else runs amok without her interest cast upon them.

More primordial fae reveals that we will be eternally watched by the goddess—as her chosen ones. I suppress the shiver that comes with that revelation.

Emrys and I have General Baphet and Tirnoc to draft a letter that we formally sign, signifying our selection for battle. For the playing field and date. The eighth of July is two and a half weeks away, and gives us enough time to prepare, as well as many lucky hours of midnight sun that we very much need to come out on top. Both males agree with our strategy and send word to their battalions. Before we hold an official announcement of our own, Emrys and I hand over two weapons and command them to follow our directions for them exactly. They are surprised but do as told.

Calling all attendees, we gather the denizens of the Seelie Court in the throne room. Standing on the golden dais, Emrys and I declare that the war has taken a new advance and has progressed with a date. We inform all—as we stand in our gilded finery—that the official war games begin in just over a fortnight. We also make it clear that neither one of us will be sitting back behind our King and Queensguards—much to said guards' displeasure.

"We are warriors," Emrys declares to the masses. "We have been trained all our lives to fight. We are the last Centurions. We are the Revenant and the Harbinger. And we will not sit idly by while we ask you to fight our battles. We are a king and a queen who fight for you, and we will not expect anything out of you that we are not willing to do ourselves."

A surprising chorus of cheers goes up at this. I didn't expect this sort of vocal support, especially considering how much we've been feeling like failures to the court. That so much has gone wrong and we have lost many fae to defection. Regardless, I take the support for what it is and prize it. Because I do not know for how much longer we will possess it.

We take questions and answer them as much as we're able. It seems to garner much appreciation from those gathered and I make a mental note to hold court after this is all over to hear our people's grievances. Emrys silently agrees. After questions finish and the fae trickle out, Julia lingers.

The beautiful human slowly approaches us, a slight flush to her cheeks that I catch even with her head ducked.

"I was wondering if I could speak to you," Julia says, not meeting our eyes but pointedly meaning me.

My brows draw together. "Of course, but about what?"

"I need to apologize."

My brows rise. "What for?"

"For Gideon. For Gideon and me, I mean. I don't want you to think—"

I hold up a hand. "Stop." I draw in a breath and shake my head. "What you do with Gideon is none of my concern. You are free to do with him as you want. I hold no claim over him, he is not mine and I am not his."

"But you are queen and he was your—"

"He was my past and that is where he will stay."

"I also want to say sorry for what you saw in the hall during the revel—"

"Please don't. You saw Emrys and I, as well. Everyone was fucking. It's your body and your consent. Let's leave it at that." I clear my throat. "Is there anything else you wished to discuss?"

Julia's cheeks flare redder. "No that's all."

The conversation abruptly ends and Julia leaves, a mild note of embarrassment in her wake. Once the leader of the Crows departs, I summon for Violante. Internally, I prepare myself for any response she might give.

Emrys paces nearby, thoughts spiraling through his head, all the kingly duties he has to adjust to, all the Revenant responsibilities he's abandoned, the court he forsook. He doesn't regret leaving the Unseelie Court, but there is a touch of sadness to his thoughts, like nostalgia. The Dark Court was his home for more than two decades, and now he has left it and virtually usurped the rival court—without the negative intentions. It's a lot for one person to feasibly take in, but he is doing so with surprising grace. I admire him all the more for it.

The young vampire girl arrives with wary crimson eyes. She is soft in so many ways, her features still shaped by the youth of the adolescence she's frozen at—the timid curve of her eyes, the fearful set of her mouth, the long waves of her hair dark brown hair. Everything about her prompts an evocation of innocence and sweetness, but I know it's just a predator's tactic. Vampire genes are tricky and they know how to mold their host to be the perfect apex predator—whether that be by intimidation of strength, seduction by sultry form, or as Violante's genes have determined; doe-like mannerisms.

"You summoned for me?"

"We did," I say softly. "As you may be aware, we have decided to fight the final battle of this war."

Violante nods. "Yes, I am. Is—is there some mission you want me to complete during it?"

"No, quite the opposite actually." I draw in a breath and put my hands flat against my thighs. "We want you to stay here, within the court for the duration of the battle."

Violante's crestfallen expression strikes directly in my heart. The disappointment that pours off her makes me feel like the worst villain.

"But...but I've been training for this. I want to help. I won't get in anyone's way."

"It's not that, it's the midnight sun. There is no true nightfall, and less than two hours of twilight on the eighth. That's not enough time to ensure we can get you in and out safely. I can't risk you in the sunlight."

"But there is some time, and there's shade..." Violante—from my understanding—was anxiety-stricken as a human, and this has been heightened tenfold with her vampiric status. The main fear being sunlight, and despite the brave front she is putting on, she is utterly terrified of the burning star. Even now, wanting to fight for us, she is shaking and terrified, but is determined to face her worst fear even if it means the risk of crossfire.

"I can't in good conscience allow it. We selected the date because we knew Caethes' vampire forces would be at a disadvantage with the sun, if there was any other way, I'd offer, but I can't. I will find you something here at the court to do to assist."

"What, like tending to the wounded?" Violante says with a surprising amount of snark. "Because everyone wants a vampire healer that just might decide to unhinge their jaw and sink their fangs into your already bleeding body."

"Perhaps not that, but—"

"This should be my choice."

Anger flares in me borne of fear. "And I am queen. What I say on this matter is the word."

"And your husband is king, he can allow it if he so chooses."

Emrys next to me, startles suddenly, like a deer caught in headlights. His golden eyes blink rapidly, and he looks between his queen-wife and the small vampire. Both of us fighting for the same court, one of us trying to protect, the other trying to prove.

"I respect and appreciate your desire to help," Emrys begins, "but I am sorry, I agree with my wife. You undertake too much risk with this offer."

Violante's nostrils flare and fine traceries of veins rise up around her eyes, filling with dark blood.

"You will let the other vampires risk themselves, but not me? How is that fair? Ever since I was forced to turn, I have been forced into doing everything Caethes bid me to do, and I am *sick* of it."

I'm reminded immediately of our first chance encounter. When I'd just survived the plane crash after Jacob Dugal abducted me. After the goddess, Lady Karma, shot it down in the middle of Unseelie wilderness. When I'd run from cannibalistic Unseelie and found a cave beneath sheets of rain. Where I'd peered out in the darkness and seen the ruby light of

Violante's eyes peering in at me. Eyes which I had thought for years were a hallucination.

"If I refused for any reason, she'd send Unseelies to hunt me down and torment me, or she'd find eager hunting vampires and send them my way just for her fun." Violante's voice is picking up fervor. "I have been commanded to spy and hunt against my will. To turn innocents over to the Dark Court. Ever since I was selected from the lottery my life has been nothing but a slave's sentence and I am *done* letting it continue. I lost everything with her rule. I chose nothing." Her eyes, no longer timid, penetrate me, as if seeing down to my very soul and the gray shroud it is. "This is something I want to choose. Let me do it. I want my life to be mine—and if my death comes, then my death will be mine."

There is silence after her passion and Emrys and I stand stock still, realizing we've underestimated her. She keeps the breaths she doesn't need, even and measured, her hands fisting at her sides, eyes hard.

"I am not fae, I am not forced into the oaths and loyalty of this court, but if I choose to fight for it, you have no control over me."

Violante vanishes before we can get a word in edgewise.

I have the worst feeling in the pit of my stomach. It lurks like a parasite, gorging itself on my anxiety and guilt. Everything sours and crawls up my throat, letting the sickness spread. I am not unused to making decisions regarding life and death, but what I am unfamiliar with is having to throw the queen title around to do it.

"Are we wrong?" I ask my husband.

Emrys shakes his head. "I truly do not know."

We are more alike than you would ever dare to admit.

Caethes's words ring through my mind, playing like a sick joke as I realize how very wrong I was, and how horribly close to a truth she is.

CHAPTER 26

I'm alone in the library when the door opens and reveals Gideon. I look up from the documents Baphet and Tirnoc have drafted, and set them down in my lap. The halfling approaches slowly, as if I'm a wild animal, and he's afraid to scare me off.

"Can I join you?"

I lift a brow. "Were you looking for me?"

"Actually, yes."

I can't tell if he's lying or not but I gesture to the chair across from me. Slipping the papers into the leather filer, I wrap the twine around it to close, and set them down. I'd been trying to distract myself after learning that Bambalina had chosen to end her life, rather than to live in a world without her sight and goddess's grace. My gorge sits uneasily and I blame myself.

I shake myself from my guilty thoughts as Gideon, meanwhile, takes the proffered seat. I push aside the dossiers, and cross my legs, the smooth leather of my slate leggings only slightly creaking.

"Well, you have my attention."

Gideon fiddles with his hands and I watch his fingers work in their clutch. He's nervous and there's guilt lining his frame.

"Are you planning an abduction attempt to turn me over to Caethes? Because I warn you, I would not attempt it this day. It's foolhardy, and I'm not in the mood."

Gideon barks a laugh and shakes his head, his black waves loose with the movement. "No, I'm not that stupid. Besides, I don't want to." He looks up at me with open amber eyes. "I don't hate you—we just weren't right for each other."

I mentally prompt Emrys through the bond, letting him know where I am and whom I'm with. I'm not asking for backup, but simply giving him the common courtesy—the decency—to know that I am currently alone with my ex-lover. It seems like basic marriage etiquette.

Emrys internally laughs, and then flashes me an image of his surroundings. It's a meeting with Enydd, Tirnoc, Baphet, and battalion leaders—the one I'd opted out of but had taken copies of notes for.

"You know, you being a liar and all makes it difficult to believe you."

Gideon sighs. "What will it take for you to trust me, again?"

I ponder a moment. When did I trust him last? When was that trust broken? Even when I thought I was human or just a solidary fae, he was a liar. There were moments I caught him in untruths or deception. Truthfully, I'd hardly had faith in him when I *did* trust him. It's nothing short of a miracle that I *did* believe him enough when I told Caethes he knew where the Harbinger was all those months ago.

It's difficult for the fae to believe the words of those who are not also faerie. If a faerie tells you they love you, you don't have to question it. When a faerie tells you they hate you, you know they do. It's different when a halfling says it.

"I don't know," I finally respond.

Gideon hangs his head. "I deserve that."

"You do."

I do not have to bring up how he turned to the Dark Court and how he knocked me out and tied me up at the Winter Carnaval. I don't have to say how he hated me, and spurned, and humiliated me there. But I also don't have to bring up how I wronged him. Dumped him and then immediately kissed Maelona in front of him. Left him abandoned in the Faerie Roads after a hate fuck with no guide. Ignored his pleas at the Unseelie Court meeting, and initially refused to rescue his father.

We were so utterly wrong for each other. Toxic in our relationship. We may have found love, but it was twisted. We were wrong for each other. Bad for each other. We brought out the worst because we clashed, rather than melded. We were just *too* different. Too incompatible.

"What if I used my remaining heart's desire commands now? Wasted them on something small?"

I startle. "That could work."

254

Gideon straightens in his chair. "Evelyn, I command you to say your soulmate's name."

I laugh, but the command easily pulls from my center. "Emrys Gwyndolyn-Vanora."

Gideon smiles. "Good. Last one. Evelyn, I command you to tell me more about Corvina." I realize he's finally getting to the point of seeking me out.

I raise a brow as the command tugs at me. "You want to know more about your dead soulmate when you have a new, living partner?" The words are harsh and brusque, brutal even to me.

Gideon's caramel complexion flushes. "So, you know about me and Julia."

"She told me. Besides, it was kind of hard to miss you two fucking in the hallway."

Gideon's head snaps up.

"Don't worry, I don't care. I already told her she's free to do with her body as she wants, just as you are. Just don't do anything that risks your position in this court—you're already on thin ice."

"I won't and—" He looks away sheepishly. It's uh...new. And not serious—yet." Gideon shakes his head. "You know, other faeries can't say things like that. They can't use figure of speech like you do."

"I suspect it has something to do with being half witch. Corvina could do it too, Emrys as well, I suspect for the same reasons."

Gideon brightens at this and suddenly, forced by the commands, I launch into story after story of Corvina. How we'd grown up in the court with Aneira as our mother, battling with wooden practice swords that soon turned to steel, faux war games with Maelona. I tell him about Corvina's penchant for parties and luxury. The elaborate tea parties she used to throw as children and then the soirees she dragged me to in our teen years. I mention the beautiful dresses she wore, how she commissioned them, and helped the tailor finish them. Her careful hands that were built for dance and art, not killing and battle like mine. I briefly gloss over her lovers, the few there were, and I let him know how loved she was by everyone. Everyone favored the dark daughter over the pale one. I was the twin of frost and deep January winters; she was the twin of summer nights and star fall.

I wonder how well matched they would have been. If her softness could smooth his hard edges, if their pieces fit together being different enough to be equal. Gideon and I are too sharp for each other, acting as whetstone to the other, constantly honing to a deadly point. Together we were two battling weapons, perpetually aimed at each other. Together, perhaps they would have been weapon and shield. Protector and comforter.

After my stories, the hold the command has on me fades and I'm let go. Suddenly, a relief so sweet, rushes through me. No one holds any sway over me any longer. No one can forcibly command me against my will. I am free of that fear.

Approaching, I sense my husband just beyond the doors. He enters the library with all the grace he possesses as the Revenant and king. He's wearing a blouse of black and white, tiny designs like constellations with the sleeves rolled, and black velvet pants tucked into shiny black boots. A black crescent moon pendant hangs against his chest, between the open buttons and there I can see the edge of the scar. He comes to my side and I twine a hand up his arm, feeling the smooth expanse of his flesh over taut muscles. I lean into him as he winds a hand into the long silvery hair at the nape of my neck.

"Hello Gideon, good to see you," Emrys says unaffectedly, but I see the flash of ire in his mind. The moment he'd stood behind Caethes at room number seven of the Aberth Inn, seeing me, mussed from bed, and Gideon shirtless behind me with scratches marring his back. The betrayal and anger that had suffused him. I temper the flare of jealousy with a brush of my fingers, banishing the intrusive thoughts with devotion of my own—pouring all my love for him into the bond.

I love you. I choose you.

I know.

"Good to see you, too, Your Majesty."

Emrys makes a face. "That feels wrong, please don't say it again."

Both my husband and I are struggling with the honorifics of our new titles.

Gideon laughs, relieved for the easy air my soulmate has given him. "Noted."

For a moment I'm thrust into a fantasy. Of this day, this scene, this place. Of Emrys and I leaning together as we are, but also of Gideon sitting in that chair with Corvina perched on the arm of it, her fingers in Gideon's hair, his hand on her waist. She's clad in silver jewels, silk of violet and lavender— Unseelie Court colors—with a silver crown of stars and roses upon her brow. We both have our dark leathery wings. I picture the four of us, laughing, happy, alive. Corvina planning a party she's desperate for me to be just as enthusiastic about, My husband eager to show me off. Gideon begrudgingly supporting it only because he wants to do whatever makes his love—his soulmate—happy. In the image we have platters of food, cheeses and meats, fruits, pastries before us, goldwine passes easily between us—because here I don't have a drinking problem. Here, I didn't undergo the trauma and loss of Drysi's death, Aneira's death, Corvina's death. Of the loss of my wings, the survival in the wasteland.

The fantasy crystallizes and breaks, Corvina vanishing from view. The ghost of her presence whispers away, leaving the arm of Gideon's chair empty, and the warm love in his face replaced by cold longing. My throat thickens at the sudden feel of irreplaceable loss. Of what goddesses and misfortune took from me.

I want to scream for our shattered fates.

CHAPTER 27

Emrys and I lead a follow-up announcement to the court that anyone who chooses not to fight in the approaching war is welcome to reside within the court, depart to safehouses, or flee to other Seelie territory around the globe. We tell them to prepare for either result and no judgement will come from fight or flight. Most Seelies choose to fight.

The following days are a rush of planning, strategy, meetings, and training. There is little to no time left for anything not court or battle related. Every night Emrys and I collapse exhausted into sleep, but we're too tired to be physical. The mental toll of ruling and plotting wears on me, and the physical ails of training make my muscles shake and ache.

Emrys and I have only managed a few quickies, and I miss my husband. The satisfaction of his touch, and the wringing of pleasure from our bodies. These are hurried and to the point, and while they are spectacular, I want more.

Anxiety ratchets up, and a heatwave begins crashing upon us. The interior of the court remains cool—albeit a few degrees warmer—outside is near excruciating in its level.

Finally, on the sixth I call it early and refuse any more meetings or training. Tomorrow we are set to leave for the cabin ruins, and I cannot take another second of politics or battle strategy. Directly in the middle of the meeting, while they speak of monitoring said ruins for traps, I stand and raise a hand.

"I am finished here. If there is anything more pertinent that I must know, speak it now, otherwise I will not be available until tomorrow."

Shocked silence follows my declaration, eyes blink at me and mouths drop.

"No? Nothing? Lovely, I will see you all tomorrow."

And with that I sweep out of the room and head for my chambers, projecting very specific thoughts to my husband. Through the bond, I see him scramble to make a similar disclosure, and then chase after me. I laugh to myself all the way to our bedroom.

I close the door behind me and carelessly shuck off my dark green dress, revealing a lacy and strappy black set of lingerie that I'd put on specifically for this occasion—a set

Emrys once wondered about. It's been more than two weeks since I've properly had my husband, and that is two weeks too long.

The lace cups my breasts in a divine push that I need, giving me cleavage I don't normally possess. The lines of it carve across my abdomen, drawing the eye to the expanse of my flat stomach and cutting high on my hip bones. The underwear is sheer lace, so sheer you can already see the wetness drenching me in anticipation. The ass of it is completely revealed, just a thin line. Garters wrap my thighs and I leave my knife-shoe heels on my feet.

Yanking my hair from its confines I shake out the tresses and stand in the middle of the chamber, waiting for my husband's quickening presence.

It had been hard to keep this slight surprise from him, keeping my mind more distracted and full than usual. I'd poured all my attention into the meetings, giving him only the barest of my regular flirtations. But now, I've opened the door to that particular secret, and he is *ravenous*.

Emrys flings open the door and he stands there in all his finery—black leather and silk, dressed as he always is in one of those slutty, salivation-worthy blouses. He takes me in with heady topaz eyes, lowered hoods meant for the bedroom, and thick lashes drawing shadows on his wicked cheekbones. That cruel and beautiful mouth of his is pulled into a devilish smile that promises to devour me whole—and fuck me, I want it.

His cock is hard, and it strains in his pants, painfully large and tight.

"Close the door," I command.

My king gives no hesitation and slams it closed. I approach slowly, my heels clicking and I come before him. I reach out and grab him by the crescent moon pendant he wears, drawing him towards the steps, down to the bed.

He reaches out for me, fingers grazing my waist and the lace there. I pull away and shake a free finger at him playfully.

"You will not touch me until I let you," I tell him, sultry, my eyes just as darkened in lust as his. I can see the form I cut in this room through the bond, the way he sees me so much like divinity. The lust he holds for me makes me so wet that I have to fight the demanding urge to jump him and ride him right then and there. But that's not what I'm planning for today. I have something else I want.

"A menace. A tease. A fucking vixen," he says, like a rapid prayer. All things he's called me before.

"And all yours."

I draw him down the stairs, still pulling his chain and I guide him to the bed. Without preamble, I shove him onto the emerald coverlet, and he lets me. He lays there, sprawled and cat-like, so hot that I want to lick every line of him.

"On the pillows," I tell him.

He complies and shucks off his boots.

Once settled, I climb over him. His hands instinctively go to my waist.

"Uh-uh, what did I say?" I chastise as I seat myself astride his still leather-clad pelvis.

I pick up his hands and draw them over his head. My breasts lower to his face and he moans with the restriction I've given him. He lifts his hips, rolling them once against my core and I have to bite my lip to keep from crying out. The friction against my lace-covered clit is bliss. My hands have taken his to the headboard and there, where I have attached leather cuffs, I lock his wrists in.

He's utterly at my mercy.

Of course, he could break out of them if he so wanted, but I know he doesn't. This—the bondage, being tied up—is something he very much enjoys.

A slight gasp catches in his throat. "Vanna." He tries the cuffs. They hold.

"Yes, husband?"

I slowly slide myself down his body, drawing my wet core down his legs. Rubbing myself on him like I'm in heat. My hands go to the bare skin at his chest, fingers digging, nails scratching. I pop the buttons free and push the silk open, exposing all his gorgeous muscles—the shape of his pecs, the cut of his abdomen. My mouth replaces where my hands once were. I leave a line of hickeys down his body, peppering his entire torso in love bites.

He smells, as always, of lemon and vetiver, leather, and home. He tastes divine, sweet and salty with a slight musk. I love it. I love *him*.

He strains as I kiss and suckle and bite. I sweep my tongue over his nipple and he groans, thrusting upwards for me, but I am not where he wants me—where he needs me. I continue my teasing ministrations until I get to the desirous cut of his V-line.

Emrys whimpers as I work the buttons from his pants.

"Do you think this cock belongs in my mouth?" I whisper as I start tugging the leather from his hips.

"Yes," he gasps as I free him.

His beautiful golden length springs free and I don't give him a moment of teasing before my mouth is on it and taking him. I sweep my tongue over the head of him as I pull him into my mouth. He groans, flexing his wrists in the cuffs, and presses his head into the pillows, tossing his head back and forth.

My lips form suction on his cock as I bob my head up and down, laving my tongue down his length and swirling it over the tip. I catch a pearl of salty arousal and lick it away. My hands rove up and down his hips and abdomen, nails dragging down to his thighs and massaging all the sensitive skin. I continue sucking him and as I do so I force the rest of his pants away, kicking them to the floor. He lays there in nothing, draped only with the open silk of his blouse and the heat of me.

Thrusting into my mouth, I take him, suppressing the gag reflex that I've never been able to master. Tears track down my face, but I continue sucking his dick, pleasuring my husband in a way he deserves.

He's managed to pull himself up some, gazing down at me as I take his member in my mouth. He's lust-addled, his golden eyes practically glowing with desire. They promise to do every dirty thing to me he can imagine. To take me in every position he can think of. To feast on me until I'm writhing beneath him—screaming. The thought sends a rush of wetness between my legs.

I meet his eyes as I take him deep, and his growl of pleasure is absolutely feral. I keep licking and sucking, and I can feel him getting close.

"Fucking hell, Vanna, you're perfection." He gasps. "Don't stop, I'm so close love."

I urge him on and suddenly I feel his cock pulse and throb, spilling his release into my mouth. He moans as he comes. I swallow him down and suck through his orgasm, drawing the waves out longer, letting his pleasure linger. When the last vestiges of his climax wane, I climb astride him.

He's breathing heavy and meets my eyes. "Sit on my face love, let me taste that pussy. Let me make you come."

"Not yet," I reply coyly as I settle my lingerie-covered core against his recently pleasured cock.

Confusion covers his face as I block my intentions from our minds, focusing on the act I'd just performed on him to maintain the surprise a while longer.

Straddling him, I run my hands over his chest, down his abdomen, and then up my own. My fingers grazing my core, my stomach, my breasts, neck, lifting my hair and settling it down my back. His eyes heat again as he watches me. My hands rove down my throat and skip over to the straps of my black lingerie. I drag a strap down my shoulder, watching him watch me.

He is utterly focused on my every move.

"*Vanna*," he manages, shocked and turned on. Awe-struck, delighted, and frustrated.

I do the same to the other strap on the opposite side, and then I trace the line of lace cupping my swelling breasts. I cup them through the fabric, lifting them, holding my husband's greedy eyes. My fingers tuck into the cups, and I tug it down a little. In the center, I loosen the stays that hold them in place. Untied, I free my breasts. My nipples are hard and peaked, painfully tight, and begging to be touched.

When my fingers brush the tips, I throw my head back and moan. I touch myself again, rolling my nipples between my thumbs and forefingers, working myself up. Pleasure zings straight down into my wet and clenching pussy, grasping at nothing. I whine a little as I flick my nipples, those pink peaks eager for the touch of my husband.

One hand continues my self-pleasuring on my breast, the other slides down my abdomen, fingers going directly over my core. I rub myself over the lace and roll my hips with the touch. The friction is teasing but not enough.

"Take it off," he begs.

I hum my indecision—playing.

My hand goes up again, and then back down, edging us both. I can feel his cock hardening again under my ass already.

Finally, I feel my own frustration pick up and I reach up to the ties holding the strappy piece together. Peeling the lace off my body, I undo the tie high at the hips that hold the fabric against my center. It all comes off and I straddle my husband, bare and smooth and sleek, left only in the lace garters and dangerous heels.

I'm so wet and aching that I debate on not continuing my teasing, but I stubbornly decide to complete what I started.

I pleasure one nipple, swirling the bud, as I reach down between my legs and spread myself for him. I am drenched and swollen for him. I let him watch as I take a finger and plunge it inside me. I moan as I clench around my own digit. Drawing it out, my finger glistens with the wetness, and I draw it over my clit, rubbing it. I groan, circling that bundle of nerves as I sit on my husband.

He watches, heated, holding himself in check. His eyes continue their illicit promises, the bond flooded with all his plans for me. Everything he wants to do right now. Most of it including his mouth on the pussy I am currently self-pleasuring.

Taking two fingers, I hook them inside myself and pump in and out, rubbing in a come-hither motion against that spot that feels so good. The heel of my hand grinds into my clit and I feel pressure build. The threat of an orgasm grows as I thrust my fingers in and out, my hand toying with my nipple, my hips rolling of their own volition.

As I finger-fuck myself, I feel some of that pressure swell and then a gush of wetness floods over my fingers. It's messy and we are both soaked, but Emrys moans with pleasure.

"Fuck Vanna. You touch yourself so well."

I mewl as I rush on the approaching orgasm, letting it slam into me. I moan as I come on top of my husband, my delicate inner walls squeezing against my fingers. I keep working myself through it, gasping on the waves that take me. Stars explode behind my eyes as I come crashing down.

Breaths heaving, I slowly draw my fingers off of and out of my body. I look at my soaked fingers, seeing the light catch the dewiness. I look at my husband deviously.

"Open your mouth."

He complies immediately. I tuck the fingers I used to make myself come into his mouth and he sucks my climax from them, his talented tongue wrapping around them. He licks up them, catching every bit of my essence. Once cleaned, he kisses my fingertips and then nips playfully.

"Thank you for such a treat, My Queen."

I clench from the way he says it. I've just had an orgasm, but already I'm greedy for another. And my husband has regained his energy, his cock painfully hard on my ass.

I shift my hips, grinding against his straining length. He lets out a broken sound and I grin. We are no where's near close to being finished.

"You've been so good for me, I figured you deserved it." I smirk. "Now, how do you want me?"

"Let me lick you. I'll make you come better and faster than you can."

I quirk a brow. "Do you have something to prove, My King?"

"Always."

Carefully I move up his body and then straddle his face. I lower my pussy against his mouth and he wastes no time feasting on me. His tongue plunges inside my core and then sweeps out, dragging against my slit and to my clit. He nips that bundle of nerves and then his tongue flicks over it, rapidly, hurrying on a climax despite my oversensitivity. I mewl and begin to see stars. My hips undulate on his face, and he manages to keep his rhythm even against my movements, his tongue talented even though his bound hands can't stay me.

"*Fuck Ryss*. I'm so close already."

He alternates between suctioning and flicking, and suddenly those stars overtake me as I come on his face, the orgasm powering through me as I grind down onto his mouth. He licks me through the last crescendo, finishing me off fully. I tremble as he flicks his tongue again, and I flinch from being so over sensitized.

I moan and shiver, climbing off him, my legs weak. His lips are glossed with my wetness and it turns me possessive and feral.

This moment between us isn't over, not yet. We haven't even reached the main event. This is a moment of treasuring before the potential end, and I want everything with him to be memorable—especially if it's going to be our last, though I don't want to think about that.

Moving back down his body, I gaze at him meaningfully as his core and mine meet. I hold a question in my silver eyes.

"*Fuck*, yes," he groans.

I don't wait any longer and I lift myself, plunging down on his cock. We moan in unison as I ride him, the sound of wet flesh smacking leads us on, our movements becoming frantic, and I throw my head back, crying out.

Bouncing up and down on him, I press my hands against his chest and force more friction to exactly where I want it. The shock and grind of my clit barrels me on to another orgasm—I've lost track of how many I've had during this lovemaking session at this point. I can feel Emrys losing control and suddenly with a broken moan he's coming. His cock pulses inside me. I come hard on him, grinding down through the motions. The throes of my climax have me mewling, crying out. I'm so soaked and sore and swollen. And a complete mess.

I collapse on top of him, sweat-soaked and sated. I'm ruined in the best of ways. Breaths heaving, and with Emrys's chest panting beneath me, I lay there for a moment. Wallowing. Languishing. Luxuriating.

Drawing myself up, I come up to my knees and unbuckle the cuffs that bind him to the bed. Just as I release him, he has one hand immediately on me. I smile and release his other, but then immediately realize my error. His other hand traps me and suddenly he has rolled me beneath him and I am pinned to his mercy.

I let out a squeal that is half fear and half delight, and all turned on.

"Emrys!"

"Shh, wife. It's my turn."

I follow his train of thought and gasp.

"I can't! Love! I have no more in me."

"Oh, we'll see about that."

Emrys takes those cuffs that I'd used to bind him and locks my wrists in them. I am face down, on my belly. He lifts my hips to his and runs his nose along my spine. I feel his lips tickle me as he kisses down every knob of my spine, and then takes his hands to my hips.

Massaging my cheeks and building anticipation, I bite my lip. Emrys smooths a hand at the base of my spine.

"Arch that back for me, love. Hold onto those bars."

My eyes roll back in pleasure. The gravelly undertone of his voice. The desire that he wrings from me despite all the previous orgasms.

"So good. Such a good girl."

Fuck, he knows how much I like that.

More wetness—I can't contemplate how—floods between my legs.

269

He takes his cock in hand and then guides it against my entrance. I am soaked and the head of him slides through effortlessly, the tip teasing my clit. I let out a breathy moan, and toss my head, my view a silvery curtain of my locks and the viridian silk of our sheets.

Sliding his length against me again, I feel it penetrate deeper, but still teasing. I groan, pushing my ass back to him, wanting all of him.

"Just wait."

I whine and wiggle my ass at him. He chuckles.

This time, when he drags his cock against my slit he slips it in and then pushes. And pushes.

"Yes. Oh fuck, yes."

I bite my lip as he sinks into my pussy, pressing to the hilt. I am so full, so stretched, so over-pleasured. And yet he's still giving me more.

I push back against him and then he begins. Plunging in and out of me, he pumps over and over, his skin slapping against my ass, sweat-slickened flesh increasing the sound. His hands coast up my sides and cup my breasts, his fingers rolling my nipples between his fingers.

How? How is he bringing me so much pleasure? How can my body take anymore?

But I am designed for him, and he for me. We take everything the other gives.

"You're so tight, My Queen. So fucking tight and all fucking mine."

"All yours," I keen. "Everything is all yours. All yours."

"I know, and this cock is yours, and you take it like the absolute fucking queen you are."

"Yes," I mewl, a climax flushing through me. "Yes, fuck, oh yes!"

My orgasm explodes within me, shattering me fully. My nerves fry and I scream. Everything is pleasure and bliss. Everything is Emrys and fucking. It's all fireworks and stars. I moan and keen, pushing my ass back as he thrusts his final thrusts. His climax taking him too as he spills inside me once again. He collapses atop me and kisses down my back, hands soothing my ribs and hips.

"I love you, so much," he whispers against my ruined body.

"I love you, too," I reply breathlessly, my eyes so heavy.

Emrys releases me from the cuffs and holds me for a moment. He then let's go, but only to get something to clean me up with. He wipes his cum from my leaking legs, and kisses my belly, my thighs, my hips. I jerk from the sensitivity. When he returns, he wraps me up and tucks me into the blankets.

His body perfectly forms to me and he places his chin against the juncture of my throat. He kisses my neck, nuzzling there. His fingers stroke against my soft flesh, soothing, not stimulating.

"Tomorrow is—" I begin but he cuts me off.

"I don't want to think about tomorrow. I just want to think about now. And now with you is peace."

"Okay."

So, we do not speak and we do not let the thoughts form. We remain wrapped in our love and silk, drifting off to sleep with pleasure-soaked forms. Because tomorrow is not peace or heaven. Tomorrow is war and hell.

CHAPTER 28

The next day I wake ridiculously early, before dawn breaks over the court. I slip from the covers, sore and aching. My husband is on his stomach, head tilted into the pillow. His face is soft in sleep, those sharp edges muffled by his slumber. The sweep of his lashes casts shadows on his cheekbones, and his splay of garnet hair is tousled upon the silk.

I lean down and kiss his brow, then change into leathers. I write a note in case for whatever reason he doesn't tune into the bond or can't.

Casting one last look over my shoulder as I leave the room, I creep down the silent hallways and into the field of the court. The sky is not golden as it is inside, it is plum with streaks of peach. Dawn approaches with its first light. The air is scented with the woods and slight chill of dew before the sun burns it off.

In the grass I spin, looking up and realize my attempt will be in error. Stepping into the woods that ring the pocket realm, I cross the threshold—the inbetween—and enter the Faerie Roads.

My trip is short and I find myself atop the highest point of my court. On the top of the Golden Hinde. The mountain I'd climbed to whisper the words for Callahan's death. Here, the air is cooler with the elevation. Wind whips my hair as I stand and watch the sun begin to rise.

"Lady Fate!" I call out into the cloud cover, over the trees, and to the fading stars. "Lady Fate, I summon you. I demand to speak to you as Queen of the Seelie Court, your chosen Centurion, your Harbinger."

I wait—knowing from Henry's revelation that she's watching—and as I do, the air changes. There is a pressure increase and a slight whisper to the wind. With it accompanies the slight tang of magic, like electricity.

Without turning I can sense the presence of divinity.

"What do you ask, young queen?"

I finally face the goddess, and I find Lady Fate in all her radiance as before. Long, wavy red hair, floating about her perfectly, completely sleek and without tangle—even in the breeze. Her mis-matched eyes, one of sapphire and one of emerald, are as vibrant as before. Her creamy skin is blemish-free, carved of marble and moonlight. She is beyond beautiful.

"I request a favor."

The goddess quirks a dark brow. "Another? I am not known to grant more than one to a single individual."

"There's a first for everything."

The goddess inclines her head. "Indeed. Well, what do you wish to speak of? Your prophecy?"

I shake my head, but the last line haunts me.

All those you have ever loved will die.

Lady Fate tilts her head, as if able to hear my thoughts. Or simply just perceptive enough to know where they went.

"I want to petition you for Henry Zhao's health."

Surprise lights the goddess. "You want to make a trade of healing for the father of your former lover? Your sister's soulmate?"

My stomach twists. "Yes."

"Why?" the goddess seems genuinely surprised. I am surprised by her not understanding, but I suppose she is a goddess and she is not influenced by the whims and emotions and morals of humans and the like.

"Because I promised him I'd try, and he seems like a good man. His health is failing."

"He is human, that does tend to happen."

"But he is still so young."

"He is."

There is a pause while I wait for her to say more, but she does not.

"Please?"

"What will you trade?"

"What do you want?"

"I want you to win the war."

"Is that all?"

Lady Fate seems to think for a second. "Yes. If you win the war, I will give you this boon. Win, and Henry Zhao's health will be restored to as it was before his injury."

Hope blossoms within me. "And there are no tricks? No strings attached?"

The goddess looks affronted and for a moment I worry that I've fucked everything up. "No, I will not trick. I am not the fae."

I flush with embarrassment.

"May I ask another question?" I try to derail the conversation away from my faux pas.

"Proceed."

"The prophecy," I begin, thinking back to her earlier assumption. "Everyone I've ever loved will die…is that set in stone?"

"It is."

My heart drops through my stomach. Like lead. Like an anvil. My belly bottoms out and fear takes me.

"But—" Hope blossoms in me as she proceeds to speak. "Not everyone who has died stays dead, do they?"

I stare at her, that desperate hope I've been secretly clinging to regarding Emrys's fate inflating. "No. They don't."

"Your soulmate has already died once. For all intents and purposes, he has fulfilled that portion of your prophecy. But that does not mean he is invincible. He can die again, but he doesn't need to."

"Is it romantic love only?" I love Maelona platonically—I always have—but the affection that I held for her romantically never crossed into love. I pray that is enough to keep her here. Living.

"No. All love, dear Evelyn. But…death sometimes only takes a second. Sometimes that second is enough to save them."

I blink. Maybe I won't lose them all. Maybe they'll be okay. And Gideon…to a degree he died already, he was dead to me. Is that enough?

"I must admit," she carries on. "I am surprised you did not ask me to bring back life again. Although, I'd have to refuse as all the deaths that have been taken are far too late to be returned. Still, I imagined your stubbornness would at least have you asking."

"I did so once, and since I have learned they say that apparently asking you to bring someone back is not worth the price you ask."

She cocks a brow. "Do you agree with them? Do you think I demanded too much for my Revenant? Your precious soulmate? If so, I could always just take him back."

My heart races and panic floods through me. I didn't mean to insult her, but yet I continuously keep putting my foot in my mouth where political semantics are concerned.

"I won't," she says after a delay. "But to answer you; I chose each cost dependent upon the individual. Perhaps whoever wrote in whichever journal you are referencing disliked what I asked. You must be aware of self-serving narratives, Evelyn. The fae tend to be my favored, but your kind can be fickle and selfish."

I begin to ask the goddess something again, but her waving hand interrupts me.

"I grow tired of this conversation. Please take your leave, young fae queen, and take with it the words I have selflessly given you today. I have gifted you more than anyone else."

Biting my tongue, I nod. "Thank you, Lady Fate."

The goddess inclines her head and then disappears from view.

I descend from the mountain top and hop through an inbetween.

Gideon is the first to find me on my return to the court. He nearly stumbles into me in a hallway and I startle back, so lost in my thoughts I hadn't realized where I was or where I was going. Nor, registered the internal alarm.

"Gideon!" I say, suddenly realizing he's exactly who I needed to speak to. "I have news."

"You do?" he quirks a midnight brow and takes a step back.

"I—" I cast a look around. "I did it. Your father will be healed."

Gideon's eyes grow comically large, whites surrounding the amber spheres. "You met with the goddess?"

I nod. "She accepted my terms."

"Which are?"

"Win the war and your father will be healed."

Relief and desperate hope clash in Gideon's eyes and silver lines the edges. Emotion, true, devastating emotion paints itself across his face. He lets out a broken sound like a sob and to my surprise he throws his arms around me.

I freeze, but he just holds me tight.

"Thank you. Thank you, so much, Evelyn."

It takes a moment for my mind to process what he's doing and what he's saying, but when he does, I gingerly wrap my arms around him too—carefully patting him on the back. His touch and smell bring mixed memories to the surface. The cedar and mint reminding me of the cabin and his rescue of me—of the hope he first instilled in me. The slight spice and musk, reminding me of the inn and the Roads.

I break from him, uneasiness from the memories working through me. I try to be as sensitive as possible, but my discomfort at his touch has me checking in on the bond. Emrys is aware, but he is okay. He understands. Thoughts are not controlled—they are also not indicative of my wants. They are just intrusive.

I do not desire him, and not a single cell in my body reacts in that manner.

Gideon steps back and quickly presses the heels of his hands against his eyes.

"Sorry, that was a little over the line. I just…I'm sorry, I'm just overwhelmed."

"Your apology is accepted."

He draws in a heavy breath and it stutters through his chest. A moment later he removes his hands from their rubbing. "So, what now?"

I shrug. "Now we prepare for war and hope with all hope that we win."

Gideon nods. "It's you, Evelyn, of course we'll win."

Feeling suddenly very awkward, I glance around. "I need to get going, we'll be leaving for the battlegrounds soon."

"Right, yeah. Of course." Gideon's voice is slightly awkward.

I nod and we go our separate ways. I quickly find my husband, but I don't have to relay the information, he already knows. Melding into his arms, I sigh and press my face to his chest, inhaling his scent—mostly vetiver today.

"I'm very sore," I complain softly.

Emrys chuckles and the sound rumbles in his chest. I cuddle in closer and he squeezes me tighter. Cupping the back of my head, he presses a kiss to the crown of my head.

"I can imagine you are." He nips the point of my ear. "Deliciously so."

I hum an agreement.

Together, the two of us meet with Enydd, Maelona, Wisteria, Julia, Baphet, Tirnoc, Bleddyn, and Aveda. Violante, barred from the upcoming war, and the fact that it is currently daylight, is not present. I still feel a surge of guilt and fear, a sick coil of dread, at preventing her from fighting as she wants to.

On the fringes, our Kings and Queensguard stand around us protectively. Far enough that the distance doesn't feel suffocating, but close enough—should we need them.

"Do you have the weapons?" Emrys asks Tirnoc and Baphet.

The males nod and Tirnoc tilts his auburn head to the door. Snapping his double-jointed fingers, servants come into the throne room, tugging carts loaded with weapons. The servants stop abruptly before the general and commander, planting the wheels down.

Drawing up a blade, Tirnoc lifts the blended metal to eye level. His brown eyes assess the sharp edge carefully before handing it to me and another to Emrys.

"Blades forged from your goddess-blessed blades will be effectively distributed to the warriors today."

Emrys and I gaze down at the daggers with longing. We'd handed off both Heart's-Desire and Oath-Sworn to be shattered and melted down, forged with new blades so that the others can stand a chance against the Wild Hunt.

I'd seen the mixed-metal blades in my vision, seeing the silver swirled with gold, and gold swirled with silver. At that moment I knew exactly what we needed to do. In addition to the advantage of midnight sun, we'll be leveling the playing field with these weapons. Against the forces of the Unseelie Court, the Vampire Court, and the Wild Hunt, our advantages with allies of the Seelie Court, House Council, and Arcana Society might be enough.

Already, I miss the blade dearly, and I know Emrys does too. He'd only just gotten his back, and already it is gone. But it is for the greater good. It is for the survival of our Court and people.

We sheath the blades we're given and nod to the commander.

"See that they're distributed evenly and caution everyone not to lose them. Should they find a stray mixed blade in battle, tell them to take it," I tell them. I do not mention how or why there would be a stray blade. I know we don't have enough to go around so whoever loses one will likely have lost their life too.

I draw in an anxious breath as Tirnoc gives everyone present a blade borne of our former goddess-blessed swords. When everyone possesses one, they sheath them, and take for the Faerie Roads, all of us departing and readying for the battle.

Maelona and several others hold packs weighted down with anti-Unseelie warded stakes that we will use for tonight before the battle tomorrow, to ward off any early attacks. It will do little if they decide to use fire or some other weaponry to cross the line, but it will keep the Unseelies physically on their side. After the night, they will then be used around the makeshift infirmary as an extra layer of protection.

I remember the warded tent stakes Gideon and I used across the Yukon as we travelled south, looking for exit. Looking for the Harbinger. A pang of nostalgia and stupidity winds through me. How different everything is now.

As everyone leaves, Emrys pulls Enydd back. Our former mentor takes a step backwards in surprise but turns to her once protégé.

"I wanted to thank you," Emrys begins, throat thick. "For everything you've done for me. For us. For being here today and for supporting us back during Century Training, even when you disapproved."

Enydd's jaw clenches and water lines her plum eyes. "You're very welcome, boy."

Emrys swallows. "I know we lose you tomorrow, so I just wanted to say…good bye, I guess. And thank you."

"I want to thank you as well, Enydd," I add. "You were the difference between us getting away and not, after Osian forced the chase. Without you, we would not be here today—in several ways."

Our former mentor looks away, uncomfortable with the influx of emotions and warmth. "I have lived a very long time, but you two have made me proud of the years I have put in. I am glad to have been part of your lives. To be so pivotal to you. Please know that you two also were significant in my life, as well."

We don't ask, but we move in unison, and my soulmate and I wrap Enydd in an embrace. She startles but after a second wraps us up too.

"We will miss you, Enydd," Emrys says.

"I will miss you both, too. You were the best Centurions I could have asked for."

Tears prickle my eyes and I force them away.

Once upon a time, Enydd was cruel and hated me, and I hated her. Now, we know tomorrow is her last day and death is knocking on her door. And I am sad for it.

What a difference all this time makes.

281

I think back to the beginning and how nothing is the same, what I was first destined for, versus what I am now. I look back upon the days in the Yukon; nobody, vulnerable, memoryless, human, Evelyn, to who I've transformed into; soulmate, wife, fae, Seelie Queen, Harbinger, and *Ceidwad Cudd,* Evelyn Corianne Gwyndolyn-Vanora. All my titles ring of power, burying the once-was as the nothing she was plucked out of and plunged into.

"We should go now," Enydd says, disentangling.

"Of course."

And then we traipse into the beginning of the end.

CHAPTER 29

The cabin ruin is the first thing we see when we step out of the Faerie Roads. The second is all the faeries and allies milling about the destroyed structure. The clearing is large and fits all of us extremely easily—especially since many trees have been removed and cleared. Tents are erected and carts of weapons are off to the side, warriors delegated by Tirnoc and Baphet handing them out. Over to the opposite side a food line is set up, stew being cooked, bread cooling, fruit sliced. Everything is in preparation for the warriors tonight, to be nourished before tomorrow's war.

Emrys and I find the designated commander's and general's tent—a giant emerald thing—and step inside. Inside is a war table surrounded by captains, commanders, and generals. I recognize a few, but namely Baphet and Tirnoc.

"What are the planned designations?" I ask, stepping up to the table.

Tirnoc immediately launches into explanation, introducing captains as he does. He tells us strategy, who will be fighting in squadrons with who, what everyone's duties are. He explains where and how the House Council and Arcana Society will assist. Gideon will be battling with the protectors of the Arcana Society, Maelona will stay near Julia and the Crows, Aveda will be working with the spy network that she is still singlehandedly upholding, Bleddyn will be paired with Tirnoc's forces, Enydd with Baphet, Wisteria will remain near Emrys and I.

It is unsaid why the Greyvale witch will be with us, but everyone knows.

Wisteria's sole mission is to take out the Unseelie Queen.

It also helps that she now possesses the healing Fairwalker power and to have a healer with the king and queen is irreplaceable. The King and Queensguard will surround us, paving the way for us to Caethes. It will be an added layer of protection for the witch. With her ability to counteract Caethes's chaos, I truly think she is the only one who will be able to get close enough to end her.

"The Arcana Society and the House Council will be bringing the vampires during the two hours of twilight we receive, after that, we lose their assistance," Baphet says. "Before and after that point we have the rest of their assistance, but it is important to note that the Unseelies will have many more vampires than us, and it will be a second wave to this battle. The vampires will be fresh and untried this night. They will be eager, and strong, and full of energy. We will be tired—but we mustn't forget."

Dread loops through me. Baphet has been through many battles, he understands these war games better than I could ever imagine. He knows these waves exist and how they come and go. This is unfamiliar territory for me. I have been in fights and on missions, in skirmishes and on assassinations, this is a whole new playing field and it is no game. Not to us.

I can practically hear Lady Fate cackling in my mind's eye.

The lullaby calls to me, repeating over and over in my head.

Rooks are crown and scorn,
She is deceit, hers was apart
Aneira and Maelona.
Knights are murder and mourn,
She is failure, her grief is heart
Julia and Wisteria.
Bishops are sacrifice and cost,
She is three, his was death
Me and Emrys.
Royals are found and lost,
She is true, his lies are breath
Corvina and Gideon.
Pawns are bait and invention,
They will die, they will define
Drysi, Elliot, Callahan, Enydd, and so many others.
Herby states the play of ascension,

A Game of Lady Fate's design.

We never did hear the Unseelie half of the ballad. It irks me that we don't know the players on Caethes's board, but for me none of that matters. She is the piece we must take to end the game.

Now, I wonder which of our pieces we must lose to formally lose our game. Our war. Aneira was a Rook and we continued on. Emrys and I are now rulers of our court but not the board, we are Bishops. We have lost our Queen piece in Corvina, does that mean losing Gideon—our King piece— defines it all? Surely not, surely this is all skewed by Lady Chaos's and Lady Karma's interception.

I feel a headache throb in my temple as I focus so hard on the lullaby, prophecy, and tactics. Emrys notices immediately and asks for water. He hands it to me wordlessly and I drink it down gratefully, taking icy swallow after icy swallow. Before I can say anything more, my husband hands me a small plate of fruit. I try to decline but he places it in my hand insistently.

"Eat," he commands. "You need to keep your strength up and the last thing you need is a headache. You don't need to be anymore sore for tomorrow."

I cock a brow, projecting thoughts of last night's antics through the bond. Emrys snorts and flushes, discreetly adjusting his pants.

Tease, he fires through the ether.

Oh, I certainly was, I tell him, sending the specific memory of me playing with myself on his bound and restrained body.

Emrys coughs and a few captains look over at him. He waves them off and sends me a dark look.

You'll pay for that.

Promise? I taunt while sucking the juice off a slice of melon and biting into it delicately.

He sends me back an image of his face between my legs, evoking all the emotion and sensation involved in it through the bond. My face flames while I chew, surprised by the zing of electricity that races straight to my clit.

More eyes land on me and bounce over to Emrys, but we both wave them off.

"Please continue," Emrys says to the gathered warriors. "You were explaining how the human Crows will be wielding iron blades."

The speaking captain, a faerie with cerulean hair and a blackout tattoo covering the entirety of his neck, goes back into detail, outlining the strategy they have previously mapped, and I have evidently completely tuned out. I continue eating my fruit in silence, alternating between eating and drinking, listening to the speakers. The headache wanes and I'm grateful for Emrys's care and concern. He flashes me a look, letting me know he read that through the bond.

The talks go on for hours, and though I know the strategizing is important, I would rather be in the moment, battling with my soulmate, than listen to tactics. I don't say this though, as I know that no one else possesses the connection Emrys and I do. No one else has a soulmate bond, no one else is a Centurion. The advantages we have in battle are unparalleled and unmatched. No one understands it.

We are mirrors. Equals. Soulmates. We are everything to each other.

Finally, it ends and Emrys and I are freed from the tent to speak with the others. We seek out Maelona first and find her with Aveda. They're holding hands.

It derails my plans of conversation a bit, but I tip my head in acknowledgement to the Admiral. "Thank you for staying with us."

Aveda inclines her head. "Maelona was my deciding factor. I have always held a fondness for her, and with you out of the way, I've finally gotten my chance."

Maelona runs a hand soothingly down Aveda's back. "I would've taken you at any opportunity."

Aveda turns, cheeks reddened, but displays her teeth playfully. "You would have, but I prize monogamy and desire commitment. You were not ready for it then."

"I was not." Maelona's tone turns richer, her hair reddening. "But I am now."

The two share a heated gaze and I glance at Emrys, suddenly feeling like an interloper. After a few pregnant moments they return their attentions to us and Aveda's softened gaze sharpens.

"I still expect you to hold up the promise of the Winter Carnaval."

"I swear to you their end will be by your hand if I can manage it."

Aveda looks at me squarely, taking me in, looking for the slightest sense of a faerie lie. The moment stretches and the Admiral works her tongue against her cheek.

"It is the deal."

Maelona twists some of Aveda's white hair in her grasp, utterly enamored with the faerie.

"What do you need?" Mae asks.

I look at Emrys awkwardly and silently ask for a private moment. Maelona also picks up on this body language and excuses herself from our partners. Together, the two of us walk a small distance away and halt near a tree line.

"I just wanted…" I trail off, emotion surging up my throat. "I just wanted a moment with my best friend."

Maelona quirks a brow. "This feels heavier than that."

I wait a beat.

"I'm scared," I admit. "Our forces are nearly matched with Caethes and even then, I know our death toll is going to be great. We will experience losses and I fear that you'll be one of them."

"You underestimate me so much?" Her tone is teasing.

She doesn't know about the prophecy that decrees everyone I have ever loved will die. She doesn't understand how severe the anxiety about this is. It's not that I am undervaluing her skills or not believing in her, it's just the forces of fate and destiny are oppressive and daunting.

"I do not underestimate Caethes."

Maelona shrugs. "She is only a queen. We are more."

"You really aren't frightful?"

"I'm terrified. But letting that fear debilitate me will do no good. I choose to focus on the facts that do not scare me. That being one of them. Knowing the Winter Carnaval cannot interfere is another." She pauses. "I thank you for that, and I thank you for rectifying the insult with Aveda." She gives me a conspiratorial look. "Her disdain for you drove her to my bed finally, so I also have you to appreciate for that."

I laugh, surprised by how easily she's lightened my doom and gloom. "I am glad you have found someone."

"Me too. I am happy with her. Far happier than I expected with commitment."

Maelona had always taken casual lovers—even we were casual affairs—but if Aveda is the one who has turned her to dedication…I am more grateful to the Seelie spy to have given that happy gift to my best friend.

"I'm so sorry for everything I've put you through. But I am so thankful you stuck by my side and put me in my place. You never let me get away with shit."

"I did not. And do not. You are my best friend, it is what I do."

Feeling a surge of emotion, I wrap my arms around her neck and pull her close. Maelona immediately returns the embrace, crushing me to her.

"I love you, Mae."

"I love you, too, Ev."

For a moment we stand together, holding each other. I smell Maelona's orchid and cherry scent with hints of Aveda's honey and amber musk. It is soothing and I breathe it in like it is the very air I need to sustain life. It isn't the all-consuming, home smell of Emrys, but it comforts me all the same.

When we pull apart, I know that we've begun a new phase, both in our lives, our relationship, and this war. I know that after tonight, nothing will be the same. And I know Maelona sees it too.

CHAPTER 30

The evening dawns on us after hours of planning, preparing, meeting, and strategizing. I am completely drained, both mentally from the day's toll, and physically aching still from mine and Emrys's exuberant lovemaking last night.

Outside the tent I have collapsed in, I hear the raucous sounds of drinks being passed around the fire, and regaling tales of old war and battle stories. Some stories I could contribute to, however less advanced my age than others, but I know my self-restraint—and in my currently exhausted position, I know I wouldn't have the will to refuse a drink. I cannot jeopardize the war on my addiction. I will not risk all these lives for a drop of liquor.

Even through the tent walls I can smell the acrid plumes of smoke and the whisper of pine on the wind. The scent of oiled steel and softened leather peppers the air, heightened by the heated summer climate. Despite it being north, it is not cold—not as cold as one would typically expect—and in the hemorrhaging heatwave, the degrees are sweltering in the day, and pleasant at night. I'm sure more than one person will be sleeping beneath the stars tonight—short duration as that may be.

Every now and then I hear a voice I distinctly recognize—Maelona, Aveda, Gideon, Julia, Wisteria, Bleddyn, and Enydd—and a few that takes me a pause to clue into—Baphet, Tirnoc, Rachel, Lorelai, and others. Beside me though, is the most familiar one of all.

"You should try to sleep, my love," Emrys soothes, running a hand down my arm.

I open my eyes, which I had been resting, trying to lapse into sleep, but anxiety prevents me from falling to slumber. And unfortunately, I am too keyed up in all the wrong ways to be soothed to bed by an orgasm or two.

Turning on my side, I face my husband, dipping my hand into the collar of his shirt. I trace the scar and stare at him—gold meeting silver. Our legs are tangled together, and a downy blanket covers us. One of his arms is wrapped beneath me, the other stroking my cheek—my shoulder, my hand.

"I wish I could."

"Tell me what's bothering you then."

"You can read my thoughts."

"Humor me."

"I'm afraid of you dying."

Emrys smiles and brushes a lock of hair behind my ear. "I am not so easy to kill. Also, Lady Fate assured your fears. I have fulfilled that portion of the prophecy once. She will not be taking me from you again."

"I'm afraid of dying, myself."

Emrys tightens his grip on me. "I won't let you."

"I'm afraid of missing out on the future I saw."

"Of our daughters."

The words strike directly into my soul. *Our daughters.* It hammers in a reality that I'd never knew could exist. Never knew I could want. But want it, I do desperately. Not right away, but one day. I can feel the void in my heart—in my soul—where they should be. Where they one day will be.

I swallow hard and nod. "I want them."

"I do too, love."

Tears burn and prickle in my eyes, my throat aches with the unshed. "One day?"

"One day," he promises.

Eventually his caresses lull me to slumber and I fall beneath the stars wrapped in the arms of my cosmically blessed, soul-bonded partner.

I'm lucid, but not awake. In a less than tangible form, I turn, searching. In my dreaming haze of unreality, I find the goddess standing behind me.

Lady Fate's scarlet hair is a war banner behind her, drifting as if in an ocean current, tendrils coiling about her frame. She is swathed in glittering white, like starlight made material. Her gemstone eyes of sapphire and emerald hold me, the mis-matching aspect lending an intense, eerie quality to her.

"On the eve of this war, I come bearing you a gift, young queen," Lady Fate intones.

I take in the goddess's tall presence, lifting a brow. "A gift?"

"You have been subjected to a time of turmoil, not how I had planned. My meddling sisters have set the board awry and the prophecies dealt are ill-fitting for their recipients. For that, I offer a boon."

I hold my breath.

"Because you wear so many new titles and names, I will show you how each of them came to pass."

Lady Fate lifts a hand and the cloudy haze I had scarcely noticed around us shifts, parting to reveal a warm cottage where a light-haired man and a dark-haired woman huddle together.

"You're certain?" the man asks.

The woman nods, and as she lifts her tear-filled eyes, my heart turns to glass—brittle and fragile.

It's Drysi.

Drysi has her hand clasped with the man's, the other over her womb. She's holding her belly protectively, and I realize she has just discovered her pregnancy.

The man laughs, tears of joy leaking from his night-dark eyes—Corvina's eyes. My glass heart cracks as I take in his appearance—truly take him in, and find more similarities. His silvery, salt-white hair despite being no more than thirty, his thickly lashed eyes, his straight nose, the jawline…

This is Rhodes Whitecrest.

My father.

Corvina's father.

Crystalline fractures spread in my chest as I wander closer, not of my own volition. I crouch beside my parents, my father placing his hand to my mother's belly, disbelief and hope burning in his gaze. I lift my hand to place it over theirs, but it drifts through like a smoky illusion. Their forms resettle and then they fold both their hands atop the small swell.

"Rhodes," Drysi starts. "I know this sounds impossible, but I think there are two."

Rhodes jolts in surprise. Beside him is a bowl of water and he takes it up. He peers in, and as he does so, he presses his hands more firmly to her. After a moment, his eyes flare wide. He lifts them to his pregnant fae love.

"You're right. Two girls."

Tears well up in Drysi's eyes and she chokes a sob. "I think I love them already."

My glass heart shatters in my chest, wrenching a broken sound from my throat. Faeries can't lie. Drysi loved us from the moment she discovered us. Silent tears track down my cheeks.

"Of course, you do." Rhodes presses a kiss to Drysi's brow. "You're going to be a wonderful mother, Acacia."

Acacia.

Not Drysi. Acacia.

I changed my name.

Drysi's—Acacia's words ring in my head. After Rhodes died, she changed her name. Did she keep the Vanora name? Is the Vanora name a true name? Or is it a façade like Drysi?

Too soon, the vision shifts and suddenly I'm standing at the base of the Seelie throne dais, Aneira sitting upon it in a dress of hunter green. At her feet is Drysi, holding two swaddled babes, sobbing, tears running down her face.

This time the tears are not of joy; they are of sorrow and grief.

My broken heart twists at the sight of the faerie who'd raised me.

"Please, My Queen," Drysi begs between sobs. "Take them, please. I have no one else, I trust no one else. You can keep them safer than I ever can. I will not rest until that traitorous coven is in the ground. My daughters will always be in jeopardy while those witches live. Please, take them while I eliminate those who stole their father. Never tell them of this. I need my girls safe."

"Acacia—"

"It's Drysi, now," she interrupts swiftly. "Please. Take care of them until I return. I cannot come back until I destroy every witch who took Rhodes from me. I swear I will decimate them all, and only then shall I return."

"Drysi, that is a severe oath to make."

"I loved him," Drysi says with a feral intensity. "But I love them more. I can't put them in danger." Drysi gazes down at her two sleeping infants, one with a shock of black hair, the other a dusting of white. "I love them with all my heart, and I will not stop, even when *it* stops beating."

"Please, Aneira. Please do this for me. I will never ask you for another thing, and I will pledge my undying loyalty and fealty to you."

Aneira's yellow eyes flare with interest. "Swear it."

Drysi does. Through a thickened throat and silent tears, she does.

Tears fall on baby Corvina and baby Evelyn as she presses kisses to their tiny foreheads.

"Mama loves you both."

Reluctantly, with her entire bleeding heart on her sleeve, Drysi hands over the dozing babes to her queen. A cracking, painful sound slips from Drysi as Aneira takes both children. Baby Evelyn immediately wakes and begins to cry, the sharp pitch making Aneira wince as Drysi hitches a sob. She grits her teeth before meeting the queen's eyes.

"Love them until I return."

And then Drysi strides out of the room, her cries shaking her shoulders as she passes through.

For a moment Aneira is alone with us, her yellow eyes staring down at infant Corvina and Evelyn. Tears gather in the corners of her eyes.

"I had a babe once," she tells us softly. "Golden eyes, garnet hair, dark wings." She strokes our leathery wings and we squirm. "I couldn't keep him. Everything about him was a painful reminder of what once was. What could have been. I told no one I was with child, but when he was born, I paid a witch in secret to bless him with luck so that he would not be killed when I surrendered him. I couldn't bear to look at him, and I thought the safest place for him was as far from me, so that's why I gave him to the Dark Court.

"He's grown a little older now, and no longer winged. A group of Unseelie cleaved them, held him down, and tore them in the nursery. It had to be done, I couldn't have them putting the pieces of his parentage together, and then after I had them killed for it."

Aneira gazes about the room, looking out over a tapestry of her likeness.

Horror winds through my gut. Aneira had Emrys's wings taken from him. Out of some sick and twisted maternal instinct to protect him—she *butchered* him. A foreign surge of hatred for Aneira rushes through me.

"I ordered all memory of my wings to be removed from art and history before he was born. Altered by hand, magic, or glamour. I made all my subjects swear never to speak of it, even pleaded with Caethes—a last favor to what we once were—to make her denizens do the same." Her voice cracks. "Perhaps she saw a likeness of what she once was in me, because she did."

Longing enters Aneira's gaze as she holds us. "Perhaps you two are my second chance, because I regret giving up my boy. I will not fail you now."

The world shifts again.

"Why are you showing me all this?" I ask desperately, clutching my chest. All of the emotions are a storm on my heart, crushing it, catching it in a whirlwind.

"Because it made you what you are," Lady Fate responds, from behind me.

Maelona stands before me, six years old and full of grief. Her hair is blue, dark like the depths of the ocean. Her sadness is as deep as a trench, coloring her every move. She fiddles with something in her hands—an orchid.

"I've never seen that flower before," a small child's voice says. I smile, remembering a time when it was soft, before it took on its signature huskiness that allowed me to pass as a male for so many years.

Young Evelyn steps into focus, silvery hair braided in two thick ropes down her back. She's dressed in fighting leathers, young Maelona is clad in a spider silk body suit.

"It was my mother's favorite," Maelona answers, dejected. "But she died."

"I don't have a mother," young Evelyn responds. "Not truly. The queen is like my mother, though."

"Did she die, too?"

"No, she just left me and my sister." An idea strikes young Evelyn. "Maybe the queen can become like your mother, too. Such a thing can be done. Queen or not."

Maelona stares at her. "You're kind of weird, you know that?"

"Yes. And most everyone says I'm not the nice sister."

"Who are you?"

"I'm Evelyn. Who are you?"

"Maelona. I think you don't need to be nice. Faeries aren't supposed to be kind, anyway."

"Really?"

Maelona shrugs. "All the ones I've known."

Young Evelyn seems to ponder this. "Do I need to try to be nice to be your friend?"

Maelona laughs. "No, but I will tell you if I don't like how you're being."

"Deal."

The two girls shake hands and the world warps again. Through a watery haze, a new scene begins to form.

He's lounging on a chaise, scandalously swathed in gauzy fabric with a young fae male draped across him and a female running her hands through his hair, his head resting in her lap. He's sixteen and I am thirteen. It's the first time I'm seeing Emrys.

My younger self stands in a gown of cobalt, leathery wings outstretched. It's a faerie revel, one hosted by a debauched Seelie who has connections to the Unseelie. Corvina, Maelona, and I had snuck out to attend it.

Emrys caresses the jaw of the male, eyes intent on me. We're strangers here, yet there's a tension. An insistent tug. A familiarity, though not understandable. He looks away.

A flash of jealousy rushes through me as I watch my husband pull the mouth of the male to his, kissing him. He was so goddess-damned beautiful, even so young. Now, as an adult, he is heart-wrenchingly gorgeous.

Corvina and Maelona suddenly bump into young Evelyn, and in that flash of a moment the connection is broken and my younger self is led away.

I'm shown brief flickers of the final Centurion battle. Of Osian surging up behind us and killing Emrys, of me screaming for his life, of commanding the goddess.

The scenery changes and now I am the Harbinger, my past self armored in gold, wings proud behind me.

It's another party, at this one, both the queens are in attendance. My heart twists when I catch sight of Aneira—warm, vibrant, alive. But the memories of how she'd wronged my soulmate so grievously sour the affection—like a rot, spreading throughout. The Seelie Queen is dressed in gold, positively dripping in pearls, diamonds, and crystals, Caethes the silver opposite. Were they lovers at this time? How could I not have known?

Among the party-goers, everyone is masked, and candles burn in recesses of rock walls, the only light provided in this cave. The cave itself is red rock and clearly divided between Seelie and Unseelie, with some gray area in the middle where a handful of members of each court interact. Interspersed throughout the room are those known—friends, enemies, allies, a couple of my former lovers—and strangers, all made up of faeries, witches, vampires, and halflings.

One such halfling is Gideon.

I draw breath, my past self none the wiser. I watch, my past self simply surveying, not assessing any threats, but being aware for my queen, as Gideon weaves through the crowd. He has an insignia on his breast, denoting the Arcana Society—back when he was a soon-to-be protector. Someone across the room catches sight of this.

Emrys is grinning as he crosses to Gideon, fitted in his anonymous, black Revenant regalia, an elaborate mask over his features, dark red hair slicked back. He is somewhat disguised, but I'd know those golden eyes anywhere.

Emrys strikes up a conversation with him, but I can't hear what they're saying at first, so I move closer. My soulmate claps my ex-lover on the shoulder.

"Then do I have a story for you. Care to hear about the dawn of the Harbinger and Revenant?" Emrys asks, eyes flickering to my past self, helmed in gold.

I realize it was him.

Emrys is the one who told Gideon the story. Emrys is who started Gideon's fascination. Emrys is how I read that journal after the cabin's arson.

It was all him. It was his last-ditch effort to get the words out and potentially jog my memory. My disguised self doesn't react to Emrys in the slightest, aside from some mild perturbance.

The sight starts wavering and suddenly I feel a presence behind me. My alarm pinging a familiar tone. One I thought I'd never feel again. My heart seizes and tears burn in my throat. I don't want to believe it.

"Evva, Evva, Evva. You were certainly holding out on me all these years, weren't you?"

I turn in disbelief, and there, wings out, long black hair a free cascade—is Corvina. Her night sky eyes smolder with warmth as she tsks.

"Married to that gorgeous fae male, and you never told me?"

"Vina?" I ask breathlessly.

She extends her arms at her sides. "In spirit. Lady Fate is giving you an unprecedented kindness."

Tears immediately course down my cheeks. "How can this be?"

Corvina shrugs. "She's a goddess, she can do what she wishes. But do not change the subject. I know you hadn't remembered everything, but you're telling me you didn't remember any of *that*?" she says, indicating Emrys's blurry form conversing with Gideon.

"That's my soulmate, you know."

"Mm, and he's speaking to mine, but you still got a taste of both. Didn't you?"

Color flushes deep on my cheeks, burning my face. The heat mixing with the tears is an overwhelming combination and I end up choking on a poorly suppressed sob.

"I didn't know. I'm sor—"

"I jest. You better not apologize for something we didn't have knowledge about. We didn't even believe soulmates were real, Evva."

"I still am, though. Sorry, that is. I just...I don't understand how it all got so fucked up. You should be here still. You're the good one. The kind one."

"I'm still fae. I do have that faerie trickery in me like everyone else. I like to tease and taunt, sister. I am not as good as you make yourself believe."

"Better than me."

She lifts a brow. "That may be so, but we were dealt different lives. I was little more than a pretty face in some gowns who could wield a knife if need warranted it. But you? You can kill with your bare hands and you will ruin anyone who hurts those you care about. That is a sort of goodness, is it not?"

"Only a faerie would equate goodness to violence."

Corvina grins. "We are Unseelie by nature and born. We were just raised Seelie."

There is silence as my twin stares after her unmet soulmate, wonder and curiosity in her face. "How different it could've all been if we'd met."

It's disconcerting to me to see my face—the identical shape and planes—look so longingly at Gideon. Once upon I time, I may have gazed at him like that, but no more—never again. Corvina simply keeps staring, softness in her eyes.

"I know he's problematic. He nearly betrayed you in some ways and outright betrayed you in others."

"You are correct."

Corvina sighs. "But I think I could fix him."

I groan and look skyward. "I wouldn't be holding my breath if I were you."

"Oh, what am I even talking about this for?" Corvina groans. Suddenly, my twin sister is crossing the gap between us, and before I can even react, she's wrapping her arms around me.

Immediately, I grow boneless. All the steel in my spine, the strength of my will, it all falters beneath my sister's touch. I've missed her so fucking much. And here she is. Warm, familiar. Her scent of night-blooming jasmine and the variety of perfumes she fancied enveloping me. It is so wholly Corvina that the tears turn to sobs as I clutch her desperately.

Her hand strokes the back of my head as I cry, and cry, and cry.

"I know, Evva. I'm so sorry." She presses a soft kiss to my temple, and it's as if I can feel the imprint of her lips there. "But I am okay. And I do not blame you. My death was not your fault. Absolve yourself of that guilt."

"I'm not—" I choke out.

"You are. Let it go," she commands.

A sob tears from my throat and with it the hidden guilt that Corvina pulled from the depths of my soul. All this time

I'd been blaming myself, shoving the pain so deep. But now, my twin allowing me to let it go—to heal—I can begin to forgive myself. Corvina can still choose to forgive me—or not lay blame—but it's going to take a little more for me to banish it.

"I have to go," she whispers as my sobs begin to ease. She pulls away from me and I clutch her like a desperate toddler, unwilling to be parted.

"Please."

"I can't," she says. She cups my face between her hands. "I love you. Now you need to live. And make that bitch pay."

I crack on a broken laugh, tears burning in my throat as I nod. "I will. I love you, too."

"Good. Now wake up."

I do with a start.

My limbs flail and immediately my husband wakes beside me. Instantly, he reads the distress through the bond and I'm bared so open that it's as if I'm flooding it with the dream—the gift from the goddess. Emrys sees it all. In a moment, it's all laid out and I begin to cry in the waking world. Wrapping my arms around my knees, I try to hold myself together. Emrys doesn't hesitate and gathers me to him, holding me close—keeping me from shattering.

"Vanna...I'm here."

"I know," I whisper brokenly. "I just need you to stay."

"Always."

My soulmate is there through the darkest of moments. The most violent of sobs. Never once does he let me go. When exhaustion claims me, he lays with me and he is awake, stroking hands through my hair, waiting until I fall to sleep again.

This time, I dream of nothing.

CHAPTER 31

Feeling as if I blinked, the entire day of the eighth comes and goes with an air of anxiety. Tension floods the atmosphere and weaves within our forces like a cloying wave. Everyone is keyed up, amped, and jittery. We are hours away from war. From the pivotal moment of the reign change, urged on by petulant goddesses.

I am stressed as I go about, finding the squadrons and battalions all in different armor, different weapons, all designated for different strategies and different tactics. Baphet and Tirnoc seem confident in the plans, but I can help but blanch, especially when I catch sight of Maelona with Julia and her murder of Crows, all dressed in black, the brunettes, Lorelai and Rachel flanking them.

Bleddyn, leading our King and Queensguard, catches my eye and makes his way over. I step away from my husband and meet with the last of Aneira's Queensguard. He holds my gaze with an air of gravity—grave and solemn and resigned. He folds his pale hands before himself in his black armor, his deep, blood red wings pinned behind him in a measure of respect. Ducking his dark head, he begins to speak.

"It has been an honor to know you, Evelyn. To have watched you grow from the infant at Aneira's footstep, to the Centurion you became, and now the queen you are." He lifts his head, his black eyes meeting me. "Whatever may happen tonight, know that I have the utmost faith in you."

Emotion thickens my throat and I can't speak. I nod and reach out a hand. Bleddyn takes my forearm and holds it. I take his. We shake up and down once.

When he releases me, I have a foreboding feeling I don't want to acknowledge.

Bleddyn's departing back is swallowed by the horde of guards and I watch him disappear within the ranks.

The House Council and Arcana Society are slowly arriving, bringing halflings, witches, and the odd werewolf. The vampires will come later. With them, preparing to fight with them, is Gideon.

I swallow thickly as I catch sight of the halfling I'd once loved. Of my sister's true love and soul-bonded partner. He had been her destiny. He was supposed to be an integral change to the courts, to the settling of the Unseelie's feral ways. But Fate had been fucked, the same way we were fucked over.

Making my way over to Gideon, he looks up with my approach. He's dressed in a protector's uniform—black canvas and leather. The uniform has always been equal amounts clinging and loose, flexible when need be and strong for others. As he makes his way over, he tightens the Velcro on the vambraces that hold an assortment of knives.

"I wanted to thank you again for choosing our side," I say awkwardly to begin. "You had many reasons to turn on me and to hate me."

Gideon shrugs. "Like we've said before, we were never meant to be and we were wrong for each other. It sounds like a broken record, but that's because it's true. I think deep down we knew, but at the same time we felt some connection." He clears his throat. "For transparency's sake; I do want to make it clear that I don't regret what we had. At the time we both needed each other."

"I agree. I do not regret it, but I do not wish for the likes of it again."

"Good," Gideon says cracking a smile. "Because you still scare the shit out of me."

I throw my head back on an unexpected laugh. "Wasn't I supposed to be different?" It's an echo of what was thrown at me at the Winter Carnaval.

"I was wrong," he says jokingly and it doesn't hit a mark that hurts.

I extend a hand out. Gideon gazes at it critically with those amber eyes for a moment before sighing, smiling, and taking it.

"To our wicked ways of delinquency?"

"May we be as cold as iron," I finish.

His warm palm heats mine and for a moment I think about the times we had together, when we were all that mattered because we were surviving and alone. Flickers of the cabin, pizza, whiskey, fire, the forest and northern lights, a tent, battles, stoking chaos, tricking a queen, plans and lies, the truth. I do not hold any blame to him any longer and I forgive him for all he has done. I will not forget, but it is all now in the past.

We break apart, understanding lingering between us.

"I hope we both come out of this alive."

"So do I," I say.

I leave with another nod.

While I'm thanking the Arcana Society and House Council for their presence and assistance here, I begin to be sucked into the recesses of my mind. Of nostalgia and memory. I slip aside and find myself within a copse of trees.

I'm staring blankly through the forest, simultaneously haunted and longing for the dreams of last night. Of Lady Fate's gift of my sister. I miss her so desperately my heart aches. I feel such a void without her. It's only Emrys that keeps me from falling from the precipice of oblivion. Not even Maelona—for all the love I hold for her—is enough to prevent that.

I break myself from the reverie and return to my soulmate. The two of us travel to our tent and don our armor.

I, for the first time since returning from my abduction, wear the golden armor I'd had crafted as my designated uniform as the Harbinger. Pure gold, shining and scalloped. The Seelie crest is emblazoned on the chest, etched ivy winding down the breastplate, stars trailing across the shoulders. The chain mail at the joints is gold too, glittering in the faint light. Etched chrysanthemums sharpen the shoulders like epaulets, petals floating down the entire piece. I do not wear the helm, no longer hiding my identity. The large openings for my wings are conspicuously visible and empty.

Emrys wears black leather everything, sensitive and vulnerable areas reinforced with patches of thicker hide. All his is newly etched. Two sets of wings are drawn across his back—his and mine, our losses. The moon cycles trace down his spine. Like me, chrysanthemums are present, but unlike me, his are on his knees. Daggers, both inscribed and veritable weapons cover his arms and legs. Stars line the collar of his baldric strapped to his person.

In our tent, alone, I let a few tears eke out.

"I love you."

"I love you, too," his whispers, pressing a chaste kiss to my mouth.

I return it, reveling in the sweetness of it all.

We make our final rounds as the clock winds down, and true evening descends. We line and group up, our forces along the forest's edge. Like chess pieces.

As we wait, my mental alarm pings and I stand at attention.

Caethes and her forces arrive. They crest a hill and traverse down the slope, filling the landscape with silver armor and beasts. The Unseelie Court has always possessed more fae beasts than the Seelie, and droves of them lead the procession. Most of them look like some amalgamation of what killed Corvina and Callahan, others more reptilian, some avian. Her fae are festooned with weaponry, the few witches she'd amassed clad in black and silver, intimidating with displays of magic—Blackthorn vines, Goldwine shields, and the like. I sense only three werewolves among her ilk.

Caethes herself arrives on the back of an enormous fae beast, something strongly resembling a dragon, its face rather wolf-like with a snout filled with razor teeth and salivating black gums. Fur melds with scales and flesh, all of it some shade of sickening, oily black. Its eyes are twin orbs of blue fire with obsidian antlers that rival her frosty ones. Its wings are tattered but they are very like the ones I once had.

I see a bridle on the beast and the spellcraft carved into it. A fae beast cursed by witches. This isn't its true form, this is a punishment derived from a coven. For all I know, this beast is truly gentry fae or higher. I wonder how many heart's desire commands Caethes has from it and how she managed them.

The Unseelie Queen is wrapped in spidersilk, a bodysuit that is skintight to her frame and legs, tucked into tall silver boots. There is an overcoat and cape that gives the illusion of a gown, her entire being silver and white like a shining beacon in the darkness. Like some sort of holy angelic salvation against the night. It's sick. The vision of benevolence she tries to display when she is the very furthest thing from it.

The Dark Court Queen makes her way through the masses and crosses the foremost line of her forces. She stops directly after them, tilting her face up at Emrys and I who are also on the frontlines. We do not hold ourselves to the second row like the Bishops the goddess determined us to be.

"So, this is where it ends," Caethes announces.

Before Emrys or I even have a chance to respond, the air suddenly charges, filled with the pause before lightning strikes. I look up to the sky where the horizon turns lavender with crackling electricity and flooded with waves of viridian akin to the northern lights. The heavens open up, and three ethereal figures descend to the earth between the battlelines.

Lady Fate lands first on delicate white feet, her scarlet hair like a war banner behind her. Mismatched eyes holding untold power. She holds herself with all the grace of her divine status, more regal than all the present royalty combined.

Flanking her, Lady Chaos, all golden and brash holds a restless energy, like an image of some Greek deity—Athena or Artemis. On the opposite side, I can only assume is Lady Karma, sapphire eyes and dark skin, long braids of darkness coil about her like snakes—likening her to Medusa, against her sister's Greek goddess.

The three goddesses take in the battle formations and the forces mustered. Everyone drops to a knee in their presence. Everyone but the fae rulers.

Shock crosses Caethes's face, but she does not show waver on her perch upon the cursed fae beast. Her midnight eyes flood wide for a moment before she composes herself. Emrys and I manage a dutiful inclination of our heads, something very close to impertinence, but more acknowledgement.

"So, it begins as it must end, the wicked Game of Lady Fate," the goddess in question starts, her voice immeasurably powerful. "Champions, Pawns, all pieces between, thank you for the role you play today. I acknowledge your presence and the sacrifices you made in the name of a change in era. Of the rule of the fae, the changing of sovereigns, the transference of power. Today, it ends, as it must, in one form or another."

Lady Chaos steps forward and when she speaks, I'm transported back to the moment she interfered with the original bargain I made for Emrys. I am haunted by her voice and I feel my hackles rise in response. If I still had my wings, they'd be flaring wide. Even now, I feel the muscles where they were once attached, twitch.

Lady Chaos seems to sense my irritation and she glances at me, smirking. My hackles rise even more. Then, as if I'm nothing, she looks away, snubbing me. I have to rein in my ire.

"We shall not return any souls from the veil of the dead, whomever passes by strike of blade or by any hand, will remain fallen," Lady Karma says. "We will not offend the universe's law during a war. What is meant to be will be, whatever is reaped, will be sown."

Lady Fate lifts her pale palms above her, cupping the setting sun. "Let the battle commence."

Lady Karma holds a silver bell and chimes it seven times—stating the hour.

And with that, the three goddesses turn into pillars of light and shoot for the stars, landing among them and burning brighter than any other.

Without further ceremony the attack begins.

CHAPTER 32

I have no time to get my bearings before the bloodshed. Swords slash and clash, around us death moans and battle cries sing to the vibrant sky, arrows twang and thwack, meeting nothing and flesh.

Caethes immediately turns tail and weaves behind her lines, retreating to a hilltop to watch the carnage from her fae-cursed perch. There's already a flush to her face, a frenetic gleam in her eyes. The chaos is beginning and she is getting drunk on it.

Emrys and I stay side by side, carving our way through, Wisteria at our heels. We cut down forces, knowing this is only the first of many waves. Come night, the vampires will descend. Come moonlight and the Wild Hunt will arrive.

I am little more than my body, my mind working with singular purpose in tandem with Emrys. A snake-scaled faerie falls beneath my blade at the same time as a fae with flesh mimicking bark gurgles on Emrys's. A spatter of crimson mars my husband's features, crossing his nose and the left side of his face. I can feel a similar pattern dripping down my neck and splattering my jaw. I do not bother to wipe it; this battle is still in its infancy and there will be much more blood drawn this night.

Our singular mission tonight is to get to Caethes and eliminate her.

I catch sight of Gideon fighting with the other protectors of the Arcana Society. He and his former comrades move as a unit, stabbing and slashing, shooting and aiming. The protectors wield blades and bows and guns, the latter cracking through the air in a wild juxtaposition.

As effective as guns can be, there are certain supernaturals that have a slight resistance to the basic bullets. Unless they're iron or silver, a blade is often times better.

With the right squadron, Maelona leads the Crows with Julia, the two of them marking the helm as the sea of black takes on the wave of silver. The humans bear arms of iron and the fae screech and fall beneath the burning metal. The warrior princess herself is clad completely in the Crow's black, leather from head to toe, her midnight hair bound in a circlet on her head.

Overhead, aerial attacks ensue. Battles are launched and swords are drawn, bodies collide and spin out together, tackling and clawing. Corpses fall, impaled on swords, crashing upon the earth or comrades or enemies. Emrys and I weave through the maze of them all, keeping alert of any sky created dangers.

The Admiral falls in line with the Crows, tagging along, not like a lost puppy, but rather a nomad that feels a temporary draw to one thing or place—at least for a short time. She rises into the air on her signature wings, sending arrows raining down like hellfire on Unseelie forces. The hail of her weaponry is unparalleled, the volley impossible to dodge. Nearly every one of her marks strikes true. After her aerial assault, she lands and once again joins her group, sidling up to Maelona.

The two battle fiercely together.

A werewolf crosses directly in front of us and tears a nearby Seelie limb from limb. Wisteria gasps, but then blasts it with a charge of chaos. The werewolf goes tumbling into the fray and I watch as Bleddyn impales it through the spine. He casts the corpse away without any acknowledgment, continuing the fight.

Afan—the turncoat Seelie—is decapitated directly in front of us by Enydd's urumi. It flashes twice before she tugs and lops off with ease. Afan's body tumbles away from his head, the two connected by a spreading pool of claret.

Witch magic lashes around us, chains of Blackthorn vines, shields of Goldwine protection, notes of Frostsinger submission. My adrenaline thrums through me, my body on constant alert from every direction, searching for any threats from the sky to the earth, both physical and magical.

I spin, sensing something amiss behind us. There, I find an Unseelie about to make a grab for Wisteria. I grab a small dirk from my arsenal and throw it with precision, directly between her brows. Red blood leaks down her face before her white eyes roll back and she crashes to the ground.

Wisteria's sclera-less black eyes widen and then fly to me. "Thanks," she rasps.

"Of course."

Emrys has continued our forward progression, and I turn just as he stabs a Blackthorn witch through the eye. Several ropes of Blackthorn briars vanish across the warzone. The body falls and we cross over it, battling back-to-back for a moment as forces attempt to attack us.

My husband and I press against each other as I take on an Unseelie and Emrys dispatches a second Blackthorn witch. In three moves each, matching, we take out our opponents.

I think about asking Wisteria to add a chaos bubble over our small party, but the witch needs to be collecting all the chaos she can. She can't risk wasting that energy when it'll all be needed to overpower the Unseelie Queen.

Beneath us, the ground is becoming mushy. Saturated with blood and overworked by countless footfalls. I feel it squelch beneath my boots, a slight slide in my step. I immediately correct my footwork—the years of Century Training coming second nature. To solidify my realization, a faerie loses their footing and slips into the muck. A reddish mixture smears across their garb. Emrys plunges his sword down into his chest, the dying faerie gurgling once, adding to the ruined earth.

A sting on my cheekbone has me hissing and I turn in the direction of the assault.

Tadgh's nameless brother stands from where the whipped blade struck me. His matching dark hair and dual-pupiled eyes takes me aback for a moment. His brother had been a softer Unseelie—weak perhaps, but not worthless, not like Caethes had determined him to be.

316

"Mutilated bitch," he hisses.

Fury flashes through me and through the soulmate bond. Emrys senses my wrath and my desire—the intention I have in ending this faerie. My soulmate passes me his sword in a one-handed toss and I catch it as easily.

In a lightning strike of a movement, I cross the two swords at the faerie's neck and scissor them—effectively relieving his head from his body. Blood spurts from the stump at his shoulders, spraying arterial over a couple surrounding faeries. He thumps to the ground while his fingers twitch with the last dying nerve endings.

A hysteric cackle sounds and I snap my gaze over. Cariad is there, tittering with a manic gleam in her eyes as she swipes her fingers through the blood newly coating her face. Cariad has always seemed a little more unhinged than other Dark Court fae, and here, it seems that atypical presentation is making her more susceptible to the chaos. I can see it in her eyes, the way that she moves. It's like she's high, basking in the sensations. That glint is still there as she licks Tadgh's brother's blood from her fingers.

The borderline cannibalistic qualities of the Unseelie have always been relegated to the more unstable of the Fair Folk. It is not an overly natural way of the fae, though it isn't frowned upon or disgraceful. But the Light Court determines that that behavior denotes the Dark Court, and as such, Seelies do not partake in, nor display those habits.

Someone knocks into me and I lose sight of Cariad as she melds into the fray, dancing through the violence.

Around us, the war wages, raging upon the earth and in the sky. Winged faeries battle above or send overhead attacks, swooping and diving, taking opponents out in a tackle or firing arrows below. Bleddyn is one such faerie, his dark red wings carrying him high up in the lavender and jade sky.

It's criminal really. How such a beautiful sky filled with goddess created Northern Lights crowns such a terrible day. Such an odious occasion. While blood runs freely upon the earth, the sky flashes and dances to a song only it can hear.

Far ahead, having circled the far reaches, Baphet and Tirnoc have their battalions attacking from opposing sides of our field. Slowly, they're converging and crushing the Unseelie forces between them. By force or death, the Unseelies fall beneath the two generals might, their battalions eager to meld together.

I don't know how much time passes, but Emrys and I carve our way. The time, however, becomes apparent when the full moon ascends in the sky and the shadows emerge.

The Wild Hunt floods the field, converging on our forces and attacking with fervor. The only thing they didn't anticipate is the goddess-forged blades. The smaller weapons—dirks and knives, blades—all now have the ability to harm and eliminate the Hunt. It significantly levels the playing field, and the Unseelies balk at their advantage being usurped.

I slice out and sever the head of an attacking shadow, his feral grin his final façade as the darkness of his skull tumbles to the ground. I stomp on it as I take on another. Emrys beside me plunges his knives through the hearts of three in quick succession. Behind us, Wisteria continues gathering the chaos, a high glittering in her black eyes, causing shakes in the hand that holds her own goddess-forged blade.

With every strike I fall further inside a space in my mind. Into a space where my consciousness ceases to exist and I am purely action. Three more opponents, and I'm lost to it.

Reality slams into me when I'm met with the deceased face of Bleddyn.

His wings are shredded, his eyes glassy, blood coats his face. My heart aches at the sight and I take the moment to crouch down and shutter his eyes. My slender fingers are completely saturated in blood. My hands look dipped in paint.

Our losses tonight have been great already, and not yet have we even received our second wave. The hour in which the vampires will join the fray.

We've been at this for hours now, slowly killing our way through the field and forest, making our way to Caethes. With every advance we make, Caethes escapes further from us. She is not fighting. Not for her people or her pride. She is watching, overseeing, cowering. She is a coward. A joke. A mockery.

I rejoin the fray with a groan. My arms ache, my body hurts, my throat is parched—desperate for water. Blood covers every inch of me, all my paleness turned garnet. My husband wears the scarlet similarly, his golden eyes standing out like twin suns beneath the gore.

"Witch, you okay back there?" I ask as I meet a crosswise strike against a member of the Hunt. I stab with my opposite hand, ending the faerie for good.

"Fine," she replies, voice tight.

I chance a look behind me and see sweat beading on her brow, sliding down her throat. Fear strikes me in response.

"Slow down on the chaos consumption, it's making you sick."

"I thought that might be what's happening," she says dryly, giggling shrilly. "I don't feel good."

Concern slices through me. I reach out to Emrys through the bond.

Wisteria needs a break; the chaos is going to give her an overdose.

There's a cliff-face up ahead, we'll stop there a moment, Emrys replies.

Working through the forces separating us from a brief reprieve, we guide Wisteria. In minutes we make it to the sheer wall of rock and I urge Wisteria to sit. Emrys and I flank her, staring out at the war waging beyond.

"Just try to breathe," I coax her.

"Gee, hadn't thought of that one, Faerie." Wisteria's breathing turns thin and reedy. "I think I'm going to be sick."

"You're welcome to use the forest floor." I soften. "If you need to let go of it then do so."

"No," Wisteria groans. "If I do that, I'll lose all this progress and feeling like shit will have meant nothing."

"You're no use to us if you can't stand long enough to kill Caethes."

"Fuck you, Faerie."

Wisteria throws up behind us.

I nod and thin my lips in a *"that's what I thought"* sort of way.

An Unseelie launches at us, and with the same care I'd use to bat a fly, I dispatch him. It continues similarly—Wisteria's sickness, Emrys's and my killing, our waiting.

Eventually, Wisteria returns to her former self. Her sweat disappears, the glassiness of her gaze vanishing, the vomiting ceasing. She straightens and gets her bearings, surprisingly lucid all things considered.

"I'm good. Let's go find this bitch."

"All right, but slow down on the chaos. Don't take so much in."

"Don't tell me what to do." She winks, laughing playfully. "But I'll be careful."

We continue our passage and onslaught through the trees. All of the animals have escaped from this war, not a single call of birdsong to be heard. No mice skitter underfoot. Ferns and berry bushes are trampled beneath the war's feet, trunks and bark bearing the marks of missed sword swings, fresh gouges leaking sap. Even though we're on the fringes of the central battle, blood muddies the ground here.

Nearby, I catch sight of Maelona and Aveda, both of them blood splattered and vicious. They lead the Crows, cutting swaths through the Dark Court numbers, the humans lashing with iron, burning and branding the Fair Folk. Both the warrior princess and Seelie spy are near unmatched in their prowess, almost rivalling Emrys and I.

Further away the Arcana Society leads a charge against a growing squadron of Unseelies. Methodically the protectors in black garb dispatch their numbers, Gideon among them. He's bloody, fangs out, knives and guns blazing. His black hair is slicked back with blood, amber eyes intent on his goal.

I realize with shock that among the numbers of protectors is Caspian. His black hair, too, is soaked with blood and pushed back. As if gelled into place. His pale skin isn't visible beneath the warpaint of death and blood. His golden eyes—so much like my husband's—are raging furiously, vengefully, determinedly. His white teeth bear his fangs in a feral grimace, shooting and slicing all enemies on all fronts.

This boy. This seventeen-year-old boy is virtually unstoppable.

I pray he makes it out of this.

We continue to our fight with Caethes.

CHAPTER 33

True night for midnight sun begins to fall, and with it my strength begins to wane. Darkness begins creeping over the horizon, threatening the arrival of both forces number of vampires. The trees begin casting more shadows, the sunlight dimming.

It'll be soon. Far too soon.

Caethes has been leading us in a circle, our attempts to cut across the battle leading us deeper into the fray. Before us is the cabin's ruins, our spiraling journey bringing us right back to the beginning of it all. Again.

She's still astride her beast just beyond the ruins—wicked and ethereal. She stares us down, watching the fight with an impassiveness that infuriates me. She sees it so clinically that she's so far removed from the situation and that without engaging in the battle it appears like a show. I curl my hands around my weapons, feeling the frustration.

Just then, the scenery changes—transforms.

The sky ripples and then like a fount of blood, redness spreads across the horizon, painting all the heavens crimson. The blood-tinged scene is eerie and macabre and very dramatic. It's certain that goddesses have a penchant for diva behavior, and this flair solidifies that.

It is officially nightfall, colored by the shade vampires are best represented by.

I brace myself and wait.

It takes only minutes for the first hisses and battle cries to fill the air. The vitalized vampires will overwhelm the tired forces and both sides will suffer many losses as a result. Moments later, and vampires appear from both sides of the opposing forces, guided by the fae, enabled by the use of the Faerie Roads.

The field floods with vampires, jaws unhinged, fangs bared, speed unmatched. Like snakes, they strike and sink their teeth into necks and tear out throats. They bleed enemies dry. They exsanguinate them and leave them for dead. It is a brutality that Joseph's court is best known for. Our vampires from the Arcana Society are more refined, though not pacifist. Still, they do seem to have qualms while Joseph Harrow's subjects do not.

Wisteria screams behind me and I whirl, finding her in a vampire's clutches. Without thinking, I simply act and drive my blade into his throat and slash it one way and then cut him the other. His head is connected by only the barest of skin and bone, flopping unsteadily. He rocks backwards, and his head hyper-extends further before he topples entirely.

I put my hands firmly on Wisteria's shoulders, looking into her Caethes-black eyes.

"Are you okay? Did he hurt you?"

Wisteria's hand goes to her throat. "I'm okay, he didn't get the chance. Thank you."

I nod and ensure Wisteria stays close to me.

We cut through two more swaths before Wisteria gasps. I prepare to attack another vampire, or faerie, or witch, or shadowy apparition, but there is none. After following Wisteria's gaze, I swear colorfully. Emrys turns next to me and does the same.

"Violante, what the fuck are you doing here?" I demand.

Violante, dressed head to toe in black, in a uniform similar to the Crows, draws her shoulders inward at the chastisement. Pieces of her long dark hair fall in front of her face, too short to be contained by the long ponytail she has tied.

"I told you—this is my choice."

"I don't want to risk you."

"I appreciate the hesitation, but I understand what I'm putting at stake here." Her red eyes are hard and resolute. "I can't stand by. If I meet my end here, so be it."

An arrow flies through the air a mere five feet from us.

"Vio..." Wisteria murmurs, pained. "I just got you back. How am I..." Wisteria loses her words.

Violante offers her a sad smile. "If I'm gone, you'll figure it out. You're strong."

Tears grow in Wisteria's eyes, so eerie in those sclera-less orbs. "I'm not nearly as strong as you think I am."

"I think it's you that is undermining your abilities." Violante steps forward and takes Wisteria's hand. "But let's not worry about that right now. Let's worry about killing this evil faerie queen." Violante's eyes flare in embarrassment. She turns to me. "I don't mean you, just for clarification."

"I didn't think you did. I wouldn't call myself evil."

Violante's face flushes but she nods.

"Stay close," I tell her softly. "If you're going to be here the best thing you can do is be another guardian for Witch, here."

Wisteria rolls her eyes but follows with Violante flitting around us. She fast—so fast—nearly blurring with her movements—jittery with anxiety and anticipation.

With the sun officially set for a few hours, all the vampires are ravenous. It is pure and utter chaos—so much blood, so much loss. We are flagging but the vampires are new.

I watch an Arcana Society vampire throw down an Unseelie, pinning her dragonfly wings in one hand and wrenching as he bares her throat. She screams as he sinks his fangs into her artery. Another vampire—one of Joseph's—snatches one of our Crows and snaps her neck before I can react, latching onto her jugular. I realize distantly that it's Lorelai.

Beside me, Emrys whirls, grappling with a vampire. As I ready to interfere, a shadow of the Hunt rushes me. My husband aims straight and true for the heart just as another jumps into the fray. I battle it out with my shadow while my soulmate takes on the second vampire.

"Vee," I shout to our young vampire. "Keep her safe, don't let anyone touch her!"

Emrys tosses his opponent bodily and he sails through the air, slamming into the Wild Hunt member I'm facing off with. The two of them go down in a sprawl, and together Emrys and I finish them off, just in time to turn to two more Unseelie opponents striking out at us. Together we move, sinuous like water, in tandem, and dispatch them with flourishes. Four more come at us.

Then more.

And more.

We become prime targets as the Dark Court forces realize the Light Court's king and queen are at the center and we have lost our guards along the way. Not that we needed them, but half of them are dead, and the other half battle it out intensely among the others.

Arrows rain down around us from archers on both sides of the fight, every so often a spear pierces through the air, sticking into a body. Bullets fly, fired from the Arcana Society, the crack of the firearms brash against the metallic shriek of swords and blades clashing. A few misfires sputter in the night, malfunctioning near wards. The screams and groans of the injured and dying storm the red-veiled world, all of these terrible sounds imprinting in my psyche—scarring me.

I chance a look over my shoulder and see Wisteria and Violante huddled together. Violante guarding her in a feral crouch like a wild cat, fangs bared, jaw unhinged, hissing at every approaching threat.

Emrys and I sink into a synchronized dance of battle. Of kill and strike and lunge and dodge, of hit and slice and plunge and swing. We are so practiced in our ways that it is second nature, all around us bearing truth to our Century Training. Our unparalleled status. Our names of Harbinger and Revenant.

327

We start trying to work back to Wisteria and Violante. We'd strayed too far and the whole point of keeping them around becomes less and less accessible.

Just as we are mere yards away, a swarm of vampires cut between us and them, attacking the four of us in a frenzy. Emrys and I cut through them with ease, but those who have elected to attack the other two become major threats.

Both Wisteria and Violante yell as their blows land. One grabs Violante, wrapping her in a vice. Furiously, the young vampire thrashes and manages to get an arm out, clawing her nails down his face. He yowls and she rakes them down again. In pain and rage, he cracks his blade hilt on the back of her head and flings Violante with all the force a vampire possesses. She soars through the air, twisting like a ragdoll until a flying Unseelie snatches her midair and pitches her into the ruins of the cabin.

"Vio!" Wisteria yells. "No! Oh fuck, please no! Not her too!" She begins sobbing, her knees buckling. Her breathing comes thready as a panic attack rises to the surface. She wobbles on her feet before she drops down.

"Wisteria!" Emrys yells as he cuts down a petite vampire with long blonde hair. "Wisteria, listen to me! We're here, you're here, we'll get to Violante. Do you hear me? I can't lie. We will get to her as soon as we can."

Wisteria continues to breakdown. "I—I—I—I can't. It can't happen again. I can't do it. I can't survive it. P—please, h—h—help her. Make sure she's o—okay."

"Fuck!" I mutter, as I relieve a head from a body.

Invigorated and infuriated, I power through opponents, fighting to get to Wisteria. My blades arc through bodies, plunge through chests, severing through arteries. It takes moments covered in blood for me to reach Wisteria. Uncaring of the scarlet that coats me, I crouch down and cup Wisteria's face—I leave bloody palmprints on her dark skin.

"If you have a breakdown here, I cannot help Violante. I'll be too distracted keeping you alive. If I can't help Violante, I can't help you. Do you understand me?" I stare into her black eyes, mine unwavering. "Do you understand me?"

Wisteria's breathing, while still thin, evens out. She nods. "I just got her back."

I nod too, still holding her face. "I cannot promise to keep her alive, but I will do everything in my power to see she survives this."

The witch manages to gather herself together. As she stands, I throw a knife over her head and lodge it in the skull of an approaching Unseelie. I walk over and take it out of the fallen corpse, wiping it on their shirt.

"Stay close, we're making our way to Violante."

"No," Wisteria says lowly. "Caethes. We make our way to Caethes. This ends here. Tonight."

I pause a breath before answering. "Okay."

Emrys returns to my side once again, and through the bond I explain the little he missed and convey how dire and desperately we need this plan to move forward. We are lagging and tired and the vampires are only going to take advantage of that.

The three of us move through the battle. I catch sight of Caethes again, this time now she has rings of the Wild Hunt circling her in shadowy protection. Over the heads of the fight, I meet her gaze, and although I can't see the micro-expressions, I know she is taunting, furious, and afraid.

"Need some help?"

Enydd suddenly appears before us, her urumi glittering as if dazzled with rubies, her emerald wings splattered with red. She grins, showing off her white teeth in a mockery of delight.

"I think there's a certain faerie queen we must dispatch."

"That would be very appreciated," I answer. "Thank you."

Together, a Pawn, two Bishops, and a Knight, cut across the war of Lady Fate's game, hoping to make the calculated moves to end it all.

CHAPTER 34

The fight, though numbers decreased, condenses. The limited magic expended is even more apparent—Blackthorn chains of lethal thorns, Goldwine shields of gilded light, a Frostsinger with her hypnotic voice, a Hazelhurst and his pattern recognition, and even more deadly powers. Everyone fights in close proximity and in groups, so due to this, friendly fire becomes a problem. As does moving across the field to get to Caethes.

The Unseelie Queen feels further than ever now, the rings of the Hunt in addition to the fray between us feels near impenetrable.

Emrys and I cut down line after line of opposition, bodies lying in our wake. Wisteria stays faithfully behind us, gathering chaos, keeping her tears at bay. My body aches, my muscles cry out. It is a spirit-deep pain. I can sense through the bond that my husband is flagging similarly, but together we draw strength in nearing the end.

We will finish this.

It's nautical twilight, and soon the vampires will have to flee, or else be caught in the rising sun's rays. Already, some escape, casting fearful glances at the horizon, while others call out insults of "coward" or "traitor" at their retreating backs. The halflings stay, as they are unaffected.

We renew our vigor, seeing our odds change, and it's as if the Wild Hunt can sense it. The shadowy apparitions converge on us, scything blades against us as our newly forged daggers meet and clash. A shadow hisses furiously as her attack is thwarted, and I draw my blade out and stab her through the chest. She crumples before she disappears in a hiss of smoke.

Visibly, I watch the sun begin its ascent and the war begins breaking up—vampires scatter, faeries take their place. It's a mess as new enemies find new foes, nemeses discover another partner, the fight continues its dance of kill, kill, kill. There are breaks and gaps in the battle and the four of us carve those spaces wider, forging our path to Caethes.

It is terrifying how fast the tide of war can change. Just like that.

The Unseelie Queen seems to realize the newfound progress we've made and startles. From her distance, she orders the Wild Hunt shielding her to come for us. There, Arawn leads the helm. Fury surges in my breast and I push harder, separating from the group by mere paces to take him on. In his shadows, he seems to grin and meets my speed.

I can sense Emrys through the bond, see through his eyes. He takes out attackers on the periphery, Enydd on the opposite side, Wisteria flanking us, collecting the chaos. I charge on and suddenly I'm locked into battle with Arawn.

"*Silly fae queen,*" he hisses mockingly, his shark-black eyes cruel and vindictive. "*You hold a title little more than false. You were not destined for the crown you wear, nor the one you seek.*"

"You speak so much, but you know so little," I retort, thrusting my blade against his parry. "The goddess does not speak for you, and you do not truly know Fate."

He chuckles, swatting me back. I absorb the blow and whirl into a dodge before I come up with a strike. Arawn meets the deft maneuver and I curse.

"*I have bedded queens and I have bedded deities. I know their secrets, even through their lies. I know how one can delude themselves to believe falsehoods ring true. How you do think the fae lie? They tell the truth they want it to be.*"

His statement throws me off. Bedding deities? Does he mean Karma? Surely not Fate. Or likely Chaos? Chaos seems more his preference, as evidenced by his attraction to Caethes. Even so, why speak about it here and now? I try to ascertain the relevancy before I realize—he meant to confuse me—to distract me. I attack messily and he leaps away, ending up behind me and elbowing me in the spine. I let out a sound of pain as air gusts out of my lungs, and stumble. When I whirl, he is not going to my exposed back, he is going to my exposed heart.

For Emrys.

Emrys is locked into battle with three members of the Hunt, a blur of motion and lethal grace. Him and our small quad have managed to move through the masses, and they are mere yards from Caethes. So close, her blood is on the tip of my tongue. Still, unknowing of the new danger, he fights. He is beautiful and deadly, painted in crimson, eyes of gold burning in darkness. He is power and skill, but he is focused, and he is not expecting Arawn—the leader of the Wild Hunt—to come upon him. I see his singular vision through the bond and I simultaneously scream at him and send alarm down the cord of our mating as I run.

"*Emrys*! Behind you!"

But he is not fast enough, and Arawn brings down his blade.

The prophecy sings through my blood, whites out my mind, screams into my very soul.

All those you have ever loved will die.

No. No, no, no. No, this isn't how it's supposed to be. He has already died once; he's met the criteria. He can't die again.

I watch the blade fall, and I am helpless in my racing against time—I am not fast enough. It descends, and I scream, terror ripping through me—ripping a shriek from my throat, renting the air and my soul.

Just as it's about to strike true, Enydd is there, flashing out with her urumi. She flicks out the whip-sword, and then the end comes down and severs Arawn's hand. The ghostly faerie shrieks and the sound is pure heaven to my ears. His dismemberment is the symphony of my husband's rescue.

One handed, Arawn takes on Enydd, their fight something strange and deadly.

"Go!" Enydd shouts at us. "End this!"

We leave Enydd behind and our trio dashes across the ruined grass. Caethes, to her credit, does not flee. She unsaddles herself from the beast and with her arms spread at her sides, she approaches, collecting chaos. She is a horrid, fantastical vision. Behind her is the scarlet skyline, lightening with the rapidly approaching dawn, she is all silver and diamond, full of magic, reeking of power. She eats up the distance between us on her graceful footfalls, and suddenly the reality slams into me.

This is it.

This is the end.

It ends here, one way or another.

It could have ended once with Aneira's death, but I was there to take up the mantle in her absence. I took the title as competitor in this war. The opposite side. The figurehead. I went from soldier to monarch. But more than that, I went from lost human girl in the woods, to terrifying, powerful Seelie Queen. I went from memoryless, to heir to the Unseelie throne.

With my husband at my side, covered in blood, we close in.

Wisteria's wrath is like a flame behind us, hot and burning and utterly out of control. She sucks all the chaos out of the air and into herself, driving us on, egging this war to its climax.

Suddenly, as we're passing a crowd of battling Crows, fae, witches, halflings, and Wild Hunt members by the cabin ruins, one shadowy faerie lunges for Wisteria. The witch screams as he latches onto her, fisting a hand in her corkscrew locks and wrenches her head back. Panic lights me as I turn, thoughts of Wisteria's death invading my mind.

Go to Caethes! I tell Emrys through the bond. *I can't kill her,* you *can.*

I curse heir and succession laws as Emrys continues on to do battle with his former queen, and I turn around to rescue our best chance of destroying her.

As if it were portrayed in slow motion, the red sun cracks the horizon and sends beams of light across the scene. The lingering vampires truly scatter, having failed in their foresight to outrun the dawn. I see those red-gold lines shape Wisteria's face, carve terror into her eyes, reveal the possibility of failure. Again, I'm not fast enough as the smoke licks up her neck, a dagger poised in the air, preparing to plunge it down—into her chest. I'm close, but a shape hurtles into me and I'm tossed to the ground.

I tumble, and without looking I slam my blade down into the attacker, killing an Unseelie and getting painted with their blood.

The knife falls.

In the sunlight, slowly turning golden and bleeding out the crimson, a dark-haired form springs from the ruins with a glittering blade held aloft. The figure comes down and stabs the blade directly through the skull of the Wild Hunter.

They freeze, eyes turning glassy in instantaneous death, their murder attempt mere inches from Wisteria's breast. They do not blink. They do not speak. They simply topple down, evaporating as their smoky form hits the forest floor.

It's then, as I hear Wisteria scream, that I realize who her rescuer was.

Violante.

Her body is charred and completely blackened in the sunlight. Her hand lifts, completely ruined, embers glittering on her skin—like a log left too long in a fire. Her hair has disintegrated, her clothes glowing with sparks. Her red eyes are the only thing discernable about her.

I've only heard Wisteria scream like this once before, and I thought I'd never have to hear that soul-wrenching sound again. It is the same heart-crushing call that erupted from her throat when Caethes killed Elliot. It, like this one, is branded into my memory for eternity now.

As the sun rises, Violante's body continues to disappear, that char turning to ash. Those scarlet eyes turning gray and black, chipping away in the wind.

The vampires that are not fast enough—that managed their time poorly or were held hostage by enemies and forced into the light—are caught in the sunrise, turning to embers and ash on the wind. Their forms light up and then crumble, drifting away and stealing lives.

Wisteria is sobbing, the chaos around her ebbing and flowing, her borrowed black eyes flooding with tears. Salt water tracks down her brown cheeks, carving lines through the blood and grime, dripping to mix with the gore on the carpet of war.

"Vee…? *VEE!*" Wisteria chokes out, reaching for Violante's corpse.

Wisteria's eyes flicker between the light of the Fairwalkers and Caethes's dark. Her hands hover over Violante's ruined form, trying to heal her. Her movements become frantic and desperate, but it becomes more and more clear that she is too late and Violante is gone. She hitches a sob, her eyes ebony orbs again, and bows over her the vampire's corpse.

I reach Wisteria before she can touch Violante. I know if she does, Violante will truly crumble and it will break her further. I crash to my knees and wrap Wisteria up in my arms, trying to be a comfort—to be soft and warm when I have only ever been sharp edges. I am not used to being the person to offer sympathy and gentleness. I am blunt and prickly. But I am all she has. I hold her, as if I can contain her grief—her magic. As if by holding her in an embrace I can contain the chaos before she lets it out.

"I'm so sorry, Wisteria," I whisper, realizing I don't think I've ever actually called her by her name.

Witch. Faerie. That has always been our go to. But this...

It changes our dynamic.

"I am so, so desperately sorry."

"She's dead! She sacrificed herself for me!" she wails. "Why would she do that?"

I hold her, cupping the back of her head. I'm covered in blood, but so is she. I keep her tucked against me. "Because she love—loved you." I have to correct myself from saying "loves", my fae nature not allowing me to tell a lie. A lie only because she no longer lives.

"I can't do this."

"Yes, you can." I cup her cheeks and force her to look at me. Her eyes are still taken from Caethes—good. I force those black depths to meet my silver ones. "Avenge her. Make Caethes pay for having taken her life. Obliterate her. Decimate her. *End* her."

Resolve forms in Wisteria's eyes, and behind it, I watch a wall of apathy form. My heart sinks, but it is something to deal with later. Now is the time for revenge. With power untold, I watch as Wisteria lifts herself up from the forest floor, and out of her grief, and walks with a single-minded stride to Caethes. Her body is an arrow strung in a bow, aimed directly at the Unseelie Queen. Let loose by an expert archer, Wisteria races on the fires of her wrath to the catalyst of her loss and anguish.

I follow her, batting away attackers, keeping a coppery head of hair in my vision and seeing Emrys's garnet locks mere yards from his former queen. He, among other fighters of our own, battle against the Wild Hunt that blocks the Dark Court Queen in concentric rings. Emrys, more talented than all of them, decimates them with his soldier's aid.

The path is carved, as if by Lady Fate's hand, and Wisteria travels it. In moments, we are within the fray that Emrys is pushing through. Bodies litter the ground, blood, and smoke, and ash. My heart tightens in fear and anticipation. We are so close now.

Through the bond, Emrys senses me and with it, Wisteria in tow. Between us, we shield Wisteria at our backs, the two of us battling in circles. I scythe down a blade while Emrys slashes his upwards, Wisteria in the middle drinks in the chaos, utterly brimming with it.

With an abruptness that startles me, a clear path opens between us and Caethes. We do not miss it and the three of us dash through before it closes. On the opposite side of the opening, we are met with Caethes's horrid and ethereal visage.

CHAPTER 35

"A chaos drinker like myself is your greatest weapon?" Caethes chortles, though fear touches her oppressive dark eyes. "All this work to carry a witch through war so that she might end me—it's nearly poetic, darling niece."

Three shadowy forms of the Wild Hunt are all that stand between the Dark Court and the Light Court. Three monarchs, one witch. With my king flanking Wisteria, chests heaving, we hold. Emrys and I silently communicate through the bond, while Wisteria continues gathering her proverbial bomb of chaos.

My lips curl back from my teeth. "You cannot kill me, as I cannot kill you, aunt."

It is a near twisted echo of what I'd once said to Emrys all those weeks ago.

You'd do well to remember that you are forbidden from killing me in my own court, the same that I am prohibited to kill you in yours.

"I bet it twists you inside that you cannot deal the death blow," Caethes taunts. "I imagine you've fantasized about my end more than once, and yet here I stand before you, and you cannot harm a hair on my head."

Fury seethes through me at her words. She isn't wrong, and that's all the more reason to drive my hatred for her onward.

"She may not be able to kill you—but I can," Wisteria hisses.

"Quaint child. Even should you succeed in your vengeance, you are filled with a void. Hollow with rage. And once that bloodlust is slaked, you will be left with nothing but the chasm of loneliness you're desperate to escape. My death will be your undoing, little Greyvale. Your revenge is your only fuel," Caethes cocks her head. "But you know this already, don't you?"

Unease slithers through me. "Wisteria, don't listen to her."

"Why not? I speak only the truth."

I bite my tongue, unable to lie.

It's unsettling to be paused in this battle. We've constantly been moving, moving, moving. Now, at a standstill, I don't know how to begin again. Luckily, Emrys rectifies that.

Lunging into action, my soulmate carves the throat from the middle hunter. They dissipate, and before they even collapse, Emrys is engaged with another. I take on the remaining shadow while Caethes watches, true fear in her eyes.

I realize she truly believed that Emrys would not forsake her as her signature anemone flower represents. That symbolic court flower guiding her belief, that perhaps at the final moment he would become the turncoat Revenant again and return to the fold. It is a falsification. It is a delusion that she has enabled herself to believe, even knowing of the soulmate bond between us. Deluding oneself is how the fae can lie, and evidently, Caethes has been lying to herself for some time. Hurt touches the lines of her face, softening it nearly imperceptibly, until it hardens with hate and anger.

Caethes turns her attention to her fae beast, standing there, frozen, as if awaiting command.

"Kill them," she directs.

I throw myself at the beast as it begins to charge forward, the two of us crashing to the undergrowth. Claws scratch against my armor as I grapple and slice. I meet fur and teeth, punching the side of the faerie's head. The beast yelps and I grab it by its silver collar and slam another punch to its face.

Wisteria, as if possessed, passes Emrys and I, and lifts her hands. All the gathered chaos bloats her aura, all the air surrounding her shimmering with compressed power. Wavering with the extreme amount of energy, the magic warbles as Wisteria forces it into an orb between her hands. Caethes, knowing what Wisteria is doing, quickly matches the action. In shock, I see the chaos take visible form. It is silvery and gold, like stardust and gold leaf. It swirls, like the surreal waves of the aurora borealis, like glitter in fancy champagne.

As Wisteria forces it into form, the waves become jerky, angry and electric.

Simultaneously, as if both the queen and the witch possess a bond, they launch the amassed chaos at each other. It strikes true, and the opposing power slams into each other, locking into a deadly battle of wills. With a sonic boom, louder than a thunderclap, the magic sounds for miles and eons. The chaos crackles and sparks, like lightning in clouds. Wisteria's hands are claws as she pushes the magic at the queen, the queen's actual claws curl as she too fights the polar magnetism-like chaos between them.

Locked into this battle, it's clear that neither of them can let go to reattack. If one should falter, the chaos will be a decimation. Whomever releases will receive the full brunt and blowback of it. I realize this is it. And so does Emrys.

"Kill her!" Caethes yells at the beast I contend with.

I watch as the opal on the beast's collar glows and come to a sudden realization.

With my free hand, I yank at the collar, trying to break it. It doesn't move. I find a keyhole and dig the once goddess-forged blade into it. It doesn't unlock. Finding the weakest forge while the beast drives itself into a frenzy becomes a dangerous endeavor, but I discover the spot. Prying the tip of the blade into it, I manage to break the seal. A flash of pure white light erupts from the collar. With both hands, I force it open and off the faerie's neck.

Suddenly, his eyes clear, and glow unearthly blue. He meets my gaze and then tosses me off his form before darting into the forest, beyond the evergreens and pines, fleeing the war and all its enemies. Running into the golden sunrise. I watch the antlered wolf-dragon disappear as Caethes screams in contempt.

Finishing off his hunter, my husband turns, and I feel through the bond as he steels himself, preparing for the death blow. Holding the blade aloft, he moves for the chaos wielder, the faerie woman who raised him when his true mother abandoned him. Conflicting feelings momentarily war within him, but he moves. He takes the first step, and then charges. Mere steps away. I join him.

Suddenly, a fearsome shadow lands before us and bodily knocks Emrys away. My husband tumbles to the ground, rolling through the blood and debris before coming up on a knee. He growls, baring his sharp teeth at the usurper.

I end the enemy before me and whirl to the new hunter. The shadowy apparition wields deadly blades and my heart stutters as I recognize Arawn. Last I'd seen him, he was fighting with Enydd. After she'd told us to run and end this. Where is she? Did she make it? Is she gone? How many have we lost now?

Emrys dodges and lunges from Arawn's merciless attacks. Something has rejuvenated Arawn, because he is fast—so fast. My husband is completely on the defensive, his blades turned to shields rather than weapons. I run to assist him, but as my feet eat up the distance between them, I'm suddenly caught by magic.

Vines of deadly black thorns wrap around me, pricks of every point pressing into me, denting my golden armor and puncturing my exposed flesh. I let out a scream as the pain registers, sharp and severe, new blood blooming like a rose on every jab. I can feel the scarlet running down my skin, my throat, cascading beneath my armor.

A Blackthorn witch pours thorns of ebony through the battle, weaving them around Seelie forces. From one witch, three chains extend. I watch as one pulps a Crow into bloody viscera—Rachel. My stomach drops through my feet and my gorge rises.

Emrys's eyes flare wide at my capture by a Blackthorn witch and Arawn uses his distraction. The hunter opens up a line on Emrys's cheekbone and he hisses in pain. My heart constricts, just like the thorns holding me captive.

Suddenly, a wet choking sound meets my ears and the vines evaporate.

Where the Blackthorn once was, Enydd now stands, urumi glittering crimson with fresh blood and the witch's head on the ground. She spares only a second's look at me before she throws herself at Arawn.

Emrys is on the ground, rolling away from the plunge of a blade. The point buries itself in the ground where Emrys was just seconds before. Arawn continues a merciless attack while my soulmate's chest heaves. Enydd joins their fray and flicks out her bladed-whip-sword. One of the lashes catches Arawn and he growls, a purely primal sound.

Nearby, Wisteria yells, sweat beading on her brow. She leans into her hands, pushing, as if the chaos were a boulder she's pushing uphill. Caethes grits her teeth, pressing forward similarly.

I rush Caethes, hoping the heir and successor laws won't prevent me from interfering with their chaos battle. Hoping that if I knock her away, Wisteria can land the killing blow. I go to tackle the Dark Court Queen and slam into an invisible wall. I'm floored as I rebound off it, wind knocked from my lungs.

Caethes hisses at me. "You dare attack me, girl?"

"Oh, don't be so surprised, Caethes," I retort, getting to my feet.

I chance a glance at Wisteria but the witch merely flickers her eyes at me and tips her head at Arawn—a clear

"I've got this" signal. Turning, I join the battle of Emrys and Enydd against Arawn.

Emrys ducks below a scything attack from Arawn and drives a blade up into the hunter's side. Arawn shouts in surprise and pain as Emrys withdraws the knife and goes for another attack. Arawn dodges it as Enydd lands a slash against his back. The shadowy apparition bellows and spins an attack, long blade outstretched. He misses, but at the same time I lunge into the fight, sliding beneath his guard and driving my blade up. It knicks his chin as he stumbles, backhanding me. My neck snaps to the side, my face stinging as I taste blood.

Go to Caethes, I tell Emrys through the bond. *Wisteria has her distracted. Now's our chance.*

Emrys spares no response and pivots, racing to the queen. Arawn senses the change and immediately whirls. A feral panic lights his frame and he rushes after him, calling out a warning. Enydd and I dive for the hunter as he plunges on after Emrys. Arawn is fast, so fast—too fast. He tackles Emrys to the ground, shadows and smoke straddling my husband as he holds a blade aloft, and drives it down.

I scream as I slam into the leader of the Wild Hunt, grappling for the blade. I toss Arawn away, and the weapon gets fumbled. The sharp edge slices into my cheek, a mirror to the slice Emrys so recently earned. The sting is hot as blood leaks from the wound, my elbow smarting from smashing into the ground. Looking up, I find Arawn crawling after Emrys, going for another attack—Arawn, horrible, awful fae he is, knows how to hit where it most secretly hurts.

Enydd whips down her urumi and it buries itself in Arawn's shoulder. The smoky faerie screams and launches himself up, demonic visage bared as he slams into my former mentor. The two of them roll together, clawing and slashing.

Unseelie enemies lunge at Emrys and I, the two of us forced into combat while Enydd and Arawn drive at one another, and while Wisteria and Caethes are still locked. I dispatch my Unseelie just as another one arrives to tear at Wisteria. This time, I *am* fast enough. I yank him back by his blue hair and slash his throat from ear to ear. He drops with a fount of blood and a gurgle. Wisteria's eyes flash with thanks.

I turn back to Enydd and Arawn, finding Emrys joining just at the wrong time. Enydd dodges, just as Arawn plunges his blade forward. My heart slams into my chest—breaking, shattering. But somehow, Arawn makes an error and stumbles, missing my soulmate. The blade goes wide, and instead of a stab it turns into a swing.

I gasp as it lands, struck halfway through the center of Enydd's chest.

My former mentor lifts shocked plum eyes to her murderer. He grins, feral, as he withdraws the blade and slams it in again. Enydd's eyes go glassy, and then she drops to the ground.

Dead.

I howl, the loss striking me deeper and truer than I could ever fathom. With grief fueling me, I seek vengeance, and crash into Arawn. I straddle the undead faerie and plunge down my blade, but he knocks my hand away and rolls us over, my back crashing into the forest's carpet. A rock digs into my neck as Arawn's hand goes for my throat, tightening, as the other grasps a blade.

Suddenly, the blade and the hand thump to the ground next to me, vanishing into a wisp of smoke. Arawn screeches as Emrys's blade returns for another attack, this time at his head. Arawn, with his stump of an arm, slams it into Emrys's solar plexus. My husband staggers back, dragging in a breath. I manage to gather my feet beneath me and buck Arawn off of me. The leader of the Hunt gets his bearings, just as Emrys repossesses his own.

Through the bond, Emrys suggests a course of action and without further conversing, I confirm.

Emrys tackles Arawn, wrapping his arms around the undead faerie, as I leap at his front, climbing up his tall frame. On his shoulders, I twist my legs around his head one way, my newly forged blade carving the other. With a wicked crunch and wrench, I tear Arawn's head from his body. Holding his head aloft by his hair, Arawn's body tumbles to the ground and I ride the corpse down, landing on a knee.

With the head in my grasp, I survey the remaining hunters and watch them all freeze. Their eyes lock on me, and suddenly, they disappear, smoke and shadows returning to the dark—vanishing.

With Arawn's death, the Wild Hunt is leaderless, disorganized. They no longer adhere to the alliance with the Dark Court, and therefore, any bond slips away—like water through one's fingers. Every last hunter departs the fight, seemingly without conscious decision to.

The vampires are gone.

The Wild Hunt is gone.

Witches have been targeted and most have been all but ended. Halflings hold their own, running low or out of bullets, turning to blades and arrows. The few wolves have been killed or have fled. The humans have managed against the fae with their iron weapons, many having fallen to the Hunt when forgetting which weapon to use. It is mostly fae left. It was mostly fae to begin with.

The war has become sparse. I can see Gideon with the rest of the Arcana society—he is bloodied, amber eyes blazing in a sea of crimson as he slams the butt of a pistol into the temple of an opposing Unseelie. Julia has a sword, and she locks into a fight with a female witch, her power evidently not offensive. Maelona and Aveda fight back-to-back, similarly splattered in gore, taking up arms against Joseph Harrow's halflings. Caspian, even more bloodied than before—still lives—fangs out as he presses a gun to the forehead of an Unseelie with one hand and pulls the trigger at the same time as he drives an iron stake into the heart of another.

Caethes looks over at the tide change and her eyes show a flicker of unease. That unease is enough for her will to waver, and Wisteria's to break through. Caethes's chaos splits, like a tree struck by lightning, and Wisteria's barrels through the center. Wisteria's chaos slices through the center of the queen's and arrows through in a singular strike. The chaos, made tangible, turns into a bolt of pure power and plows through Caethes's heart.

The Dark Court Queen staggers, gasping.

A smoking black hole burns through the Unseelie Queen's breast, so deadly one can see through her body. The edges are charred—cauterized. Caethes looks down in disbelief and horror, white specks of chaos like stardust flickering at the edges of the fatal wound.

"For Elliot," Wisteria enunciates slowly. Lethally. She steps forward, punctuating each word with a footfall. "For Violante." She amasses another blow of chaos. "For Aberth." The orb of silver-white-gold grows and burns. She readies it to throw, her borrowed black eyes illuminated by her magic. "*For me.*"

She lets the chaos go.

CHAPTER 36

Caethes's split magic streams freely out of her, spinning wildly out of control. The unleashed power hits any, and all forms with no discrimination. I watch it blast into Aveda and knock her flat, Maelona ducking down to her side with a yell, cradling her. Another flash of it catching Commander Tirnoc and slamming him bodily into a tree—he makes a terrible crunch.

More gouts of chaos flare about in friendly fire as the queen loses control, her entire chest obliterated.

Emrys tackles me to the ground, holding me down and safe as chaos jets overhead right where we stood. My husband presses his chest against me, the two of us bleeding on one another. His golden eyes seek mine, begging the two of us to make it out of this alive.

Wisteria is on her knees, spent. All her chaos has emptied out of her and plowed into the Unseelie Queen. The witch hangs her coppery head, her dark hands pressing against the earth.

Caethes blinks, shock the only thing keeping her living. She opens her mouth and then suddenly those sclera-less black eyes turn glassy and roll back. The Unseelie Queen crumples gracefully, and then falls aside, arm outstretched, as if trying to reach for the Revenant one last time. Never to touch him again.

Caethes's antlers break on impact, a tine burrowing into the bloody ground, a fresh snap on the hoary lines—sharp, illuminated against the peeking sun. She is sightless, the gaping hole in her chest exposing what little of her heart remains— between her cruelty and Wisteria's obliteration, there is a scrap left.

When the chaos unleashed it was virtually a pause button on the war. Now, someone has yet to resume the scene. Everyone is frozen, staring at the three of us surrounding Caethes—the survivors against the Dark Court Queen.

"You did it, Witch," I whisper.

Wisteria glances up, her eyes once again her own teak-brown. She smiles weakly, and then collapses.

A nearby Crow limps over and takes stock of Wisteria—Tim or Andrew, I don't recall his name, and he's not familiar enough to me to see beneath the gore. He assesses her vitals and seems unconcerned.

Emrys and I get to our feet, the King and Queen of the Seelie Court together, united, in the victory of this war. I kneel down next to Caethes's corpse and pull the diadem from her brow. The Unseelie Crown does not brand me this time. I am the heir to the Unseelie Court, the crown is mine by right and by blood with Caethes's death.

In my hand, the crown transforms, the silver turning to mercury—a fluid metal, reforged. The crown warps until it becomes a pair of antlers woven into a circlet, three roses with diamonds in their center at the brow, an arch dangling with opals and crystals hovering above it all like a flipped halo.

My Unseelie Crown.

The crown transformed, as it should be as mine.

I stare down at it in a mix of horror and curiosity, woven with fascination and pride. I possess crowns and thrones of both fae courts. I alone. Never has this ever been done. Never in history has it been documented or precedented.

Blood-soaked, aching, burning with a soul-deep exhaustion, Emrys and I clasp hands. I thrust the crown up into the air, dawn light catching all the edges and jewels. A bright, pure spot in the field of darkness and bloodshed.

"The Unseelie Queen is dead!" Emrys calls out, voice hoarse. "The war is over. Surrender, or pay the ultimate price."

"Heed the direction of your Seelie King!" I shout. "Listen to my command! As Queen of both the Seelie and Unseelie Courts, I command it!"

Shock floods the Unseelie wasteland but they do as they're told.

All the Unseelie forces lay down arms, the blades falling with a metallic clatter, a cacophony of a disorganized orchestra, and bow to us. The remaining Seelies forces stand and remove the weapons from those who'd given them up.

Blood and death are thick in the air, a cloying, coppery scent that sours my stomach and wrinkles my nose.

"Take the surrenders into custody, they will have further options," Emrys pronounces, voice loud above the sudden, horrible silence.

Maelona gets Aveda to her feet, the Admiral pressing a hand to her chest, as if ensuring her heart is still beating. Julia stands surrounded by her Crows, success a burning pride on her features. The Arcana Society is scattered about, but are drawing together as they gather up those that have surrendered, Caspian, bloodied, is at the helm of it all. General Baphet is at Commander Tirnoc's side, seeking a pulse—his hanging head indicates he doesn't find one. Gideon, despite all the betrayals, against all odds, stands with the halflings.

Emrys squeezes my hands, heaving a disbelieving, despairing breath. I can feel the need to sob grow in his chest, the want of a bed, the utter exhaustion plaguing him. I know it because I feel it too, regardless of the bond.

"It's done," I whisper, only loud enough for my soulmate to hear.

"We made it," he returns.

A single tear tracks down my face, and a brittle smile trembles on my lips. Emrys leans down, ignoring the blood, and presses a kiss to my mouth. It is a hard press, mouths closed. Blood paints our faces, but I clutch his jaw with both hands anyway. One tear leaks out from Emrys's eye and trails over my fingers. We break apart as our forces begin taking away the opposition in earnest. Together, we walk through the devastation.

I meet Gideon's face across the expanse of the battlefield, an odd sort of camaraderie settling between us. Blood covers him from head to toe, his black waves matted with it, his hands gloved with it. His amber eyes glow with warmth and hope, as if he has finally proven himself. Showing he fought for the right side. I offer him a small smile, and he shares the same one.

That smile falls as a blade slams through his chest.

I scream.

Seeing where I look, Julia turns, and she too, screams.

Gideon looks down in shock, seeing the point of a silver blade splitting his heart in half. He turns, horrid wonderment on his face, needing to discover who stabbed him in the back.

There, standing behind him, long auburn hair waving past her outstretched moth wings, white petal lashes fluttering over orange eyes, is Cariad. The Unseelie titters a maniacal laugh, blood streaming down her wrist from the plunge of her dagger.

Before anyone can react, Julia takes up a bow from a shocked archer, and releases a deadly arrow directly between Cariad's eyes. The Unseelie falls, eyes glassy and gone before she even hits the ground.

Julia casts the bow aside and leaps over bodies, rushing to Gideon's side as he falls to his knees. I can see the glitter of tears already etching lines down her cheeks. I chase after her, my husband at my heels. We dodge the obstacles of discarded weapons and decaying bodies, wounded soldiers moaning and crying and unconscious. Julia comes to a sliding halt by Gideon first. She cradles his head while blood burbles from between his full lips. Tears freely cascade down her cheeks.

"No, no, no, please no!" Julia sobs, she whips her blue-gold eyes to me. They're shiny and red. "Do something! Fix this! You're the queen of two courts, can't you do *something?*"

"I…" I hesitate and glance at Emrys, seeking answers where I find none. "I am not a goddess. I am just a queen." I kneel at Gideon's other side and look down at my once lover. My sister's soulmate. "I'm sorry."

The goddess's words ring through my head and I curse her.

Julia cries out, a sound of pain and stumbles off. Her pain is visceral and it takes her, as if intoxicated, to the edge of the woods, to retch and cry.

Wisteria is unconscious so her Fairwalker healing is out of reach. If she were still awake, she'd be able fix this. She took Maelona from the brink of the edge, the death calling her name as surely as it's calling Gideon's. But she is not, so it is for naught.

I look down at Gideon, his eyes fading. I can see blood flooding around the knife-wound. I place a hand to his. His skin is already cooling.

"I'm so sorry," I repeat.

He cracks a bloody smile, his vision unseeing beyond me. "It's okay. It's not your fault," he rasps. "Maybe I'll see Corvina on the other side."

Fresh tears slip down my cheeks. "Give her my love if you do."

"I will."

And that's the last thing Gideon Zhao ever says as he slips from this world.

I bow over his corpse, mixed feelings ripping through me. Regret, grief, anger, hate, confusion, loss, love, pain. It all courses like a virulent plague, like a vicious current. I'm slipping beneath the waters of it all, drowning in it. I didn't expect this. I never expected to feel this torturous loss over someone who'd once betrayed me. But here I am, seeing someone I once loved, so completely lost to me.

All those you've ever loved will die.

Gideon fulfilled my prophecy. Goddess, I was so fucking stupid to believe we'd all make it out of this alive. This is war—fucking war—of course it would end like this. This isn't some storybook ending where we celebrate with mead and song and festivities. Where we all make it out alive. This is reality. This is an abomination. And it's all my fault.

I started this war for him.

And he was our final casualty.

I want to scream. I want to cry. I want to not feel any of this. This is a nightmare—a fucking nightmare. I feel like I want to explode, my chest feels tight with it. Gideon just got his father back, and now he is gone forever.

My husband wraps me in his arms. He holds my head to his chest, not judging my feelings, letting me feel them. Letting me rage through them. I haul in staggering breaths, black pinpricking my vision. Anxiety threatens to take me over the edge and my soulmate senses it through the bond. Carefully, he tugs me away from the new death, away from Gideon's body.

"He doesn't blame you. He said it wasn't your fault," Emrys whispers. I know he's telling the truth, the fae can't lie—but it still feels wrong.

At the fringes of the forest, I collapse. Darkness overtaking me as my husband carries me through it. His hands are bloody, but soft and gentle. His touch is the only thing I want. His reassurance the salve to this hurt.

"I've got you, Vanna."

CHAPTER 37

Emrys and I are alone for only moments before new screams rent the dawn. My gaze whips to the source and I find the goddess descending onto the battlefield. She stands against the tree line, sunlight filtering through the boughs above. Over the decimation is an illusion of a chessboard, flickering with a wave of Lady Fate's hands. Instead of the typical white and black tile, the squares are iridescent silver and gold. The board fades away as Lady Fate steps forward, eyes locked onto me.

I stomp over to her, fury in every line of my body. Emrys follows, similar anger fueling his steps. I still hold the Unseelie Court crown in my hand. Before the goddess of blood red hair, I throw down my weapons and brandish my new crown.

"So, this is it?" I demand. "Your game is over; the reigns of monarchs have changed. The fae have a new ruler. Is this what you wanted?"

Lady Fate cocks a brow and inclines her head. "No, it isn't. But I managed the hand I was dealt. You'd do well to practice the same."

"No cosmic wisdom now? No predestined plan?"

"Not for you," Lady Fate offers a trickster's smile, her eyes flickering to Caspian. "But there are still threads in play, and I am not yet done. Though when it comes to my meddling, your story is done—you are free to live as you wish."

"Such a gift," I scoff. "Should I be grateful?"

"You should. You, girl-queen, can keep your soulmate when I have every capability to pluck the life I returned and sever that life thread." Lady Fate smirks. "Farewell, Harbinger, I do not think we shall meet again. Not according to my plan." She turns to Emrys. "Enjoy your reign, Revenant."

With that, Lady Fate erupts in a pillar of light and disappears to the heavens.

Everything after Lady Fate's final visit is a blur. Tasks are doled out, water is fetched, food is cooked, bodies are carted off and prepared for funeral pyres. The corpses are separated by allegiance, the Unseelie to the left, Seelie to the right. The wounded are addressed by able-bodied volunteers, the death toll is counted, trauma is wracked in every individual. So many designations are made, delegations assigned.

General Baphet takes on a massive role in organizing soldiers and running a list. The general is more experienced in these sorts of battles than I. I am more familiar with missions, spy assignments, guarding a ruler. I am not fully equipped to tidy up after a war. But I try.

Emrys and I do not leave each other's sides—anything that needs to be done, we do together. We give Maelona a leadership role and she drags Aveda along with her. Julia, new in her grief, dives into helping the wounded. Wisteria is still unconscious.

All my movements feel mechanical. My processes just a list of commands like a servant. I am barely hanging on by a thread.

The aftermath of the war takes days.

The bodies are all burned the following evening, and I still fucking hate funerals. There are rows upon rows of pyres, bodies laid upon hundreds of final beds. I thank everyone for their sacrifices, and their honor, and loyalty. I give personal thanks upon Bleddyn's pyre, for everything he was to me and to my mother. Then I move to Enydd's, telling her body that she's the only reason we made it out of Century Training alive. That she was the difference in us winning this war. When I stop before Gideon's pyre, my throat thickens. I swallow heavily, tears pricking in my eyes. I open my mouth and close it. Once. Twice. I clear my throat, my jaw working, trying to keep the waterworks at bay.

"I loved you, and I hated you," I whisper, only loud enough for me to hear, to Gideon's gray corpse. "But I am not glad you are gone. I will miss you—you will not be forgotten..." I look up to the sky, the first tears are falling. "Not while I live. And I hope you've found her, because she was wonderful."

The flames devour the dry timber and hundreds of bodies burn at twilight.

Gideon's parents stand at the base of their son's pyre. Natalia was brought via the Faerie Roads after the war's commencement so she could see her son's final resting. Her face is a mask of cold rage. She doesn't look at me, just past me, and I can see every wall up past the sky in her eyes. I do not try to engage.

I'd never seen her up close, but she's pretty. Shoulder-length dark hair, green eyes, smooth skin with the first signs of true aging—she was young when she had Gideon. Despite her pain, she stands tall, her slender frame held ramrod straight.

Henry stands beside his wife, now the perfect picture of health from Lady Fate's blessing, grieving the son he chose. Gideon wasn't his blooded son, but as Aneira was a mother to me, he was his father. Tears streak down Henry's face, sorrow bowing his spine.

I shutter my eyes and offer Henry Zhao my condolences.

"He proved himself a true ally to the Seelie Court," I tell him softly. "As queen, that is the greatest honor I can bestow. As a person? As someone who once loved him...those words feel like bullshit, and no flattery will ease your pain. For that, I will forever be sorry." I turn the slightest to Natalia. "I am sorry," I say, hardly a breath.

Henry cracks on a sob and he nods, words beyond him. I pat his shoulder, and leave him to the crackling flames that consume, and his grieving wife.

I travel to the far side and there, I bear witness to the final decimation and destruction of the Unseelie Queen. Caethes, once the pale queen of white and silver, of savage cruelty and eerie beauty, turns to a blackened husk. I stand watch long enough to see her turn to ash.

After being on the bloody grass all day, after fighting in a war and hauling bodies, I am filthier than I've been in my entire life.

Before any insurrection can start, I send loyal forces to the Unseelie Court to hold it down until I can figure out what I'm doing with it. General Baphet along with several soldiers are dispatched there along with Aveda.

Back at the court, I dump my armor in the throne room. I never want to see it again. It is dented and ruined and covered in blood. It is covered in all the memories of this war I do not wish to remember. It has absorbed the personality of a life I no longer live. That armor was that of the Harbinger. I am the Seelie Queen now.

I am no longer just a warrior.

I am a warrior queen.

Dull and gold, I leave the armor to be forsaken.

In our room, Emrys and I cut the clothes from our bodies and stuff them into the trash to be lit on fire. We stand in our tub and dump buckets of water over our soiled bodies. So much blood covers us. So much grime and dirt and gore. The water runs crimson. After a dozen buckets it begins to turn pink. Half a dozen more it finally begins to clear. We help each other scrub the grit from our hair, horrified to find bits of bone and flesh. Our nails are cracked and black beneath the crescents. It takes an aggressive amount of scrubbing to remove it all.

Finally, somewhat cleaned of the visible filth, we fill the giant bath with steaming hot water, adding scented oils of lemon, verbena, and ginseng. Even though it's large enough to sit in it and not touch, I lean against Emrys's front as he wraps his arms around me, luxuriating in his touch. My muscles weep from relief. The uncoiling of tension a near painful thing to experience. I moan as the hot water works its magic. My husband slides his fingers through my hair, massaging my scalp. Despite the nudity and the touch, there is nothing inherently sexual about the moment. We are simply a comfort to each other. We've been through so much, it's difficult to believe that the worst of it is behind us.

"I think I've decided what I'm going to do with the Unseelie Court," I tell Emrys slowly, eyes fluttering.

He presses a kiss to my brow. "Tell me later. For now, take your mind off everything."

We soak a while longer before sleep nearly claims us both. Limbs slumber-heavy, we manage to crash into our bed together, curled up, arms and legs laced. When I fall asleep it is with a lead-weight heaviness that steals dreams.

When I wake, I know more than a day has passed. Between the gnawing in my stomach and the fullness of my bladder alone, I know the hours have been long. When I look out the window, it is pitch black—which affirms my theory as it was midnight dark when we went to sleep last. I slip from the bed to see to my needs. When I return, Emrys is stirring.

Sensing through the bond, Emrys begins to rise. I crawl back into the bed as he lifts himself onto an elbow. I trail my fingers across his chest, down his arm, to his hand, twining our fingers together.

"May I tell you my plans now?" I ask.

Emrys smiles, those sharp teeth that I'd once remarked only a lover would be close enough to see, on display.

"Please do, My Queen."

I do.

I wait in the throne room alone, dressed in satin white, like moonlight made material. The gown glides over my skin like water, cutting lines in a deep plunge down my cleavage, and up a hip-high slit. On my brow is the golden Seelie crown, roses, thorns, spikes, and all in its glory. I resist the urge to pace, shifting in my gilded heels, fiddling with my bracelets and rings. A Queen's Glamour cloaks me.

Finally, she arrives wearing a gown of black velvet.

"You summoned for me?"

"Don't be so formal," I say softly.

"You are queen two times over, now. It's hard not to be," Maelona replies.

"That may be so, but you are still my best friend."

Maelona cracks a smile. "I suppose so. But why did you ask me here?"

I tip my head to the side. "Take a walk with me."

She comes to match my stride as we travel through the curtain of ivy and onto the Faerie Roads. The warm tunnel welcomes us, I can feel the power rippling through it, the distinct absence of the Wild Hunt now. With Arawn's death the Hunt is listless and disorganized—it'll take some time for them to return to a semblance of what they once were, and a battle such as the recent war has taken a toll on their energies.

The path we take is too familiar, one I have traveled many times, even reluctantly. As we reach the gabbro staircase and the statues of Emrys and I, Maelona and I ascend to the Unseelie Court throne room. Together, the two of us stand in the glass and diamond mountaintop expanse of the Unseelie Court. Baphet and several other guards are stationed about the space.

I cast a new Queen's Glamour over the two of us, blocking our conversation from eavesdroppers, obscuring their visions from this bubble.

"What are we doing here?" Maelona asks, a brow arched. Her hair is its natural black, freely flowing, no adornment or braids to be found.

Removing the first Queen's Glamour I'd casted back in the Seelie Court, I produce the Unseelie Court crown. "Will you be Queen of the Unseelie Court?"

Maelona's rich brown eyes flare wide, and her hair bleaches white in shock. "I beg your pardon?"

"You heard me. What did you expect me to be saying when I dragged you to the Unseelie Court?"

"I don't know, but it wasn't this!"

"Well, will you?"

"How could I accept?"

"Easily. You simply say yes, and I abdicate the Unseelie throne."

"This is madness."

"I disagree. Does this truly seem so ridiculous when you think about it? There is no way I can rule both courts. The fae are simply too different, there is too much bad blood to mix the two and force them to coexist as one. But with you as queen, we can forge a true alliance. Together, we can bring a real reign of peace. It will take work for our denizens to adhere to the new rules we instill, but this is a real opportunity, and I would trust no other to rule as you will." I hold out the crown. "You were always meant to be a queen one day; it just turns out that it's not of the court we expected.

"Will you do it?"

Maelona bites her lip and then nods quickly.

"Then kneel," I tell her and hold the Unseelie Court crown between my two hands.

Maelona drops down, the midnight gown spilling like ink on the ground around her.

"I, Evelyn Corianne Gwyndolyn-Vanora, Queen of both the Seelie and Unseelie Courts, hereby abdicate my claim on the Unseelie Court throne and present my heir, Lady Maelona Eidolon as successor to the Dark Crown." I feel the magic ripple through the crown, twisting it into the human-deemed shape of fleur-de-lis. "As sovereign of the Light Court, I crown you, Queen of the Unseelie Court."

And then gently, I set the silver crown atop Maelona's head.

Instantly the silver crown changes. On her brow, it warps and twists like water in a storm until it becomes anew. Spikes erupt from it, sailing upwards in three spires. Two wings, like that of a butterfly sprout from the center and span the width of the circlet. In the center, right against her forehead a marquis diamond forms, flanked by moonstones. A corona arches atop the circle of the crown, dangling with shards of crystal and obsidian and silver chain. All of it comes together in a perfect design specifically altered for her.

When it's done, Maelona looks up and meets my gaze—smiling.

"Glad to see it worked this time," Maelona quips.

I laugh. "As am I." Maelona rises and I smile. "So, would you care for an official coronation, or is this sufficient?"

"Are you joking? Of course, I demand a party. I am a queen, you know, and I shall be celebrated as such."

My laugh returns, a warm sound that I haven't felt for days. "Then we'll start planning it."

Maelona taking over the court isn't so simple as just handing over the reins. It takes time and tireless effort, the Unseelies begrudgingly accepting her. Maelona receives a tour of her new court by trusted individuals my husband recommends, Emrys also assists with adjusting—as the Dark Court was his home up until recently.

"*You* are my home," he corrects when I state this. I grin and he pulls me into a kiss, pressing words to my mouth. "There is nowhere else I'd rather be."

Unseelies who'd been mostly playacting under Caethes's monarchy come forward, admitting their fears and their desire to be more like Seelies. They undergo a rigorous interview process and questioning before they're accepted to be part of Maelona's advisors and inner circle. Emrys vets Unseelie warriors to assign her a Queensguard.

Meanwhile, Julia and Wisteria are both desperate to help plan Maelona's coronation, the former eager to forget her grief with Gideon's loss, the latter filling the empty void her revenge fueled with the party. The two of them are like a machine, functioning in perfect synchronicity, not forgoing a single detail.

Few of the Crows made it out of the war alive. Most of them elect to further their training in becoming spies—humans are essential for the art of lying and deception—or warriors. Some follow Maelona and train under her and her new guard, while the remainder decide to give up the title and live simpler lives. I respect the decision, but I am aware of how difficult the transition from battle to civil life will be, and vow to do whatever in my power to ensure they are well.

Aveda, with her new relationship with Maelona, surprisingly stays loyal to the Seelie Court. However, she does request Ghislain gift her with an official emissary mark so she can foster diplomatic relations between the courts further. The tattoo is done and the Admiral seeks me out.

"I still want to take down the Winter Carnaval, but I will not do it without the court's backing and I will not risk it now when Maelona's reign is so new. She will have enough struggle keeping hold of her head in the Dark Court, I'll not add to it. I will wait until the timeframe you promised has elapsed, and then I expect both the courts to work together to decimate it."

"I swear it," I tell her.

Aveda smiles, baring white teeth—a match to half the hair on her head. "Good."

I am not so disillusioned to believe that everything will be sunshine and rainbows between the courts. There is so much old and bad blood. Current hostilities between people still exist despite the queens being the dearest of friends. There are many, many, many meetings in the future to lay out alliances and terms. But I will do it. For Mae.

Gideon's family didn't wish to speak to us any further, but I leave them with the offer of welcome in the Light Court, and my aid should they request it. I'm unsure if they'll ever take it, nor would I blame them if they don't. They lost their child. It is no small thing and surely a conversation of why his demise happened would be like a cruel reminder. After reviewing the facts, I'm certain they will try to let my existence fade from their lives. And that is okay.

Aberth is decimated. The entire town torched in an arson. I have no idea if it was Seelies or Unseelies, human or Crow. No one has come forward yet, but all that is clear is that it is completely gone now and fully abandoned. I don't know how I feel about it.

The Arcana Society sustained heavy losses, and for that I offer the haven a gift—a vial of golden Seelie elixir, that when smashed, will summon a court warrior in a time of need. Anytime. Anywhere. Sonya Deveraux accepts this gift with grace and fear.

Somehow, Caspian has inserted himself into the visit and joins Sonya and others when accepting the vial. I pull him aside when I note his presence, and Sonya becomes distracted by Emrys guiding her to Maelona, trying to forge an alliance. The new queen only visits temporarily—it's unsafe to leave her new court for long periods in this unrest.

"How are you doing?" I ask Caspian, taking in his appearance.

It would be a lie to say he looked well. His golden eyes—the Lockwood eyes—are haunted, and one of them is ringed by a puffy green and purple bruise. His left cheekbone is swollen, and his lower lip sports a split down the center, and a nasty cut lines the lower edge of his jaw.

He shrugs and winces as he does so, hidden injuries making themselves known. "I've been worse." A dark flicker moves through his eyes—blatant memories from the Winter Carnaval.

"I know," I say softly, leaving the past hanging in the air. I change directions. "If you ever need anything, please do not hesitate to reach out to us personally."

"You know, I'll likely take you up on that offer. One day, I'm going to destroy the Winter Carnaval." A menacing gleam rises in his gaze and the power behind it startles me. "One day, I'll make them all pay for what they did to me. To the others. Especially Joseph Harrow. I am going to find those girls he experimented to create, and then I will ruin him."

I meet that vicious look with one of my own. "We will be right behind you in his destruction."

Caspian chuckles. "That's what family is for, right?"

CHAPTER 38

I've never seen the Unseelie Court look so beautiful. As always, it is the eternal night skyline view, with wintry mountains despite being the end of July. The glass walls and ceiling glitter with swaths of white lights and garlands of glittering white flowers with purple centers. Silver silks drape the space overhead and in corners, creating an airy canopy. Ivory votives in tall glass vases line the aisle, the candles flickering and catching the light—fracturing iridescence. Silver chairs have been set out and every one of them is filled by those allied to both courts.

As with mine and Emrys's coronation, the opposite court must be invited, but as we are not currently in a war, nor are we enemies, the coronation is a peaceful event—a party, something much needed after so much strife. It is awkward, however, so many of the fae having fought in the war as foes, many still sporting injuries of every sort in the aftermath. Not to mention the grudges for deaths wrought. Due to this tension, Emrys and I willingly accept our King and Queensguards. Though, it is mostly overkill as no bloodshed can occur during a coronation until the clock strikes midnight. Even so, as an added precaution, every attendee must swear to peace after such time.

Emrys and I sit in a place of honor at the front—as if this were a wedding and we sit where the bridesmaids and groomsmen would stand. In fact, we are not the only ones graced with such a placement. Joining us, surrounding the diamond Unseelie throne are Aveda and Julia. The missing presences of Gideon and Violante are painfully tangible.

The air is filled with the sounds of murmurs and whispers, accompanied by a softly playing violinist, cellist, and flutist. There is the softer swish and shuffle of fabric moving, feet tapping, and wings fluttering. Among the freesia is the scent of cherry blossoms, as well as cinnamon, leather, and the distinct bite of winter.

The dress I wear is long-sleeved and black, with a neckline that plunges to the navel and two ever present thigh slits. Beneath the dress I wear a body chain of gold links, diamonds studding it like drops of stars down my sternum. On my feet are my favorite knife shoes with the pearl blade switch. The entire ensemble—particularly the body chain—has Emrys ravenous for me and I can sense through the bond all the depraved things he wants to do to me. I tilt my crowned head, my silver hair falling in a long cascade of free tresses, and I lean into my soulmate's ear. As I do, I whisper.

"Keep thinking those naughty things and I'll drag you into a corner, collar first, and have my way with you."

Emrys groans. "Is that a promise?"

I nip his earlobe. "Care to test me?"

My husband wears a golden circlet about his throat, similar bands wrap his wrists. He wears a gorgeous green and gold brocade blouse, as always in his tempting attire, it's unbuttoned scandalously low, parted wide enough to display the scar from the death blow he took for me. It doesn't escape my note that others notice it. His pants are smooth, buttery leather—I know because I more than once caressed the ass that looks incredible in them.

"Vanna, this is your best friend's coronation," he says, sufferingly. His fantasies have ramped up. "It may be best to finish up your daydreams."

"Or perhaps, I suggest you countdown to the moment her crowning ends so I can finish *you*."

Emrys bites his lip, stilling the moan that wants to escape his throat as I send him a very graphic mental image of me on my knees, unbuttoning his pants, while licking my lips.

Just then, the heavy silver doors open, and Wisteria strides out wearing a coronet of stars, draped in swaths of white moonlight silk over her lush curves. Her face is painted with flourishes of silver around her cheekbones and eyes, lids and cheeks dusted with shimmer, lips painted black. A small silver ring replaces the gold hoop that was in her nose, the septum piercing flashing in the light. Around her throat is an elaborate choker of silver-encrusted black opals, dripping down her collarbones and over her breasts. In her beringed hands, set upon a violet pillow is the Unseelie crown.

With her head held high, grief hiding in her eyes, Wisteria strides forward so she can be the one to crown the new Unseelie Queen.

Standing at the base of the throne is Ghislain's twin sister, Lylian, the only other faerie to possess the sort of magic he does. Instead of gold Seelie magic flooding through her veins, silver Unseelie power flows through hers. She may be his twin, but they look alike only in the most basic way with their features. Her hair is a pale fall of lavender, her eyes powdery blue, with the slightest pinkening of her cheeks and nose. She is soft and lovely-looking. Too soft for the brutality of the Unseelie Court—at least the court beneath Caethes's reign.

Wisteria stands opposite Lylian, staring over at the crowd, awaiting the crowning.

Finally, the silver doors open again and Maelona steps out in absolute grandeur. The silver gown she wears is diaphanous, skirts upon skirts that hold constellations of starlight made of diamonds, the dress spanning as wide as the aisle. The train drags behind her, the entire thing covered in glass beadwork, forming swirling curlicues. The neckline is a sweetheart, the bodice corseted with every inch of it covered in clear gems or milky white stones. With every step I see heels of silver, opals on the toes, silver filigree travelling up her ankle. Her black hair is done up in elaborate coils, crystals, diamonds, and pearls worked through the styling. Jewels drip from her ears and throat, every single inch of her screaming decadence.

She looks like a queen.

Maelona holds her head up high in such a queenly manner that I have to keep myself from snickering—she was made for this. She was always meant to be a queen whether Lady Fate designed it or not.

When she arrives before the throne she kneels with a prompt from Lylian. As she sinks down, the layers of silver finery around her like a pool of mercury, I can see the affirmation in her face. This is what she wanted. What she wanted, but never let herself dream of having while Aneira was alive.

This is her destiny.

"Tonight is the official coronation of the new Unseelie Queen. Tonight, we celebrate the end of an era, and the dawn of a new reign—one touched by the goddesses of Fate, Chaos, and Karma." Lylian takes up the crown from Wisteria's pillow. "I, Lylian Ellorian of the Dark Court, hereby crown Maelona Eidolon as Queen of the Unseelie Court." She turns her attention of Maelona now. "Do you swear to defend this realm and be the shield that stands for the people of the Dark Court?"

"I do," Maelona answers firmly, anticipation making her hair flicker.

"Do you swear to protect the hearts of the Unseelie Court and reign over it until the end of your life or abdication?"

"I do."

"And do you swear to uphold the tentative peace forged with the Light Court?"

Maelona smiles at this one. "I do."

The crown slowly descends from Lylian's hands and onto Maelona's head. "I now proclaim you *queen*. May the goddesses bless your rule." Lylian raises her arms up, as if cupping the moon. "Rise, Queen Maelona Eidolon, reigning monarch of the Unseelie Court."

Maelona stands with that silver creation sitting upon her brow, and then applause erupts. Maelona inclines her head and stares out over the crowd. Over her people. And then she grins.

The coronation devolves into a revel with food, drink, music, and dance. I abstain from the drinking with Emrys at my side, my husband similarly avoiding alcohol in solidarity. Aerial artists spin from the silks on the ceiling, swathed in bodysuits of silver and white, all graceful limbs and fluid movements. Attendees dance and writhe against each other on the dancefloor, merry and horny, and bright and vivacious.

Julia, dressed in a violet gown, takes to a corner with a smoking stick between her fingers—something I imagine is some sort of mood-altering substance. She takes a drag on it and blows it out to the ceiling, sighing. Wisteria soon joins her and wordlessly holds her hand out for the stick. Julia silently hands it over, crossing her arms over her chest, and leaning against the wall, a foot kicked back against it. The witch inhales, staining it black from her lipstick as she holds the substance in her lungs, then slowly releases it.

"Welcome to the Dead Boyfriend Club," Wisteria says dryly. "It sucks, but it gets easier."

Julia chokes on a shocked laugh, sad and humorous tears leaking from her eyes. She takes the proffered drug from Wisteria again.

"I think I'm lost. I don't know where to go," she remarks idly to the witch.

"Me neither. I think I'll stick around the court, and be lost a while."

"Then I'll stay lost with you—for a little longer at least."

I turn my attention to where Maelona lounges casually on her throne, the picture of Renaissance elegance. In her hand dangles of chalice of goldwine, silver and black clad guards surrounding her seat of power. The new queen takes it all in and as she surveys the crowd, her eyes fall on me and she smiles. Queen to queen. Best friend to best friend.

Nearby Maelona is Aveda, the faerie with butterfly wings, dances in front of the throne—captivating Maelona's attention. The new queen's eyes are drawn to the sensual movements of the fae woman and I watch her hair flicker pink, lust red, and black—over and over.

I am glad for Mae. Her and I were not meant to be, but perhaps her and Aveda are. It makes my heart warm to see her have someone.

It, surprisingly enough, even made me happy to see Gideon with someone. Until…

The unprecedented grief threatens to swallow me on the tide of its wave, but Emrys is there to pull me from the undertow. I don't love Gideon any longer—I haven't for a while—but I still cared about him, and his loss is poignant.

Physically, Emrys tugs me away and I let him. Suddenly, we find ourselves in an alcove, obscured by silver curtains. Then his mouth falls against my throat.

My eyes roll back as he places hot, open-mouthed kisses along my throat, my collarbones, my jaw. I grasp his shoulders, hands traveling down his arms, across his stomach, my fingers finding the gold buttons on the blouse and plunging between them. His skin his hot, surely as hot as mine is burning from the arousal coursing through my blood.

"Ryss," I whisper.

Emrys's hand goes to my throat, tipping my head back against the wall, hitching my leg on his hip. Grinding upward in one hard thrust, I feel the hardness in his pants eagerly pushing against my core. I groan and lean into him, nipping his ear, my tongue following the line of gold hoops there. Lust glazes my skin and saturates my blood. It is everywhere in and on me, and I desire my husband so desperately that I have turned animalistic in my drive to have him.

My hands are tugging his shirt open, roving over his abdomen, and slipping beneath the waistband of his pants. There, I find his hard cock, painfully pressing into my hand. He moans, my hand caught between the two of us as he rolls his hips again.

"Fuck, Vanna."

My soulmate presses me harder into the wall, and suddenly my other leg is hitched over his hips too. My ankles lock behind his back, but he figures out how to fit his hand between us and his fingers dip beneath my dress. He easily finds my clit, and I am soaked. He sweeps two fingers through the wetness of my pussy and then comes up to circle that nub, massaging it in the harsh, demanding strokes I like. My head knocks against the wall as he begins working me into a frenzy.

The throb of his hardening cock in my hand has me curling my fingers around him, pumping him firmly. Our mouths meet in a wild dance, teeth and tongues as we fuck each other with our hands. Wetness drips from between my legs, across his fingers, and down his wrist. I can hear the slick sounds he elicits from me and I have to bite my lip at the extremely lurid things that cross my mind. I grind my hips into his hand, using the wall to push off of and my ankles to pull him into me.

My hand is on the side of his neck, guiding his lips to mine, my fingers teasing those dark red waves.

"I love you so much," I rush against his lips.

"I love you, too." He kisses harder. "So much."

Emrys tugs my dress down my shoulders, the deep neckline causing it to fall around my waist. My breasts are completely bared to him, caressed by the golden body chain that slides between my cleavage and curves around my ribs in graceful arcs. His free hand goes to my nipple, rolling the hardened peak between his thumb and forefinger.

I let out a pitchy mewl as the sensation heightens drastically, the arousal scorching through me. I can feel my climax building inside me, begging for release.

Suddenly, his hand disappears from between my legs and I let out a sound of outrage. His cock slips from my hand, my fingers sliding against his skin. But just as quickly as he disappeared, does he drop to his knees and his mouth replaces where his fingers just were. I slam the back of my skull against the wall as the thrill of his tongue strikes me, not caring about the pain in my head.

Emrys's talented tongue dances across my clit, flicking it, swirling against it, sucking at it. The combination of suction and the movements of his tongue has my orgasm cresting, hard and bright. My hands are fused in his hair, pulling him by the roots against my center.

"I'm so close, please don't stop," I beg.

He does not stop. He keeps going, fucking me with that majestic tongue, and that perfect mouth of his before I come undone on his face. The orgasm slams into me, rippling through every inch of my body, soaring through my blood. I let out a gasp and then I moan sharply as Emrys's hand comes up to clap over my mouth, muffling the sound. My moans follow the wave of my climax as I slowly come down from the high.

I'm breathing heavy as Emrys rises from beneath my perch at his face, sliding our faces to the same level. My legs wrap around him again and he presses his face to my throat, inhaling my scent, nipping me.

"Let's go home," he murmurs. "I'm not done with you yet, and as used to an audience as we are—this is your best friend's coronation, and we should let her have her moment."

"We should," I agree.

We disentangle and step from the curtains of the alcove, and onto the Faerie Roads—crossing the inbetween of our private space and the throne room. The Faerie Roads are welcoming, soft and earthen. Emrys is a few paces ahead of me, but I see the way his ass moves in those leather pants and I can't help myself.

I attack my husband's form, tackling him to the ground. He turns in time, and we crash to the ground together, my hands wild at his pants, finding the buttons and pulling him out. His cock is proud and extremely hard beneath my touch, and I spare only seconds pushing my dress out of the way before sinking down onto him.

He groans, so low and sexy in his throat that I feel it in my core. I take him deep, and ride him, feeling the exquisite fullness of his cock stretching me. His hands go to my breasts, tweaking my nipples, causing me to throw my head back in ecstasy. My hips grind down on him, the most incredible friction on my clit from this position as he works me over.

I'm fucking him, another climax threatening me, feeling his cock pulse, when suddenly, he flips us over on the floor of the Roads and fucks me into the ground. His hands grasp both cheeks of my ass, kneading them in his fingers as he lifts my hips up and exposes me completely to him.

"Look at this pretty little pussy taking me so well," he growls and pushes the image through the bond.

A flash of unadulterated lust courses through me from his viewpoint—me splayed to him, wet pussy swallowing his thick cock, wetness soaking both of us, my breasts heavy and peaked with arousal, the pink tips hard, begging for his mouth.

My cheeks are flushed, rosy, even beneath the blue glimmer of the bioluminescent mushrooms.

He thrusts in and out of me, hammering me with his beautiful cock. Completely at his mercy, and loving it. We fuck like we fight—matched and the perfect mirror for the other.

I take him as he takes me, and through the bond, I feel him nearing his orgasm. My back arches and my pussy clenches, squeezing him as his rhythm speeds up to a punishing pace. I scream as my climax slams through me, hitting me without any momentum. My nails rake into the earth of the Faerie Roads while Emrys moans as he comes, filling me with his release. His cock throbs as he spends himself, his strokes slowing.

We separate and stand, fixing my dress and putting his cock away. We are filthy—covered in dirt from the Roads—and our hair is mussed—clearly from sex tousling. Despite it all, we don't care and we grin at each other.

"That was fun, want to try it again sometime?"

Emrys laughs at me and cups my cheeks in his hands and presses a passionate kiss to my lips. It's brief but all consuming. He pulls back and gazes into my eyes.

"Do I really get to keep you?"

"For as long as you want me."

"I'll always want you, Vanna."

"Then it sounds like a plan."

He kisses me again.

We finally finish our traveling of the Faerie Roads, realizing as we near our court that we completely disregarded our guard. Unfortunately, it is one of the downsides of not being used to being protected—we're not used to alerting anyone to our whereabouts. When we return to the Seelie Court, we find the first servant we can find and ask them to send a messenger to the Unseelie Court to inform the guard of our return.

The washing in our bathing chamber leads to more fucking—with our hands slathering soap all over the other's body, feeling the firm and soft lines and curves and planes, how could we not? Emrys bends me over the edge of the tub and takes me, pulling my hair in his grasp, the other one on my lower back, pushing me down, arching my spine into the perfect position for him. He plunges into me so deep I have to bite my hand to keep from screaming out as loudly as I want. He's just so good, and thick, and talented.

My eyes roll back as he comes, my own climax following as his hand plays my clit like a violin—strung tight and released. He collapses against my back, kissing down my spine, stroking my ribs.

"Would it be sacrilege to say you're like a goddess?"

I smirk. "I don't care, call me whatever you want. But just so you know, I'm not the biggest admirer of all the goddesses we've met, and I wouldn't take too kindly to you wanting to fuck any of them."

He laughs against my shoulder blade. "The only person I want to fuck is you. I'm yours."

"As I am yours."

"Forever."

"Forever," I agree.

CHAPTER 39

As the dust finally begins to settle on everything that has come to pass, a realization strikes me. I jolt up from the bed that Emrys and I are laying in, a book splayed open before me, my husband lounging next to me with a book of his own. We are equally unclothed.

"What is it, Vanna?"

"There's something I need to do."

He cocks a brow and I tell him. A mixture of happiness and sadness crosses his face as I explain what it is and why I must do it. He deposits the book he was holding on his side of the bed and crawls over to me, kissing me tenderly.

"That is awfully kind of you," he comments, hands stroking down my spine. "A sweet sentiment from a faerie, in fact. One that once called herself a monster."

"I *am* a monster."

"Well now I know faeries can lie because that simply isn't true."

I roll my lips between my teeth. "I've done terrible things."

"As have I," he says moving lower.

"I've done terrible things to you."

"I have made my mistakes, also." He pauses. "Unless you are referring to the filthy things in bed, because in that case, I say 'please continue them' instead."

He's at my hips and comes up behind me, mouth dipping down. He nips at the supple curve of my ass cheek, leaving a love bite there, a finger tracing the seam of my backside. I lick my lips at his touches, anticipation making me wet.

"Do you truly think you're still a monster, Vanna? After everything you've done for so many people? Truly think on it, because I cannot bear the thought of you thinking so little of yourself."

"No," I sigh, heart hammering. "I don't."

Because it's true. I don't. I have done many terrible things, as I have stated before, but many of those terrible things were done with good intentions. But even with those deeds in mind, I have still done more good. I have saved more, protected more, rescued more. Surely, Caspian doesn't imagine me a monster. Surely, Caethes's fae beast does not consider me one either. Surely, there are others who feel the same way.

"I think that acceptance deserves a reward."

And with that, he lifts my hips, bites my ass, and then slips his cock into my aching core again.

It's still summer, but the seasons are giving way to autumn. Soon it will be time for Maelona to complete her Equinox Revel, just as Emrys and I completed the one for the solstice. My husband and I stand on the sidewalk before an apartment complex. We're both glamoured, but for an added measure, we wear a second glamour of civilian clothes—human clothes. In reality we wear leathers, but to the eye, Emrys is in black slacks and a thin dress-shirt, sleeves rolled to the elbows, several buttons undone—old habits die hard. I'm in a plain tee-shirt, white sneakers, and pair of jeans—like a relic from my human days in the Unseelie territory.

A human, or so I'd thought. Now…a faerie queen. How has my life changed so drastically?

"Do you want me to come with you?"

"No," I tell my soulmate. "I think I need to do this alone."

"I'm here if you need me."

I squeeze his hand. "Thank you."

As I approach the building, I'm hyper-aware of how others will perceive me. I've altered my looks ever so slightly, turned my pale hair to a more natural ash blonde, my eyes not so unearthly silver, added a healthy tan, and hidden most of my scars. I'm crossing to the front door when a slender woman exits, a tote bag on her arm, a file folder in her hand, phone in her other one.

I'm so startled that I speak before I think. "Amari?"

The woman stops abruptly and looks at me quizzically and suspiciously. "Yes, can I help you?"

She has long black and red braids, deep brown skin, and thickly lashed dark eyes. She's dressed in a blazer and matching pants, ironed, fitted, and tailored, with a very expensive white shirt beneath it. On her feet are shiny heels of brightest scarlet.

I inhale sharply. This was the woman Callahan wanted to marry. Sweet, ambitious Callahan that just wanted to do good for the world and was taken by faeries, his dreams shattered with the death they brought. I still remember his last words like they were yesterday.

If you ever find her, tell-tell Amari I love her, okay? And I'm sorry about leaving the shoes in the hallway. Tell her I wish I'd married her.

Gideon had promised to tell her on his behalf. But Gideon is gone now, too. It's just me, and though I'd never promised myself, I'm compelled to carry out this final wish for him. They're both dead now. Now ash. Only memories.

...save the world if you have to...just live.

"I...I—" I swallow, not able to lie. "I knew Callahan."

Amari immediately picks up on my use of past tense and her shoulders sink. "He's dead, isn't he?"

I thin my lips and nod. "He is, I'm sorry."

"How?"

I have to form my words carefully so that I'm not caught in a lie I can't tell. "He was attacked while writing his article on climate change by one of the natural predators of the

Yukon. My friend and I were hiking when we found him, and we decided to group up. He…there was another attack."

Amari watches me stone-faced, her brown eyes like tourmaline. "Is that your friend over there?" She indicates with her chin at Emrys.

I give a start. She shouldn't be able to see him. Not while glamoured, not with a King's Glamour. I suddenly feel very self-conscious about my own glamour. Is it working? Does she see me as I truly am? It's exceedingly rare, but there have been instances of humans with the natural ability to see through magic—True Sight. Does Amari have it?

"N-no," I stutter, taken off guard. "That's my husband. My friend…ah, he didn't make either."

"I'm sorry for your loss. Was he a faerie, too?"

My eyes widen to the size of saucers. "You know of the fae?"

Amari gives a short bark of laughter, but I can still see the pain in her eyes. From knowing about Callahan's death. I know that loss is now fresh. "Of course, I do, I've just tried to steer clear because where there are fae, there's trouble."

I can't deny that. Maybe it wasn't my use of past tense that elicited the dejected reaction in her. Maybe it was the fact I'm fae and mentioned Callahan and her brain went to the most likely result.

"Do you and your husband want to come inside and tell me what really happened to my boyfriend?"

I hesitate, but relay the information through the bond. Emrys begins striding towards us.

Amari lets us both in. She has a ground floor apartment, so it's a short walk. The space is done up in shades of beige and terracotta, the sofa caramel leather, a large macrame decoration hanging on the wall behind it. Emrys and I stand awkwardly in the open concept layout, Amari leans against the island arms crossed.

"Well?"

"He was killed by Unseelies while we were trying to escape their territory."

She exhales, chin quivering. "Fuck," she whispers, looking away. She swipes a hand beneath her eye. She composes herself, clearing her throat. "Okay. All right, well are you from that secret society or whatever?"

"What?" I ask, drawing my brows together. "No, we're from the Seelie Court. What are you talking about?"

"Some secret society has been trying to get me to work for them for years. Apparently, I saw someone I wasn't supposed to, and they figured out I had the Sight."

"Was it the Arcana Society?" Why hadn't they said anything when I contacted them to falsify police reports and hospital records for Callahan?

"No, I've never heard of them. It's called the Winter Carnaval. Do you know of it?"

My blood runs cold.

"Amari," I say warningly. "I'm not trying to scare you, but you need to stay as far as possible from the Carnaval. Do you understand?"

Amari straightens. "Why? What is it?"

"It's the supernatural black market, specializing in trafficking."

All the blood drains from Amari's face.

"How many times have they tried to contact you?"

"Three times." Amari swallows.

Emrys curses under his breath. "I'm going to put you in contact with someone, and you need to explain this to them," Emrys pronounces, finding sticky notes on Amari's counter and scribbling on them. "If the Carnaval wants you, they're not going to stop, and eventually they're going to take you by force."

"Why should I trust you?" she questions.

"Are you aware of the fact that faeries can't lie?" Emrys asks, still writing.

"Yes…" Amari replies, a question in her voice.

Without looking up, Emrys speaks. "We are the king and queen of the Seelie Court." He pulls the note from the stack. "Please call this number."

After Amari's initial shock wears off, she does as bid and within the hour, our King and Queensguard, the Arcana Society, and the remaining member of the House Council arrive. They debrief her, and Amari takes it all in stride. After a lengthy conversation, Amari nods and it's like a trigger. The Arcana Society moves into action and begins packing up her apartment and explaining her new life, and everything she has just accepted. It's mere moments later and Amari's entire life is neatly boxed up and taken away.

Along with Carmella, Amari will be one of the new members of the House Council—the supernatural government still healing from the vicious attack only months before. They—meaning Carmella—has decided a human is essential to ward against biases. Amari lets them lead her out, but suddenly the entire reason we came here strikes me.

"He wanted you to know he loved you," I blurt out. Amari's eyes swing to me. "And that he wanted to marry you."

She smiles, sadness in her eyes. "I know. I found the ring."

With that, she slips out the door with the Arcana Society, leaving her old life behind.

Emrys and I stand shocked for a moment. This did not go as planned, but in some way, I think we were meant to be here. To tell her this. To learn of her ability and the Winter Carnaval's seeking of her. It all feels connected.

As Emrys and I leave, I catch sight of something unnaturally red and I freeze. No. There's no way. But my husband saw it too, and the two of us follow the figure. Just as we step into the alley she disappeared into, we find ourselves transported onto the Faerie Roads.

There, standing in the middle of the Roads, lighted and eerie blue from the bioluminescent mushrooms, is Lady Fate.

"You've just changed the course of fate," the goddess says flatly.

I straighten. "With Amari?"

"With Amari," she confirms. "She was not part of your story. She was meant to be part of another's. But I suppose the meddling my sisters have done to your board have ramifications spawning lengths that I have yet to see. I should find it humorous that your further meddling is muddying the waters of destiny even more."

I don't even know if I'm supposed to apologize. I do not know if she's even angry. She seems...perturbed, but also amused.

"What does this mean then?"

"It means that I have to take matters into my own hands," she sighs dramatically.

"Are...are you going back on your bargain?" Emrys asks, fear painting every line of his body, staining his soul. The same alarm courses through the bond and bleeds into me. My heart hammers desperately.

No. No, not after everything we've been through. We've just survived hell. We just survived a war and came out the other side alive. She couldn't be so cruel as to take him after all of that.

"No. No, I quite enjoy you living, Revenant. I will not be taking what I gave Evelyn Vanora. No, I have something else in mind. You two won't be able to help them when the time comes. You've tipped the scales too far one way, and I must tip them back."

"What does that mean? What time will this be?" I press.

"You will learn. But don't fret, little queen. I have put you through enough, it will be a happy occasion. Perhaps three," she says winking meaningfully and glancing downwards. "Not yet, but eventually, my Harbinger. Eventually, your vision will come to pass."

I suck in a breath so short and sharp that it squeezes my lungs. Emrys glances at me and reads through the bond.

My vision.

Three.

Three daughters.

Red of hair, black of hair, white of hair. Eyes of gold, silver, and black. Winged.

Emrys virtually melts next to me. His eyes softening, his hands going up, moving as if to touch me. To touch the belly that is currently empty—for now.

That is the future that Lady Fate is currently dangling in front of our faces. The promise that those girls—our children, our *daughters*—will prevent us from fucking up her next game. The shock and the anticipation overpowers any anger I may feel at threatening fate. I've learned my lesson from her before—I won't play with that fire again. She gave me my husband back, yes. She has given me kindness, yes. But I haven't forgotten for one moment that she is a goddess and she is fickle, and she can take it all away just as easily as blowing out a candle.

"But it is still our choice," I counter.

Lady Fate smiles, and I can't tell if it's a sweet, or a venomous one. "It is, but I think you've found you've already made up your minds."

We have. I can see it shining through the bond clear as day. The want. The longing. Not yet. Not for a little while. But soon enough. She also knows as well as I do that I won't make Drysi's mistakes. I won't risk not having my daughters for anything—even revenge.

"Rule your court, young monarchs," Lady Fate says with command lacing her tone. "Enjoy the new era you're ringing in. But do not stray too close to another's board, or I may have to…redirect you." She gives a small finger wave. "Farewell my darlings, it was a pleasure."

With that, Lady Fate backs away and slips around a corner, completely disappearing from the embrace of the Faerie Roads.

In her absence there is a hush and for a moment we wait, letting the air adjust to the aftermath of a goddess. When some of the silent eeriness fades, Emrys and I turn to look at one another.

"Three daughters," I whisper.

"Three daughters," he echoes.

"Are you disappointed with no sons?"

Before he even answers, I can see the answer flash through the bond. "Why would I be disappointed? Their gender will not dictate any difference to me. You are the fiercest warrior I know, and your sex has never stopped you."

"Well," I begin flirtatiously. "Sex has certainly stopped me more than once when it comes to you."

Emrys chuckles. "Not what I meant, but I appreciate it nonetheless." Slowly, he cups my cheek. "I will be honored to raise our children better than we were brought up. They will be loved, and they will be treasured. Never once will they question where they belong, because they will belong with us."

Tears shimmer in my eyes, blurring my vision. I nod. "I like the sound of that."

"Good." He kisses me quickly before tugging me along the Roads, back to our court.

I feel...*lighter*, somehow, passing through the gilded curtain of ivy separating the throne room from the Roads. Crossing the polished, earthen floor with Emrys at my side, I feel at peace. Ascending the dais with my husband, I feel settled. Placing a hand upon the throne, my soulmate copying the action, I feel *whole*.

Summoning the Seelie crown, the comfortable weight settles upon my brow with divine, uncontested purpose. Emrys's glints gold and ebony upon his garnet waves as together, the two of us in unison pour intention between the bond and into the throne. There, all the Seelie magic in the court alights with incandescent brightness. The false gold sky burns with heavenly fire, the veins of magic that cross the throne flare, and suddenly, the throne fills with a hum. Pushing more magic into the throne, Emrys and I delve into the gold together—the magic that blesses us with our heightened King's and Queen's Glamours, the sensitivity to the intricacies of our court, all of it—and then we cleave.

In one smooth motion, as if it always was, the great Seelie throne of three gnarled and proud tree trunks— separates. The branches remain tangled overhead, golden lines like webs still weaving between, but now rather than one throne, there is two.

As Emrys had pulled apart his crown to form mine, have we split the massive seat of power for our own.

They are identical seats, neither boasting more than the other. It is as we are.

Opposites.

Equals.

Mirrors.

Mates.

"So now it begins," Emrys whispers to me, releasing his hold on the magic streaming through us and the bond. "Our rule of peace."

There is so much we have lost. So much we still have to repair. And while there is still so much uncertainty, I know with unconditional clarity that anything felt between my soulmate and I is not part of it.

I love Emrys Gwyndolyn-Vanora with everything in my heart. I will love him until my last breath. The moment my heart stops beating. And if there is an afterlife for me, I will love him beyond that. He is my reason, my everything, my all. Even if it is all unknown, our love will always hold true.

And I know he loves me, too.

I know that he would call down a goddess for me, as I did for him.

Emrys wraps his arms around my waist, fingers trailing on my ribs, and I lock mine around his neck, pulling him down to my level. Our lips brush, just slightly.

"Any commands, My King?"

Emrys smiles against my mouth as he ghosts his teeth against my lips. "Oh, many My Queen, but let's just start with kiss me."

I laugh softly at his jaw. "As you wish."

Our mouths meet, and with that kiss we promise eternity.

THE END

PRONUNCIATION GUIDE

CHARACTERS

Evelyn: EVAH-LINN

Gideon: GID-EE-UN

Maelona: MAE-LOW-NA

Aneira: AH-NAY-YA

Caethes: KI-THES

Violante: VEE-OH-LAN-TAY

Enydd: EN-NED

Tirnoc: TEER-NOK

Cariad: CARE-EE-AD

Emrys: EM-RISS

Tegwyn: TEGG-WIN

Tadhg: TAIG

Róisín: RO-SHEEN

Arawn: AIR-RAWN

Osian: OH-SHAN

Aveda: AH-VED-AH

Baphet: BAF-ET

OTHER

Ceidwad Cudd: KAI-YD-WAH COO

Aberth: AH-BEH-TH

Kayla McGrath

ACKNOWLEDGEMENTS

I'm sitting here, stunned, staring at my keyboard with the realization that this trilogy has concluded. It's over. It's done. It's finished. I'm in disbelief; but while Evelyn and Emrys's love story has reached its happy ending, I am not finished with this world—one day I will return, and it will be Caspian's story. I couldn't have completed this book—and especially this trilogy without so many people around me. I am incredibly grateful to everyone who has picked up and read my books, and as much as I'd love to thank every person each and individually, this would turn into its own novel. So, without further ado—and in no order—I begin my thank yous.

To Michael, my loving and endlessly supportive and devoted husband. My god, the world knows I couldn't have done this without you—you are the person who wanted me to indie pub years ago, and without you working your ass off each and every day, this would not be feasible. Thank you, my love, endlessly and forever. I love you more every day.

Rebecca F. Kenney—I feel like I thank you every time, but you have been integral to my career—thank you for this gorgeous cover, it's my favorite of the series. Thank you for all your support and wisdom and patience, you are one of the most inspiring people I've ever met.

To Ali, without you Emrys would not be who is he is. Without that fated conversation we had over the course of a several hour FaceTime to confirm that he was the right endgame, thank you. And thank you for all the support and roasts.

My gosh, thank you to Cydney Daemon, one of the kindest people on IG. Your passion and love for these books has me all sorts of emotional. Thank you for being the wonderful person you are, you are an absolute treasure and I'm so lucky to have connected with you.

To each and every person who has shared my posts, thank you. You have kept me motivated and passionate about my books and writing. Special thanks J.D. Yanez, Ellee Rhea, Karissa Kinword, Whitney Dean, Jess Lampe, Enna Hawthorn, Catherine Labadie, Kaja McDonald, K.P. Burchfield, Jae Waller, and so many more, for sharing or interacting with almost all of my stuff. I appreciate you all.

To my safe space—you know who you are—thank you from the bottom of my heart. Y'all are wonderful and I'm the luckiest person to have you in my life.

My daughters, Vivienne and Rosalie, without you, I wouldn't be me—thank you. You don't realize it yet, but you are my everything. I love you both.

My parents and my siblings, thank you for not judging me for my social media marketing—we don't have to talk about it. I love you all.

Thank you, as always to Sierra and Maria, y'all are my rock and I love you. Thank you for listening to my unsufferable complaints and rants and stresses. Thank you for the memes and support.

Also, a big thank you to Sherilyn, who has read everything I've written and wants even more. Your enthusiasm is a huge motivator and I am so glad you've enjoyed my books so much. I appreciate you!

Literally thank you to every single person who has read my trilogy. It's unbelievable that people have loved these characters I've created. Thank you for reading along with Evelyn and her journey.

And as always, thank you dear reader, for everything. Thank you for taking a chance on a little indie author like me—as I like to jokingly say, Your Favorite Baby Indie Author—it's my favorite thing to know people are reading my books.

If you feel like it and you're comfortable doing so, I would be incredibly grateful if you'd consider leaving a review for Our Shattered Fates!

Thank you for reading, and I hope you consider keeping an eye out for what I put out next, I have so much planned.

Kayla McGrath

ABOUT THE AUTHOR

Kayla McGrath has been writing since the age of thirteen out of spite, having read a book with a love triangle that didn't go her way. After that, it became a passion. If she's not writing, then she's reading, or drinking endless cups of chai. Kayla lives on Vancouver Island with her husband, two daughters, and two boxers.

She is the author of the Cold as Iron trilogy and the Infernal Curses series. Our Shattered Fates is her fourth book.

You can find her on Twitter (@KaylaMcGrath_), TikTok (@kaylamcgrath_), and on Instagram/Threads (@kaylamcgrathbooks).

Kayla McGrath

OTHER BOOKS BY
KAYLA MCGRATH

THE COLD AS IRON TRILOGY
This Broken Memory
These Ruined Dreams
Our Shattered Fates

INFERNAL CURSES
The Nightmare Curse
THC (Coming Fall 2024)

A DEATHLESS EMPIRE
A Deathless Empire (Coming Summer 2024)

Kayla McGrath

"It all began, once upon a nightmare curse…"

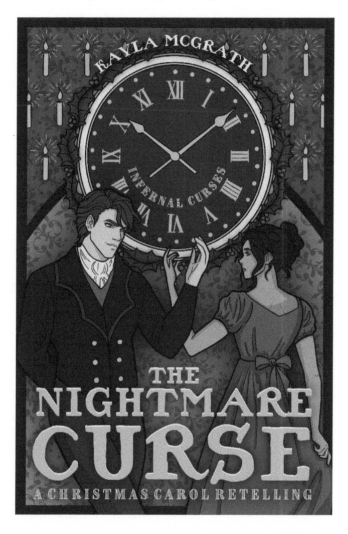

Book one in the Infernal Curses series, available in paperback, e-book, and on Kindle Unlimited.
Turn the page for the first chapter!

Kayla McGrath

ADELAIDE KANE

DECEMBER 24, 1866

Vanity was the hardest sin to rid oneself of and such pride would be Adelaide Kane's demise. She was kind to a fault, but that, paired with her exquisite beauty, and miserly hands made her the perfect victim of jealousy. And the ruinous Nightmare Curse.

"Please," she begged the demon whose face was an abyss of stars beneath an ivory hood. "I repent, I truly do! I see the error of my ways, I will share my coin, donate to charity, I will live in a ramshackle hovel. Please, let me leave this dreaded nightmare with my life."

Someone had hated or envied her enough to cast a killing curse on her, willing to risk their own life in exchange for hers—should she succeed in change. The demons didn't care who lived or who died, they collected a soul either way.

"And what of your beauty? Would you forfeit that?" the demon asked in an echoing voice that prompted existential fear.

Adelaide pressed a dainty hand to her creamy cheek. Her fingers were slender, but not bony, her nails perfect, pink ovals. She felt the softness of her skin, the heat of her rosy cheeks. She was in her seventh decade, but due to having performed the Staying in her thirtieth year, she appeared not a day more.

"Would you still scorn those who do not possess the same radiance as you?" The demon drew closer and lifted a cosmic hand, its not-skin swirling as its eldritch fingers captured a golden ringlet and spun it. "Dedicate less to how you look? To let society judge you at your most natural?"

The horror that shivered through Adelaide was a physical thing and she couldn't help pulling away from the last demon. She couldn't lie to the demons who visited her, it was a compulsion of the curse. Even if she wanted to deny it, to lie to herself even, she could not. It was a physical impossibility and she couldn't force her tongue to move around the untruth.

Her eyes flickered to the frozen grave that yawned open from the snowy ground. They were in a cemetery past midnight and were utterly alone—not even a mouse scurried within the demon's presence. Wind howled through the skeletal branches of the dark trees and beneath the moonless night—not even shadows played upon the untouched snow. The edges of the grave had roots like corpse fingers, reaching up from the pits of Hell to drag her down. The hole was so deep she could not see the bottom. And she did not want to. What lurked below terrified her beyond measure.

"I—" she opened her mouth to answer the demon, but despite her fear, she could not.

Hellhounds of smoke and darkness paced by the demon, their eyes molten embers of red-hot flame. Lips pulled back from teeth with the promise to devour her if she threatened to run. She had been warned they would drag her to her demise, should she try to flee.

"You do not truly mean to change your ways, therefore I shall take your soul and feast on it."

The demon lifted its hands in summoning. Ghostly chains of black iron appeared from the ether, wreathed in deepest crimson light. The haunted chains danced in the air, puppets of the final demon's ministrations. Undulating like snakes, they slithered on the frosty air and slid around Adelaide.

Tears spilled and froze on Adelaide's cheeks as she subjected herself to the phantom links that would drag her to the underworld. The weight of her sins—pride and greed— bound the chains and pressed into her, crushing her, suffocating her. The dark magic forced itself into her mouth and down her throat, clogging her air and stealing her breath. She gorged herself on greed and squeezed her lungs with vanity.

The pain was excruciating, so much agony that she could not scream, could not plead, could not pray. She was jailed to her form without reprieve, suffused in endless suffering. It was endless and it was seconds. Time ceased to mean anything. All was pain.

The hellhounds yipped with excitement and anticipation, increasing their prancing and snarls.

Bones crunched, skin split, ivory protruding from the scarlet and viscera. Her once beautiful face purpled and bloated as the chains continued wrapping, compressing her skull.

The demon cast her into her oblivion-grave where her physical form finally gave way and she was nothing but mist and blood, gore and shards. Splatters of blood arced from the hole and scattered on the snow, leaving perfect frozen rubies in the glittering white.

Her soul screamed on the descent to Hell, as it would for all eternity until some beast swallowed the final morsel of her spirit. Divining on her agony like a delicacy.

The demon watched facelessly, and vanished with the hellhounds, concluding the night's end.

In the morning, the church bells unknowingly called out Adelaide Kane's death knell on Christmas Day, pronouncing her as the twenty-first victim of the Nightmare Curse.

9 781738 226528